However Many Must Die

The Blood Scouts

Book 1

PHIL WILLIAMS

MMXXIII

ISBN-13: 978-1-913468-24-8

Cover art by Stefan Koidl
Cover design by P. Williams

Published by Rumian Publishing

Visit **www.phil-williams.co.uk** online for more information and
regular news regarding the writing of Phil Williams.
Join the newsletter to be the first to hear about new projects.

Map of Boldarow, c. 721

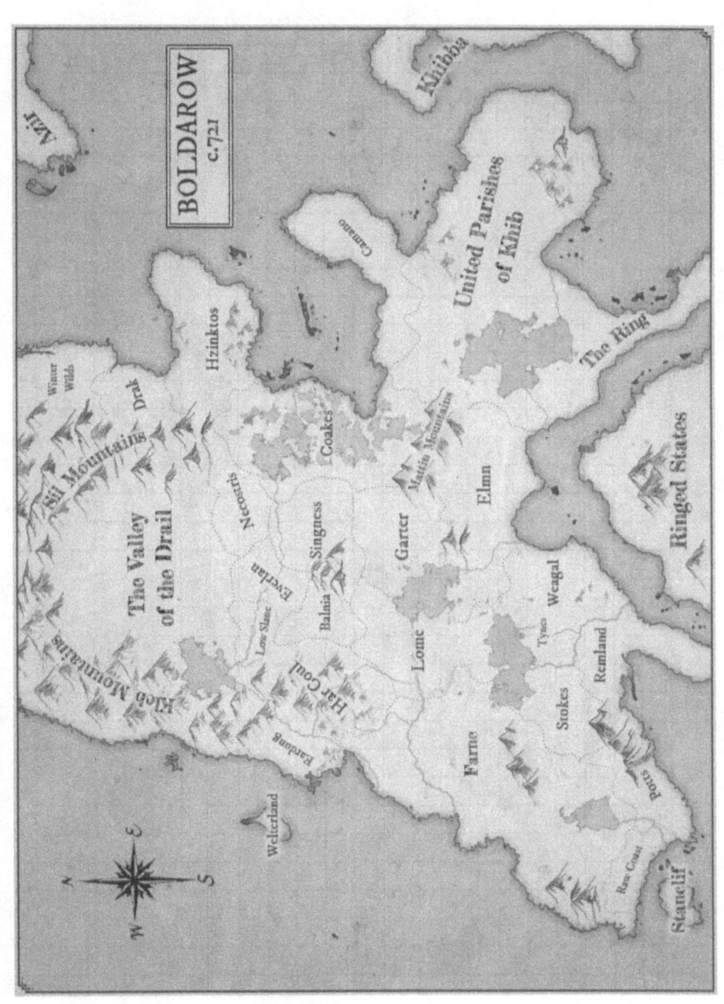

Languid's Glossary

Abridged from "Languid's Glossary", *Languid's Everyman Guide to Fierce Women of The One War (Issue 4: The Blood Scouts)***, p. i-iii**

Psst. Want to know a bit about this world, and the people in it, before you dive in? The what and the where and the why and the who of this particular stage of The One War? Then, mate, I've got your back.

We're going to be following the glorious Blood Scouts during their escapades in the Western Theatre, circa mid-720, so here's a bunch of background you might find relevant. You don't need to brush up on all this now, it's here just in case. And I'm gonna assume you know nothing because let's be fair, some of you don't. Not judging; I'm here to help the everyman, that's my whole point. So, from the top, here's what you're dealing with:

Lay of the World

The Rocc: *the stone we stand on; everything, this whole world. You know this.*
Boldarow: *the biggest and baddest central continent of the Rocc.*
The One War: *global conflict where empires clashed, 719-728.*
The Drail Empire (people: Drail / the Drail (collective), adj: Drail): *an empire comprising (dominating) seven nations in the Valley of the Drail, headed by Drail itself and bolstered by Low Slane, Har Coul and that lot; these fiends promoted "Purification", meaning, the more you stuck to their ideals, the safer you were.*
The Comity: *countries unified in taking down the Drail, led by Stanclif and Khibba.*
Imperial Stanclif (people: Cliffer(s), adj: Stanish): *an empire with a seat of power in the small southwestern isle*

of Stanclif. These lads promoted the secular "Civilisation" movement, essentially putting material wealth and snooty values above all.

Khibba (people: Khib(s), adj: Khib): *a monstrously big empire way off in the Eastern Continent, with old-fashioned religious values and a big melting pot of inhuman races.*

Azir (people: Azirian(s), adj: Azrian): *large, broadly isolated empire far north of Khibba, variously got in on the action on both sides.*

Low Slane (people: Slane(s), adj: Slanik): *a small but powerful principality within the Drail Empire, famed for housing monsters and the elite Dread Corps.*

Har Coul (people: Coul(s), adj: Coulard): *mountainous western region of the Drail Empire, balanced primitive tech and civilisation with barbaric fighting styles.*

Farne (people: Farne(s), adj: Farnish): *empire and large western land mass mostly decimated in the early stages of the war.*

Garter (people: Garter(s), adj. Garter): *large central nation overrun by imperial fighting, previously the seat of a hugely powerful empire (centuries earlier).*

Olon (the Ringed States): *mostly colonised group of nomadic nations south of Boldarow, encircled by the Ring Sea.*

Singness, Elmn and Coak: *countries east of Garter and Drail.*

The Emerging Isles: *way distant bunch of islands far south of Khibba, colonised late in the day, including Gonland and Carper.*

Places of Interest

Arrow City: *capital of Drail.*
Vasseer: *capital of Stanclif.*
Kleb / Sil Mountains: *vast ranges that respectively flank the east and west flanks of the Valley of the Drail.*

Heaven's Eye: *great lake with shore territories spanning both Drail and Har Coul, collectively known as Lakeland / the Lakelands.*
Tynes: *city state, southwest of Garter.*
Green Rise: *site of a spectacular battle in Farne, 721.*
Wick: *walled city on the southern border of Farne and Har Coul.*
Highscythe, Cleave, Fever and Null: *central and eastern Drail strongholds.*
Blythe: *a pool town north of Green Rise.*
Swelig: *a small village in Stanclif.*

Institutions

The Arbitration: *international regulators of safe and proper magic use.*
The Purification: *the Drail's widespread network of "secret" police.*
The Dread Corps: *crack Slanik military unit with a unique ranking system, including (in order of seniority) battle chiefs, kill chiefs, shocksmiths, killsmiths and fearsmiths.*
The Church of the Venerate Flesh: *once dominant religion that followed prophet Bly Castor's Book of the Body; acolytes commonly called "Vens".*
Revery of the Cane Saints: *ancient religion following diverse prophets and personified deities, partially documented in Tikan Mythology.*
The Movement of Knowledge: *secular revolution placing science and materialism above religion and magic (eventually underpinning Stanish 'Civilisation').*
Mortal Magic (or witlacing, flesh weaving, blood corrupting): *magical practice relating to living flesh and consciousness. Broadly grouped into four schools: intention, will, flesh and parsing.*
Earth-touching (or dirt-minding, mindlessness): *magical practice concerned with manipulating the physical world,*

of and relating to the environment.

Spirit Work: *various disputed schools of alternative magic, such as the Ringed menafis (witches) who supposedly empower mesita (conduit warriors). (Don't worry, this stuff's rare.)*

Leaders of Interest

Statesmen Dowel: *the nominal head of Imperial Stanclif (supported by lords).*

Patrain Vinkent Narroway: *head of the Drail (supported by Prognanes, like lords).*

Screaming Prince Proud: head of Low Slane.

General Easter: *commander of Stanclif's 6th ("Sick") Brigade.*

General Kettal: *commander of Stanclif's 2nd "southern" Brigade.*

General Amalric: *commander of the Drail's 8th Division.*

General Foul: *commander of the Drail's 3rd Division.*

Battle Chiefs Ways, Hark, Baron and Gloven: commanders in the Dread Corps.

Sin Sight Panderlair: *seasoned Purification inquisitor.*

Thorn Red: *seasoned Purification inquisitor.*

Captain Brade: *famed Stanclif adventurer.*

Notable Members of the Blood Scouts Platoon

Squad Leaders: *Captain "Tenacious" Tate (Sun Squad), Larkin (Sabre Squad), Harmon (Rock Squad), Sarge (Boot Squad)*

Magic support: *Dollemore (witlacer), Emi (dirt-minder)*

Snipers: *Four Skills (Sabre), Oksy (Rock), Wild Wish (Boot)*

Heavy weapons and demolitions: *Pound (Boot), Cade (Rock), Fuse (Rock)*

Medical support: *Fixit (Boot), Ill Dog (Rock)*

Boot Squad Grunts: *Rue, Loose, Dakoda, Small, Colt*

Notable Races/Species

Arrexes: *large insectile flying creatures, occasionally bred for riding.*

Barkmen: *elusive inhabitants of the Eardung forest.*

Coakels (worm-eyes): *part invertebrate, part fish, from the Coak wetlands.*

Cirga: *large insectile centaurs with a hard carapace.*

Degrebus: *leathery, devious winged creatures found in mountainous regions.*

Giants: *enormous bipeds of various types, including skalk, hawk and swamp.*

Goblins: *green-skinned bipeds, about half human size and low in intelligence; including harker, lowbite, pack and weed.*

Gonish (waders): *diminutive but intelligent race from the Emerging Isles.*

Grekkels: *part lupine (wolfy), part lacertillian (lizardy) bipeds native to Low Slane – fast, strong and vicious.*

Humans: *the prominent, powerful and most common bunch of bipeds.*

Matticks (trunks): *stocky humanoids with heads in their chests.*

Spidroms: *robust arachnid-featured folk principally from Azir.*

Wyrlings: *big flying worm things.*

1

The Battle of Green Rise, 720, saw one of the war's great early upsets. The Drail's immense 8th Division had the high ground and fresh reinforcements, and were rightly confident to advance on Stanclif's "Sick" Brigade. But this would be a harsh lesson in how modern technology could take advantage of even the smallest chinks. How different might things have been if not for a single unguarded path?
Dueley's Comprehensive: The One War in 10 Volumes (Vol. 4), p. 31

Wild Wish chased behind her battle sisters to where the dense tree-line met the base of the cliff. The battle was thundering above, on the plateau that topped the hundred metres of sheer rock, so they were clearly late. Not that anyone wanted to be early to this party. Captain Tate complained about the male officers always being too hesitant to unleash the Blood Scouts, but Wish secretly suspected every one of those delays saved them at least a little bloodshed and dismemberment. Besides, they were here now and the fight was still raging and she was near the brave, stupid front. Telling herself not to worry, there wouldn't be any resistance. If the Drail were aware of this path, they would've used it themselves.

No, the scouts were going to scale this cliff unseen and jam a knife in the enemy's side, then sit around laughing about how easy it had been.

As Wish's friends ran out from the trees ahead of her, a soldier came running the other way and popped that little dream. Loose jumped him, clamped a hand on his mouth, and pushed him quickly against the rock face. For a moment, his alarmed expression turned hopeful at seeing his attacker was a young woman. Then her knife tore his throat out. It was a deep, unclean cut, with Loose taking no chances. She leapt back from the spray and raised her hands in innocence as he thudded into the dirt.

Rue hissed, "Bloody well soaked yourself."

"Maybe it'll scare the rest off?" Loose laughed nervously, teeth shining through splattered gore. Her blonde hair hung free from her helmet, framing startling blue eyes, in a contrast that made her look positively demonic. At once smiling, vibrant, and unhesitating in that deadly attack. It gave Wish a confusing thrill she didn't need right now. There were worse ways to go, she supposed, than in Loose's hands. She had lost enough sleep considering her own brutal death, as this war had created a great many new opportunities for it. To get around that, sharing a tent *so close* to Rue and Loose, one of Wish's favourite tactics was to replace thoughts of dying with thoughts of her beautiful friend's embrace. Now, she might find it harder to separate the two.

Lieutenant Larkin jogged past, up the path, with only a brief look at the dead man, whose head lolled obscenely, eyes empty, locked in surprise. She soon skipped back down the slope announcing, "On his own. Must be a deserter, maybe got lucky, spotted the path while hiding in the trees."

That silenced the girls. He was missing a good part of his neck. Granted, he'd got closer to Loose than most guys did, but, on balance, *lucky* didn't quite cut it. But they couldn't take prisoners or risk anyone giving them away. And there *were* worse ways to die. Even if half the platoon would've done it cleaner.

Putting it quickly behind them, Larkin barked and clapped to drive them onto the path. No formation to it, squads intermingling as the scouts hurried on. The rocks rose straight up to the side, so severe it was hard to see much further than above their heads. The switchback barely jutted out two feet, steeper than most stairs, and after two turns of climbing it presented a jagged drop over the edge. Wild Wish scrambled gracelessly up, trying not to look down. Her companions huddled nose to arse on the tier below, helmets bobbing along with the fall getting rapidly higher.

Eyes ahead, focus on the next step, don't think about it.

Rue was in front of Wish, greatcoat flapping as she hustled after Loose – Loose in the lead again, elated from that first kill, eager to show everyone how it was done. Like a warrior princess or an avenging angel, washed in blood and glowing on her way to glory. Wish was going to hug her hard when this was over. Acceptable behaviour after a good fight.

The noise got louder as they climbed. Gunfire and cannons and screams. The crackle of thunderous magic and the roars of beasts best avoided. The scouts added forty chants of heavy breathing and the clatter of equipment to the din. The ground below became a distant shadow of tree cover.

Loose skidded to a stop and Rue almost bumped into her – Wild Wish almost slammed into Rue, and so down the line. Over Rue's shoulder, Wish saw the path had evened slightly, towards another curve around the rock, and another man in a green coat was right there. A moment's stunned stillness as he, like his dead comrade, wondered at this beautiful (bloody) woman before him. Loose regained her senses first; she swung her gun up and pulled the trigger. The rifle clicked – jammed – and the man suddenly lumbered towards her, no weapon in hand but desperate murder in his eyes. Loose swore and tugged at the rifle bolt, trying to clear the jam as Rue pushed to get around her. The man shouted and Loose looked up.

"No –" she said, not quick enough to block him. A big hand grabbed her head, smashed it sideways into the rock, then thrust her the other way. She flew off the path, four limbs flailing through the sky. She and Rue screamed at the same time, and Rue fired from the hip, up through the man's jaw, exploding half his face. He bounced into the rock before toppling over the edge, too.

Rue stopped to look down after Loose but someone pushed Wild Wish on, into her.

"Go, go! They'll have heard!"

Moving without thinking, Wish pressed Rue forward and Rue snapped, charging ahead with an animal snarl. Wish picked up her pace to catch up. Didn't dare look aside, to where Loose had disappeared. Gone so quickly.

Don't think about it now.

They turned another corner and Rue fired again, knocking another man down. They jumped over the body and kept going, up, a final climb and they were there. The rocks gave way to sharp, leafless hedging. Only the trees of dark woodland stood sentry before them. Beyond, gunfire roared. Men shouted senselessly.

Rue stopped, torso heaving. Wild Wish stumbled to her side, ready to collapse from the climb as more girls hurried past. Pound went to Rue and whispered encouragement. They bumped helmets and moved into the trees. The platoon continued swarming past Wish, fanning out.

"Here – *here* Wild," someone called. Four Skills, waving an end of rope. Wild Wish moved on automatic and took the rope to wind around a thick tree trunk, then they threaded it through a pulley and tightened the ratchet without a word. The background noise of gunfire and pain was as steady and indistinct as the crashing of waves, with occasional louder blasts shaking the cliff beneath. But a quiet, plaintive word filled Wish's mind, as she recalled Loose's *No –*

"Ready," Four Skills announced, throwing the rest of the spooled rope over the cliff. She shook it out, to be sure it'd reach the bottom, and they waited. Back through the trees, two dozen women now formed a semi-circle around them. Wish's thoughts expanded beyond Loose falling. One death in millions. People drowned in mud. Witlacing magic could peel men's flesh from their bodies. Poison gases made soldiers cough up their lungs. But Loose had just been unlucky and that somehow seemed worse than everything. Her gun should have worked and she should have survived to travel back home and see Wish's farm. They should've been laughing and hugging this evening. It was possible, an hour ago.

A minute passed before the rope went taut, and then three tugs – the signal. Wish shook herself from her thoughts to join Four Skills and two others in heaving on the rope, to slowly, slowly, raise the Reaper. Occasional muted shouts came from points down the path where others helped guide the weapon up. Captain Tate strode up to Wish's side, watched briefly, then joined in pulling.

With a final heave, it was up: forty kilos of matte metal, wheels, carriage and all. Wish helped turn it around, ready for dragging, then Four Skills slapped her arm to move. She let Skills guide her through the trees, trusting she had some idea where she was going. Towards the sounds of hell.

Light flashed through the tree-line, the field almost visible now. They arrived at the edge of cover together, fell behind trees and peered ahead. A tightly packed army of hundreds, maybe thousands, of men were moving over the grass, left to right, parallel to the tree-line but thirty metres off, armour and blades dull in the morning haze. Far away in their midst lumbered a great humanoid shape: a rock troll or hawk giant, at a guess, from its uneven bulges. Its head was draped in a cowl of what could be hair or armour. Whatever it was, it was out of place; the biggest, nastiest beasts of the Drail's 8th Division should've already struck the Stanclif front line. Holding a giant in reserve put their own troops at risk. But General Amalric had also left this flank open because it ran alongside an impassable cliff, with supposedly no paths up. Silly Drail hubris.

That monster aside, the field was packed with ordinary soldiers. Green coats flapped over metal chest plates as they pushed each other along, shouting for blood. Wish couldn't see any Stanclif blue beyond the chaos, meaning the scouts were in a good spot. Tactically, at least. If the gamble didn't pay off, they'd be mud. This copse was the only cover in an otherwise bare two kilometres of sloped grassland and there was a thin, thin line between bravely clever and outright irresponsibly mad.

Boots tramped up behind Wild Wish as the others spread out, and a small group swung the Reaper into position. Three girls stacked sandbags and rocks under and around it, for a makeshift pillbox.

"Give me a leg up," Four Skills said, pushing Wish's arm. Like Wish was activated by shoves. Which she was. She set her back against the tree and made a lattice of fingers for Skills' boot. She took her friend's weight with a gasp as Four Skills stepped from her hands up onto her shoulders. Then Skills was gone, and Wish saw her swivelling to lie on a huge branch. She'd be doomed if they pinned down her position, but it was an excellent vantage point otherwise.

Wish checked side to side to find a perch of her own, but Tate pointed to the Reaper. "Wild, you're up!"

Wish gawked, pointing a finger back at herself to ask, *why me, with four people already there and the wasted rifle on my back?* Where was the rest of Boot Squad? Tate had spoken, though, and marched off, so Wish swallowed her complaints. She settled in behind the four-foot hunk of metal and took hold of both handles. The others took up positions by trees or rocks, except for Dakoda who crouched over the ammo belt.

"We're good," she said, then faced forward, hand on Wish's shoulder.

Good, sure, like that throatless soldier was *lucky*. Like Loose –

A massive cloud of dirt and smoke erupted far beyond the giant, earth and bodies thrown high in the air, as an artillery shell hit home.

Wish blinked, slowly.

Thirty metres of space separated her from an impossibly large throng of men, charging down the hill to grind the heel of Drail into the world. They were fuelled by a savage will to stomp everything into their empire's mould, when all Wish wanted was for everyone to just stop. Just. Damn. Stop. So we can all go home – to our homes, not *yours*.

The scouts had forty guns in the trees now, a firing squad with Wish at its centre, sweaty palms slick on a monster gun. Someone with thicker arms really should have been on it, like Pound. Dakoda's breath was shallow, by Wish's ear. She squeezed her shoulder and Wish nodded understanding, probably unseen.

"Got the standard," Four Skills announced from up high. Ridiculously calm. The 8th Division flag was flying at least a hundred metres off, a wall of murky cloth hanging from a tall cross-bar, showing a trumpet over a wing.

"Gentlemen!" Tate shouted, though the scouts were neither gentle nor men. "Time to knock on the door! Stanclif! Boorah!"

The chant might have been ironic, but forty voices roared it back, Wish included. "Boorah – Stanclif!"

Four Skills fired first, the crack of her giant-slayer rifle triggering everyone else's guns. Wild Wish squeezed and the Reaper spat a thunderous rattle of rounds. Wish screamed to add to the noise, taken by the sheer power of the gun shuddering in her hands. She swept the sights across the army ahead as Dakoda frantically fed the flaring beast. The nearest flank of enemies went down. The next line went down. Way behind them, the 8th's standard swayed, slowly toppling. Wild Wish raked the gun from side to side as men turned her way, forty, eighty, hundreds disappearing in little puffs of blood. She slipped up only when a stream of fire flew out from the trees, bursting across the clearing to engulf another ten, twenty men? Most likely Emi, their dirt-minded mage – a theory confirmed by a mean laugh that followed, so loud it was audible over the gunfire.

By the time 8th Division realised they'd been flanked, their losses must've pushed four figures. The Reaper spat six hundred rounds a minute. The ammo box contained a chain of thousands. The men were routed, panicking, knocking each other over in a mad dash to get away. Those brave few who tried to punch through to the scouts were dead in seconds.

The gun clicked dry, and Wild Wish stopped yelling, breathing almost as fast as the gun had fired. Dakoda shouted reassurances she didn't hear, feeding in the next chain of bullets the same time she kicked the spent box away. All around, the scouts kept firing and shouting, making as big a noise as they could to drive fear into the Drail. Rue cursed louder than all the rest. Behind that racket, a drum started, down the hill.

"The battalion are advancing!" Tate shouted. "One more chain on the Reaper, then we're coming for them! Send them home!"

Dakoda slapped the gun and shouted it was ready. Wish nodded.

The drum rapped out a steady martial beat, bouncing through the trees. Out on the field, a great bloody mass of 8th Division were mangled on the ground. The rest were falling over themselves to get away. Further back, their forces were grinding to a standstill, meeting new resistance. Over their heads, the great shape of their giant tore an arm upwards, some poor victim flying weightlessly up into the sky. Flying as Loose had done. *No –*

"Fucking fire!" Dakoda screamed in Wish's ear, and she squeezed the trigger, screaming back. Sweeping the gun left and right again, catching men in their unarmoured, fleeing backs. Wild Wish screamed louder, eyes narrowing, trying not to see the dying. She pulled the gun up slightly, bullets ripping through heads before clearing them totally. She released the trigger with half the belt remaining. Before Dakoda could scold her into firing again, the platoon sprung up on Tate's command.

The Blood Scouts charged out of the trees in a sporadic wave. Dakoda tore her disapproving look away from Wish to join then, and Wish kicked off from the Reaper and ran sidelong into a tree, snatching up her Long 0.48. Leaning against the tree, she looked through the scope. Between the charging backs of her friends, Drail soldiers were turning around, aware they couldn't flee fast enough. Some drew swords against the scouts' guns. Four Skills fired from above, a steady, casual culling, one by one.

Wild Wish probed the battle with her scope. The Stanclif forces were visible now, storming the slope to the right, hundreds of riflemen with vehicles trundling behind them. Closer, there was Rue, gun down at her side in favour of a hatchet that she swung into someone's face. Aside, Larkin put all her weight into her rifle, bayonet driven through a man's crotch. Over their heads, Wild Wish picked out the giant, a long way off, retreating with the rest. A hawk giant, right enough, feathered with panels of loose skin, flapping like badly woven capes. Wish got its bobbing head in her cross-hairs. Too far to hit, and why bother – it was crushing its own comrades as it fled.

Back to the centre, and there was the standard, being raised again. Some Drail hero was trying to rally the troops, blood all over his face, one last attempt to show they had some fight left. It was actually working, as men rushed to his side shakily aiming rifles any which way; never underestimate a flag. As the bar slowly lifted, the man rose from a knee, straining against the heavy weight, and the mud-stained flag caught the wind. Some Drail cheered. But the drum was drumming and the girls were carving a path towards him as the full might of Sick Brigade caught up.

Wish held him in her sights as he looked up at the resurrected flag with a death-stare grin for this symbol that made sense of the world and this war and the thousands dead. A valiant rise, with so much hope in his face. A shame. Wish fired her last shot of the day and the flag fell. The Drail choked on their cheers. She imagined one whimpering "No –" before Rue split his head open.

2

With the unprecedented scale of the fighting, and armies ill-equipped to deal with the aftermath, entire fields of corpses became breeding grounds for pestilence. The most effective solution was fire – but this caused friction with the Church of the Venerate Flesh. To counter the Church's influence, Stanclif propagandists produced one of the more outrageous claims of the war, and used fear of Drail necromancy, rather than disease, to justify the burnings.
Sickness and Sin: Medicine and Religion Through the Ages, Grunberg, p. 476

This wasn't much fun anymore.

Of course, no one ever said that it was *supposed* to be fun – though the hawkers and posters back home heavily implied it. They used words like glory and honour and superlatives about reaching your full potential, and between the lines you knew they were really telling you that war was *exciting*. And it was, frequently, especially if you grew up in a shabby little place like Swelig, where there were precisely two other people your own age and the most drama you were likely to see concerned arguments haggling at the farmers market. Sneaking out to join the war effort, to *travel* and take risks, had been a world apart from Wild Wish's grey prospects in her hometown. It'd been terrifying and brutal and at times deeply traumatic – crossing the sea, slumming on the front line, being pushed to physical prowess, dodging blades and bullets. But it had also been exhilarating and, impossibly, introduced Wish to dozens of amazing girls she would never have met otherwise.

It *was* fun and it *was* good. Sometimes.

Then some days it was really, really bad.

Wild Wish was trying to count the positives of this day, though. Most of them had survived. They'd won the battle. And she'd found a comfortable mound of broken earth to rest on and reflect, while everyone else was busy. But there were dead men as far as she could see. Or at least bits of them. Smoke rose from the churned mud and blood formed puddles like it'd been raining all morning, glinting bright red in the sun. Once the gun smoke cleared, the other smell would become unbearable. The stench of death. And Loose was gone. Colt, Boot Squad's only cook, and Pally of Sabre Squad, were dead, too. Three out of forty. A dozen more battles like this and there would be no scouts left. Then, with a dozen more battles like this everyone else might be dead, too. Those few who survived could take a castle each. A country, maybe?

Wish's fellow Blood Scouts had spread out across the battlefield, joining the few hundred straggling Stanclif soldiers left looting or looking for some other release. Rue was stomping between bodies, occasionally striking down with her axe. She would have done it even if she hadn't watched her lover die, that was just Rue. A wiry yet muscular brute of a woman and Wish's closest but most unlikely friend. Loyal, honest and good for drinking with, and for hugs too firm to be misunderstood, but also quick to violence and slow to stop. After massacres like this (there had been a few now), Wish preferred to let Rue do her thing while she retreated to thoughts of her dream-farm, with its cosy wooden cottages and soft-tongued donkeys, and all the girls tending lush green fields together. Under a dazzling blue sky not unlike this one.

Except Loose wouldn't be there, now, and *here* the dazzling sky only helped illuminate the carnage. There was little green left in the churned mud and seamless gore of Green Rise, and in place of laughter and birdsong there were only the occasional pleas of the dying as scavengers finished them off.

Strictly speaking, Stanclif condemned violence outside the heat of battle – it wasn't *Civilised* – but the only judgement here came from the waves of Ven Zealots shouting to stop purgers from burning bodies. The zealots appeared without fail after every battle, as though they'd been hiding in the weeds, to preach about the

Sacred Flesh and the anathema of the flame. Wish admired their passion, kind of, but there was a time and a place for screaming vitriol and it wasn't just after surviving a nightmare, when you were trying to imagine nice things.

A skinny guy in ragged robes and chains was flapping his arms around a pair of young men who were trying to drag bodies to a makeshift pit. A bomb crater, half full of corpses already. They kept losing their grip as the zealot shrieked in their faces then bounced away as they swatted at him. Both men looked deeply tired – they'd obviously drawn short straws while the bulk of 6th Brigade had already left the slaughter behind.

Wild Wish hoped they'd leave soon, too, to give her some peace.

Sarge cast a shadow over that thought. She asked, "Not helping clear up?"

Wish squinted at her, silhouetted against the bright sky, and chose attack as the best defence: "We agreed I wouldn't have to man the Reaper."

"Tate's orders, not my fault if she saw you available. Were you lost in your own thoughts then, too?"

"I'm not lost if I *like* the thoughts. You know how many rounds we got through? Four figures, Sarge. That's not me. I'm a precision tool, you point me at the right target and I end wars with the *minimum* damage."

Sarge got an ugly sceptical look on her face. She had a thick-skinned, deep-lined countenance that could show kind, experienced understanding, or, as now, stony hardness. Wish suspected she'd once been a librarian. "When did you ever end a war, Wild?"

Wish scuffed a boot through the mud. "Not today, obviously. Unless we just convinced Vinkent Narroway to surrender his entire empire?"

"Hardly," Sarge snorted. "The Drail have fled to Wick, and it'll be a while before we get any designs on taking that fortress. General Easter's having everyone settle on the river bend – everyone but Command, who have their eye on a pool town over the ridge. Blythe. They're sending a company to secure it."

"And you're telling me because he needs my approval?" Wish prompted.

"We're the advance party. More specifically, you are. Take Oksy, follow the stream upriver three miles and you'll find Blythe. We'll follow on, just want to get eyes ahead."

"Is this because I got to sit down at that damn gun while everyone else was running about squealing? Because I did not *want* to sit at that gun. It's Rock Squad's gun."

"This is because you're a good scout, Wish. That's all."

"Then why Oksy? Can't I go with Four?"

Sarge's scolding face told her not to be childish. "Four's already on her way, with Emi, taking the road – *you* get the quieter route. Less exposed. That's your reward for manning the Reaper, Wild. Count it a blessing."

"A single blessing balanced by Oksy."

"Suck it up – someone else is gonna mule your stuff up there for you, after all. And be careful; if Command think it's a sensible place to set up camp, then the Drail probably did, too." She patted Wish's arm and paused as if about to say something encouraging. How Wish had been a real hero today, sorry about Loose, these hard times would pass, something like that. But Sarge just grunted like whatever she wanted to say was obvious, then trudged off.

Wild Wish stood, stamped her feet, shouldered her rifle and traipsed off the other way. Reconnoitring a town was better than handling the dead, she supposed – and the chances were she could find a billet there, no tent tonight. There might even be booze and fresh underwear and food.

Oksy was standing over a body with Corporal Brogan, a Cheaster Battalion rifleman the scouts kept crossing paths with. They both smiled the knowing smirks of a too-pretty, preternaturally friendly couple. Oksy was a sturdy girl, with long black hair and a scar over her left eye, smooth-skinned, soft-voiced and always around offering advice on *everything*. Brogan was cutting a dead man's teeth out. He said, "Heard that was your work on the gun, Wild. We all owe you one. Their charge fell apart right when things were getting nasty."

Wish raised an eyebrow and indicated the field around them – he didn't call that nasty? There was a pair of legs erect like fence posts three paces away. Just legs.

Brogan shrugged. "Could've been us, without your help."

"Our guns and a load of glass bombs dropped over" – Oksy pointed, as though the exact location mattered – "by the east flank. And we had four earth-minders who caused a quake to cave in the Drail reserve artillery. We had them convinced they were surrounded, pretty much. Must've been ten or fifteen thousand Drail on the field. Against Sick Brigade's eight thousand, max. This was a coup."

"Uh-huh," Wild Wish said, barely listening. "As a reward, Oksy, you and me are going for a walk. There's a little town that's ours for the taking."

It wasn't that Wish was jealous of all the information her fellow scout was quick to offer, and maybe her pretty looks and effortless charm, but just that Oksy seemed to know *too much*. The first day they'd met, in a barricaded cellar between battles, Oksy had asked Wish if she was into girls – with smirking sympathy, which was worse than mockery.

Oksy wore a knowing half-smile now, too. Always amused by Wish. She said, "We've been invited to party. Brogan's guys have a keg of maltique."

Wish paused. The thick, biscuity liquor of maltique, so common at home, was a luxury on the front line. All this country had was weak, fancy wines. Brogan pumped an eyebrow and she said, "Our town could probably accommodate a few guests. But you might have to keep the noise down around General Easter."

Brogan's face fell. "You're securing a place for Command?"

"We are." Wish slipped a hand through Oksy's arm and started walking her away. Oksy called back promises to regroup later as she skipped over a couple of dead bodies. "Four Skills is already on her way, let's beat her to it."

"Ah." Oksy pulled her arm free and fell into step. Her knowing smirk was back. "And are we expecting resistance? Or a friendly welcome?"

Wild Wish gave her a wan smile. When were they ever welcome, really? By now, the liberated civilians were too bitter that their homes were burning to be thankful about being liberated. In the south of Farne, when they'd quickly reclaimed big patches of land, the locals had been delighted to see a blue uniform, but up here, the army had been dug in for months mulching the countryside. Wish had received buckets of malicious looks and a man had even spat at Small, the least offensive of all the scouts. If they didn't have each other, this would be a distinctly horrible place to be all round. But they did have each other. Every night, Wish thanked the stars, the Saints, the Book of Body, Cane, the Knowledge and every other belief-system for giving her the Blood Scouts. Well, most of them. Oksy was still annoying.

Wish and Oksy cut a path between corpses and body parts. A severed hand, bones sticking out. A broken rifle, snapped in two – had a poor fool been shot through the gun? Unable to defend himself, same as Loose. Wild Wish closed her eyes against the memory, and felt Oksy soften alongside her. *No –*

"You okay, Wild? I know how much you liked her. You were there, weren't you, when –"

"Yeah," Wish said, curt enough to stop her asking more.

Oksy waited. Figuring Wild Wish would confess what? She liked Loose. Beautiful, fun, generous – *everyone* liked Loose. It wasn't easy seeing her with Rue night after night, and it was even less fun knowing Wish would never get a chance now. Not even a last bloody hug. Loose was gone, same as the thousands of dead they were walking into the ground. The best Wish could do – the best anyone could do – was accept this win, seek out a nice bed and drink enough to stop thinking about anything ever again.

Another Ven Zealot started shouting, across the field, and the soldiers near him shouted back. He'd climbed on top of the scorched shell of a tank and men threw stones at him to get down. "Forgiveness starts here! Do not waste your sacrifice!"

"You know Harmon's taken a few girls back down for the rest of the supplies," Oksy said. "They'll give Loose a proper pyre. Maybe you want to fall back and join them. I can go on ahead."

Wild Wish slowed down. From a fall that high, whatever they found, it wouldn't exactly be Loose. She didn't need to see that. "Think I'd prefer to be useful."

They hiked up a ridge above the devastation, to where the grass thrived again. There was the stream on the other side, snaking back along hedges and through little clumps of trees. As they continued, Oksy described where the morning had left them, tactically. Wish ignored the numerical details of different Drail divisions regrouping at Wick Fortress, but latched onto the possibility that defeating them there could leave all of Farne in the Comity's hands. After Farne came Har Coul, and from there it was a clear line onto the heart of Drail itself. Following a year of unthinkable bloodshed, maybe this *was* the tipping point. Maybe Wild Wish's slaughter would open the way for the united Comity of Imperial Stanclif and Khibba to finally secure global peace. Home by Relight Festival, as they promised. A year late, perhaps, but still. It was only a three-thousand-mile march to the Drail capital, Arrow City, at twenty miles a day –

Only, Oksy kept talking, and she had other details, about every conflict across the three theatres of war. Countless border shifts that Wish didn't even try to follow. The bottom line was that everything was too complicated to guarantee anything. A case in point, Oksy said, was that the Stanclif earth-minders had done well in today's battle, but could just as easily have been killed, dealing them an awful blow. Dirt-minding, as everyone who wasn't as carefully precise as Oksy called it, was a devastating magic, but risky to use, as it cost little bits of the mage's sanity, which generally didn't work out well in the midst of battle.

To prevent a complete rundown of the ins and outs of the entire global conflict, Wish eventually said, "Okay sure, Oksy. But like, on a scale of one to thirteen, how much closer would you say I came to ending the war today?"

Oksy's trademark smirk was back. "Well, the Battle of Green Rise has redrawn the lines by a couple of miles, but we're still outgunned by 8th Division and now they're dug in hard."

"I must've killed *hundreds* of people today," Wish said. "Loose died. That nice hill back there will never be the same. It was worth more than a bunch of nonsense names in a bunch of nonsense places, wasn't it?"

Oksy didn't answer, because they both knew it probably wasn't. Instead, she looked back reflectively to the mess of Green Rise and maybe thought what Wish was thinking: the hill might recover, at least, but everything else was fucked.

The walk up the clear stream, under the shade of trees, helped. No blood in the water or bodies on the banks; they could almost have been home. Give it an hour or two and half the army would descend on the stream to wash, but for now it was just Wish and Oksy on a country stroll. Rifles slung over their shoulders, hands swinging close to touching – even if Oksy was *so annoying*, Wish could pretend she was someone else.

Better than nothing. Back home she had nothing.

Those thoughts survived mere minutes until the sight of Blythe rudely interrupted. From the cover of trees, Wish saw a small settlement penned in by red-brick walls, the tiled roofs of circular towers rising from the centre. An unpaved road veered away from its entrance through another patch of woodland off to the right. An open pair of cast-iron double-doors led into the town, twelve feet high and surrounded by green-coats. A swarm of men, hurrying crates through the doors to a flat-bed carriage, strapped to a pair of impatiently stomping pack beasts – armour-hided, five-legged animals, bigger than horses, stronger than bulls. It was a transport barely cheaper than a petrol engine, likely slower. And the men were shouting in Slanik, the language of the Drail's creepiest allies, Low Slane. Between that transport and the men's shouts, someone – or some*thing* – important was being removed from the site.

"I count at least eight," Oksy whispered, watching through her rifle scope.

It was possible there wouldn't be many more inside, given how these ones were preparing to leave. They could just let them go. Hadn't today already been enough? Yet Wild Wish unslung her gun and quietly drew back the bolt. They had the trees for cover, and the advantage of surprise, though the green-coats might quickly close those gates or run out of sight. If she shot the pack-beasts, though? Hells, why not add murdering innocent animals to the tally.

A glint of light caught Wish's eye. She raised a hand to shade her face. Across the other side of the road, a mirror was signalling out of the trees. Four Skills, already in position. And if she was there, Emi was too – their dirt-minder would heavily tip things in the scouts' favour. Yes. If anyone could secure a town, it was them – Wish, the once inoffensive daughter of a bootmaker from Swelig, now deadly at distances of up to two hundred metres, with Oksy her (maybe, not quite) equal, and Four Skills even better. The Blood Scouts' sniping elite. Wish couldn't remember what clean hair smelt like, but she knew the three of them could kill ten men in five seconds. And Emi – she could do so much more.

The men were trying to flee, not ready for a fight – maybe they could kill them before they reacted. They could take a town. With precision and skill. Blythe looked sturdy, inviting. A big chimney was smoking inside. Maybe they had fresh bread. The soldiers were the only problem; once they were gone Wish would devour *all* the bread. A triumph to make the day sort of good again. Wish whispered the best part, "The animals can live."

"We're going for the soldiers, then?" Oksy said.

"Get the ones nearest the gate," Wild Wish said. "Let's keep the doors open."

3

The Blood Scouts (as the 28th Light Scouts Platoon were commonly known) are not well documented, but we believe they conducted a robust campaign of subterfuge and guerrilla attacks on behalf of "Sick" Brigade. They were the collected battle daughters of one Captain "Tenacious" Tate, a war widow who disappeared from official records after the Battle of the Basin. Estimated to comprise some three or four dozen women, including sappers, snipers and even the odd magic user, they had a reputation as unruly outcasts. Statesman Dowel once referred to the Blood Scouts as "our deadliest and most shameful secret", referring to the unthinkable practice of seeing women turned warrior.

Dueley's Comprehensive: The One War in 10 Volumes (Vol. 4), p. 35

Wish fired first and shifted, to fire again, as the others joined in with a quick barrage of shots. The green-coats fell like fairground targets, with only a handful left to dive for cover. But the gates squeaked, shifting – dammit, there were a couple inside, closing them out. Two men fired back blindly from behind the carriage, as the metal frame sparked with shots from Four Skills. Wish quickly sighted a knee sticking out from the carriage and shot, knocking the soldier down. Oksy finished him. But the doors were creaking closed, with one green-coat left outside, still firing randomly across the road. No time, had to move – Wild Wish half rose, but Oksy gave her a warning glance. Daft idea.

"We can't let them –"

Something cracked thunderously in the far trees, the branches and leaves shaking. Four Skills stopped firing. The girls froze, same as the green-coats around the entrance. The trees shook and snapped and Wild Wish stood up to watch. Did the Slanik soldiers have some other fiend waiting for them? Another giant or some other earth shaker? With an immense, wrenching crack, a huge shape flew out from the trees and Wish ducked despite the distance. The pillar of a dismembered tree trunk launched through the sky as though fired from a crossbow. The soldiers in town yelled in fear as the man behind the carriage bolted to get inside. The trunk flew through him and into the doors with a terrific bang. One door flung wide open over whoever was behind it as the other snapped off its hinges and thunked into the earth, before toppling onto the felled tree.

Wish gaped in awe. There were smears of blood around the edges of the broken doors. An instant ruin of a previously sturdy defence, and no sign of life beyond it now. If any green-coats remained, that demonstration would have them running.

The still moment was broken by a high, savage screech of a laugh. A cackle, really, starting nasty and getting worse. The mad, terrifying laughter of someone severed from their senses. Emi, paying the price for such a fierce stroke of magic. The pack beasts kicked and stomped and huffed in growing panic, straining against the carriage but held in place by a brake lever. If the hurled tree hadn't been enough to scare anyone beyond those walls, that laugh would be – it belonged to a ragged witch dragging herself out of a tomb. The carriage brake snapped and the two beasts pulled their yoke to shreds in desperation to get away, stampeding off the road, trailing broken wood behind them. Emi laughed and laughed, and even Oksy looked unsettled.

"We'd better get in there," Wild Wish suggested, knowing Four Skills would already be doing whatever could be done for Emi. "Before they dig in."

Oksy nodded, and together they ran across empty ground to the broken doors, glancing up at the ramparts to be sure they weren't being watched. As they reached the gates, skipping over the green-coats' bodies, Emi's cackles died down, wavering between laughs and whimpers. Oksy rushed to the left and Wild Wish skirted the fallen tree, both with their rifles up. Through the gap, Wish saw the main street into Blythe – a wide, unpaved road flanked by a mix of timber-framed stone huts and modern brick houses. Another green-coat lay lifeless about twenty metres back, face down. No other movement. Wish nodded to Oksy and she ducked under the tree branches, slipping inside in a crouch, scanning for window lookouts. Wild Wish followed, moving around the other door, opening up the view.

As a pool town, Blythe presented a warren of possibilities for hiding beyond that main road. The place was built over its own personal reservoir, taking advantage of Farne's frequent rainfall with gutters lining every spare path, channelling water through subterranean turbines to turn mill-wheels and pumps. Narrow canals ran in front of all the buildings, while bridges and walkways connected them at higher levels. If the scouts left the cover of the gates there'd be a million places to find enemies, and Wild Wish shared a sceptical look with Oksy. Her friend looked neutral, serious, not prepared to step inside either.

Emi's laughter finished at last. Four Skills would catch up soon, and they could cover the entrance together until backup arrived. But as they waited, watching the dead town in silence, a window squeaked open and Wish swung her scope to it. A hand came up, shaking, fingers splayed. Waving for peace? Then another hand, something bunched up in it. Material that both hands quickly worked to hang out the window. It unravelled into the familiar crimson rock-gate flag of Imperial Stanclif. The person shouted in Farnish, a hoarse male voice. He added words they were more likely to understand, first in Stanish, "Hail Stanclif! Boorah!" then Khib, covering all the bases, "Nit Khibba! Nit!"

Wish kept watching, in case it was a trick, and the flag was waved more fervently as the man repeated those words, voice growing hopeful, seeing as they hadn't murdered him yet. More windows opened, more hands waved, and a door opened. Oksy snapped her rifle to it, but an old lady hobbled into the road, hands raised high, and shouted, "Welcome Stanclif! Welcome!"

Wild Wish lowered her rifle. It was over. Time to reap the heroes' benefits.

She nodded to Oksy. They walked side-by-side into Blythe, heads high. Small cheers rose around them, maybe a half-dozen civilians hooting and banging on pans, tears in their voices. The old lady rushed closer, pointing up the road as the scouts passed the remains of the green-coats caught by the flying tree. Three, or maybe four, men had been behind the doors. Their coats covered darker uniforms underneath. Black? One of the men wasn't quite dead, and started crawling on his belly, coughing, legs apparently not working. He breathed heavily, looking up as the people of the town emerged from their doorways. He glanced at Wish, frightened, mouth covered in blood. She returned the look uncertainly, a question shared that neither knew the answer to: was she going to finish him off?

But someone ran past and a booted foot came out of nowhere to catch his jaw. The soldier jerked into the ground as three villagers crowded him, kicking furiously, slobbering with pent up rage.

Wish cleared her throat and braced herself to intervene, not really wanting to. More villagers arrived to pull the others back, though, in a mess of emotion – they insisted it was over, don't stoop to their level. The soldier was motionless. Wish gave Oksy a sideways glance and muttered, "He was dying anyway, wasn't he?"

The old lady tugged at her sleeve to pull her away, leaving that unanswered, urging them to follow. She blabbered in Farnish. If it meant leaving this mess behind, Wish was happy to go.

"What's she saying?" she asked Oksy, fount of all knowledge, who helpfully replied, "She wants us to follow her."

Wish rolled her eyes and continued along the street. They passed what the Slanik soldiers had been moving: three more crates, one of them larger than the others, open with bits of metal and wiring hanging out. The town's united celebration grew in volume and the main street filled with everyone in calling distance, maybe twenty people now, a paltry number considering Blythe's size. The old lady stopped in front of a large building, some kind of storehouse with doors big enough to admit a dragon. She rattled a padlocked chain on the door, getting more excited as she demanded Wish open it. The other locals pressed in – an impoverished, thin-fleshed bunch, hollow faces watching. They were dirty, underfed, and frightened despite the liberation. The old lady took Wish's hand and insisted something, pointing at the chained doors, eager to free whatever was inside.

Wish looked back across the town, past a lot of expectant, anxious faces, to the entrance where Four Skills and Emi were walking in, watching her. Wish shrugged, gestured for the old lady to step back and lifted her rifle. She shot through the padlock and the civilians rushed past to wrench the chains free. Oksy and Wish were pushed back as the crowd heaved the doors open and let sunlight into the cavernous interior. The locals ran in with shouts mixed between worry and delight. They started pouring out moments later, taking more people with them, swarming around the scouts – they were hurriedly reclaiming family, friends, neighbours who'd been locked away. More than one wail of despair came out – not everyone inside had made it.

Why would the Drail lock up the townsfolk like this? Wish wondered. Had there been an uprising? As the growing crowd filtered out, it got stranger. There were other races in there, not just the Farnish humans: a couple of shin-high waders darted between their legs; a stout trunk lumbered out, squinting its big eyes against the sunlight; and what looked like a family of spidroms scuttled by at the fringes, careful not to alarm anyone with their many chittering legs. Either Blythe was a crazily cosmopolitan town, or the Drail had gathered a *very* strange group of prisoners here.

There were black uniforms under the soldiers' coats, Wish recalled. The Slanik Dread Corps wore black. They were said to do scary things . . .

The questions were for later, though, as the escaped prisoners spread out around the scouts, their hugs and deep breaths of fresh air subsiding into realisation of who had saved them. They cheered and smiled at Wild Wish. Her cheeks flushed; a whole town's adoration was a lot. But she'd allow it. Then a young woman burst out of the crowd – a dark, terrifying shadow – too fast for either scout to defend against. She jumped Wish, clamping her hands on either side of her face, and planted a heavy kiss on Wish's lips. She pulled back and kissed again. She squeezed her arms around Wish and said, with husky relief, "Thank you!"

Wild Wish was stiff as a plank as she accepted the thanks, unable to keep from smiling. Hell, she *knew* this kind of gratitude from beautiful strangers was possible, no matter what the others kept saying. Oksy's smirk told her to enjoy it while it lasted.

"When you're done taking advantage of young ladies who think you're a guy," Four Skills called out, beyond the hubbub, "take a look."

Wild Wish drew back to glance her way. The sniper had passed the crowd with Emi, and the pair were staring further into town. Wish craned to see what they were looking at, something in the direction of the smoking chimney she'd noticed from outside.

Emi said, "That is a *nasty* pile of bodies."

4

Two of the three dominant global powers had proudly separated religion from state by the turn of the 8th century. However, it is arguable that they merely traded one form of faith for another: Stanclif high society extolled the advance of rational science and their institution of Civilised Society with a dangerously exclusionary fervour, while the Drail leadership conducted a nationalist crusade through the "Purification".
A Primer of Modern Thought, H. Minant, p. 175

Constans Maringdale held down a retch. She was not squeamish, but anyone would struggle to keep their breakfast just seeing a worm-eye, let alone having to interrogate one. The experience was especially bad for her, a third-class intention mage, thanks to the barrage of *feelings* the creature put out. Humans were rarely capable of more than two conflicting feelings at once, but these things, with countless sensory receptors, were a confused, skittish subspecies, full of chaotic emotions that Maringdale had to work hard at filtering out.

Such was the life of a Purification officer, hunting internal threats to the Drail Empire: after you tracked vermin through swamps and tunnels and dragged them screaming back to the cells, you had to unravel their thoughts, too.

Maringdale didn't know how her partner (she refused to call him *supervisor*) could stomach touching them, but Sin Sight Panderlair emotionlessly clamped one of the writhing captive's sensory tendrils between forceps as he held his other hand out for another tool. He said, "Words, soldier, it is only words! A location for your comrades and this all ends."

Maringdale grimaced as Panderlair took the scalpel and the worm-eye exhaled hot, ugly pain. Their aide, Donut, hovered by the wall, refusing to look. The thing's fish-like mouth gasped for mercy. It was no soldier and barely needed breaking, but Panderlair was a perfectionist. Maringdale could parse the rebels' location with trial and error, through her witlacing – they could name possibilities and she would sense the worm-eye's truest response as easily as reading an expression. But Panderlair wanted to make an example of these irate fishermen, to limit further resistance to the Drail occupation of the Coak wetlands. As always, he wanted not just to triumph over their enemies, but to utterly break them, as was the Drail way.

Worm-eyes were barely humanoid: though bipedal, their upper limbs (not exactly arms) protruded from waist-height, with claw-like hands. Their domed heads had gaping jaws, around which probing tendrils stuck out like fleshy whiskers. Their sensory receptors, always moving, writhed as if the things' faces were alive with maggots. As Panderlair cut those feelers, each one produced another sensation that Maringdale had to block out if she wished to stay focused on the information they needed. Here a sharp sense of imminent danger, there a confused spark of heat.

"Don't know, don't know!" the worm-eye insisted, using one of only a handful of Drail phrases it had been drilled to say. It was a lie.

"This doesn't stop," Panderlair promised, his dry tone offset only by the strain of squeezing harder. "No one cares what we do to you. No one started a war over Coak. Your people aren't even protected under the Treaty of Tynes."

That was also a lie, but the worm-eye writhed, making a noise that could've been weeping. These things *seeped*, too – murky liquid dripping out of a mouth that didn't seem to properly close. It reached for memories of home and family and love, Maringdale sensed. Everything betrayed and abandoned, as Panderlair claimed.

Of course, though worm-eyes actually were protected by the Treaty of Tynes, that only mattered if you left witnesses. And when Vinkent Narroway had announced the repulsive worm-eyes' expulsion from the Drail Valley, the international community did nothing. Maringdale had been happy to see a Coakel family guiding a wagon out of her neighbourhood in Pace. Leaving the streets cleaner of slobber. She wasn't a bigot – she merely understood they were better off in their eastern swamps, where they belonged, the same way the Drail were better off not having to watch their language in taverns. To say nothing of witlacers like her, who wouldn't have to endure the barrage of their unfiltered, clumsy feelings anymore.

Besides, there was logic behind the divisions involved in the rewritten boundaries of the Drail Empire. Trunks were relocated to the lands of factories and mines because their stout bodies were built for labour. The Garter moneylenders *needed* breaking up, with their monopolies harming small, local businesses. Every race under the great Drail umbrella needed organisation, to best support the Empire – what did the Drail stand for, if not working towards a common goal? If they didn't restructure the Boldarow continent, then Stanclif and Khibba would roll over them and they'd all be slaves of a vile foreign power.

The process might be harsh, but Maringdale believed in it. She only wished she could do more than hunting snivelling civilians for piecemeal results. She and Panderlair, together with their lackey Donut, had thwarted their share of insidious plots, but Maringdale hadn't signed onto the war effort to chase insignificant Eastern Front bugs. The Drail could give up their gains in the backwards countries out here, let the Khib advance as far as the Garter frontiers, and what would be lost? Savage lands better left to savage people. No, an intention mage of her calibre, with her fighting experience, belonged on the Western Front where the real battles would be won. She longed to pit her skills against the pompous Stanclif, instead of this diaspora of ugly races that Khibba controlled. Yet it was the recurring story of her life that she should be downplayed. Her talents surpassed those of many men who had been awarded higher Intention classes, just as her skills had been superior to those of most men above her in the tax office.

But the war had brought new opportunities. She was making a mark, in her way.

After a squelching pop that made Maringdale wince, the worm-eye finally bleated submission, waving a little claw to indicate the map Donut was holding. He brought it over and the bleeding, sobbing creature dragged a claw over it, searching for the right spot. It pointed hard, determined to get this done. That was where its friends were hiding. The worm-eye slumped with whimpering shame into the iron chair.

Panderlair stood, holding the map tenderly, and turned his one eye to Maringdale for confirmation. She rolled her own eyes at the theatre of it all, then nodded, yes, it was telling the truth. Panderlair nodded back. Again, Maringdale didn't need her powers to understand it was an order. As he marched out of the door, she drew her four-shot revolver. The worm-eye barely had a chance to raise what few twitching sensors still worked before she fired. The abomination was thrown back in the chair, domed head erupting over the wall behind it.

A mercy. It would only suffer, living with the damage they'd done to it. Imprisoned in Drail camps, it would've known untold nightmares. It was as much a mercy to the creature as it was to anyone who'd have had to keep looking at the revolting thing.

Maringdale and Donut said little as they burned the body, behind the concrete bunker. Donut was a big man, more fat than muscle, who looked perpetually confused. He was too slow and good-natured to make a proper soldier, and came from a wealthy family with enough clout, and sense, to keep him far from the front line. His parents likely hadn't counted on the horrors he'd see with Panderlair and Maringdale as babysitters, though. Over three months of this work, Donut hadn't quite hardened to it yet, but he kept going, without complaint. Maringdale knew when he was upset, or doubted their violence, or would just rather be anywhere else, but he never voiced such thoughts, and made a diligent dogsbody. Given enough food and rest, he did not dwell on what was happening in between.

The worm-eye almost teased a new reaction from him, which Maringdale studied carefully. Donut's face was ashen as they sat after finishing their work. Back in the mess hall, with bowls of gruel, she sensed his doubts over eating, possibly for the first time in his life. But Donut's rusty cogs turned and he gave a light shrug before lifting his spoon.

"Not even after the sight of a mutilated worm-eye," Maringdale muttered. He looked up, not quite hearing, and she gave him a light smile, showing off her three gold teeth.

Rather than try to figure her out, he announced around a slobbering mouthful, "Is good."

"It's not good," Maringdale said. "It's never good." She stirred her own bowl of grey slush, oats stewed in water with a vague, woody spice meant to convince the soldiers it was nutritious. On the best days, they tossed in ground-up slop left over from the officers' mess, dregs fed to dogs in peace time, but today was not one of those days. A layer of skin caught on Maringdale's spoon — hopefully trimmed from a vegetable.

Donut swallowed his mouthful, preparing to say something. Another question about her witlacing, which kept proving conceptually above him. "So, do worm-eyes think in Drail? You don't speak their language, do you? Like, what did he sound like in his mind?"

"Intention doesn't require words, or sound," Maringdale told him. As she had a thousand times before. She couldn't be mad at Donut, though; most people doubted her talents, whereas he just struggled to understand. "But how do *you* know it was a he?"

"In the" — Donut gestured to somewhere vaguely below his chest — "you know."

Maringdale did not know, nor did she want to. "Intention magic works the same way you know that. We just know."

Donut accepted it with a profound nod and continued eating. Safe in the knowledge that he had made an attempt at understanding, his day's work could now be considered complete. Maringdale tried to feel as satisfied herself. Little by little, they were weeding the Empire — so the Purification preached. But she imagined soldiers in the trenches, with none of her talents, could merely raise their heads and gun down a score of worm-eyes in a matter of minutes – actual, Khib soldiers – while *she* spent a week hounding disruptive fishermen.

Too valuable, was the excuse she'd been given when she last applied for a military assignment. The same they said when she first enlisted: *you are more valuable in a civilian role*. Never mind she could read their real intentions. No woman belonged in the actual fighting; the concept itself was offensive to Drail sensibilities. Never mind she bore the scars of someone who fought most weekends back in Pace, merely to keep herself entertained. They thought her appearance, the crookedly reset nose and gold teeth, scarred chin and practical clothing, were all a show. She stabbed at her gruel, wishing it was one of those bastards' faces.

Panderlair strode in, stiff-legged, to interrupt her brooding. Bald, gaunt, wrinkled and missing an eye, his grim face fit his perpetually grim mood. With his scarring, it looked like he had a prolapsed arse where his left eye should be. He'd turned the weakness to a strength, insisting his one eye saw evil better by making up for its lost twin, but Maringdale caught a hint of insecurity every time he said it. He also dressed better than Maringdale or Donut to make up for those looks, with a thick gold chain around his neck, the white and cream livery of the Purification, and his velveteen cloak putting their bulky, utilitarian greatcoats to shame. He was truly proud of what they did, believing, in no small way, that the war effort rested on their shoulders. He'd made a sound mentor, over the eleven months Maringdale had trudged around this war, but he was a reject from the real war effort, the same as her, unable to see straight and occasionally slipping into moments of confused distraction.

Sitting down, pulling over a bowl of gruel for himself, Panderlair announced, "We've received orders. Garter. An outpost bordering the Mattin foothills. We're to investigate an explosion and punish those responsible. Without delay." The other side of the Mattin Mountains would put them on the south front. Not much further west, but better than here, at least. "We leave in an hour."

Maringdale jerked upright. "After three days of swamps and

fucking worm-eyes? I need to soak for at least a day."

"You've got an hour," Panderlair said, coldly. "We'll clear the Fell Pass before nightfall, to make it to Camp Raven in time to join a convoy heading through the tunnel to Dose. Those are the orders."

Those were always the orders. Push, push, push. Maringdale gave him a disapproving look and folded her arms over her chest, but said nothing more. His mind was set – another crusade to approach with full zeal, no matter how menial. They would march proudly into another small mess, and bring Glory for Drail. Maringdale asked, "The target?"

Panderlair looked up from his gruel. A glint in his eye said she'd like the next part. He'd been holding back, the sly dog – she hadn't even noted a feint. "It would seem someone has compromised a Slanik Dread company."

"Oh?" Maringdale started to smile.

"A Dread company?" Donut echoed fearfully, not sharing her enthusiasm.

"That's right, Donut," Maringdale said. "The nastiest, most elite sons of bitches in the Drail Empire. I'll happily march through the night to get in bed with *them*."

5

Fullbred's got five armies, from sea to shining sea,
A million men to march with, but it's Easter's lot for me.
Not Ulcer nor Clentarvin, and I'm no Fen bunny,
Vivan keep the navy, it's Easter's lot for me.
Sick, Sick, Sick Brigade, this is Poldrake's way!
Sick, Sick, Sick Brigade, we'll make the green-coats' day!
Sixth ("Sick") Brigade Marching Song

After a litre or more of local wine and little food (there was no fresh bread), Wild Wish was struggling to decide whether or not she wanted to forget the day. On the one hand, she'd been hailed as a hero, not just by the people of Blythe, but also by her fellow Blood Scouts and Sick Brigade's chiefs, who arrived shortly after. Captain Tate patted her on the back and said General Easter himself was impressed by their efforts both on the battlefield and in securing the town. Wish had spotted the general rolling in on a tracked steam engine with an escort of metal-plated imperial guards. *Rolling* literally; he came off the truck in his famous wheelchair, thick-tyred and armoured like a chariot, and he waved at the gathered scouts, on their rag-tag perch around the tavern doors, before he entered the more respectable council house. Easter carried gravitas with him, his bald head refusing to shine in the sun, scarred skin warning the world that even without legs he was formidable. And he gave the scouts a wave. Maybe there would be medals.

Then there was the tavern itself – a finer building than any Wish had been in for months, and one of a handful that the townsfolk had volunteered for use. The town wasn't exactly a throwback to domesticity, the mess and stink of the recently billeted green-coats made sure of that, and food stocks were low. But to sleep on a mattress in an actual room was a blessing Wish hadn't known since outside Redstow, where they had first joined this leg of the war. The tavern was a dream of heavy oak furniture and warm gas lights, with an open fireplace and a long, inviting bar. Sitting at a big circular table with most of Boot Squad, and Oksy and Dollemore, Wish took it all in fondly. The wider hall was big enough to fit their entire platoon, along with a handful of Command's less discerning men, and some of the locals, including Wish's other treat of the day: that eager young woman who'd *kissed* her.

The woman, a Ringed State native with the darkest skin Wish had seen, hovered in a corner, nursing rations and occasionally throwing the scouts looks. Her hair hung in glorious heavy curls, she was tall, and she was decorated with bone-white tattoos of strange lines and symbols running over her arms and face. Everyone kept their distance – ordinary ringers, the distant races that inhabited the colonised lands encircled by the Ring Sea, weren't trusted. The tattoos marked her as a menafis, though – especially spooky. It was one of many exotic, misunderstood magics that didn't fit into the either of the two schools of witlacing and dirt-minding, both feared and derided by regular folk, and barely understood by Wish. But those kisses and her embrace were a magic all of their own, so Wish had decided she must be a good witch.

That said, the ringer had kept her distance ever since the impulsive kiss. She had slipped back into the throng of onlookers as the other Stanish soldiers came into town, and Wish was reduced to snatching distant glances as the bustle increased. Could there have been more if they hadn't been interrupted?

More would've been nice. That little bit more *might* have tipped the balance against the bad of the day that clouded the other half of Wish's thoughts. The bloodbath of Green Rise, with hundreds shredded at her fingers. Then the pyre of dismembered corpses they'd found here in Blythe – limbs, heads and torsos from a score of different species, burnt to cinders. It stank worse than the battlefield pyres, and was only one of four piles they found evidence of, the other charred remains long burnt out. And behind those horrors, there was Loose, gone forever. That little cry, "No –"

Had those piled on the pyres said the same, facing the Drail butchers? Or had they died kicking and screaming, fighting till the end? What was worse?

Better not to know. Wild Wish downed what was left of her mug of wine. She slammed it on the table and called for another, drawing a cheer from her battle sisters. Oksy watched her kindly, but had said little since they'd entered Blythe. Processing, analysing, no doubt. Emi and Four Skills had started putting together theories on the bodies, together with their other resident mage, the tall and eminently sensible Dollemore, as the rest of the scouts showed up hauling their gear. From the scant remains of what hadn't been destroyed when the pack beasts stampeded, it was clear that the Slanik soldiers had been moving experimental equipment, perhaps one large machine that had been dismantled; something that the locals said had been tested in a mill house, producing sparks and screams. The Drail's 8th Division had held the line above Green Rise for two months before today's battle, and they had taken Blythe right at the start of that period. Half the townsfolk had been chained and sent to work camps deeper in the Drail Empire, while the rest were left to serve the occupying soldiers – men who locked carts of different races in the storehouse before dragging them to the mill for experiments. Hundreds had been killed with no clear results.

The tests were connected to witlacing, Dollemore said. It was her discipline, she should know. Witlacers usually drew energy from their own resources, weakening themselves to produce great feats, but there were some that sought to draw energy from others. There had been rumours even before the war that the Drail were creating weapons from such abuses. They would use machines in place of mages, if they could find a way. But these were crackpot theories, Dollemore insisted. At the least, you needed someone powerful to form a conduit, because witlacing by its very nature was a thing tied to *life*. And the machine clearly wasn't effective, or they would've used it during the battle instead of just burning the evidence.

Fixit, Boot Squad's medic, was especially disgusted. As the

scouts' resident Ven, the mousy, bespectacled Fixit had mostly made her peace with the burning of bodies after battle, but found it hard to stomach the Slanik experimenters' atrocities. Bad enough that people were tortured and killed, but then committed to the fire, denied salvation – for what? To gain a military advantage? It was a blasphemy that made the nervy woman squeeze her wine mug so hard the metal bent. As the others drank and shifted away from such topics, she settled into preaching to Sarge, again, about the Church of the Venerate Flesh. Sarge did a good job of pretending to listen.

Small, the shortest and generally cheeriest member of the group, suggested a game of shake-bone, taking out her pouch of dice before anyone could disagree. Pound, a thickset, rarely responsible mother who'd left her kids behind to join the war, threw some coins down and Fixit took her cue to leave. She wasn't averse to gambling, but not with bones – another slight to the Ven ways. With her gone, Sarge left too, mumbling about checking their orders. Rue hunched forward, throwing some coins in, face darker than ever, and round it went until they'd all put in a stake and they started rolling, joking, behaving like the day had never happened. Like Loose and Colt were just taking a break and might rejoin them any second.

Wild Wish drank and played, smiling, occasionally glancing at the ringer. She loved all her friends equally but their ribbing humour wasn't filling the hole right now. The wine was spinning her head without numbing her thoughts. The ringer's kiss, fingers on her – *strong* – that had felt good. But what of Loose's face, disbelieving, about to die? Had Wish even seen it? She closed her eyes and saw men explode into red mist instead. Bullets from the Reaper popping bodies like bubbles. And the man outside Blythe, his knee bursting –

"Just give her a bloody slap," Rue's voice cut through Wish's thoughts, loud with impatience. Wild Wish looked up with surprise, finding her friends staring, some mid-speech as though they'd been trying to get her attention. Mostly amused.

"Is it my turn?" she said.

"Only for about an hour," Oksy said.

"Where were you this time, boating on a Gull Creak barge?" Small joked.

Wild Wish grinned as other suggestions of her fancies followed. Hiking the Mattin Mountains, dressed for a Vasseer ball. No one appreciated her mind could go dark places, too. She took her roll, was thankful it was no good, and pushed away from the table. "I'm gonna grab some air."

"Is that her name?" Oksy said, to a couple of sniggers and questions from those not aware that Wild Wish had been fawning. She couldn't help another look at the ringer, who was actually unashamedly looking at her.

"Oh Wild don't go *there*," Pound laughed. "She'll swallow your damn *soul!*"

Wild Wish smiled but the woman did, indeed, suddenly look ominous. She had to be a head taller than Wish, sturdy, shoulders set with confidence. Maybe this required more thought. A strategy. Wish left the table and found the floor swayed like a boat deck. No, that was just her. Getting some air *was* a good idea. She used other scouts and tables to support herself as she eased her way through the crowd and down some steps, over to the exit and out into the night. As the doors swung shut behind her, she breathed in the chilly Farnish evening and scanned the unlit surrounds. The waterways between buildings reflected light from inside as glittering guidelines.

Wish walked into the street. The council house was four buildings down, with Easter's truck and a bunch of horses hitched outside. Guards lingered stiffly outside. And was that – yes, Wild Wish raised a hand in a wave to Tate and Sarge, the pair chatting on the steps of the building with a man in a pressed uniform. Sarge gave Wish a subtle *not-now* nod.

The tavern door opened and Wish turned to find the ringer standing there. She froze rigid as the woman's eyes met hers, searchingly. She'd followed her – what for? Earlier was a passionate mistake, surely, as she mistook Wild Wish for a male soldier. Or considered *any* rescuer worth a kiss. But she had been hovering all alone, watching, so maybe there was something. *Was this love?* She stared silently, something to say but assessing Wish carefully before saying it.

Wish bit the side of her lower lip and tried to help, "About earlier, I'm sorry if you thought I was –"

"I want to go with you," the woman said, firmly.

"Huh?" Wish said. "We just met –"

"I want to fight with you, to stop the Drail." Her voice had a strong timbre and fine accent; she'd been taught Stanish well. She stepped closer, within arms' reach. "I'm one of the greatest blade-fighters of my people. The Khib don't want women to fight, but you do."

"Stanclif aren't too happy about it either," Wish said, slowly. Their allies, the great nation of Khibba, were actually known to be a lot more diverse than Stanclif. In truth, the scouts' platoon was formed precisely because it helped Stanclif Command keep track of the women who swindled their way into the forces. It meant they could hide them all away together. "We're not exactly popular – honestly, I can't recommend it."

The woman stared with unfaltering intensity. She was almost one with the shadow, silhouetted against the light spilling from the frosted tavern windows, but her eyes were bright, and the tattoos on her cheeks and arms shone like moonlight. Two straight lines ran down her left cheek, a series of jagged triangles on the right, combining with circles that widened towards her ear. It all accentuated a long, beautiful face with thick lips and invitingly bright eyes. The overlapping shapes on her muscular arms formed a fierce collection of knives and bones. Definitely menafis markings. Wish had never been so close to a ringer mage; in fact, she had only ever seen one other, running a stall of charms at the annual Swelig fair. But she knew mages, and could imagine how Emi or Dollemore would react if told they should sit out the war. Still, while this one was wonderful, and tempting, even the scouts would have reservations about fighting alongside a ringer. Wish cleared her throat. "It's just, wouldn't you feel more at home with – I mean – your own people?"

"My own people?" The woman's hard face fell. So much

disappointment in one look. "Fireti has no army. We raised three thousand warriors and marched alone. Those who survived were disbanded. Captured or thrown aside."

"You fought the Drail alone? Where was – what was –" Wild Wish's stuttering went quiet. She wasn't even sure where Fireti was. Was it a country or a town or what? Maybe just some guy who raised three thousand warriors? Wish cleared her throat, starting over. "I'm sorry. But if you're serious, then I don't know if the scouts –" She faltered again, recalling the hope she'd felt herself, when Sarge first found her crouched in a sodden foxhole. There had only been two Blood Scout squads, then, but the promise of a group where she belonged had been a revelation. And Sarge always complained that Boot Squad could do with their own mage. Or a sapper. All the other squads had magic or bombs. Wish glanced back to the command building, to see Tate had disappeared and Sarge was saying goodbye to the man. "We'd need to ask Sarge. She's coming over now." The ringer's face brightened. "She might say no, okay?"

Sarge almost strode right past them.

"Sarge!" Wish said. "Hey! I want you to meet – what was your name?"

"Newk," the ringer said.

"Not now, Wild," Sarge said, hand already on the door.

"She wants to join up!" Wish blurted out.

Sarge gave her a weary look. Tired and pissed that the day hadn't ended yet. "This isn't the time. I'm starting to wish you'd turned down this assignment."

"What? That was an option?" Wish frowned. "But this place is adorable – have you seen the beds? And the people –" She stumbled as she stepped closer to Newk, trying to put an arm around her shoulders, finding they were much higher than her own. Newk stood proudly, nonetheless. "Doesn't she look like prime scout material to you?"

Sarge looked Newk up and down. "A menafis? You want to fight? For Stanclif?"

"Yes, ma'am," Newk nodded, her own arm coming around Wild

Wish's shoulders, bonding them with a hand that stayed put. "Stanclif has the finest soldiers, I saw them in action today. This hero bravely saved me from captivity. I was foolishly taken on the road to General Kettal's southern brigade, but I promise it won't happen again. I'll do whatever it takes to crush the Drail and deliver civilisation to all lands."

"Huh." Sarge said. "So you're a Civist?" An adjective for the most loyal Stanclif colonials, which rather thinly disguised her obvious concern that Newk was a ringer.

"I'm motivated," Newk said. "The Drail came to my land decades ago. They murdered the Seventeen Families to conquer Fireti, and we've fought for revolution ever since. I will take ten heads for each of the Seventeen. My sword is yours if you'll have it."

Wish quickly processed that. "One hundred and seventy heads?"

"You think it can't be done?" Newk asked, insisting it very much could.

Wish puffed out her cheeks, brows raised. The hand was still on her shoulder. "No, it can. I killed, what" – Wish looked at Sarge – "six or seven hundred men today?"

"Wish," Sarge said, as a one-word warning. Don't bring it up again, it's war, we've all got our burdens. To Newk, she said, "You were captured by the people here? Any idea what they were up to?"

"Torture," Newk said. "I heard screams and saw lights, but I regret that is all I know. They tied me tight – stronger than the others – otherwise I would've done something, I promise. But they feared me and kept constant watch. They wanted me for later. They wanted to improve their work before testing it on me."

"Because you're a menafis?" Sarge said.

"Also one of the best blade-fighters in Fireti," Wish said. Sarge stared at her rather than the ringer – particularly at the hand *still* on Wish's shoulder. Her eyes asked whether this was just an attempt to get laid. Wish gave her an encouraging smile that didn't help.

"Come by in the morning," Sarge said. "Give me time to think, and the rest of the girls a chance to unwind before we toss them any new complications."

"They'll love her," Wish promised. "I'll handle Rue, if she's your worry."

Sarge gave her a sceptical look. "All right. In the morning. Get some rest, Wish."

Wish shrugged, and Sarge continued into the tavern, a burst of noise spilling out after her. "Well, that went well." Wish smiled at Newk's fingers on her shoulders again, and Newk suddenly pulled away – hadn't she realised they'd been touching all that time?

"I'm sorry. I apologise for earlier, too. The kiss."

"Oh, no," Wish started – she did *not* have to apologise for that. "Why don't you come in for a drink –"

"I shouldn't." Shit, was she embarrassed now? Running. "I'll see you in the morning."

"Okay," Wish said, hiding her disappointment as Newk awkwardly darted through the door. "I guess I'll . . . soften up Rue."

Yes. Rue. The woman who'd once told Wish, with the best intentions, that together with Loose, their trio had the most trustworthy skin in the platoon. She'd loved fair Loose, a white angel. *No* – Wish closed her eyes.

She needed more drink.

6

Many cures were researched for the so-called "Hero's Hangover", as military leaders recognised a drop in effectiveness the day after a victory. Of all the pills, tinctures and elixirs invested in, only Robenson's Bung Oil consistently removed the worst side-effects of alcohol consumption, but this was taken out of circulation when it was discovered to contain human blood. The details of how it worked were classified under an order that suggested magical interference.

**Sickness and Sin: Medicine and Religion
Through the Ages, Grunberg, p. 489**

On waking, Wild Wish's head throbbed like it was being squeezed between a rock troll's fists. What had happened? She recalled playing dice, and a lot of hard "bread" and something that pretended to be a cheese, and there might have been singing and arguing – but she did not remember changing out of her uniform into this night-slip, nor getting into this lumpy bed. Thankfully, Drunk Wish had secured a bucket of water that she drank from and splashed over her face. She used the remains to dab at some of her worst smelling patches. The empty bed suggested it'd been a lonely night, in the end, but the memory of the mysterious ringed woman resurfaced. An illicit conversation outside that went . . . nowhere. Newk had disappeared into the night, and Wish had kept drinking with her squad. She had apparently found a whole room to herself, for the first time in forever.

She tied back her hair, gathered her uniform from the floor and exited onto a narrow corridor. Too clean and quiet for the inn. She crept down the tight stairs into a living area, with a small wooden table and overturned stools. She found the kitchen with cupboards open and bare. The empty bottle of liquor on the counter looked fresh.

"Anyone here?" Wish called out, voice croaky. No answer.

She stopped short in the hallway at the sight of a broken door, dropping her clothes, hand going for a pistol, axe, anything. As she realised none of her weapons were there, she also appreciated the door had been broken a while ago. Another memory came back. Her own boot kicking that handle in, because no one was answering? Dammit Wish, some hero.

Pulling on her trousers, Wild Wish exited onto a charming street, lined with tiny timber houses all running together. The light stung her eyes as she noticed a figure standing a few doors down. No, not standing – leaning against the post of another house's porch.

"Rue?" Wish called, and Rue startled awake, spinning with a hand on her hatchet. She paused, recognising where she was. At least partially.

"I fall asleep in the street?"

"Standing up, by the looks of it," Wish said. "I'm impressed."

"You" – Rue drew the axe anyway, pointing it at her – "you said we'd get beds. Supposed to sleep well." She took a step away from her post and almost fell; Wild Wish rushed to catch her, but Rue swung the axe loosely, backing off with a sneer. Her heavy brow, thick jaw and flat-lined face was severe at the best of times, but became a few shades darker when she woke grumpy. Hungover Rue could be scary (even more so than Regular Rue), but Wish knew she was a big softy deep down. If she liked you. For some reason, she liked Wish.

Wild Wish stepped back. From the light, it was still early, moisture on the windows suggesting the mist had barely cleared. Curtains were open but no one appeared to be home. One end of the street joined a wider road, but the other finished in a tall brick wall. The Blythe perimeter – she remembered now. They'd stumbled off looking to get away from the noise. Rue had cursed and cursed over the loss of Loose.

She straightened up with defiance, appearing to remember that herself. She attempted to flatten her short brown hair, never quite possible due to general scarring. "You slept in there? Any food?"

Wish shook her head. "But I did find this fetching night gown. Want to see what else they've got?"

Rue grunted assent, never one to turn down a pillage, and they went back inside. Once they had secured a couple of armfuls of undergarments and Wish was back in her uniform and boots – no sign of her gun or short-blade – they headed back towards the centre of town. Voices were rising ahead.

"I hurt anyone last night?" Rue asked as they turned onto a street and found more soldiers gathered than the night before. A company were securing Blythe, setting up sandbags and wire-traps.

"Not that I'm aware of," Wish said. But hadn't Rue been yelling from up on a tabletop?

"You should've got yourself some local arse instead of keeping me company."

"Nah." Wish offered a smile. "Loose was my friend, too, remember."

It made Rue snort. "Sure." Fair – it was a rather one-sided friendship, which Wish hadn't minded. "Well you've got the right idea, anyway, Wish. Don't let anyone close. Not worth it in this bloody meat grinder. We'll be lucky to make snowfall with half our mates still breathing."

Wild Wish frowned, not sure that was her idea at all. She thought the time Rue had with Loose had still been worth it. Even if it hurt now. Just sharing a tent with Loose and hearing her voice had been worth it. Back home, they had small ideas and limited conversational skills. Here, they joked, they sang and enjoyed every moment that wasn't bloody slaughter. They were comfortable with each other, shared each other's space, breathed each other's air. The war brought people to life before it killed them. And when it finished – when it finished they'd remember, wouldn't they, what it meant to live?

Wish would have her farm, with running water and rolling hills, and she'd still have *them*. They would drink and share stories, living for themselves instead of the slaughter. Four Skills hunting for dinner, Fixit tending to neighbours' ailments, Pound and Rue building – extending the country palace of Lavender Manor. They'd make snowfall and beyond, she was sure. They'd make it all the way to the end.

"Shame, seems like a big town," Rue was grumbling when Wish brought herself back to the moment. The tavern lay ahead. "Should be *some* women here. Wasn't anyone worth a lay, Wish?"

"The green-coats drove them out. Or killed them. Mostly killed them, I think."

"Typical." Rue paused. "Still, least you didn't get with that ringer. Creepy as sin, her."

Wish held her tongue. She remembered Newk's hand on her shoulder. The possibility of her coming with them? There had been a vague plan that she'd ease that over with Rue. Oh.

The pair entered the tavern and stopped in the doorway, thirty pairs of eyes turning to them. The whole platoon was gathered before Captain Tate, up on the small band stage. The scouts were grouped by squad, Sun near Tate, Sabre around the entrance, Rock by the bar. Boot, their girls, were scattered up the stairs. Apparently the pair were late to a meeting, and entering with arms full of underwear. Against a couple of knowing leers, Rue snapped, "Don't get any ideas, we were *not* together."

She made it sound unthinkable. Which it was, but come on – it wasn't *her* place to be offended. The looks that might've turned to mockery fixed on the clothes, though, with admiration. Wild Wish shuffled to an empty table, saying, "I'll just put these . . . here."

"You been trading with the locals?" Larkin, the head of Sabre and the closest officer, asked. Wish gave a smile rather than lie. Rue, with less apology, flung her load down and thumped through the room to join Boot Squad. Wish followed with small nods and whispered hellos. She watched out for a superior look from Oksy, but her fellow sniper wasn't by the bar – not here at all, in fact, so at least they weren't the only stop-outs.

"Now we're all here?" Tate's voice carried across the crowd as Wish settled onto a step next to Small. "Orders are simple. We're waiting on word from the insert, so take the break you all deserve for the next couple of days, with occasional northward patrols. Rock and Sabre, that's you. Boot, you're on provisions – seeing as you've already made a start" – that got a few chuckles – "and Sun are coordinating with Sick Brigade. Make the most of it, we'll be moving again before you know it."

Simple orders, but Wish understood she had missed the meat of it. What *insert?*

Tate marched for the door, cutting off the meeting with her customary abruptness. The room fell into chatter. Some girls turned questions to Wish and Rue, but their squad leaders drew everyone back for specific orders. Sarge, halfway up the stairs, gestured Boot closer. They squeezed in together, with Fixit and Dakoda leaning over the banister up top.

"Usual deal," Sarge said. "Check storehouses, cellars, for food. Don't worry about ammo, the Brigade's here for that – put your hand down Wild, you got a question just bloody ask."

"Sorry," Wish said. "But what's going on?"

"In honour of our bravery and skill exhibited on the field yesterday," Dakoda offered, snidely, "and for so swiftly securing Blythe, General Easter has awarded the Blood Scouts with the highest honour of all. A swift death sentence."

"Enough, Dakoda," Sarge said, weary enough to say she didn't disagree. Brazen and cynical as sandy-haired, sallow Dakoda could be, she was generally right. "We're on standby to head north. Same as usual."

"Be fair, Sarge," Pound said, "it's not *quite* the same."

Sarge grunted. Yeah, this was bad. "We might be bound for Slanik territory." Wish and Rue both started with incomprehensible noises of complaint, and Sarge raised a hand for quiet with a nod that said yes, yes, they'd been through this already. Low Slane sat deep in Drail lands, a principality that the Comity would avoid touching entirely if they could. It was nestled between Har Coul in the west and the divided Fallen Empire of Balnever to the south and east – either of which presented far more hospitable paths into the Valley of the Drail.

"Might've been better you let those green-coats go, yesterday,"

Fixit said, above Sarge. "That gear they left behind put an itch in Command's pants."

"Why?" Wish asked, unsure she wanted to know. Low Slane and magical torture experiments all pointed to Something Very Bad. Not to mention they hadn't actually been green-coats, had they? They wore black. Dread Corps black.

"It's not all on us," Sarge explained. "They had rumours about this already; turned out Blythe was marked for an agent to investigate. The equipment has a sigil that he's been tracing, and the prisoners confirmed the men in charge were Slanik Dread Corps." (Called it.) "Bald bastards with piercings down the left side of their body – wearing Dread robes, chanting, all that crap. They're working on a wit weapon, Wild. From the way Command are talking about it, they're scared it could take things to another level of Fucked."

Rue swore as Wild Wish frowned. They'd seen some pretty severe levels of Fucked already. This war had delivered artillery batteries that could pulverise armies from a mile away, and there were rumours of gasses out east that made you chuck up your lungs. It had been clear since the start of summer that this was unlike any fighting the world had seen before – what the Reaper did made that plain enough. What was the next level from *that?*

Wish's face must've asked the question, because Sarge said, "We'll know more when they extract their agent. Last contact was in Wick Fortress, a day from here. Where the Drail are making their current stand. He's been telling Command we can't ignore Slane any longer for a while, they say, and after what we pulled off yesterday, Easter realised he's got an option other than marching the full army into the wilderness."

"This is what we get for being noticed," Wish said.

"It's nothing we haven't done before," Sarge said. "Stretching a little further into enemy territory, but the principle's the same. Move quiet, move quick, get out."

"Respectfully," Rue said, in a tone anything but respectful, "there's a difference between going a little further and striking to the black heart of bloody Drail. No one's ever got close to taking the Weeping Citadel. Not in this war or a hundred before."

"That's not our mission. And we're not arguing about it. We're gathering provisions and otherwise taking it easy. Unless you'd rather request new orders?"

"No, sir," Rue said, voice teetering on aggression. "I'd rather we weren't acting on the word of some damn ungrateful foreign prisoners that didn't belong anywhere near here to begin with. How do we know it's even real – if there was a Dread mage here, why wasn't he at Green Rise yesterday? We're supposed to take the word of some thick-shit trunks or a filthy ringer?"

Sarge held Rue's eyes firmly as the squad went quiet. At the top of the stairs, Dakoda shifted to the side, making clear why the rest of them were suddenly so uncomfortable. In the shadows on the balcony, behind the group, stood Newk, arm's folded in a silent challenge.

Rue glared like she was the one who had been insulted. "What's she doing here?"

"Meet our newest recruit, Rue," Sarge said.

Rue swallowed anger. "Come again?"

"*She* got in bright and early. Gave a strong account of herself, I'd say. I'm surprised Wild Wish didn't mention it, seeing as she's the one who vouched for her."

Wish squirmed as the squad stared. Rue turned away. "Forget this."

"You'll miss breakfast," Sarge said, not entirely bothered.

"Let me, let me," Pound said, shoving after Rue.

"I take it you didn't discuss it?" Sarge asked Wish, who responded with a nonplussed look. "Well, you calmed her down last night, at least. Wasn't any more trouble?"

"No?" Wish replied, unsure what trouble there'd been to begin with, let alone if there had been more.

"We'll all keep an eye on her. But right now, seeing as we've extra work to do, Newk's on board. I want you take her to the quartermaster to get kitted out."

Wild Wish looked up and found Newk decidedly sterner in the light of day. Judging her for keeping company with Rue? The other squad members smiled with an unspoken message that none of them had wanted this task. Wish glanced hopelessly after Pound, thinking she should've chased after Rue herself, to avoid the attention. Her good idea in the night now seemed ready to bite her. But she said, weakly, "Sure Sarge. No problem."

7

Though written history tends to focus on the clashes between the western empires, it is worth keeping in mind that much of the complexity of modern politics is rooted in the ancient conflicts between the central southern and eastern territories of Boldarow and the Ringed States. Of particular significance, the boundary between industrial Garter and rural Elmn was redrawn no less than a dozen times in the 8th century alone; towns in the Vantac Split famously had streets where you might find residents claiming different nationality depending on which household you spoke to.

Empires of the Rocc, Xanthial, p. 672

Cantering closer to the so-called city of Cleave, down from the outskirts of the Mattin foothills, Maringdale and her companions slowed their horses to take in the gibbets along one side of the road. Scores of them marked the city's approach, as jagged and slanted as the buildings, and populated with corpses, each hanging upside down from a chain attached to one foot. Spare legs hung free and crooked, arms hung to two feet from the ground, but most of the bodies were incomplete. Animals had chewed bits away.

Donut covered his mouth and nose, hiding a bleat of disgust.

"Our enemies deserve no better," Panderlair said with satisfaction and trotted on.

Maringdale inspected the bodies as they passed. What was left of their clothing was bloodstained and torn by animals or gunfire, but khaki colours and Khib battle badges were evident. The triple triangle of a Khib sergeant, stitched into one sleeve. The circle and wick of a Khib bomber, dangling from a chest. Such common prisoners should have been protected from execution, but Panderlair was right, all enemies of the Drail – of civilisation itself – deserved death. Further down the line, though, Maringdale saw the dark green of Drail uniforms. Four bodies, fresher than the rest. One had his throat cut, face trapped in horror behind streams of blood that had dried over empty eye sockets. Maringdale paused, transfixed for a moment. So young, so *harmless*. She shook herself from the thought and spat at the traitor before riding on.

This was the way of the Slanik Dread Corps, of course. They were direct and merciless. Maringdale respected that. She had encountered Dread soldiers only once before, when in northern Singness, pursuing a corporal who had "accidentally" shot his commanding officer in battle and fled. During their stay, Maringdale saw three black-clad Dread soldiers in a drinking yurt, their armour-plating lined with bone patterns, faces covered with half-skulls, sharp and ugly like insect jaws. After the spy hunters' quick capture of the traitor, one of those Dread soldiers came to perform the execution himself. It was done in private, but Maringdale heard the screams. *Everyone* heard the screams.

This latest assignment, Maringdale hoped, would be more educational than that.

Cleave City, a rear outpost supporting the Drail's 4th Division, was a city in name alone. It comprised a haunted spattering of wooden shacks, few higher than two storeys and all charred rather than painted, irregularly shaped like the architects (carpenters) had made things up as they went along. Maringdale imagined they didn't even finish what they had started, with no two adjoining walls erected by the same person, and all of them drunk. That would be fitting for Southern Garters, or Northern Elmnish, whichever territory Cleave fell into: it was hard to keep track, and at the end of the day it didn't make any difference. They were disagreeable, nomadic folk, both sides of the border. Merchants, swindlers or unreliable craftsmen, the lot.

Maringdale followed Panderlair through Cleave's walls – thin palisades – but instead of stout, fearsome Dread soldiers she found only ranks and ranks of frail, dead-eyed men in dull Drail green.

They wore the ivory-coloured bars of Low Slane over their breasts, but these men were nursing bandaged limbs or heads and looked hollow with resignation. They worked lamely to shift supplies onto or off wagons, and were strangely quiet. Half alive.

"Hitch here," Panderlair instructed, at a small house flying an officers' flag.

Maringdale jumped down into the mud, no paving or even wooden boards to temper the torn-up earth. She tied off the horse and followed Panderlair into a dimly lit building, kicking a fist-sized chunk of mud off her boot. Donut cried complaint as it splattered his shin.

A Slanik officer was hunched by a low fire, a thick woollen blanket over his shoulders. The only light was from the low flames, and the deep shadows accentuated his Slanik features: high cheek bones, a sharp nose and sleek, straight black hair. He barely looked up as the trio entered, but sniffed, hard, as some kind of greeting.

"Major Gair?" Panderlair said.

The officer sniffed again and shook his head. He spoke hoarsely: "Captain Ogard. But if you've come to hold the man in charge to account, that'd be me. Sniper did for the major four days ago."

"We were told there was a Dread company here," Maringdale said.

That got a snort of dark laughter from Ogard, which made him cough and he doubled over his knees. He didn't stop. Donut fumbled at his kit bag and drew out a water flask. Ogard flapped a hand to keep him back. He turned from the fire and Donut gasped. Maringdale barely held in her own shock at the sight. Ogard's skin under his eyes, and down the right side of his neck, spreading under his shirt, was pronounced by thick black lines, as though someone had vividly tattooed the pattern of his veins. In the half-light, his flesh looked cracked. He croaked through broken lips, "Water won't help. And you do not want to share your flask with me." As one, the trio took a step back, giving him what little space was available in the tight room. "Yeah. We're back from the trenches, where *something* happened. Probably gas, but we didn't see it. I've heard they've been using gas over in Farne, making men vomit their innards." Ogard looked down at his fingers. They looked shrivelled with dehydration, similarly mapped with dark veins. "Whatever it is, burnt the blood inside us. Turned it to charcoal. Got men who seized up and died just like that, others with appendages falling off. I've been lucky, all considered. Only half-congealed." He said it flatly, and Maringdale sensed his true feelings: the lucky ones died quickly.

He continued, "You saw those Khib brutes hanging on the way to town? We got them as good as they got us, at least. Dread company went after some of our own who they counted responsible, too. If you came to do more than that, you'll find few friends here."

"There was an insurgence in town," Panderlair said. "We're here to hunt out all the true enemies of the Empire. We'll do our job, wherever that leads us."

Ogard nodded as though he expected nothing less. "Then listen. The warehouse that exploded, it was separated from our other stores. Colonel Ways was particular about keeping us out, and the way it went up" – he exhaled at length – "I'm *glad* it had nothing to do with us. Lit up the night like the Winter Brights. They ordered us to stay well clear, even with nothing left to see – but we don't *want* to go near it."

"Colonel Ways is in charge of the Dread company?" Maringdale asked.

Ogard rested back in his chair to focus on her, cracked lips stretched to a weary smile. Recognising for the first time she was present, his doubts and fears faded to the usual feelings Maringdale sensed from men on the front. Her stern face, bandoleers, and wide-brimmed riding hat didn't detract from the simple truth she was a woman, drawing a yearning for more than dreams of sex and romance – it spoke of nostalgia for normalcy. The wives, mothers, daughters and girls-not-yet-met all left behind in a former life. She pushed back her coat tails to better show her tatty sword scabbard and pistol holster, and doubt crept back into Ogard's mind. He said, "Will you be investigating them?"

"Them being the ones that were attacked?" Maringdale replied quickly, and read his concerns. Part of him blamed the Dread company themselves. Not for the bombing, but for his own fate. As his eyes shifted from her to Panderlair, his hopes for justice faded. Like most people, Ogard balked at Panderlair's one-eyed stare. He turned to warm his hands before the fire. He breathed hard, struggling to fill his lungs, then said, "They've relocated, up the road to someplace smaller and better secured. But watch yourselves, talking to them – Ways is ruthless. The guards that got strung up were those closest to the warehouse, including a couple of his own men, but this obviously wasn't the work of rookies. Someone knew what they were after and hit that Dread site hard. You got any idea what those boys were doing here? We don't, and I figure if we did, we'd be in a lot more danger. They're reporting to a Dread doctor. Seriously think any Drail would risk crossing that?"

The spy hunters let silence confirm it was doubtful. The Dread Corps' so-called "doctors" were scientists who experimented with the horrific creatures of the Slanik wilds and the darkest applications of magic. Maringdale felt her heart burning at the thought of such elements at work here; this investigation could prove doubly important. If they could ingratiate themselves with this company, contribute to something truly important . . .

The captain concluded, sullenly, "Take the road through the woods out of town, there's a ruined castle. That's where you'll find them."

Maringdale sensed, then, that with this dismissal he intended to relieve one of his last responsibilities. She got a flash of his deeper intentions. Within a few days, suffering whatever pain those clogged black veins gave him, he would put his own revolver in his mouth. A few words of hope now might convince him otherwise; he only needed to hear that there were ways he was still valuable, that he could yet survive to enjoy all he'd left behind in Low Slane – for however little time he had left. It didn't need to end here.

But with Ogard hunched towards the fire, the back of his head inviting them to leave, Maringdale said nothing. She was not here, after all, to hold the hands of men without the stomach for war.

***

Leaving Captain Ogard to his fire, the spy hunters regrouped outside, where Panderlair scanned the road. Would they stay to make life miserable for these battered soldiers, when the Dread soldiers had already left their mark? His single eye fixed on Maringdale and she sensed his usual thoroughness bubbling up. He said, "Let's take a look at the forbidden blast site before we continue."

"Where they –" Donut exclaimed. "With the –"

He was unable to complete the clear fear that they would be courting trouble with the Dread company. Maringdale hesitated, too. Panderlair saw no order as standing above the work of the Purification; he would accuse the Dread soldiers themselves if he found reason to, and he probably felt bitter that they'd already robbed him of disciplining the few guards that could be easily held responsible. Nevertheless, it was a step towards the company. Maringdale patted Donut's arm and walked past to show it was okay.

They mounted their horses and followed the roads past more weary soldiers, up through the north of the city to where the lodgings thinned out to make way for storage buildings and workhouses. Coming to the edge of Cleave City, they met a blockade of barbed wire and clumsily stacked wooden stakes, where two guardsmen stamped their feet to keep warm – Ogard's men, not remnant Dread soldiers.

"No passage this way," one said, with little conviction.

"We're with the Purification," Panderlair replied, and the familiar dance of conflicted emotions played out across the man's face. A second's disbelief, followed by panic, suddenly wanting nothing to do with this conversation, then resistance as he recalled he had orders, even in the face of inquisitors. It all passed in an instant, before the soldier decided it wasn't worth his effort. He stepped aside. They guided their horses around the pointless barricade and Maringdale smirked at the mutterings of the soldiers behind them. Frightened men calling her trio creeps.

The road rose between two large wooden structures, and turned a corner onto the scene they weren't supposed to see. Panderlair stopped and huffed. Maringdale drew up alongside him and Donut held back, muttering a curse. There was almost nothing left of the building that had stood here and the ground was burnt in an enormous black star that spread across the road and through the wall of the next nearest building, now a burnt-out husk. There was a crater at the centre of the site and the barest fragments of debris. Scorched bricks, the twisted metal of a decimated piece of furniture. A hint of a body part.

The scale and devastation of the explosion was made more eerie by the way the entire site steamed, a mist rolling off the blast mark as though the explosion had occurred hours ago, not days. It was a blue mist, ethereal, unnatural. Panderlair's eye roamed over every detail, a hunter coming to life.

"Oh Saints, is that – is that –" Donut stuttered, no more articulate than before.

"We're not *supposed* to know what it is," Maringdale said. That kind of unreal mist, with that kind of colour, had the hallmarks of a parser's magic – the school of witlacing most applicable for battle. Ogard's concerns about this being linked to his illness were understandable. Such magic was the domain of life energy, and the mysterious thread that existed between living things. It could both protect and drain, and it could harm them even at this distance.

"This site had great value," Panderlair said, with deep, rumbling judgement. He bristled at his own pronouncement, his thoughts clear: someone had destroyed technology far advanced beyond whatever Khibba had to offer. This destruction was what happened when their superior ways were unprotected from the ignorant masses beyond their borders. This was why they fought. The Dread company, Maringdale knew, would understand that better than everyone.

8

"Stamps: Keeping Stanclif's Boys Marching Since 642!"
Slogan for Stamps Boots, of Stanclif Pride Footwear
(made in Olon)

The brigade's quartermaster was set up behind Command's council-house HQ, which had become a fortress overnight, with piles of sandbags around the base, metal plating over the windows, and gun barrels sticking out from the roof. The guards outside pointed Wish in the right direction, around a corner to where the street was blocked by a wide tent, concealing the entrance to the large building. As Wish escorted Newk, dozens of soldiers watched them. Men tended to get tense and confused by the presence of armed women in ragged uniforms. Wish thought they should be pleased to see a refreshingly pretty face amongst the crowds of grubby combatants – it pleased *her* – but mostly they got insecure and claimed the scouts were putting them all at risk.

Wild Wish rarely rose to such remarks, except to smile sweetly. She *could* explain that she had already killed more men than they were ever likely to meet, but no one would believe her. Most nights she tried not to believe it herself.

The looks the men reserved for Newk were worse than usual, though; they were hostile, as though Wish was walking with a green-coat. She kept quiet, not quite sure what to say to make it better. The quartermaster was no exception, a portly guy with a bulbous, jovial face that turned to a grimace as he laid eyes on them. His snarl showed off an iron front tooth – a man who took advantage of his own stock – as he said, "You one of the darlings that's been popping Drail from the treetops?"

He made it sound like Wish should be ashamed, so she replied,

"Yes, but we've come down from the branches just to see you. We need full gunner kit." She gave Newk a quick look. Her leather sandals were worn thin. "With some small stamps."

"Stamps?" the quartermaster scoffed. "For you, I've got bovers. Command keep us equipped for their female staff –"

"And their female staff can keep their bovers. No, no" – Wish shook her head – "got to be stamps, Captain's orders. And gunner kit, please. The full bag."

The quartermaster's face turned to stone. "Which captain?"

"Tate. The one responsible for winning the day yesterday. Or didn't you hear?" The man's stare intensified, so Wish leaned closer and whispered, conspiratorially, "Do you want me to put in a word with her for you? I've heard she's a real backbreaker. Especially when it comes to guys who don't follow her orders."

He grunted, a derisive noise that might've been disgust at her attitude or the idea of a female captain. Either way, he gave up negotiating, wanting no more part of this conversation. He turned to gather what she'd asked for and Wish whispered to Newk, "Gunner kit is light, meant for soldiers in armour placements. It's not the best protection on a battlefield, but it lets us move fast and" – she further lowered her voice – "it's the easiest to adjust. Which we do ourselves. If you suggested it to them, they'd call us difficult. But try marching fifty miles in trousers too big and see what your chafing thighs have to say. Same with the stamps. Best boots in the Five Continents, even if they're made for men. I can adjust them myself – my dad's a cobbler. Don't ever let them fob you off with the women's kit. It's made for clerks."

Newk took all this in with silent study.

"What weapons do you favour? Most of the platoon carry the Bowstown Mumbler – the most popular, reliable rifle in Stanclif – but we've got a few that prefer the stubby Submitter. I've got a Long 0.48 myself, but that's for marksmen. How well can you shoot?"

Newk considered this and answered seriously, "I'd like a sword."

"Sure, we've all got either a Stalwart Sideblade or the Flink hatchet as standard. Some of the girls carry a bone hammer or chain blades. But I'm talking about for a main weapon."

"That is my main weapon. I'm a blade-fighter, I told you. I can best anyone with a blade."

Wish gave her a worried look, remembering that the full force of Newk's mighty nation had been wiped out. This might be why. Granted, there were plenty of soldiers on both sides that insisted on sticking to melee charges, and sometimes that worked when two such platoons clashed, but the world was rapidly learning that honourable battles were good for little more than mass graves. Wish said, "It's mostly people with guns that you need to beat."

"I've never fired a gun." Slight worry creased Newk's brow. "But I promise, I can fight."

"Okay, okay." Wish patted her arm. "Leave it to me."

The quartermaster reappeared to pile the kit on the counter and huffed, "Anything else?"

"A mumbler?" Wish suggested, the most accessible rifle. "And ammo."

"What?" This threw him again. "This isn't for *her,* is it?"

"It's for the Blood Scouts," Wish said. "Is that a problem?"

"Generally, I don't go giving weapons to women, and most particularly not to *savages.*" He stared hard at Newk and she frowned back. "What she even need a gun for? With them tattoos and that mean look, sure she's fine fighting tooth and claw."

"Do you want to test that yourself?" Wish shot back. "You'll lose your teeth." She paused in his shock. "Lose *more* of your teeth, I mean. And she will still need a gun to protect the Empire from the hordes of Slane."

"Slane?" The quartermaster scoffed. "No Slanik hordes out here."

"Tell that to the six I killed yesterday. We're about to take the fight to them. Isn't it your job to help us? Or should I get my supplies from someone who actually wants to win the war?"

The quartermaster grumbled threats she could barely hear, his lowered volume signalling reluctant defeat. He turned to grab the weapon.

As he put down a rifle and two magazines of bullets, Wish said, "And a long sword." She twisted back to Newk. "Any particular kind?"

"Sharp," Newk said.

The quartermaster offered a disapproving look but didn't argue again. He pulled up a particularly wide blade, almost three feet long and slightly curved, with a twisted metal handle. "Got some Khib salvage I'm happy to get rid of, should suit you."

"Great," Wish said and turned to Newk. "Take the pack, shove it all in. Throw on the boots, leave that crap behind." She watched Newk fumble with the clothes, hurrying to get everything in the bag. She slung it over her shoulder then kicked off her makeshift footwear and tripped into the boots. Newk took up the rifle gingerly, so Wish gave her an encouraging smile, then she shouldered its strap and took the sword to test its weight. She spun it expertly, with a flourish that removed any doubt she could use it. Wish watched with wonder, then thumbed the direction back to the inn, thanking the quartermaster. He regarded them like eels that had sprouted legs.

Walking up the street, Newk said, softly, "Thank you, for all this."

"It's nothing. No sense you joining us ill-equipped. They always give us trouble, though. Unless you can turn on the charm like Loose, she'd have –" Wish faltered, grin stalling as the thought popped in a cliff-side scream.

"Did I meet Loose?" Newk asked.

"No. You won't." Wish hurried on. "Your people never had guns? At all?"

"Not like this. We had muskets."

"Muskets? *Powder* rifles?" Wish whistled. "What were you doing with muskets in Firesti?"

"Fireti," Newk corrected. "We traded for them. That was the best Stanclif could offer us." She didn't say it with malice, but Wish felt a pang of guilt. "We hadn't much use for them before. Blade-fighting is our culture. We are intimate with death. We are only a small nation in the central Ringed Plains, near Dunbeal Lake – what your people call the Fire Sea."

Rather than betray her lack of knowledge of pretty much anywhere in the Ringed States, or how the location related to death and sword-fighting, Wish dwelt on that word *intimate*. Newk made the brutality of fighting sound alluring. Wish said, "Stanclif is such a big empire, they couldn't have had a chance to reach all the colonies properly, to best equip you."

"Yes," Newk said. "We were under the hammer of the Drail for many years. Men who came demanding ownership of the land. Trading for it. As if land can be owned." She scoffed. "We had little chance to let Stanclif in, but I know your Civilisation would be different."

Wish frowned, not entirely following. She wanted to ask what exactly was going on in Fireti before the empires came duelling over who owned what land, but she didn't get the chance. A chirpy voice interrupted: "Hey!"

Wild Wish jumped as Emi appeared next to them with a bounce. The dirt-minder was grinning, never good at hiding her scheming nature. She stood a little taller than most of the scouts (though to her chagrin slightly shorter than Dollemore, her magical rival) and hid her standard light uniform under a perpetually dusty, overlarge navy greatcoat. Her face had an unusual prettiness: a wide mouth, a slightly upturned nose and bulging eyes that might've been froglike if they weren't so fiercely intelligent. Emi was the scouts' most dangerous, scariest and least predictable member, who Wish found it best to avoid. Yet the magic-wielding loon often gravitated towards her with sly looks and teasing smiles. Wild Wish had had more than one embarrassing dream about her (about being at her mercy), and she was quite sure Emi knew it. Maybe even made it happen. Mind control belonged thoroughly in the camp of the witlacers, who Emi loathed, but she had wiles all of her own. She said, "How're you settling in? A fine set of stamps, good start. Sadly conventional rifle, though."

Newk flashed Wish a worried look. "You said –"

"The mumbler is the staple of the Stanclif Empire," Wish promised. "Don't listen to her, she doesn't even own a gun."

"I just imagined *you* would go with something more interesting,"

Emi said, pressing closer. She twisted snakelike around Newk, taking in the sword sheath. "Although that is curious. We haven't been introduced. I'm the Blood Scouts' dirt-minder. Some would say our only true magic worker. Or at least I *was*. Emi." She held up a hand. Wish didn't mention that Dollemore was not only senior in rank but also generally more respected as a mage. She wasn't getting in the middle of that again.

Newk shook Emi's hand and said, "Newk. Of Fireti."

"I've never heard of a Newk of Fireti," Emi said. "I did know a potent menafis called Diniki. Lost himself in glue wine in Tynes. Did you know him?"

"I have heard of him," Newk said. "He fell from the Queen's grace when he did not return to Fireti to report on his expedition."

"That doesn't surprise me." Emi laughed. "Another victim of *living*. Have you been practising menafi long? We should compare notes."

Newk shook her head with an uncomfortable smile. "I am mesita, not menafis. A blade-fighter, that's all."

Emi scanned her. "That's all?"

"A very fine blade-fighter," Newk added, her confidence warming Wish.

"Ah. Well, we'll use what we can get, won't we?" Emi said. "I've duties, sadly, but we'll have time together on the road. Menafis or mesita, we'll *commune*."

"Like witches?" Wish suggested, to draw a line under all this magic jargon she couldn't follow. This was *her* new recruit, after all. She pointed over Emi's shoulder, to where Tate and a few others from Sabre Squad were preparing to go somewhere. "Looks like the captain's getting impatient."

"Indeed." Emi leered. "I will see you later." She spun away with a flourish of her coat – the main reason she wore the vast thing – and skipped off towards the others. Newk watched her leave with an unsettled expression.

"I haven't met many dirt-minders," Wish confided, "but I hear she's worse than most. It's not the magic that does it; Emi's just Emi. We love her. But also hate her."

"Oh," Newk said, not, apparently, having connected the slightly manic encounter with the general fear that dirt-minding turned its practitioners mad. Its use took a clear and immediate toll on Emi, for sure, but her default was hardly normal. Newk would see that soon enough.

Wish wanted to ask what a mesita was, not entirely sure what the difference was between that and a menafis, the tattooed magic-workers of the Ringed States, but she wanted more to put Emi's interruption behind them. She said, "Let's get you changed and claim some gruel."

They walked back to the tavern, quickly passing the remnants of Sun Squad and Wish's friends' table, up to a room strewn with kit bags. There was Wish's rifle and her little blade, her body remembering the location she'd forgotten. She told Newk to change behind a partition and sat on the bed. Why had she vouched for this rather quiet ringed woman who showed no natural propensity for weaponry? She knew nothing about her, except that she gave a good kiss, and that the other scouts distrusted her. And that she was amazing.

"Newk," Wild Wish said, louder than necessary. "About yesterday. When we met –"

"I said sorry?" Newk worriedly poked her head out. Bare shoulders and her thick locks hanging loose, curving over something more. "I forgot myself, after my captivity. It was inappropriate. I'll remember Stanclif values in future."

"Yeah, okay," Wish replied quietly, willing the red out of her cheeks.

Newk ducked back out of view. After some quick shuffling, she appeared again, her warrior's body hidden by Stanish blue-grey. The padded slacks, hard-wearing boots and loose linen undershirt all looked good on her, though. Made her look even tougher. It was hard to imagine the Drail taking her prisoner, especially considering those magic markings on her.

"Is something wrong?" Newk asked.

Wish had been staring, and blurted out, "No. Absolutely not. We'll get the trousers taken in, sort out those boots, but you look like a scout already. We've never had a menafis in the scouts. I've never actually seen one at work. Besides a traveller in my village, when I was little, but I think he painted his skin and I'm quite sure he used strings to move things. *Can* menafis move puppets?"

"That is more the domain of your magics, I think."

"Ah." Wish waited a moment, for Newk to maybe explain where she actually sat in the magic spectrum.

Instead, Newk changed the subject: "Is the Blood Scouts an old company? You look very experienced."

Wish laughed, but saw she was serious. "Sorry. I don't think there's much that's *old* left in this war, save the leaders at the very top. I signed up ten months ago, and I'm probably one of the best snipers Stanclif has. Because the others keep dying."

The answer troubled Newk for a second; had she dreamt they were all immortal veterans? No, the Empire's elite were the first to die. Newk asked, "But are you good?" She nodded to the Long 0.48 by Wish's feet. It had a thicker barrel and chunkier carriage than most rifles, along with a brass and leather telescopic scope like something stolen from a ship's bridge. "Could you teach me?"

"Could I –" Wish caught her own surprise. Taking responsibility for enlisting a recruit was daunting enough. Training her with a rifle? Lying close to her lining up sights – faces touching? Wish bit her lip. "I mean, I can give you a couple of pointers. But Four Skills is the one you want. She's the best."

"Four Skills?" Newk echoed.

"She's very focused," Wild Wish explained. "Does four things *very* well, so she says. One of them is shooting. You can ask her about the others yourself." Wish stood. "Speaking of which, let's do some introductions. You'll find the Blood Scouts are nothing if not welcoming."

"I don't want to share a bloody tent with a ringer, that's all I'm saying," Pound's voice rose up as Wish led Newk down the stairs. The creaking boards made the squad look up as one. Pound mugged sheepishly – heavyset, loud, and frequently speaking without thinking, she was used to these situations, and her crooked grin announced her trained response: pretend it hadn't happened. "All kitted out, are you?"

"Yeah," Wild Wish replied, approaching slowly. With Pound were Small and Dakoda, half-empty metal bowls of gruel in front of them. A couple of full bowls sat to one side. "That for us?"

"Cold by now," Dakoda said. "But still full of good, good nutrients."

Though quite sure it wasn't, Wish led by example, sitting and digging into the lukewarm sludge of the tavern's porridge. Newk followed cautiously, but didn't take the spare bowl with all the girls watching her. Wish eyed the others, not stopping her sloppy eating, to force someone else to speak.

Small broke first, sitting closest, and pushed the other full bowl towards Newk. "Come on and eat, you gotta have energy if you're gonna carry our bags."

"Carry –" Newk started.

"Don't listen to her," Dakoda said. "Small needs all the help she can get, look at those scrawny limbs."

"Aw come on, she'd have done it!" Small complained, genuinely believing it.

Newk smiled, at last, and bent over the bowl for a taste. She'd been locked up for who knew how long, on Slanik prisoner rations, yet still reeled from the poor breakfast.

"Make the most of it," Pound advised. "It's a step up from the hardtack we'll have once we get moving."

"*That* depends on us," Wish said, around a mouthful. "With that stream nearby and this fine town, I think we can come away with some fish. Bit of game from the forest, cook up some jerky while we wait on Command?"

"In case no one's warned you yet," Pound told Newk, pointing a stubby finger Wish's way. "Don't listen to a damn thing this one says. She's always got her head in the clouds, dreaming big. If she didn't, she mightn't have roped you into this madness."

"I wanted to join," Newk replied.

"And take care to keep your belt tight," Pound went on as though she hadn't spoken. "She's been gagging for company since we set out from Bulkheel." Newk tried to hide her surprise. "Only she doesn't know how to get laid. If she starts writing you poetry or something, tell us, we'll set her straight."

"Okay."

"Seriously," Dakoda said. "Do you know what you're doing? You could go home. You don't belong here – in this fight, with us, whatever."

Newk put down her spoon, face steeling.

Dakoda waved a dismissive hand. "I don't mean you're not welcome. Ignore Pound, we'll take anyone mad enough to join. I mean this mess is between the Stanclif statesmen and the Drail Prognane, with us skewered in the middle. What's it to the Ringed States? Go home and enjoy the sun."

Newk considered an answer carefully, then said, "No one can enjoy the sun under the Drail shadow. Our homes are all connected to this war. And we have a Stanclif railroad. Part of one, anyway."

The table took in her point, then Small smirked and said, "Have you been practising that?"

She started laughing and Pound echoed Newk's words in a deep, dramatic voice, "No sun under the shadow of the Drail."

Newk looked hurt and added, "They killed my family."

The two scouts went quiet, but Dakoda, rarely sympathetic, said, "We've all lost family. Taken families, too. Wish must've ruined a thousand families all by herself just yesterday, isn't that right?"

Wish looked up over her gruel and said nothing.

"No sense coming here for revenge, or anything noble, that's all I'm saying," Dakoda sighed. "Nothing noble in this war. If you *have* to fight, find another motivation fast."

Newk looked chastised. "What other motivation is there?"

"You tell her about the farm yet?" Dakoda asked Wish, who quickly shook her head. She was wary of confiding her hopes to newcomers. Not everyone got it. But in time-honoured scout tradition, Dakoda confided for her: "Wish is gonna take us all back to Swelig. North-east Stanclif, far enough from Vasseer to be isolated without being too remote from the city. An easy life in beautiful countryside, self-sustaining, looking out for each other. All it needs is for this damn war to end."

"Right now, all farm produce gets committed to the central stockpile," Wish explained quietly. "We'd never hear the end of it."

"And everyone will go back there?" Newk smiled, finding the suggestion cute? Or was it sympathy? Pity? What had Newk said about the absurdity of owning land?

"Everyone would be welcome," Wish said. "Dakoda says she's good with cattle, so she's definitely coming."

Dakoda bared her teeth in something between a grimace and a grin; she had an aversion to just smiling like a normal person. "Sure, you end this war and I'll make all your wishes come true, Wild."

"Well *I'm* here for the booze rations." Small beamed.

"Biscuits, for me," Pound said. "Bland, hateful biscuits, but they're free as long as we keep killing for them. Well, that and this was a great chance to get away from my bloody kids."

"Her family thought she went out to get milk!" Small cried, slapping the table in her never-ending disbelief at Pound's surely invented sign-up story. "They don't even know she's here!"

Newk turned to Wish as they folded into laughter. "I would like to see it. Your farm."

Wild Wish swallowed her mouthful. The others went quiet, eyeing her with keen humour. They'd say it if she didn't admit it herself. "It's a work in progress. I don't actually own it yet. But it is there – and we'll come out of this rich enough to take advantage, trust me."

"Wild's not even a farmer," Pound said, with a laugh. "But considering how many people she's killed, I don't see anyone getting in her way."

"Yeah," Dakoda joined in. "She'll definitely be at home in the slaughterhouse."

Wish forced a smile too, and focused on her gruel. Newk's expression had shifted back to uncertain. Tackling, perhaps, the same question that sometimes troubled Wish. Could this merriment, and cute dreams, really make up for the terrors that were still to come?

9

The practice of folding myriad creatures into the various empires' war efforts was at once liberating and diminishing. Many races found themselves granted greater equality, called upon to work or fight for their countries – but all were reduced to their most basic assets. Stout trunks packed the mines, wyrlings braved projectiles scouting from the skies, armoured cirga were ridden hard as messengers on the front lines. To have a physical advantage, now, was to have a defined place in the war effort.

Empires of the Rocc, Xanthial, p. 692

Panicked shouts and gunfire woke Wild Wish. She was up in seconds. She leapt down the stairs shunting into her boots and trousers in a wave of scouts all doing the same. She ran with them through the tavern, banging past tables, shouting in confusion, "What's going on?"

More gunfire, beyond the walls, spurred them right out the door, and Wish almost leapt back in as Tate yelled right in her face, her revolver raised.

"Rock Squad, Sun, with me, to the gates! Sabre and Boot on the walls – we've got company, cover us!"

No one needed telling twice, even half-dressed and half-asleep. The scouts chambered bullets and stagger-ran through Blythe. Jostling alongside Larkin, Wild Wish glanced back, watching Newk's uncertain head bob between the others. Two days in Blythe and the ringed woman had lingered near (but not quite by) Wish, saying little, having barely got beyond the theory side of their first few hours of rifle instruction. Now, at the first sign of trouble, she looked lost. Wish waved for her, called her name. Newk hurried closer and together they sprinted to catch up. Others were already piling up the two ladders closest to Blythe's entrance – gates permanently open after the damage Emi had done. Cracks of rifle fire came from outside, returned by soldiers on the ramparts. Men shouted commands to one another.

"Let me through, let me through!" Wild Wish insisted, shoving for space on the small ledge, holding her rifle over her head as much to avoid knocking people over as to show she needed a place at the front. They parted for her, pushed her on, and finally she skidded down next to Four Skills, who already had her gun poking out through a crenel. Neither of them had their helmets on, Wild Wish realised, with all this happening too fast. She tucked her hair back behind her ear. Through her scope, Wish saw movement in the trees, far back. Big shapes – riders, twisting and turning in the shadows. At least four or five enemies sheltering in the tree-line. One fired with a flash and a bullet thumped into the earth midway between the walls and trees, where a man was dragging himself forward on his elbows.

"Hundred twenty yards," Four Skills announced, and Wish adjusted her scope. Along the wall, soldiers took useless pot-shots at the trees, lucky to even hit the bark but keeping the riders back. No one had left the gates, but they were urging the man on below. He waved a hand and irritably swore at them. Newk somehow made it down alongside Wish, watching with fascinated horror.

"Covering!" Wild Wish announced, at the top of her voice, and fired into one of the riders' shadows. The shape bucked and she slid back the bolt for another shot. Four Skills fired, too, chambered a bullet and fired again. The trees erupted. Cries of big animals pierced the air. Wish fired twice more and the movement stopped, her target either dead or retreating. On the grass, the man had twisted around to shout goading remarks at the enemy. Soldiers were finally running out to him, four with their heads down, two more either side with rifles up and firing to provide cover. All Blood Scouts. They reached the man in seconds, and as they took him up an enemy burst from the trees, firing. It shot one of the girls in the shoulder, knocking her into the arms of another.

Wish caught her breath, not was hit, and gave herself a second to take in the attacker. A cirga – the great, plated race of Drak, with four legs, a torso as powerful as a horse's, terrifying spiky clawed limbs, and an insectile head. She aimed beneath the mandibles – a weak spot? – but the bullet sparked off its chest-plate. Four Skills fired, catching the side of its head. That knocked it stumbling to one side, screeching, as the girls on the grass dragged the wounded man in. The cirga recovered while its companions kept firing from the trees.

"Can you do something?" Larkin hissed, the other side of Newk. Wish threw her a look, seeing Newk shake her head.

Skills' shot had made the cirga mad, and it spun on the spot, thrusting a rifle above its head, roaring war cries. More shots from the ramparts came nowhere near hitting it, as if the warrior's bravery defied them, and when Wish fired she only clipped the side of its leg – the bullet again twanged off.

"Should've stayed in the trees," Emi growled ominously from a few bodies down, leaning over the ramparts. She made a tense, furious noise as her hands squeezed into the brickwork and Four Skills took another shot that snapped the cirga's head back. It recovered again, this time bowing low, preparing for a charge. The ground erupted underneath it, chunks of earth jarring up and catching its legs in different places with awful snaps. The warrior dropped and rolled, screeching pain, but even as it tumbled to a stop it clutched at its rifle, turning it their way. Emi slipped back from the wall sniggering, muttering nonsense words, shaking her head to prepare for more, but both Wild Wish and Four Skills were ready and they fired as one at the beast's exposed, softer underbelly. The cirga's shot went far overhead as its stomach exploded.

By virtue of being up top, where officers had been watching, Wish got swept along back towards the command building, as she saw Sun and Rock squads moving out into the country to pursue the remaining cirga, and to check there were no more surprises waiting.

Most of the others, following Fixit, were rushing the wounded girl back to the tavern. Wish's crowd took her quickly into a grand hall where high-ranking soldiers gathered around the rescued man. She found herself with Dollemore, Four Skills, Larkin, Emi and Newk, between dour older men in tight uniforms. General Easter himself, a battle-worn, deeply scarred man, sat in his wheelchair of pipes and wires, ordering that they save the newcomer. The air was electric in the wait of this man's report, and Wish had a strong feeling she was in the presence of Something Important. If she kept very still and very quiet, she might be part of it.

Dollemore worked rapidly alongside Command's best medic, doing what they could to dress the man's leg – he had taken a bullet in the thigh. He lay on a table at the centre of the room, a lean, dark-haired man with a thin moustache and a jagged nose, a natural shadiness around his eyes. He wore tailored civilian's trousers and a fine jacket, now plastered with mud and blood, and he spoke in a pronounced High Stanclif accent, loudly: "Buggers tracked me with a degrebus. I only spotted it about ten miles back." A flying creature, more common on the Eastern Front, where they were used as messengers and spies. "Devilish thing must've got a signal off before I shot it out the sky. They caught up to me a mile or so out – worst luck – ah, would you *watch* that? Don't mistake my calm tenor for an inability to feel pain – no, no don't lay *your* hands on me, I'd sooner feel it than not!" He was waving Dollemore back the same time as instructing the medic, distrusting of witlacing and disapproving of the medic. "There were five on me. How many did you knock down? I'd recommend not letting any get back across the river."

People looked to the scouts and Wild Wish looked to Four Skills, who said, "We killed one for sure. I doubt we stopped any in the trees."

"Then pray your people catch up. Ah, what am I saying – you'll not stop them now. Have you got a wyrling handy? There's a narrow crossing at the river. That's where I slipped through, you can cut them off." He scanned the officers and Wish tried to look inconspicuous, in case she was sent in pursuit and missed this conversation.

Easter nodded to one of his commanders, who rushed out of the room.

The injured man continued, "I'm disappointed, got to say, that no one met me on the road. Didn't fancy my chances after getting routed in Wick, but when I heard you'd taken Blythe I thought things were turning my way. You knew I was coming, didn't you? What in demon's blood were you waiting for?" The room took a collective breath at him addressing Easter so bluntly. The general glared back. Wish couldn't wait to tell the girls about this. The injured man rested on his elbows. "Forgive me, General, I've had a hard ride. I thought my messages were clear, though. The Slanik forces are making progress. The rumours of the Dread company stationed within Highscythe Ward –"

"Are rumours," General Easter said. "We cannot divert 6th Brigade on rumours."

"Absolutely. But they are *terrible* rumours. I've seen the Slanik mages myself, I've seen their convoys. Didn't you find evidence here?" He scanned the room, looking for someone, anyone that might support him. His eyes fell on Newk. "You've a metafis? Between you and this one – my dear, I'm sorry for snapping before, I do *respect* mortal magic but I'm slow to trust. If you'd get this *blasted* fool back" – he swatted at the medic, who stepped off with hands raised, and addressed Dollemore – "I'd appreciate whatever aide your magic can offer. And tell me: between yourself and your Ringed colleague, aren't you concerned with what was happening here?"

"It's not my place to speculate," Dollemore murmured as she laid her hands on the leg wound. He winced, giving the room a chance to chime in.

One of General Easter's lieutenants stepped forward, his scarlet cloak and officer's hat marking him as a high-level witlacer himself. About a million years older than Dollemore, with a hollow face. He said, "Captain Brade your reports are the stuff of paranoia and anti-magic propaganda. Your fears are unthinkable, quite literally. The Arbitrators would not allow it."

"The Arbitrators did nothing," the man, Captain Brade, said, "when the Drail dirt-minders buried the Cundarn munitions factory in an avalanche of rock."

"Never proved," the mage snorted. "It may have been explosive charges."

"It was dirt-minders," Emi volunteered. "We all know that. The captain's right, the Arbitrators haven't messed with Drail affairs since before Garter fell. How could they?"

The superior mage bristled at being contradicted, by Emi of all people (looking pleased with herself), and Wish had to put a hand over her mouth to hide a smile. Captain Brade said, "See, she knows. You're a magic worker too? You have a whole council, General, surely they've advised you."

"We're not exactly" – Emi grinned around the room – "meant to be here."

"Enough, enough," General Easter said. "Is his leg fixed?"

"Yes." Dollemore rose, showing her palms. "Stay off it for a day or two, but you'll be fine. Drink lots of –"

"Later. What I want now, Brade, is to know what *concrete* evidence you have for us."

"What I've seen with my own eyes," Brade said, bitterly. "What I've heard with my ears. And I have this." He fished in his jacket and held up a faded, torn scrap of paper. "A route. Through the Kleb Mountains, right behind the Drail's backs. It'll take us –" The other generals erupted in disagreement and irritation, some making noises that didn't sound like words at all, just heckling him down. Childish. Brade spoke over them all: "It'll take us all the way into Slane, unseen! Give me a company, that's all I need! Two hundred men, no armour, just enough to take a town. I am certain –"

"We cannot listen to this man," another officer rumbled. "All he's done is bring *cirga* to our door – exposed our command station – sown chaos! I wouldn't trust him with two of my men, forget two hundred."

"I wouldn't want two hundred of *your* men, Commander Uhlred."

"Enough!" General Easter boomed, restoring order in an instant. "I'll hear your report in full, Brade. In private. Then I'll decide."

With that, he pivoted his chair away, and as soon as the door closed behind him the other commanders resumed their protests. They argued over imagined redirected resources as Uhlred boastfully attempted to defend his honour. Brade dropped back onto his table breathing deeply, apparently done, and one of the lower-rank officers turned to the scouts and whispered that they should go. Wild Wish lingered as long as possible, watching the man who'd ruffled so many feathers, and he caught her staring through the crowd and winked. Between the scant details she'd been able to follow and the reactions of Easter's staff, she had a strong idea that things were about to get a lot more complicated for everyone.

10

It is precisely because the Dread Corps of Low Slane were so effective at creating an aura of fear and mystery that so little recorded about them is verifiable. They were, however, the very pinnacle of Screaming Prince Proud's penchant for combining the theatrical with the truly horrifying. Though much about their presence in the war may have been manufactured, the threat was no less real.

**Dueley's Comprehensive: The One War in
10 Volumes (Vol. 4), p. 142**

Maringdale's eagerness to meet the Dread company somehow showed, because she was sure it was the main reason Panderlair delayed until the next day. Instead, he started a circuit questioning the soldiers around town, who generally claimed complete ignorance of the explosion. Maringdale's senses confirmed they were telling the truth.

Panderlair checked them into a tavern busy with wounded soldiers, insisting they rest. After dinner, as he puffed on his Azrian leaf pipe, he warned that they might have trouble with the Dread company itself. Be ready for it. The Dread Corps were known for their rigorous initiation procedures, breaking men down and building them up again. It made them fiercely loyal, fanatical soldiers, which Panderlair distrusted – as a fiercely loyal fanatic of a different creed. Maringdale swallowed it. Let him cause a fuss; she could impress the Dread soldiers on her own and convince them to cut her free from the Purification entirely.

The spy hunters were only able to secure a single room, where Panderlair took the bed and Maringdale lay on the hardwood floor, trying to ignore Donut's wheezing snores. Between that and her anticipation, she was barely able to sleep, so was quick to react to the sense of someone watching her. Maringdale rolled off her mat to whip up her pistol from a chair and turned in a crouch to find a man in the unlit room, standing over her. She sensed no malice in him, but growled, "Announce yourself or die."

The intruder spread his hands, unarmed, but his armour, silhouetted against the half-light of the ajar door, was threatening on its own. Black, blocky panels, decorated with angular bone. And he'd just been standing over them, watching them sleep? He said, "Killsmith Hill. Here to talk."

"So you crept in?" Maringdale demanded, seeing in her peripherals that Panderlair was drawing his own pistol from by the bed. Donut stirred more slowly, grumbling, before noticing the intruder and startling backwards with a yelp.

The man wore no helmet and had a strong jaw, a thick head of fair hair. Handsome, Maringdale could tell, even in the dim light. He spoke with friendly confidence: "Lower the weapons. If I wanted to hurt you, I would've done."

"And if you wanted to talk, you should've knocked," Panderlair said.

"Perhaps. But where's the fun in that? I'm here to escort you. Battle Chief Ways wants a word."

"In the dead of night? You'll go back to your commander and instruct him we'll be with you in the morning, when *we* deem fit."

"I'll go," Hill said, "to the front of the tavern, where I'll wait precisely ten minutes. If you're not ready by then, Ways will not see you. Tonight or ever. Your choice."

Maringdale felt his confidence brimming through – he knew they wanted what he was offering. Despite herself, she felt a smile forming, for his attitude and for the opportunity, a summons to the brazen Dread Corps.

But Panderlair got hotter, used to being feared and respected. "We are officers of the Purification. How dare you presume to insult us like this?"

"No insult meant," Hill said, hands raised slightly higher. "This is when we're willing to open our doors to you, that's all. Don't come and we'll know it's not meant to be."

With that, he turned and left the room. Panderlair leapt up a second later, to slam the door as though other unwanted guests might gust in. He muttered insults while Maringdale whipped on her boots and coat. She all but kicked Donut to his feet. Panderlair glared and she said, "If it'll get us an audience, so what?"

She raced down to get the horses herself rather than wait for Donut, worried Killsmith Hill might disappear in a puff of smoke if they were late. She came to the front to find him sitting tall on his own horse, holding a gas lantern like a ward against evil, a dark knight lined with bone markings. He smirked as she waved the other two out of the building and she felt him observing her. No nostalgic longing here, but curiosity, shamelessly taking her in, imagining what kind of woman she was. Donut moved like he was still half asleep and Panderlair dragged his heels with reluctance. But he had on his livery and cloak, the Purification medallion on show, and he gave no more complaint as he mounted his horse.

"It's not a long ride," Hill said, "and the night air will do you good."

He rode fast, and they had to kick their horses to stay in the pool of his lantern. The road soon dipped into forestland, dark trees walling them in, but Hill led them without hesitation, until the trees broke to reveal a small castle. A shell of an old stone fort, one tower standing, another half collapsed, the windows high off the ground all barred or boarded up. A truck sat in front of it, before an arched set of oak double doors, but the place was unlit and looked dead.

Hill jumped down and knocked as the spy hunters joined him. A mechanism turned and a lock was lifted, before one door swung out, giving space to guide the horses in. Another Dread soldier stood with a lantern of his own, a man similar in height to Hill, the same armour, but a less friendly aura, chin lined with scars and ragged black hair loose over his brow. Hill introduced him as they guided the horses in: "Killsmith Mercer."

Maringdale recognised their shared title: a Dread company rank? She parked that question and turned her attention instead to the courtyard. It had only enough space to unload an old wagon, with a stout single-storey storehouse adjoining the remains of the broken tower and little else besides. The towers appeared to be this castle's sole living space.

While Mercer stayed back to secure the horses, they followed Hill into the solid tower, to a circular reception chamber. A stone staircase followed the wall up to the next level, while dusty old armchairs sat amongst boxes and rolled up carpet as though someone had started emptying the castle then given up.

"Wait here," Hill said, and continued through a door onto a descending stair. He went down, and the sound of something whirring and male voices chanting escaped the tunnel before the door closed behind him.

Maringdale looked to Panderlair to get his read. He stood in front of one of the beaten chairs, not sitting, and she sensed mixed defiance and worry. Asking himself, was he about to clash with a Dread officer? To hell with that, they'd been invited here. Maringdale dropped into a chair and sank heavily, lower than expected, with a cloud of dust that made her cough. She was still choking on it, flapping a hand, when the door reopened and a massive man walked in. She tried and failed to stop coughing, hand over her mouth, as Battle Chief Ways, presumably, glared at her. Bald and mad-eyed, he had a mountain's worth of muscle caged within an intricately plated suit of black armour, so scratched and dented that his skeletal decorations were distorted into something more disturbing. He had no weapons Maringdale could see, but his body itself was a war machine, and she sensed a hard quality in his mind: a direct, almost emotionless drive to get what he wanted.

"You're the officers they sent?" Ways started, accusatory. His eyes ran over each of them. Panderlair did not move, Donut squirmed with a weak sound, and Maringdale shifted in her chair but did not stand. "An old cripple, a fat-arse and a woman?"

Panderlair's shoulders tightened and Maringdale sensed neither he nor Ways would appreciate her insisting they were the best inquisitors in the Empire. Well, except Donut. Panderlair said, "You knew we were coming, it would have been wise to wait for us in Cleave City."

Ways stepped closer, a full head taller than the spy hunter. Hill lingered in the doorway behind him, watching with amusement. The battle chief said, "We conducted our investigation and were satisfied to leave. Our work doesn't want attention."

"Yes, well," Panderlair replied, "you'd have drawn less attention by allowing *us* to decide who to punish for your transgressions."

"Transgressions? You're saying I'm responsible?"

"I doubt very much the disaster in Cleave City would've happened *without* your presence, wouldn't you say?" Panderlair said, then quickly added, "We are officers of the Purification, Colonel Ways. We do not defer to military authority on our path to ensuring the Empire is safe from enemies within."

Ways narrowed his eyes, moving even closer. Maringdale shared a look with Hill, warning him that her man was worth watching, too. This frail-looking bureaucrat showed such unwavering confidence in his office that he would stand up to literal giants. Battle Chief Ways' considerable bulk swelled with that realisation. Then he let it out, taking a step back, and said, in an almost amiable tone, "Good. As it should be. You're able trackers?"

"Colonel Ways –" Panderlair started, about to try and take charge.

Ways cut him off. "Battle Chief. In the Dread Corps, my assignment is Battle Chief. You have stepped into our world, you'll find we do many things differently."

"As evidenced by the men you murdered because you failed to keep your house in order."

Maringdale sat far forward, waiting for Ways to break Panderlair's spine. Her interest gave the battle chief an out, though, as he caught her staring. He said, "You flout convention yourselves, in the Purification. Slane would never permit women in their military ranks." It was a challenge that Maringdale saw he wanted her to meet.

She smiled. "As well as a first-rate inquisitor, I am also a highly proficient intention mage."

Ways kept his face impassive, but he was impressed. "Then you'll know I speak the truth when I say those men we punished in

Cleave failed to do their job. I would have done the same, or worse, to my own guards, but they were lost in the explosion."

"You're sure about that?" Maringdale raised an eyebrow, and she sensed approval rising from Hill.

"We don't enlist traitors in the Dread Corps," Ways said.

"Funny thing about traitors," Maringdale countered, "is they only tend to appear where there's trust."

"You were targeted specifically," Panderlair said. "Why don't we start with who knew what you were doing."

Ways scoffed. "It was no secret we were in Cleave City. Even without knowing our purpose, a Dread company is always the biggest target in a given area."

Maringdale could imagine that was true. But Panderlair continued, in a tone too reverent to be real, "Humour me, Battle Chief."

"I'm less interested in *why*," Ways replied, not playing, "and more interested in *how*. I don't believe ordinary Khib insurgents could have gained access to that building. The enemy set charges without being seen and disappeared without a trace. And my mages detected no magic use in the area. No alarm was raised."

"Dread soldiers are too tough for a slit throat?" Maringdale couldn't resist. "Poison?"

"Yes," Ways answered plainly. "We're trained in poison-taking. My men drink it for sport. And the guards were staggered to give a clear view of each other's positions. No man could have got close unseen."

"No man," Panderlair echoed. "In our experience, non-human agents are even less subtle. Trunks are clumsy, rock mites slow and ungainly, sky wretches far too loud."

"The Gonish, though, are another matter."

As the others fell quiet, Donut exclaimed disbelief, using the common slur for the Gonish people: *"Waders?"*

Maringdale was alarmed at her sense that Ways was serious. What self-respecting *Battle Chief* could lay blame for something like this on waders? *Waders* was a favourite line of desperate prisoners, trying to pin crimes on an enemy small enough to hide anywhere. They were rarely more than a foot high, very resourceful, and intelligent. In an age of bloody conquest, Gonland had somehow talked their way into an imperial partnership with Khib invaders without violence. But what those desperate prisoners who cried wader failed to appreciate, most likely having never seen one, was that waders were also notoriously isolationist and risk-averse. In all her time hunting spies, Maringdale had never seen credible proof of the Gonish being involved in the war anywhere, let alone creeping around behind enemy lines.

"Do you have any evidence of this?" Panderlair said, dry enough that he might be taking the claim seriously. Internally, he was seething at Ways' audacity, seeing it as indicating guilt. Damn, Ways had triggered the righteous fool.

"Process of deduction," Ways said. "You're aware of the claims that have been made along the south?" When Panderlair did not react, the battle chief gestured for Hill to explain, as though rumours were more appropriately presented by a man of lower rank.

"There's between six and ten of these disruptive fuckers," Hill said. "Thought to be responsible for poisoning Count Fedora's staff, and the sabotage of a high-bore artillery company near Boyne. Khib prisoners have been boasting about it, spreading stories that these little bastards are sticking it to us without us even knowing it. One of your own people, Thorn Red, confirmed it."

"Thorn's been here?" Panderlair said, with animosity for the Purification's most celebrated officer.

"No, but he will be," Hill said. "He wired that they've been tracking the Gonish infiltrators for the past month or so."

"Then I suppose we're not needed," Panderlair said, dryly.

"No, you're not," Ways replied. "But if you insist on being here, you can chase these rebels down."

"Indeed?" Panderlair replied. "Unfortunately, we're not here to do your bidding. We –"

"Our site in Cleave City contained sensitive information," Ways spoke over him, loudly. "Whoever gained entry will be preparing to use that information or pass it on."

Panderlair frowned. "And what would they have found?"

"The locations of five sites linked to our own," Ways said. "Coded, but that'd only last so long. One is being moved in the next few days, another is almost done with their research and two are on watch. The last one, the closest to us, we've lost contact with. It's the north side of Fever Forest, right on the front line. A day's ride away. I've sent my own men ahead to the site, but as you're trackers you could catch these waders on the way."

Panderlair was silent as the room waited for his assessment. He usually couldn't resist a chase, but Ways had already pushed the wrong buttons. He said, "We will gladly hunt down these insurgents." Then, after the briefest pause, "Just as soon as we establish your own lack of guilt."

"Are you –" Ways started, but Panderlair continued.

"The Purification does not bow to individual command. All must be held to account to keep this machine running. We will examine the facts as they stand – including what you've been doing here, as well as the legitimacy of the executions in Cleave City. If our investigations validate yours, then, and only then, shall we continue to Fever Forest."

Ways didn't protest. His restrained expression said he had the one-eyed bastard's whole measure: not someone you threatened or bargained with. Merely someone you tolerated. He addressed Maringdale instead: "He speaks for you all?"

Maringdale saw the meaning in his eyes, bolstered by Hill shifting behind him, a shrewd look on his face. She felt *both* of them willing her to defy the Purification. The Dread Corps would take care of her. But she felt Panderlair too. Show any doubt and she'd face his wrath. She had worked with him for a year; his eyesight might not be perfect, but his wits were sharp enough, and he would not tolerate betrayal. He had a hand on his revolver already.

"He's the boss," Maringdale said, through a grim, humourless smile.

"Take the night to think about it," Ways said. "You can lodge here –"

"Back at our inn will be fine," Panderlair said. "We will reconvene in the morning. And next time you have an urge to visit us as we sleep, I strongly advise you reconsider."

Ways' face split in a smile that said so be it, all chance of their future collaboration dead. Maringdale met Hill's eye, though, before they could go their separate ways, and gave him a look to indicate she might not be *entirely* above renegotiating.

After the meeting with Ways, the spy hunters did not go quickly back to sleep, as Maringdale was treated to an extended sermon from Panderlair on the evils of those that would compromise the Purification for their own interests. The pinnacle of a civilised society, after all, was one where no man was above the law, and all infractions faced the discipline they deserved. What were they fighting for, after all, if they weren't able to come out of this as champions not just on the battlefield, but within their own borders?

The late-night meeting had lit a fire in the old man, and where Maringdale had seen the opportunity to work with the Dread Corps, he saw the opportunity to demonstrate that *none* were safe from justice. Even if they were not responsible for the explosion, they had sacrificed good soldiers as scapegoats for their own failings. They had tried to hide important work that no doubt concerned all the Empire. They had believed themselves above the Purification, and worst of all, ha ha, with a finger pointing in the air, they had underestimated the Empire's most strident soldier of peace, the legendary Sin Sight Panderlair – shifting into third person, as he did when he *really* wanted to sound important.

Maringdale wasn't sure quite how it happened, but it was at about this point that she realised she had stuck a knife deep into his throat, and her hands were warm with the mess of his blood. Donut made gasping noises, clattering back into the wall in shock, as Maringdale lowered Panderlair to the floor, the man's wicked single eye staring at her with horrified disbelief. He gagged, blood in his mouth, not unlike that gasping worm-eye as it succumbed to its dismal fate. Maringdale turned away but could still hear his gags as the blood glooped out. She wiped the blade clean on the closest object – the bed sheet – and the man finally went quiet and still. She turned to Donut and smiled over their former superior's corpse.

"*I* think we should go with Battle Chief Ways' suggested plan of action, don't you?" she asked, brightly. Donut was pale, temporarily incapable of words or even blinking, hands pressed to the wall, but he managed to nod. Maringdale continued, "The Purification does not tolerate those who think themselves above others, after all."

11

Following the Battle of Green Rise, the remnants of the Drail 8th Division fled to a position fortified by 13th Division, just outside Wick, to form the Drail's last bastion south of the bend in the Step River. New trenches were dug where a great field separated the Comity forces from Wick Fortress itself. It was a triumph for Stanclif to push them so far back, and the Drail forces were temporarily diminished, but the ground that had been gained offered little additional value. At the end of the day, both forces found themselves once again sunk in the ground, separated by a no man's land no more than four-hundred metres wide.

The Great Ebb and Flow: Reflections on Modern Trench Warfare, Sommer, p. 452

Wish grew vaguely aware of the thunder of battle returning, somewhere past the hill and trees that shielded Blythe from the new front line. Artillery fired sporadically through the afternoon of gathering supplies, into early evening as the scouts gathered again in the inn, waiting for fresh orders. Jules from Rock Squad was the one injured saving Brade; a friend of Oksy's but not someone Wish knew well. She might never use her right arm again. But Tate had drummed up another two recruits since Green Rise, from the front line, including a freckled redhead who Rock Squad snatched up because she claimed she could cook.

The imperial troops meanwhile redeployed around Blythe, with additional Sick Brigade soldiers reinforcing the battlements, fearing another cirga attack. The scouts had followed the insectile centaurs as far as the Step River, but stood no chance of catching up. It was anyone's guess now if Easter's man with a wyrling had stopped the monsters. Wild Wish imagined a horrendous clash of horse-sized insect and flying lizard. The stranger creatures of the empires were rare and seldom met on the battlefield, but she imagined it must happen occasionally, with spectacular results. Mostly, it was just men shooting holes in each other.

Into dusk, Rue got into her drink with her heavy brow getting heavier, some of those looks reserved for Newk, who hovered away from the main group. Wild Wish saw a positive, because she realised if Rue wasn't happy about Newk's company, it meant she wasn't going to claim her as a battle wife, to replace Loose. With that happy thought, Wish suggested to Newk they do a walk of the battlements, to get out of the stuffy tavern. They were barely up a ladder when they found Dollemore talking to a soldier on watch – a man masked by the shadow of a helmet and stubble across his jaw. He offered cigarettes which Wish and Newk refused, then he paused at a trio of short, distant blasts, his own cigarette raised in thought.

"That's Colonel Hangtail's mortars," he said. "They'll go for another fifteen minutes."

The burst was followed by more pops that could've been small fireworks in another life, another world. But the faint glow on the horizon, like a city's light at a great distance, spoke of something much more extreme.

The soldier said he could recognise the pattern of all Sick Brigade's artillery units, as well as most of 8th Division's. Something different was blasting tonight, a big-bore weapon set up in Wick to reinforce the Drail. Dollemore said the new trenches were already peppered with craters and severed limbs. She'd been to the front recruiting, and they might as well have stayed at the bottom of Green Rise, for all that had changed.

"You had more luck recruiting here, Wild." Dollemore studied Newk with interest; she took *everything* in with interest, this straight-backed blond with her angular face and crinkle-free uniform. Not always clean, but *always* crinkle free. "Emi speaks highly of you."

"That's generous," Wish said. "She barely got beyond hello." Despite her worries Emi might steal Newk away, or drive her away, the dirt-minder hadn't resurfaced yet. Too busy brushing shoulders with the important men in the command centre, scheming. Scheming and arguing. Mostly arguing.

"I knew she was lying." Dollemore turned her nose up with satisfaction. There was no hiding that she came from some place better than all of them – Vasseer, the Stanclif capital, obviously, but one of the really nice parts, where silent men in suits opened doors for you. She'd been tighter with Command than Emi, right in her element. Without elaborating on the specifics of Emi's lies, Dollemore added, "Do me a favour and avoid her. She'll get you in trouble."

Newk looked to Wild Wish for guidance and Wish shrugged. They turned to watch the night sky again, more blasts sounding, and Wish said, "Any news on Jules?"

"She'll live," Dollemore said. "But her war's done. I'm sorry I couldn't do more. If I'd been with her instead of Captain Brade . . ."

"Then he might've lost his leg," Wish suggested.

"No, Major Sagat is a powerful witlacer, he could've taken over from me at any time. Though I suppose it's not the done thing for an officer to practice magic in front of his peers. In the war room." Bitter? Perhaps. Dollemore turned to Newk. "I didn't see you attack the cirga. You are a menafis, do you have battle magic?"

Newk stiffened in the way she had with Emi – between this reluctance to talk and her response to Larkin's demands on the battlements, Wish got the idea there was something up with her magic. Newk said, "I've little experience."

Dollemore peered at her tattoos. Even Wish knew that so many body markings suggested more than a little experience.

A creak on the ramparts drew their attention back – someone approaching. An odd sound came from the shadows, squeaking, heavy. A machine? Wish braced a hand on her side-blade as the soldier readied his gun. General Easter's wheelchair rolled into view. The solider jumped to attention. "Sir, General, sir!"

"At ease, at ease," General Easter murmured, pushing his wheels to come closer. His piercing eyes took in the small group.

"What –" Wish blurted. "How did you get up –" She caught herself in his metallic stare, realising the mobility of the empire's most celebrated commander was not her business.

"I climbed the ladder," Easter told her without insult, though. He rattled a thick leather strap across his lap. "This comes attached. I didn't realise I'd be interrupting a party, though. I was looking for a word with the life mage."

"Sir." Dollemore straightened up. "I would've come to you, there was no need –"

"Don't." It was an order. Zero tolerance for charity. "I want to discuss this Slane business. Away from Command."

"Of course, sir," Dollemore said. "Though I'm not sure I have much to add."

"We shall see. Major Sagat is dismissive of Brade's fears because he is rigid in his thinking about how war should be waged. But if I said to you, conceive the most devastating, terrible attack you can, with no limitations – what would you be capable of?"

The question made Dollemore tease the cuff of her opposite sleeve, a slight and rare hint at her discomfort. "In terms of witlacing? Generating a force more powerful than one of your mortar blasts would drain any mortal mage; to find means to enhance that power would call repercussions from the Arbitrators. However lenient they've been so far, if the Treaty of Tynes was broken that severely, they would come out in force."

Tynes was a buzzword every soldier clung onto; Wish herself cried it with great drama whenever Rue gave her a playful thump. The accords, first established fifty years ago, sought to regulate the brutality of modern war, with rules for the treatment of the wounded and prisoners, and an international agreement over corruptions of magic. This covered things of legend that few believed were real – like death magic and bloodmancy – giving Wish some idea that Easter's thoughts were going to especially dark places. When you took the dirt-minders' ability to commune with the inanimate and the witlacers' ability to warp living systems, the combination blurred the line between the living world and the dead.

"That's not what I asked," Easter said. "Is there more to the fears than simple superstition?"

"Proven? No. General Easter, witlacers manipulate life flow – by fracturing his own energy, a mage could stop another man's heart in his chest. Enough mages working together, with a power source large enough, *theoretically* they could kill an army without pulling a trigger. But it would cost too many mages' lives experimenting to reach a level where they might kill even a score of men. Considering the other weapons we have at our disposal, it doesn't make sense that anyone would risk that."

"But they were trying something here," Easter said. "So, to face that risk, they must be working on something more devastating than artillery. Tell me honestly. You could go a lot further than stopping hearts, couldn't you?"

Dollemore paused again. She clearly knew what the general was getting at and didn't want to say it.

"You, ringer," he addressed Newk instead, "must have gained some impression of the dark arts they were testing?"

"I saw nothing, sir," Newk replied quietly. "I heard screams. No one came back."

"Did the Drail not talk?" Easter said. "Did they not interrogate you as to your own arts? They gathered a mix of races here for a reason."

"Respectfully, sir," Dollemore came in, "it's a common misconception that the shadow schools of the Ringed States produce dark magic. If the Drail were looking towards mass destruction, or raising the dead or baiting demons, if such things were at all realistic, then all the scholarship in those areas rejects any menafis practice. My understanding is that Ringed magic is more concerned with abstractions – dancing for star gods, communing with the weather. Drawing external power to the individual. The Drail consider them primitive. They may not have credited her with learning at all."

Newk looked taken aback by this dismissal of her culture, but as Easter kept his eyes on her, she remained quiet in tacit agreement. He said, "The menafis have a spirit of lost souls, I believe."

"Hed," Newk said. "Yes. He walks across the oil that divides the living and the dead, to deliver souls to Sali."

"Then the Drail could've conceived a connection to manipulating such forces."

"Maybe, sir," Newk said, humbly, "but they didn't speak to me. I think they had the information they needed. They were just testing it."

"Yet with your background, you were able to divine no hint as to *what* they were testing? Do you wear those bones for fun?"

"Sir?" Newk faltered. "Apologies, sir, I am mesita, not menafis. My relationship with the spirits is limited to where it is channelled by our mages. I am a conduit."

"Indulge an old cripple," Easter said, sternly, "by using your imagination."

Newk's stare hardened at being talked to like an idiot. Wish really hoped she wasn't going to push their great general off the wall. But she answered evenly, "Menafi is not like Stanclif magic. Or Drail magic. It is communication with the spirits. The asking and receiving of help. It does not change the natural order, it just redirects it."

"Meaning what?"

"My understanding, sir," Dollemore said, "is that the menafis perform meditative and rather personal magic. Ideas associated with luck and charms."

"Which is to say," Easter said, "you, too, don't credit them for anything at all."

Dollemore didn't answer, avoiding looking at Newk.

"I suppose that gives us one less thing to worry about. But I'm certain the Drail *would* break Tynes. If that does not lead to the magical horrors of legend, it leads somewhere worse."

"What exactly does Captain Brade suspect of them?" Wild Wish asked, drawing a regrettable glare from the general. Two insubordinate questions in one conversation, she was doing great.

But Easter's need to discuss it trumped his disdain, and he answered, "He leans towards the *somewhere worse*. He believes the Drail wish to combine the mortal abilities of witlacing with the earth-channelling abilities of dirt-minding. Discounting the mythic ideas, what else might that do?"

"Create some kind of chain-effect?" Dollemore suggested. The idea clearly wasn't new to her; magic-users probably discussed such fantasies regularly over beer, between insulting their conflicting schools of thought. She shook her head. "Again, the cost to those experimenting would be too high. Too dangerous."

"Perhaps. But we have fallen a step behind, either way. Our battle mages are top class, but the Drail have made moves that bureaucrats like Sagat lack the imagination for. Rather damning for humanity, isn't it?"

No one touched that one. Having seen millions die in the space of a year, humanity was already pretty well damned. Wild Wish gave Newk a sideways look to share that, and this time drew Easter's attention without talking: "You there. You're a sharpshooter, yes?"

"Yes, sir," Wish croaked.

"Perhaps you're the one I should be talking to."

"Me?" Wish squeaked.

"Yes. Sharpshooting is a new discipline. We considered it beyond the scope of the job before, to train excessive accuracy, considering the sheer strength of these weapons. Others thought it unsportsmanlike. We adapted only because the Drail got there first, again, pinning us down with snipers along the front. Now, do you consider your role excessive? Unsportsmanlike? Or do you spend time finding new and more effective ways to do your previously frowned-upon job?"

Wish gawked, not sure that he really wanted an answer, basically saying she was part of what made modern war so corrupt. Forget sharpshooting, did he know she had carved through hundreds of people with a machine gun?

"Indeed, this is no time to hold back, or to believe for a moment that our enemies aren't capable of the absolute worst," Easter went on, satisfied by his own conclusions. Wish bristled at the idea of *absolute worst* being inspired by her presence. "This war has made monsters of us all. Good night, ladies. Corporal."

The soldier saluted as General Easter rolled back the way he had come. No one spoke for a moment, though Wish frowned at how was he going to get back down the ladder. She'd like to see that. He rolled into the shadows, taking his dark thoughts and the mystery of that descent with him. Wish turned to Dollemore, and said hopefully, "Well, now he's gone you can tell us how baseless that fun chat was."

The mage looked worried, though. "No. Whatever the Drail were up to here, it's not hard to imagine it started with a similar conversation."

"Oh."

The solider on duty took a big drag on his cigarette and turned away. Another blast sounded from the horizon, thick in timbre. He said, "That'll be the Basin Screw. Vile piece of kit. Designed to make craters filled with shredding shrapnel, maiming rather than killing. *That's* something only the Drail could conceive of."

Wish gave him an unpleasant look, his attempt to dismiss the topic no better than Dollemore's. Their own side had obviously conceived things just as bad, and if they hadn't yet, they would do so in response. As they had with snipers, evidently. The sky rumbled on that dour thought. Thunder, far to the south, louder than the artillery, as nature reminded them of its own powerful force. The sky lit with flashes, a storm coming in.

Dollemore said, almost wistfully, "There's truth in it, though. If they were ruthless enough to make the sacrifices, and mad enough to try it, the darkest effects of mortal magic *might* be channelled through the most powerful channels of natural magic."

"Right," Wish replied, with a weak smile, "good thing the Dread Corps are known for their kindness and sanity."

The rain became a deluge, forcing Wish into the cover of an awning, a block from the tavern. Newk joined her breathing heavily, black locks glistening wet. The Farne storms were infrequent but could fill trenches in minutes if the correct guttering wasn't in place. Thousands had learnt that the hard way, back in the early months of the war, and even now a shower like this could cost as many lives as those artillery barrages.

But in the safety of Blythe, having escaped their immediate soaking, it was an invigorating distraction. Newk breathed it in like she hadn't tasted fresh water on the air in months, and Wish watched her, thrilled at her delight. Life went on; the biggest disasters would pass. Friends died but others came. The world turned. At least, it would until Easter's imagined psycho-mages ended it.

"Enjoy it while you can," Wild Wish pushed Newk's shoulder, shouting above the rain. "Once we're marching, try keeping dry in a tent. Not fun."

"I've travelled through storms before," Newk replied. "I rode the Good Ship Lovat from the Port of Casteen. We saw waves as high as mountains."

"But you had a boat? I'm not sure you got my point."

Newk smiled. She got it.

Wish said, "Look. About this menafis business. What's . . . Well, any of it?"

"The tattoos channel the will of the Mes," Newk explained. "The strength of Goda, the courage of Tol, the speed of a Canchik. The menafis prayers fill us with this energy and it lasts as long as it lasts." Her look darkened. "I haven't felt it since leaving Fireti."

"Ah. Well, at least it's not mixed up in whatever chaos they were talking about."

"Your magics aren't so different. You put magic into objects. Create metals that cannot be penetrated. Shields in the air."

"I don't know about air shields," Wish replied loudly, "but touched metals, those ones the dirt-minders reinforce, they're rare as hell. Us lowly troops can't get anywhere near them. I've heard the Davenport Cavalry have touched armour though. Madmen on horses."

"Oh?" Newk frowned. "I thought with your dirt-minder's help, I might . . ." She didn't say what she might and Wish dreaded to think. Probably something sword-based and likely to get her hurt.

"I wouldn't," Wish said. "Emi's dangerous. And she would *love* to have something to hold over you. Anything."

"You don't like her?"

Wish laughed. "I love her, I love all my scouts. I'm just looking out for you."

"You love all the scouts?"

That came as a challenge, but Wish replied honestly, "Yes, all of them. We're a family, ugly bits and all. Rue's got a hard head but a good heart. Somewhere in there. And she's *tough*. I've seen her arm wrestle guys twice her size. I swear, underneath that uniform she's ripped with –" Wish stopped, realising how this sounded. "She'll do all the heavy lifting on the farm, when this is over, that's all I'm saying. You'll see how valuable she is then."

"And Emi?" Newk shifted the conversation back.

"She'll be there too." Wish shrugged. "Every scout that survives this war is welcome, or rather *expected*, at Lavender Manor. We'll have fields, cattle, everything. Room for forty girls at least. With the pay from this tour, especially if some of us chip together, it'll happen. It's not that unrealistic. You're welcome, too. You can reach things from the top shelves, for example."

"I suppose you need ringers for that. You are all so small."

"But big in heart. You'll see. Once we end this war. With the power of the weapons out there, I guess that might be over sooner than we think."

She meant it as light-hearted, but Newk's face grew graver. It'd been going all right for a minute; they'd almost got away from the topic. Newk said, "Can your magics really do such terrible things?"

"I mean . . ." Wish trailed off, unable to dismiss it. "Maybe. Maybe they'll screw everything."

"Unless we stop them," Newk said.

"Yeah," Wish said, and turned away. She nodded to the torrential rain. "It's thinning. Come get a drink with the girls? I promise they'll be your new best friends. Whatever else happens, we'll have fun along the way."

Newk watched the rain, if anything heavier than before. But she nodded back. Also, thankfully, willing to put off the world's darkening truths for that little bit longer.

12

Without going too far into the question of shooting, it will suffice to say that of each hundred students submitted to a course, roughly seventy-five went back quite useful shots. Many rose far above "quite useful" and the competition for the top champion shot could indeed be quite fierce. But shooting was a small part of what was taught, with observation being another chief skill, and it was those who combined both disciplines best that went on to be truly great snipers.

Sniping in Farne, Heskeph, p. 62

Wild Wish had lain awake making plans: get up early, lead Newk out of town to a secluded spot and teach her properly about sharpshooting, reap adoration. She racked her brains for all the lessons Four Skills had offered when Wish first joined the scouts – tips taken from the esteemed Major Heskeph, pioneer of sniping schools for the Stanclif Empire and an object of admiration for scouts everywhere. There were concepts of breathing, observing, choosing a scope – those were the dull ones. Practice, that was the good bit. How to hold the gun, adjust the scopes to score a hit. If Newk got the principles down, she'd be able to observe well enough to be a spotter, even if she couldn't shoot. As a spotter, she could stick close for long periods waiting, with whispered discussions about their past and futures.

It made sense to teach Newk one-to-one, Wish told herself, as she hadn't seemed comfortable talking in a crowd the evening before. Much like she'd slipped into the background after that welcome kiss – that welcome kiss! – she'd preferred to listen than talk when they joined Boot Squad in the tavern. Pound told her about her two children back home (filthy little troublemakers), in the care of their grandparents; Small described her future husband, a dashing young blonde fighting with 2nd Brigade, who didn't exactly know she existed yet; Fixit tried to bring in comments about religion, via medicine, and got roundly talked down. Conversation turned to gaming, and Pound enthusiastically tried to teach a tiring, slightly inebriated Newk how to roll bones. Rue kept her distance, thumping shots of alcohol on the bar and scowling. Not necessarily at them; Sarge assured the others she just had some things to work through.

Morning came with sunlight and potential, the tremendous storm over. Wild Wish bounced down the stairs for another sloppy breakfast and told Sarge she'd take Newk to train, and Sarge immediately ruined everything: "That's great, Rue can join you."

"Rue –" Wish started with shock, but noticed Rue, having somehow missed her before, sitting beside Sarge looking grim. Dark around the eyes, red within them, a hot drink clutched in a fist.

"She needs some air, and if your new hire's to fit in, I want you getting along."

Great. So instead of shooting practice, this would be a Make Rue Less Aggressive challenge. Rue didn't meet her gaze, not happy about the proposition herself, and Wish said, through gritted teeth, "Glad to have her."

Without much more than mumbling, Rue joined Wish in collecting Newk from a table where she sat alone eating porridge. Wild Wish led them out the gates of Blythe in a deeply uncomfortable silence. It was almost a relief to be interrupted by a lumbering trunk who crossed their path. It was five feet tall, with limbs twice as thick as a human's and a stout body built like a tree-trunk – hence the nickname. The trunk's wide face, sunk into where a humans' chest would be, had big, worried eyes and its mouth hung open like a toad's. It had a companion, hanging back by the town walls, and Wild Wish recognised them as the pair she'd liberated from the Drail prison barn.

"Want to come with you!" the trunk announced, spitting as its thick tongue muddled the words. "Please."

"We're doing training, scout business," Wild Wish replied uncertainly. "Sorry."

"Want scout business!" the trunk bounced enthusiastically. It wasn't well-versed in Stanish. "Me – fight hard. And he." It pointed to its companion, who tried to hide its face, not really possible given their frames.

Wish stared. Oksy or Emi or Sarge, they were good with strangers. She was likely to say something wrong. And did: "We're a human platoon."

"But took her!" The trunk pointed at Newk and Rue scoffed, marking her own doubts there.

"She is *clearly* human," Wish answered with shock. "But listen, you do *not* want to be a scout, it's hell out there. We go deep into dangerous territory, we'll all be killed – you're much better asking to be transferred down the line. The Farnish Army have some excellent inter-species divisions –"

"Farnish fuck," the trunk spat, conveying, fairly, that the Farnish were most definitely second-best. Well, fifth or sixth, in this war.

With no idea how to handle trunks, Wish merely gave up and said, "Sorry. I'm sorry."

"No – want join –"

"She said no, you trunk bastard!" Rue stepped in, with a push that sent the trunk a few steps back. It had an excellent centre of gravity; most species would be flattened by Rue's push. It was also incensed, big eyes narrowing and lips folding in a grimace. Low and heavy as they were, trunks were a great deal more powerful than the average human. But Rue wasn't an average human and she stood over it fired up with fists ready. More importantly, the imperial soldiers around the gates took notice, looking their way with guns ready.

The trunk huffed and grumbled, holding back its frustration.

"That's enough, come on," Wild Wish said, brushing Rue's arm. "Let's go." She led by example and strode out the gates, careful not to look back. Rue fell in alongside her, grunting under her breath and mocking the poor trunk. Newk followed at a distance, and Wish caught her glancing back.

Making no more reference to the encounter, Wild Wish led them at a quick pace through the trees, down to the stream and along it, out to a field with low grass. There, she positioned a rock, took them back to the edge of the field and handed Newk her telescopic rifle. Newk was holding down unsettled thoughts, the same as Rue, but with the gun in hand, she would have to move on. She lifted it, testing its weight, and Wish gave a quick tut and held a hand out to take Newk's own rifle from her shoulder.

"That's just to hold onto while I demonstrate," Wish said. "You'll start without sights, on a cheaper rifle because – this is lesson one – a well-used gun barrel gets less accurate. Meaning we save the good guns" – she pointed at her Long 0.48 – "for when the shots matter most. Now, we already covered holding –"

"Why can't you take non-humans?" Newk cut in. Wish froze, meeting her eye for the first time since the trunk encounter, finding what she'd feared would be there. Judgement.

"Um." Wish fought for an explanation that didn't sound awful.

Rue folded her arms. "Yeah, come on Wild. This is what we're really here for, isn't it?"

"No. Not at all. Newk's not familiar with guns –"

"Oh, this just gets better."

"I can fight," Newk said. "Better than most."

"With sticks and stones?" Rue shot back. "Surprised you're not dragging a bone club."

"With a blade," Newk answered sharply. "Which can cut as deep as any bullet. The Matticks can fight, too."

"All the more reason not to have them around," Rue said. "Trust a bloody savage to think we want dangerous animals watching our backs."

"I'm no savage."

"Girls, please –" Wish said.

"Look like one to me." Rue pressed closer to Newk. About the same height as Wish, she had to look up into Newk's face, but that didn't make her any less menacing. "You wanna hit me and prove otherwise?"

Newk's nostrils flared as her grip twisted on Wish's gun, but she held in her anger.

"It's not practical," Wild Wish said, desperately wanting to diffuse this. "Taking in other species. We move at a different pace, have different needs. It's why the Blood Scouts exist to begin with. Similar builds, the same needs." She forced a laugh. "We work together to keep up supplies of clean underwear, for starters. But you bring in other species, it gets too complicated."

Newk slowly turned her glare to Wish and made her feel a couple of inches tall, knowing it was nonsense. But Wish went on, "We're forty strangers thrown together to fight through hell. It's challenging enough without added cultural differences."

"Like mine," Newk said.

"Exactly," Rue snarled, but Wish stepped between them. The tension had dropped just enough that she could guide Rue back with a little push.

"No," Wish said. "We're not so different. We've talked." *Kissed.* "It's not the same. You know it's not, both of you. Newk's great, Rue, she's got skills and a fire in her that you'll love when you see her in action. But the trunks, that's not something Command would even consider. Even if they went to Tate, or Easter himself –"

"But that man didn't. He approached you," Newk said. "That's *why* he approached you. And they're not *trunks*, they're Matticks. From the Mattin Mountains."

Wish paused, aware suddenly of how that distinction affected Newk herself. She didn't even know what you were supposed to call someone from Fireti. Newk stared, waiting, and Rue joined her, pleased that Wish could see it was difficult to handle a ringer.

Whatever Sarge had in mind here, Wish suspected she'd blown it, and stood there mutely until a shout blessedly interrupted from the trees.

"Wild Wish!" It sounded like Dakoda. "Rue? You there?"

"Wish?" Another voice – Small, the girls searching for them.

"Over here!" Wild Wish cried relief. Damned if she was going to finish this conversation. She ran for the trees. "What's up?"

"Haul arse back to base!" Dakoda shouted. "We're moving out."

Wish raced through the trees, gesturing for the other two to follow her, so thankful for the distraction that she ignored the fact she was leaving them alone together. She found Dakoda walking up the path, rifle over her shoulder. "What are the orders?"

"Oh." Dakoda wore a sick, humourless smile. "It's our lucky day. General Easter figures if anyone can infiltrate Slane, it's us."

Any scant attachment Wild Wish might have developed to Blythe was swept away in a flurry of packing supplies and a general rush out the gates to make the most of the daylight. They could've been warned sooner, to march at sunrise, but apparently Tate had been arguing with Command. General Easter had decided it fell to the Blood Scouts to tackle Captain Brade's concerns, which Tate considered to be a suicide mission on hazy intel. It was unclear if Easter really thought the scouts were Stanclif's best option to face a terrible problem, or if they were merely conveniently placed, and expendable enough, to take the issue off everyone's minds. Before giving in, Tate had spent the morning going over the details again and again, until satisfied with a viable route north. It would begin with a rapid departure to cover a good distance by nightfall. On the plus side, the exodus was so hurried that Newk was folded into the ranks without further question and Wish didn't have to deal with Rue.

Captain Brade shared a carriage with the Reaper, which Rock Squad refused to leave behind, while Tate's officers and the mages secured horses and everyone else had to walk. Fully stocked, allegedly rested, the scouts set out marching to skirt the front line and take sporadically unfortified territory into the Kleb Mountains. Wish estimated her pack was thirty or so kilos, hardly putting the light in Light Infantry. But lots of that was food, so she wasn't complaining, even if it was mostly Farnish hardbread.

The first leg of the journey would be an easy hike, they were told – the immediate area was safe from Drail forces, as far as the river. The bridge crossings were heavily protected and Easter had no immediate plans to cross the river himself, as it would leave his rear exposed to the Drail dug in around Wick. But Brade knew of a fallen tree that formed an unchecked entrance into Drail territory. Patrols were light in that region, far up the Drail's western flank, because the terrain quickly rose into impassable mountain trails and cliff faces with machine gun nests. Wild Wish wanted to know what they'd do when they reached *those*, but that was apparently a problem for the scouts of another day.

They had until the river, at least, to hike as a platoon. It gave Wish the full gamut of scouts to choose from as walking mates, and after the morning's abortive training she struck out for the front to avoid both Newk and Rue. Walking by Brade's carriage and not far behind Emi on her horse, she fell into step with Oksy and offered sympathy over Jules. Oksy nodded thanks, regretting she'd missed the cirga attack herself. She'd been instructing Cheaster soldiers at the front, meaning she'd been with Brogan. But Oksy's usual proud posture was slumped and Wish overcompensated with smiles to try and cheer her up. Didn't really work.

They reached the river shortly after noon and broke to rest; Wish found a good spot on thick grass and shook off her boots to flex her toes. Tucking into the bread, she watched Tate fuss over maps with her officers before their dive into Drail land. They had all crossed back and forth into Drail territory numerous times in the past few months, so this wasn't exactly new, but usually their orders took them a few miles at most, with a clearly defined return journey. Tate kept throwing Brade unhappy looks, blaming him for this new danger. He, in turn, nodded respectfully at her, playing things cool.

Fuse and Cade, a boisterous pair from Rock Squad, lingered by the carriage chatting to him, out of earshot of Wish, and he smiled along. He wasn't classically handsome, but in his asymmetrical, sharp-featured way, there was something striking about him. That charm was accentuated standing between the two Rock Squad sappers – both short and dumpy dark-haired women with flat, round faces, who looked so alike they should be sisters, but weren't. They were a scrappy, soot-and-grease pair who'd joined the scouts together after forging a friendship digging tunnels under trenches. Though Brade was dressed down in a tatty civilian suit, with his thin moustache the only well-maintained thing about him, next to them, he was a gentleman.

"What do you make of him?" Emi asked, dropping to a cross-legged seat beside Wish, making her jump and almost drop her bread. Emi grinned.

"You'd know better than us," Oksy said. "How's his leg?"

Emi shrugged. "Don't know, they're only witlacing it. More fool them." She sounded affronted, that mortal magic would be chosen over dirt-minding, though the two disciplines were never combined, for medical purposes or otherwise.

"He looks like he could be a school teacher," Wish mused. "But also a master pirate. Or, if he's *super* intelligent, a school teacher passing himself off as a master pirate pretending to look like a school teacher. Tricking you into thinking he's interesting."

"He's been out in Drail territory for months, they say," Oksy said. "I'm pretty sure he's not pretending to be interesting."

Wish narrowed her eyes, wondering if Oksy would be over there with Fuse and Cade if she hadn't been already got her leg over with Brogan.

"But do we *trust* him?" Emi said, darkly quiet.

They all watched Brade say something that made Fuse giggle. Anyone daring to flirt with that pair of sappers was definitely dangerous.

"He's been out in Drail territory for months," Oksy repeated, now as a negative.

"And he might have us do the same," Emi noted.

Wild Wish huffed, as if any of them needed reminding how far this mission might take them. "On my farm, Emi, you will only be allowed to say positive things."

"On your farm, Wish," Emi replied, "I will have nice things to say. Out here, what have we got that's *nice?*"

She said it with one of her usual wicked leers, head to one side in a manner that invited the answer. *Each other*, Wild Wish wanted to say. She looked back to catch Newk's eye. The ringer was with Small, who looked especially small next to her, neither talking. No sign of Rue, who had fallen in with one of the other squads, probably smoking with Harmon or Gray. This wasn't exactly a smooth start, and considering their destination, maybe them all being together was a bad thing.

13

Those that hold local above national shall be purified.
Those that hold friend above countryman shall be purified.
Those that hold personal above communal shall be purified.
Those that hold private above social shall be purified.
Those that hold animal above human shall be purified.
Ten Thousand Tenets of Purity, **Official**
Purification Handbook, Psalm 43

Everyone hated the Purification. For the most part, it meant lonely drinks and obstructive conversations. When it came to Panderlair's death, though, it meant minimal fuss. The soldiers Maringdale alerted bought her story that rebels had crept in and murdered him while she and Donut were tending the horses. They suspected those responsible left without risking further trouble, not deeming her or Donut worth it.

Captain Ogard regarded the news with a sense of relief, though he eyed Maringdale with measured scepticism. He accepted her account, and Donut's uneasy nodding, as he checked the body himself, then grumbled, "We can't double the guard, seeing as we already did, and you won't have anyone left to punish if you expand your investigation now."

"No," Maringdale replied. "We have it on good authority that the insurgents are likely aiming for Fever Forest. They intended to stop us following them, so that's where we'll go."

"Mm," Captain Ogard said. Maringdale knew he was concerned that other Purification agents might follow to replace them, but their departure might be one less complication, to take him a step back from that gun in his mouth. Still, he couldn't quite let it lie. "You would think they'd try to finish the job, though."

"I would think they might be worried I could sense them coming," Maringdale replied. "And they might believe they can spread more fear by showing they are capable of such horrors without alerting those nearby. It's one thing to kill a legend like Sin Sight Panderlair, a force of his own – but to do so in the unknowing presence of Constans Maringdale?" She whistled, as though almost impressed.

Ogard wore an expression of distrust, but he nodded, accepting her word. He dismissed them, promising he'd take care of everything here, so they could hunt the killers – *elsewhere* – and as they parted Maringdale saw him give a sympathetic look to Donut, who shied away. When the pair of spy hunters were riding back to the Dread company, Maringdale assured her companion, "This'll be good for us, Donut. You can't honestly tell me you'll miss that one-eyed psycho."

"No," Donut said, finally mustering the courage to talk. He continued thoughtfully, with an explanation that likely took him all morning to come up with. "I suppose, actually, that by wanting to stay here, and not follow Colonel Ways' advice, Mr Panderlair might have given the insurgents a chance to strike again. Which is as good as *helping* them, isn't it?"

That, of course, and Panderlair was a prick who had it coming. Maringdale merely smiled, letting her gold teeth tell Donut he was thinking straight.

At the Dread company's ruined castle, the pair found Hill and Mercer carrying a crate out to the truck. They loaded it as the spy hunters dismounted.

"Going somewhere?" Maringdale asked.

"No business left here," Hill said, clapping dust off his hands. "This position's become untenable. Where's the old man?"

"Strangest thing," Maringdale said, "but your waders must've been afraid he'd catch up to them" – she made a *crrkk* noise as she dragged a finger under her throat – "and did him in his sleep. No idea how they got in or out, just like with your factory."

"Just like it," Donut agreed, to affirm his now-decided position.

"That's unfortunate." Hill was careful not to smile, but Maringdale could feel his pleasure. He liked her. "What does that mean for your investigation here in Cleave?"

"We'll chase after these bastards at once. So maybe you don't need to load that truck."

"Ah." Hill flapped a hand to the vehicle. "We're moving anyway. But if your aim's to get to Fever Forest, we should talk." He looked to Mercer, who was leaning against the truck, less welcoming. "You good for a second?" Mercer grunted and shrugged, and Hill flashed Maringdale a smile. "Please, wait here."

He disappeared into the castle, leaving Mercer to lurk near the truck, not continuing with his work but watching them like a guard dog. Maringdale turned away rather than deal with his face, and Donut moved closer to her, wanting to say something but not sure what.

Hill returned ten minutes later with a large canvas bag slung over one shoulder, a rifle over the other. He whistled at Mercer to stop what he wasn't doing and unload the truck again. He pointed at Maringdale. "If we're to head these people off, horses aren't good enough. Jump in the truck."

She cocked her head to one side. "You want to join us?"

"I'm already there." Hill swept around to the back of the truck and threw his things in. "Ways can commandeer more transport from town and I'm better on the road than lugging equipment. Right, Mercer?"

"The Battle Chief want me with you?" Mercer asked.

"Only needs one guide." Hill grinned. "What do you say, officers, you ready to get moving?"

Maringdale regretted, for a second, that she'd be taken from Ways, but the battle chief clearly had no intention of re-emerging. Probably not a daylight person. They could reach Fever Forest in half a day with this truck, though, and their success rested on them being able to cut off the insurgents *before* they reached the next target. She'd also have a Dread soldier for a shadow, someone to learn from – someone plainly on her side – and with luck, he might even have some idea how to find the waders, impossible as that seemed.

They helped replace the truck's cargo with their own supplies, and Maringdale climbed aboard. She had ridden private motor vehicles before, but this one was bigger, setting them high above the ground, and it rumbled importantly when Hill started the engine. It was fast, bumping over the rutted ground, at least twice the speed of a horse at sprint, and there was power behind it, the sort that could smash through walls. It was noisy, fitting to its size, and duelling smells of grease and burnt oil wafted from its shaking engine. Maringdale found herself grinning, even as her fingers dug into the hard seat for stability. Donut perched on a short bench in the back, coughing occasionally on the fumes.

Away from Cleave, they drove between open fields that rose in gentle hills, the clouds parting for a pleasant day made chilly by the air blowing through the half-open windows. Hill drove like he'd been born with this vehicle beneath him, hands flitting from the big steering wheel to the stick down by his side. He had a rare contentment about him, exuding no fear or even thoughtfulness. Just happy to be there, flashing Maringdale occasional glances.

He spoke, at last, loud over the engine, "There's a gorge, two thirds to Fever. Only remotely direct path goes over the Fever Crossing. Sound like a good place to start to you?"

Maringdale shouted back, "It'll do."

"So how do you wanna run the investigation?" Hill asked. "Must make for easy work when you can read men's minds." His smile suggested he expected her to study his feelings.

Maringdale struggled not to smile, too. "I read intentions, not minds – it's different."

"Ah. Been doing it long?"

"Since I was a girl. My dad stayed out late and lied about it. I didn't even know what I was doing when I set him straight, but he knew. It wasn't much fun back then."

"Seems you did well out of it eventually – Purification don't take on just anyone."

"Thank the war," Maringdale said. "They wouldn't have me in law offices and shipping businesses in Pace. I had to gut fish before I settled into menial tax enquiries. With the war, people got desperate enough to give me a chance to do something important. But they still stuck me out in the wastelands."

"With that one-eyed blowhard?" Hill shook his head, like he knew all too well the yoke of superior bastards. "Well, you're in the right company now, I guarantee it. Dread Corps takes care of its own and this mission is important as hell. That and" – he gave her another slanted smile, one eye on the road – "I'm looking forward to knowing you better."

Maringdale was glad as ever for her skills, to know he was genuine, not just trying to get laid. There was curiosity in him. Wonder. But her old instincts shone through as she said, "Well I'm here to do a job, first." It came out harsh and his mood faltered. She quickly went on, "What exactly are your company up to?"

"Highly classified," Hill said, cheekily, and that sealed Maringdale's firmness.

"Seriously. I need to do my job. You really think the insurgents didn't know what they were attacking?"

"It's possible." Hill adjusted his grip on the wheel. "But if they didn't know when they broke in, they know now. I don't doubt they'll have gone directly to the next site, quick as they could."

Maringdale nodded. She was right to follow this path and not let Panderlair get in the way. Hell, *Donut* was right – by not helping, her ex-partner was damaging the war effort. She pressed, "Give me a broad idea, then. What are you developing?"

Hill hesitated. It was good, in a way; much as he wanted to please her, he was still a loyal soldier. It would be a problem if he threw caution away on her behalf. He said, "I can't go into details, but put it this way: those Khib gas clouds can kill hundreds, uncontrolled? They've got bombs that can level a building? We're looking to repay the favour a hundredfold." His eyes glazed a little, imagining the possibilities in the road ahead. "Trust me, in Slane we don't fuck around. We're ready to dance with the devils others don't dare to."

Maringdale could imagine Donut in back, if he could hear any of this, tightening in fear, but it was nothing she hadn't heard before. Wasn't that exactly what she was doing herself, after all? Dancing with the devils of the Dread Corps. Because sometimes you needed to enlist dark forces to bring about good. What was the Drail Empire, after all, if not the living embodiment of the ability to bring order to savagery?

The spy hunters followed a supply line north through Garter, passing retreating carriages of injured soldiers more often than fresh reinforcements going the other way. Crossing an iron bridge over the River Dare, Maringdale took in an elevated view of a field where canvas-wrapped bodies lay in rows. Scores and scores of men. Had they died quickly, under hails of ferocious bullets, or slowly, poisoned like Ogard's men? She looked forward to helping the Dread mages repay the Comity.

The milieu of war aside, Garter was an expansive and empty place. By the time they reached Fever Crossing, they had passed only two small villages and one heavily billeted town, little bigger than Cleave City. Otherwise, this area was nothing but farmland and vineyards – very few places for enemies to hide along this route, unless they burrowed underground.

The crossing itself was essentially a trading post, but it showed signs of the improving quality of life as they travelled west. The road was cobbled, making for a smoother, if noisier, ride, and the houses were timber-framed, gabled, with tiles on the roofs. No signs of damage from bullet or bomb, no barbed wire or sharpened fences here. This place could've been in peacetime. The scattering of buildings stopped abruptly at the edge of Hill's promised gorge, a drop of maybe a hundred metres, with a fast river running through the middle, breaking against rocks. A bridge, just wide enough for the truck, connected two clusters of houses, the town split in half either side of this perilous divide. There was a stone tower on the opposite side, a Drail flag hanging from its window, with a green military car at its base.

Hill drove over the bridge slowly and stopped as two soldiers came out of the tower. They shook hands, exchanged ranks, offered cigarettes and invited the spy hunters inside. Even the soldiers here seemed a better class, separated from the war. The man in charge was a portly white-bearded man who'd apparently been put out to stud on guard duty after decades of service. He poured them all shots of a fiery alcohol and rattled out what he knew of the war from his vantage point. Khibba had made advances near Fever Forest, true, but Drail had swept down into Elmn proper, ten miles further west. They were moving too quickly to dig new trenches, each side recycling the defences of dead men as they retrod ground already fought over. If the battalion in Fever could hold out a few more weeks, the officer insisted, reinforcements would arrive from Singness, where the 4th Battalion were securely dug in. Weeks, to Maringdale, sounded nightmarish. How many good men would die in a matter of weeks?

She shifted the topic to ask who had come through the crossing recently. The guard reported Ways' men had passed two days ago and a platoon of armoured hogs had moved the other way, three days before that. That aside, as many as three messengers a day came through on motorised bikes or horses. The odd degrebus, too, the officer noted; they were under orders to record all sightings of them, as some of the flying creatures had been trained by the other side, and there was little way of knowing who one belonged to until you brought it down and recovered its message. Maringdale was all too familiar with that problem. The degrebus, though looking like an overgrown bat mated with a giant hornet, was only a creature of middling intelligence, capable of basic vocalisation, and could be trained to repeat particular messages. Both the Drail and the Khib employed them to send messages or scout enemy lines, and spy hunters frequently gained tips from captured creatures.

"What about," Hill said, "any word of waders?"

The old guard saw it wasn't a joke a split-second before letting out a big laugh, and only just held it in. He shook his head. "Wouldn't be welcome here. Waders, Azrian stalks, flutes, none of that Eastern nonsense welcome here. Honestly, any non-human would be hard-pressed crossing the gorge without accounting for himself."

"But stalks and flutes tend to be bigger than humans,"

Maringdale said. "Waders, on the other hand, are small. So maybe consider the question more carefully."

He gave her a pitying look, which she didn't need her skills to interpret: typical, ignorant woman. "Sweetheart, a rock mite couldn't cross that bridge without me knowing. We're doing our job. We got warnings to be on the lookout for Stanclif spies, sure, but they're further west, and I wouldn't take that to mean *waders*."

Maringdale glared hard. At moments like this, Panderlair would offer an upturned palm, visible only to her, to signal calm. But he wasn't here, so she took a hot breath, unclipping her pistol holster under the table. She said, "And if a wader stowed away in a messenger's bag? You'd see through it, would you?"

The guard gave another condescending smile and said, *"Honey, there's –"*

"My name is Constans Maringdale," she cut in. "Intention mage and Officer of the Purification. I have zero tolerance for those who undermine the Drail Empire, whether through subterfuge, sabotage or incompetence." That last word sunk in hard as he stared wide-eyed at her pistol, which now lay on the table between them. His eyes shot to Hill, as if asking if he was going to allow this, but the Dread soldier regarded Maringdale with forced blankness. Outwardly ready to support her, inwardly thrilled at her boldness. She said, "Now answer the question properly, before I start to suspect you're involved."

The guard swallowed, slipping into the fearful territory she was more comfortable with. "No. I mean, that is" – he ran a hand around his collar – "we check everyone coming this way for papers. Those without documents we turn back or hold until we have an idea. Those with cargo, we check carefully. *Everyone*. I'm serious, not even a wader could've got past. I only thought you were joking before. It's something people say for fun. Wader did this, wader did that. What're they good for, waders? They're not even in the war, so I didn't –"

"They're allied to the Stanclif Empire," Hill said. "Whether they fight or not."

The guard swallowed again, fear increasing as the Dread soldier joined in. This was good. Maringdale could see working with Hill – he shared her wavelength, was smooth but firm. Much more pleasing on the eye than Panderlair, too. The officer said, "True, yes that's true, but if there had been waders, anywhere near here, there'd have been talk about it, that's all I'm saying. They didn't come this way, I promise you."

"Didn't come this way *yet,*" Donut corrected. He was standing by the door like a servant, roundly forgotten but waiting for a chance to put something in that would help remind Maringdale he was part of the team. His self-satisfied nod let her know she was welcome.

"What about the Dread company operating in Fever Forest?" Hill asked. "Any news from them?"

"Your people?" the soldier said quickly, moving on to something he could be more helpful with. "They came through a month ago and settled into Walton's Nook, that's the last I heard. If they're holding the line in Fever, I'd say the Nook is still secure."

"Meaning they're still there?" Hill said, and the soldier froze in fear that any further talk would drop him into a trap. "No word of any part of the Dread company leaving the area?" The officer shook his head and Hill cursed. Turning to Maringdale, he said, "They either haven't received the message or didn't take it seriously. I can press on ahead if you stay here and keep watch."

"Nonsense," Maringdale said. "Donut can stay. I'm going into the forest."

14

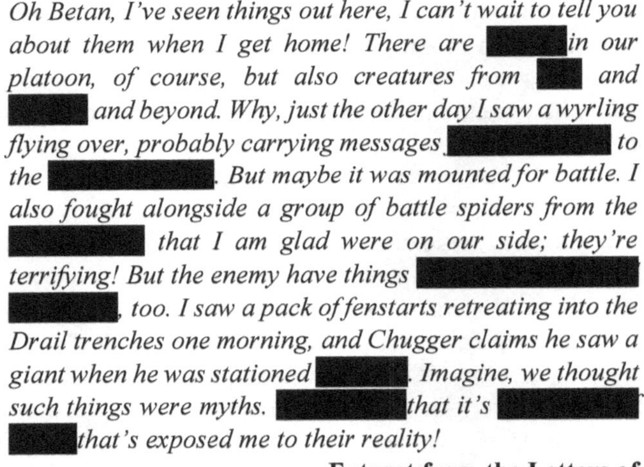

Oh Betan, I've seen things out here, I can't wait to tell you about them when I get home! There are ███████ *in our platoon, of course, but also creatures from* ███ *and* ███████ *and beyond. Why, just the other day I saw a wyrling flying over, probably carrying messages* ███████████ *to the* ███████████. *But maybe it was mounted for battle. I also fought alongside a group of battle spiders from the* ███████████ *that I am glad were on our side; they're terrifying! But the enemy have things* ███████████████ ███████, *too. I saw a pack of fenstarts retreating into the Drail trenches one morning, and Chugger claims he saw a giant when he was stationed* ███████. *Imagine, we thought such things were myths.* ███████████ *that it's* ███████████ ███████ *that's exposed me to their reality!*

**Extract from the Letters of
Corporal T. Sander, Balnia, 719**

Leaving the carriage and horses behind, the scouts broke into their squads after crossing the river, to fan out over craggy hills that were slowly becoming mountains. They marked an abandoned lumber mill on their maps as a destination, per Brade's instructions, taking separate routes there to avoid clustering. Sun Squad would travel slowest, escorting Brade, giving the others a chance to secure the path. Boot Squad moved up steep slopes through tree cover, and Wild Wish was happy to breathe in the country air, fresh and crisp after recent rainfall. The sun was out, the surroundings were quiet, untouched by war, and the dreaded Drail territory, it turned out, wasn't much different from the peaceful Comity lands.

That feeling disappeared when the squad crested a large rock that overlooked the road. Sarge ordered everyone to keep down and invited Wild Wish forward with her scope.

The road had been churned up in a series of craters, three or four feet wide, caused by impacts rather than explosives. Something huge had crossed the road and trampled the rock face on the other side.

"Giant of some sort," Wild Wish concluded. "Taking a shortcut. Probably best we head the other way, leave markers indicating the others be cautious."

"Except that way" – Sarge indicated the direction of the monster's tracks – "is where the lumberyard is. Not another mile on."

Wild Wish stared at the enormous footprints. Nothing good lay at the end of that trail, but they had been lucky enough to spot the tracks ahead of finding the beast. The others might not. "Guess we'll have to check it out."

It was a hawk giant. A humanoid biped, sitting with its legs outstretched as it rested its back against the biggest building in the lumberyard. The soles of its feet were clod with mounds of mud and rock from its advance over these mountainous paths, while its hands, with jagged fingers the size of human legs, were dark with filth and possibly blood. The creature wore a vast, grimy canvas sheet over its torso, draping down from chest to crotch, though it was hard to discern given the flaps of flesh that hung around it. Hawk giants were distinguishable by two major characteristics: the body was covered with an outer layer of skin plates, hundreds of panels of armour-like flesh that hung loose like feathers, and a great portion of its large head was made up of a stubby curved beak. This one had long draping hair, down over its shoulders, and was generally the shade of a scorched mountainside.

Wild Wish was certain it was the same beast that had made a trampling retreat from Green Rise. She'd had it in her sights then. Could've shot it without the thing ever knowing she existed. But here they sat – barely an hour into Drail territory and Boot Squad were gathered looking at the worst, and most unlikely, kind of obstacle. The myriad races were more common in the east. Wish imagined the battlefields of central and eastern Boldarow to be cauldrons of horror, swarming with enormous insects, winged beasts and ways to die that made guns and blades look pleasant. The enemies they faced in the Western Theatre were mostly human.

Why did this giant have to be here?

There were about half a dozen small buildings in the clearing but no trees. Sheer walls of rock rose to one side of the lumber mill, with a stretch of long-felled woodland off to the other. A small track led on through the rocks. The route they would need to use to continue. It was perfectly possible they might all sneak past the giant while it slept, slipping from their position by the outermost rocks to the nearest buildings and beyond, but it was a lot of open ground for ten scouts to cover unnoticed. And with another thirty soldiers to come, unawares.

"What I wouldn't give for a sapper right now," Sarge said, quietly. "As usual. You know how to kill a hawk giant, Wild?"

Wish froze. She was going there? "The same way as most things? Aim for the head." That was to be sure; the heart was usually a safer shot, but the giant's head was a much bigger target than most, and the only part of the body that wasn't covered in scales.

"Go with your first instinct, Sarge," Rue said. "We've got enough grenades between us to toss a dozen in its lap."

"Which you'd have to get close to do," Sarge said. "No. They have a weak spot between the beak and the eyes. Dead centre of its face. The rest of its skull is thick like rock, and its body too insulated to be sure you'd hit anything vital." She leaned around the corner of the rock. "We'll move closer, get a better angle from behind that hut. Best chance we'll get to put this thing down."

"Without waiting for the others?" Wish said.

"Longer we wait, the more likely it'll wake up. The others might even wake it themselves." Sarge formed a quick plan, scanning the site. "Small, you're with me and Wild. Rue, take Fixit and the new girl down the left, past that big building." Rue made a noise, and Sarge gave her a look to say, in no uncertain terms, that there wasn't going to be a problem with that. "Dakoda, Pound, to the right, go for that rock cover. We'll aim to end this with one shot, but if it goes wrong, everyone's to punch this thing with all you've got till it goes down."

"Aiming for the head," Pound said.

"No pressure," Wild Wish muttered, to a general quiet. From the hut up to the giant's face couldn't be more than a hundred yards, and specific as its weak-spot was, that was a target maybe two feet wide. An easy shot. But with an unpredictable prey.

"Questions?" Sarge said, and didn't wait for an answer. "Good, let's move."

She led the way, keeping low, with a trained step more silent than most in the platoon. Small patted Wish's back, and the other girls gave her nods as she sped out after Sarge. Small fell in behind, then the others panned out to get into position. The hut hardly felt like cover, a log cabin serving as an office or welcome lodge for the site, four metres wide. Shouldn't matter, Wish told herself. This shot was a cert. She crouched by the hut and prepped her rifle, finding the giant's grim face in her scope. Its eyes were closed in flesh folded like rock, the skin sunken dark behind the tip of its crusty beak.

"All in position," Sarge announced with a whisper. "Take it from here."

Wild Wish settled in, steadying her breath, rifle up. Cross-hairs squared right between the eyes. Big monster, easier to hit.

She pulled the trigger.

The boom of the Long 0.48 tore through the mountain and the bullet chinked off the side of the giant's head with a spurt of shredded cheek. Wish went rigid with alarm as the giant woke with a roar, great, lizard-slit yellow eyes opening and beak stretching wide enough to hide the rest of its face. She fired again, into its maw, but the angle was off and it shattered through the beak, rather than going back into the head. Then the giant was up, pushing itself off the mill to stand, as the clatter of heavy rifle fire started from the right – Pound's 56 thumping into its side. It turned towards the gunfire with a huge stride, foot slamming into the ground metres away from Wish's position, making Small yelp and jump up. More gunfire came from the opposite side, Rue and the others trying to hammer the monster. Wild Wish and Sarge dropped against the wall as the creature loomed over them, raising its arms defensively and screeching at an ear-splitting volume. The bullets kept it pinned with disorientation, chipping at its hardened skin flaps, but barely seemed to harm it. It steadied itself, searching for a target – and a cluster of pack goblins came screaming out of the main mill, four-foot green-skins hefting rifles bigger than them. One pointed towards the hut, yelling mad commands.

"Run!" Small shouted, as the earth creaked around the giant's shifting weight. If it hadn't spotted them before, it had now. Small sprinted out of cover as Sarge slammed a shoulder into the hut's door. The goblins opened fire and the girls shot back. Wish and Sarge bowled into the building, rolling onto the floor and twisting around just in time to see the giant's foot crashing down where they'd been. The hut shook, window frames snapping and walls swaying, ready to collapse.

"Other side!" Sarge pushed Wish on, through a room cluttered with a desk and cabinets. There were chest-high windows, no other exit. Through them Wish saw one of the goblins being ripped down by bullets. Sarge smashed a window, and Wish looked back to see Small running out in the open with no hope of cover. The giant's weight shifted again under the foot blocking the door, the lodge cracking, and a shadow swept over Small.

"Look out!" Rue yelled from far away, giving Small just enough time to twist back and see what was descending on her. Small gave a short, desperate scream before disappearing under the giant's other foot as it slammed into the ground.

Too stunned to move, Wish was pulled back, Sarge directing her to the broken window. Wish dumbly clambered through on automatic, getting caught on her belly. The guns kept firing outside, but not as many – the other scouts repositioning? Wish flopped gracelessly out of the hut, falling onto her hands and knees, and turned back to help Sarge. She was halfway out when the giant slammed through the hut. It exploded in a mist of shattered wood and Sarge was tossed into a roll while Wish was thrown on her back. As the debris settled, the giant rose over them with a screech, then swung an immense arm down. Sarge feebly drew the pistol from her hip, too late as the monster's hand closed on her. It tore her up into the air in a fist, twenty-feet high in a second, and regarded her angrily. Wish pushed up onto her elbows, desperately trying to catch her breath, searching for her fallen rifle. Another shot snapped from nearer the lumber mill – Pound again, in a better position – and the giant screeched irritation. It closed its fist with a loud crack that cut off a yell of pain from Sarge, then tossed her aside to take a big stride towards the next nuisance.

Wish couldn't see her rifle – didn't know what to do – but the monster was stepping over her, hadn't seen her, a huge shadow eclipsing the sky. She patted herself down, caught a hand on her short-blade. Not useful – went to her other harness – grenades. Wish pushed herself onto hands and knees, taking out an explosive tube. One of the giant's stumpy feet crashed into the earth two metres ahead of her, its ankle flaps bouncing as it did. She snapped off the grenade's catch and half ran, half jumped for the monster's heel. It started lifting as she caught hold of it, throwing her off, but she jammed the grenade up between two plates before letting go.

Hitting the ground hard, Wish rolled and coughed, breath knocked out of her again. She came still in time to see the giant had faltered, noticing the pest on its heel, and the foot slammed down short, close to the lumber mill. It was twisting around, looking back over its shoulder at her. The savage beak contorted in its permanent snarl, death in its eyes. Those eyes opened wide as the grenade exploded, shaking the mountain worse than any of the monster's strides. The hawk giant screeched again, leg coming up smoking, flinging blood and chunks of flesh across the clearing, and its huge arms spiralled as it came toppling down. Wish winced as the giant crashed through the lumber mill itself, with a great crack of rock as it smacked its head on the way down. Though weakened, and momentarily legless, it shifted, squealing, arms reaching out for purchase.

"In, in, finish it!" Rue screamed, running across the clearing, gun up. Newk was close behind. They let off a volley of shots, and more came from the other direction. The giant's screeches cut off and with another series of heavy crashes its limbs flopped to the ground.

Wild Wish rested back, straining to feel her legs, staring up at the blue sky. The girls were yelling at each other, running – Fixit shouting at Sarge, someone moving the other way, shouting about help. A goblin shriek made Wish look to the side, one of the little bastards running out of cover, gun raised, coming right at her. A gunshot came from the side and it flinched. Surprised it had been shot at and even more surprised it was still alive. It bared fanged teeth and swung its gun around with another shriek, just as Newk, rifle abandoned, flew through the air with a blade flashing. The goblin's head came clean off as Wish sat dumbly staring.

Newk ran a few extra paces to steady herself, sword at her side, and calm started to settle on the scene. Beyond Newk, Wish saw Rue watching. She focused on her mildly impressed expression, rather than the carnage.

15

The advancements in equality that the war forced upon society were evident within the military itself. Before 720, the privileged and elite controlled all the major military forces of the Rocc. Officers exclusively came from families of wealth and education. After the summer of 719, however, the rich recognised two things: to be an officer was riskier than ever before, and to be high born was not a natural indicator of military prowess.

Necessity bred a fluidity in ranks, whereby a lord's shamed son could find himself polishing shoes and a quick-witted tiler from the Vasseer slums could find himself commanding an entire brigade.

Dueley's Comprehensive: The One War in
10 Volumes (Vol. 2), p. 150

Wild Wish perched on a rock watching the scouts gathering, regrouping, coping. Sabre Squad hadn't been far behind, and attended to Sarge's body. They did whatever they could with what was left of Small, too. If Boot had waited ten minutes, maybe, then Four Skills, or Emi, or their combined forces alone . . . But Wish tried not to think like that.

She had come away with nothing more than bruises.

While Fixit gave her a scan, most of Boot Squad filled in their arriving friends. Then Fixit broke down in tears, and Oksy and Dakoda came to steer her away.

Dakoda held back, eyes warily on Wish, and asked, "What the hell happened?"

"Misfired," Wish said, quietly.

"At that distance?" Dakoda demanded, with echoes of her

attitude from Green Rise. Wary that Wish wasn't all there.

"Must've been the scope. It was off. The bullet tracked a foot to the left."

"The hell do you mean the scope was off? You preen over that thing day and night. Always saying no one's to touch it."

Wild Wish paused. She'd checked it yesterday, when she had a practice with Four Skills. It'd been firing perfectly when they faced the cirga. She said, "Maybe it got knocked in the hike." But that made no sense, not with her elk-skin padded case and a history of that *never* happening. Her friend looked equally sceptical, and Wish had to look away. Across to the others. Newk was staring at her, ignoring Pound as the latter tried to give her some kind of pep talk. The morning's argument seemed decades ago now. But it made Wish frown. They were supposed to practise shooting before leaving. She'd given Newk her rifle to hold. She whispered, "Oh no."

"What?" Dakoda followed her gaze to Newk.

Wish spoke again quickly, before Dakoda could draw any conclusions. "I must've adjusted it for shooting practice. Forgot to double-check." No good would come from assigning blame. But damn, that was it. Newk had touched the scope and Wish never thought to recheck it. Not even faced with shooting a giant. It seemed like such an easy shot.

"This is – this –" Dakoda balled her fists, not sure where she wanted to go with it. She looked back over to the wrecked mill and the giant's body. It was partly veiled by what was left of the lumber mill's walls, partly buried by the rubble of brick and wood. She huffed. "We got it, I guess. That's what counts, in the end. No telling what other damage it would've done down the line. They found body parts round back, you know? No prizes for guessing what this thing's been eating up here."

Wish preferred not to think about it. Beyond them, the scouts were starting to gather at the centre of the clearing. Tate and Larkin broke off to come their way. Brade followed, limping as he leaned against Spyke, Sun Squad's second-in-command. Wish said, "Here comes trouble."

Dakoda gave her a sympathetic look and backed off to make space for the officers. As she did so, Rue came over too, watching the group suspiciously.

Tate, whose expression was severe at the best of times, had a particularly severe expression now. She had an ever-serious countenance, her short black hair always packed into a flat, peaked cap, and she carried herself with the rigidness of a quick puncher. They'd spoken a few times personally, when Wish first joined the scouts, but since maintained a relationship buffered by rank. Wish shied under her gaze.

"Ladies." Tate nodded to them all. "You're all holding up?"

"Can't complain," Rue grumbled.

"Sarge was a good woman. One of our best."

Wish looked to where they'd laid their leader. Fixit was on the ground down at Sarge's side, with Oksy's arm around her. Not saying much. It was a bad way to go. Wish had heard Sarge wheezing her last painful breaths.

"But this is a blow for the Drail," Tate continued. "That giant would've rejoined their ranks eventually. Sarge would've been proud. Wild Wish, you cogent for a talk?"

"Captain," Wish replied meekly. Here it came, and with Brade to watch, leaning hard on Spyke. She looked miserable about being his crutch, an intimidating little woman, and her scowling presence wouldn't make this dressing-down any easier.

"Rue, Dakoda, I'm glad you're here to hear this," Tate said. Great, a whole show. "Boot's short a leader, Wish. It's yours if you'll have it."

Oh no – this was worse than a dressing-down. Wild Wish squeaked, "Me?"

"I trust you with it. You've got seniority, your squad's respect." Tate gave the others a look and Wish almost didn't dare follow it. Rue, arms folded, gave a big shrug, with no aspirations of command herself. Dakoda, strangely, smiled. "I'll count on you two to back her. And I'm transferring Emi to Boot for now."

"Oh no." Wish said it out loud this time.

"Problem?" Tate frowned.

Wish shook her head, an instinct not to complain. But it was one thing to have command over her friends, another to bring in their most powerful and least predictable member. Sarge could've handled it, Sarge was solid, brilliant, responsible – but Sarge was *gone*, because Wish missed the shot.

Tate continued, "Good. This'll mean immediate promotion. Larkin and Captain Brade will fill you in on exactly where we're at, get you sorted out. After you've rallied the squad and we've finished up here. We'll be moving in half an hour."

"Half an hour?" Rue said.

"Just long enough to lay Sarge to rest," Larkin said.

"We're not even going to stay the night, after all we did to secure this place?"

"You didn't so much secure it as destroy it," Brade said. "The little shelter left isn't worth holing up in, especially after you just announced our presence to half the continent."

"Hey, where do you get the –" Rue took a step towards him.

"Mind yourself, Rue," Tate said. "Captain Brade might not be one of us but he *is* a captain." She didn't sound happy about it herself. "And he's right. We can't stay. There should be a hunting lodge an hour or two further up." Without further discussion, Tate turned and shouted, "Boot Squad, over here! Everyone else, we're prepping a pyre."

"What?" Fixit cried, jumping up. "You can't –"

"Take it up with Wish," Tate barked authority. It confused Fixit enough to stop her protests, and as Tate marched away, she offered a parting comment: "Consider this your first challenge, Wish."

Wild Wish stared with alarm as the rest of Boot Squad converged on her and Tate's officers filtered out. Brade gave her a lingering, half-encouraging smile. Maybe mocking? But Spyke was quick to keep him moving, off to somewhere she could dump him. Pound and Newk arrived just ahead of Fixit with her funeral qualms. All Wish's command, about to see her try and tackle *religion*.

Wish had learnt about the Church of the Venerate Flesh in school, along with the myths of Ancient Singness and the plays of Artur Ferrybank, and racked her brain for details to use with Fixit.

The religion thrived under the Blessed Garter Empire, when Emperor Dunn used teachings from the prophet Bly Castor's Book of the Body to create a system of control over Boldarow. The Vens held that every living body was a small part of the immortal spirit and that on death the body must be returned to nature to complete its spiritual journey. Burial was acceptable in modern times, but true zealots believed at least part of the flesh must be consumed.

The Movement of Knowledge took over only a few centuries ago, when people started to decide that eating the dead was kind of unpleasant. The scientists agreed that the spirit and the body were linked, but so too were their deaths. The spirit was not transferred through consumption, burial or anything else. Attitudes shifted over generations, until the Stanclif Renovation, when the Church's influence was thrown into the sea together with the monarchy. There was no room for the old ways in the Stanclif Empire.

Except when you had a friend whose family hadn't got the message.

Fixit stared from one face to another, a manic look in her eye. She demanded, "What's this about Wish? Why's she sending me to you?"

"You're looking at your new sergeant," Dakoda announced, with just a twist of cruelty. Fixit's face went slack as her eyes fell on Wish to confirm it. The medic was older than the others, hair thinner, lines around her bespectacled eyes. Didn't she have seniority? Is that what she was thinking?

"Great, well, you can tell the captain to screw off then," Fixit decided, head bobbing with a new plan. "You get it don't you, Wish? Sarge and me talked. She didn't want the fire – she was ready to hear the word."

"Ready to hear it, not accept it," Rue said, bluntly. "Sarge didn't care for your shit any more than the rest of us, Fixit. She was just more polite about it."

"That's not true!" Fixit pointed a sharp finger. "Just back in Blythe, she said she was taking the V, once we got settled on this assignment she was going to –"

"Oh jog off a cliff!" Rue puffed up, ready to strike out.

"What's the V?" Newk asked quietly.

Pound said, "The scar of the Venerates, let's you know they don't want to be burned." Fixit pulled up her sleeve to demonstrate her own raggedly scarred V brand.

"You're not familiar with the church?" Rue said to Newk, like it should be right up her alley. "These wackos eat each other's flesh. Or use it for damn ornaments."

Newk shook her head. "The Drail didn't bring that to Fireti. Only their Doctrine of Knowledge."

"Yeah, well, Sarge wouldn't want nothing to do with it, anyway."

"You don't know, Rue," Fixit said. "When did you ever care for anyone's opinion but your own? Dakoda, didn't she talk to you?"

"You leave me out of this. I got less time for religion that I do for shitting in public."

Wild Wish tried to intervene: "Um."

"You need to listen to me," Fixit continued, tears in her eyes. "I knew her wishes. Think of her lasting soul. I've put up with so much, but this is Sarge – this *matters*."

"That's the point!" Rue said. "Give her some dignity in death."

"Stop, *stop!*" Wish insisted, firm enough to make them all go quiet. Now she had to make a decision. And damn it was an ugly one. No one in the platoon would agree with Fixit on this – she was the only Ven among them, and the rest distrusted the church. But this was a question of putting Sarge to rest the way she wanted. Was it possible she was swayed, even slightly, by Fixit's preaching? Wild Wish said, "I'm not saying we're committing to a thing, okay – but humour us, Fixit. What exactly are you proposing?"

Fixit had to take a second, not expecting to be heard. She straightened herself up. "If I can set up the ritual, we'd all take part, together. We'd divide her, over the fire, and consume her. Lay to rest what cannot be imbued."

She was speaking as though reciting scripture, and it left the whole squad staring stunned. Wish spoke before Rue could rally her aggression: "Yeah that's a hard no, Fixit, there's no way Sarge wanted that. We can go with an alternative."

The medic eyes went hard, but she held her tongue. Maybe it was

Wish's calm tone or maybe the six girls staring in horror. A tear rolled out as Fixit accepted it wasn't going to happen. "Can . . . can we at least return her to the earth? Not the fire."

Wild Wish looked to where the other scouts were gathering wood for a pyre. She said, "You lot get some tools to start digging, I'll sort it out with the captain."

Fixit nodded, too close to sobs to say more. They moved away. Pound put an arm around Fixit, offering her reassurances. Dakoda lingered, to share a parting look with Wish, maybe saying that went okay. Then there was just Newk, staring questioningly.

Wish gave her a weak smile, that lovely face an oasis in this horrific afternoon. She said, "You saved my life."

"I don't think so," Newk said. "Those goblins couldn't hit a wall."

Wish's smile wavered. Was that a joke aimed at Newk's own poor shooting? "All right. I won't owe you."

Newk offered a simple smile back and turned to follow the others.

Someone else cleared her throat, making Wish spin. Emi. Bloody Emi was sitting on a rock a short distance away, knees up to her chin. She winked and jumped down. "Wild. What would you have *me* do?"

"Er," Wish replied, eloquently. Emi sauntered closer. She could probably rip open a grave in a second. "You want to help dig?"

"I don't think that's appropriate." Emi made it sound like Wish should *really* know better, but didn't explain. Because you shouldn't order mages to do menial work? Because Emi was too new to the squad for such a sensitive responsibility? The mage held up two fingers. "I can offer two pieces of advice, though. To help you lead. One, always choose quickly and confidently. It's better for a leader to be wrong than indecisive."

"What?" Wish tried to follow. "That doesn't sound right."

"Think about it." Emi walked past without offering the second piece of advice.

Wish fought the urge to ask, as that was probably exactly what the mage wanted. She merely watched her go, longing to turn back time to two hours ago.

16

The Campaign for Fever Forest notably skewed towards personal, small-scale confrontations akin to the urban warfare of cities such as Llankton and Carp. The Fever battles took place in the countryside, but it was a countryside of dense woodland, caves and chasms. The confusion over the terrain, ripe for hiding yet difficult to structurally secure, and the singularly close quarters of the fighting, led to the region changing hands frequently.
The Great Ebb and Flow: Reflections on Modern Trench Warfare, Sommer, p. 348

Fever Forest was a dark, desperate place, with trees painted black and white where they'd been variously licked by fire or dusted with ash. Maringdale and Hill said little as they drove in, though she sensed he wanted to talk. To ask about her magic, her background, her plans. He gave occasional inviting smiles, which she returned, but the sounds of battle soon became clear, and the torn-up road required all of Hill's attention.

They were forced to abandon their truck and continue on foot. The ground shook regularly underneath them. Here, impolite spatters of gunfire and explosions and an exodus of green-cloaked soldiers made conversation impossible. Maringdale chased after Hill's heels, ducking at sounds that could have been a mile away. It would wait, Maringdale told herself, putting more effort into blocking out the oppressive fear and panic emanating from nearby men. Once they were done, a good day's work complete, she would see about bunking somewhere with Hill.

Passing soldiers shouted that they should turn back – General Foul was calling for a retreat, to abandon Fever Forest. Hill caught a sergeant's collar and demanded more, and the man promised he had no idea of the details. They were reserves, these hundreds of fleeing men with horse-drawn guns on large wheels. Not yet called into battle, he said. Fever had been in chaos for weeks, and he was glad to be rid of it. They would retreat to a nearby field, where Foul would flank the Khib scum.

Hill only asked Maringdale once if she wished to turn back, and she refused. They weren't close to the front yet, she told herself. The real danger was a long way off, no matter how loud the great weapons sounded. Hill led her between trees, light on his feet, only occasionally stopping to check their directions with soldiers going the other way. The further they went, the worse condition the soldiers were in, most with faces drawn down by exhaustion, many filthy from mud and debris, some wild-eyed from nerves and others bleeding. All eager to escape this cursed place.

Maringdale saw no such qualms in Hill, though, as he pressed on, rifle raised as though the Khib might jump out at any second. She could ride his coattails right into the Dread Corps, a man as youthful and powerful as Panderlair had been decrepit and slow.

It took an hour of crowded advance through the troops and trees before they broke clear of all the hubbub to an empty stretch of woodland. Another mile or so on and they found Walton's Nook and finally slowed down. Wooden and metal crates emblazoned with the bone symbols of the Dread Corps littered the entrance to a broad, moss-covered cave entrance, a great rocky arch that dipped into darkness. Hill's wary look said he sensed exactly what Maringdale felt: the company were gone, and, as their supplies had been left out in the open, they'd gone in a hurry. If they had made it out.

Hill grabbed a gas torch and continued into the dark as Maringdale hesitated, ears pricking to the sounds of violence drawing closer through the trees. The gunfire was getting steadier, the shouting worse, and she could pick out stray Drail voices clearly now – grizzled squad commanders shouting orders, "Stand fast!", "Fall back!"

Maringdale wanted to warn Hill, but he was gone. She rushed

into the dark after him. Around a corner of rocks, she picked out a light, bobbing ahead as he moved deeper into the cave. She tripped on a box and cursed but kept going, scanning what little detail she could make out: bed rolls, clothing and armour scattered about, the remnants of a fire.

Voices echoed through the cave ahead and Maringdale rushed to catch up. She turned another corner and found Hill helping another man in black armour unspool a cable. The other man instructed quickly, pointing to where Hill needed to attach something, and Hill gave Maringdale his torch to help guide them, taking out his short sword. The cave kept going beyond them, with this a mere way-point, a couple boxes and no sign of what work was being done here. The man Hill was helping was a short, slight, weaselly soldier, who looked out of place in Dread Corps armour. He explained with a whiny Singnic accent, "Gloven pulled us out this morning. We got word before General Foul's orders reached the others. Rest of the company cut north to Junker Station, aiming to catch the Iron Barge. We were all but finished here anyway."

"Our messengers never arrived?" Hill asked, hammering on something with the hilt of his sword. They were setting charges, digging spikes into the rock.

"Haven't had word from outside Fever for a fortnight or more," the man said. "The 32nd Legion were supposed to be repairing the comms line but I guess they never got there." He paused to take in Maringdale, quickly wiped a hand on his dusty uniform and held it out. "Fearsmith Netts, pleasure to meet you, ma'am."

Maringdale stared back for a second, unsure how this whelp had made it through the Dread initiations.

Hill continued over the attempted introduction, "We sent two men. You didn't hear any word of them trying to reach you?" He asked it hopefully, as though he didn't quite believe those men had been intercepted between here and the Fever Crossing. There was a lot of open space between the two places, ample countryside to hide bodies, but waders couldn't have got ahead of men with a motor vehicle, could they?

A blast outside shook the earth and made them all flinch. Dust rained from the ceiling.

"Don't know what to tell you," Netts said, ignoring the attack. "We've been on our own a while – it would've been pretty memorable, someone coming through. Okay, we're done. Puls!" He shouted, voice echoing through the cave. "We're pulling out!"

"Gimme a second!" a gruff voice shouted back.

"Move, move." Netts gestured, trotting up the cave, unravelling his cable.

Maringdale and Hill followed, the latter keeping the conversation going even as they fled. "We're chasing word of spies in the area. Partisans bombed the Dread outpost in Cleave City."

The Singnic man faltered, a curious eyebrow raised. He said, "If they were headed here, they're too late. Gloven issued retreat orders for us even before Foul started to give up the forest." He pressed on, racing out of the cave mouth, then quickly tied his cable to an ignition box. Maringdale looked through the trees, watching for movement. There were lots of men running in the direction they'd arrived from. The gunfire was close now, beyond a din of confused orders.

"We should go," she said, but was ignored.

"You're going after Gloven," Hill said, "you can pass on our message."

"No, sir," Netts said, standing, ready to set off his charge. He looked over a shoulder, the attack getting closer. "We learnt enough here to return to the Citadel, so Gloven's headed there, already gone. The rest of us are off to Highscythe Ward, reinforce the position there. Hence the Iron Barge."

Echoing footfalls came hurrying from the cave as an older, portly soldier charged out headlong, almost doubled-over for the effort. He skidded past them, panting, then glanced at Hill and Maringdale. He nodded to Netts, all ready, and the younger man returned a nod, then flipped a switch.

Maringdale jumped as the charges exploded in the cave, the ground shifting, and a burst of dust and debris sprayed out over them. She covered her mouth with an arm and yelled, "You might've warned us!"

Her complaints were lost amid the noisy collapse of the cave. The older man, Puls, shouted, "This way, there's a path out of here!"

Maringdale squinted, dust stinging her eyes, as the two soldiers turned to run into the trees. A firm hand gripped hers, and Maringdale turned fiercely on Hill, right by her. He said, "We'll go with them."

He half guided, half dragged her through the dust cloud, onto Puls' path, a narrow trail up a slope through the trees. Hill released Maringdale so she could move ahead, briefly looking back. The gunshots were almost on top of them.

"Whoa, hell – they're moving quicker than a whip-snake!" Netts whooped ahead.

"Fucking General Foul!" Puls growled. "Had to retreat now!"

Maringdale ran as the shouts shifted to the deranged roars of battle, Khib and Drail men finally clashing. She wanted to ask why he blamed Foul, when it was the Khib who had broken through the forest, but she saved her breath for running.

"Mind the gap," Puls instructed, and the group followed the path over a break between rocks. He paused to let the others pass, pointing. "If we keep –"

A gunshot cracked from down the slope and the tree by his head burst into splinters, making him duck and swear. Hill spun into a crouch and whipped his rifle up to return fire. He got off a shot then shouldered Maringdale to go on.

"Castor that was close," Puls huffed under his breath. Netts had pulled ahead, disappearing into the trees, and Puls paused to shout at him, but a barrage of gunshots cut him off. Maringdale flinched again as bullets tore through the trees and Puls was knocked down with a wet thud. He gagged with muted pain.

Maringdale sprinted, alongside Hill, heart pounding. He bounded effortlessly through the trees, rifle steady, leaving the gunshots behind, and offered a sideways glance, a hint at something almost like a wink. This was under control. Just keep running. She could have smiled back.

Then another shot came, closer, from another angle – a Khib had got around them – and the right side of Hill's head broke open like a bloody egg. He dropped, single remaining eye startled but lifeless. Maringdale dropped onto the ground and rolled through twigs and leaves. The killer charged on her position with clumsy footfalls, breathing heavily, whispering in jagged Khib, *I got one, I got one.*

Maringdale rolled and pushed herself back up as the soldier came through the trees, dirty khaki coat flapping about his legs. He spotted Hill's body, wide eyes terrified of what he'd done, what he still had to do. Then he saw Maringdale, his face almost apologetic, just as she fired her pistol. He slammed back into a tree and went down as Maringdale stood. She gave Hill one last look and sprinted after Netts.

On the north side of Fever Forest, a muddy expanse separated the trees from a ruined town, half a mile off. It was lined with barbed wire, sandbags and metal panelling, along with two huge vehicles, sitting on tyres bigger than tractors, cannons at their centre. Maringdale followed a scattering of troops racing over the field to the town, keeping Netts' black uniform in sight. When they got halfway to the buildings, the barricades and broken windows started lighting up with gun flashes. Scores of Drail troops were positioned inside, firing around them at the trees as their comrades escaped. The cannons boomed, tearing craters into the earth, felling trees, and the Khib advance was halted. They'd taken the forest, but had to stop at the tree-line.

A break was made in the barricade to let Netts, Maringdale and a handful of others through, before being quickly secured again. The gunfire lasted only a few minutes before the town went quiet but for cries of pain. Maringdale followed Netts as they were guided across a rubble street to a hollowed-out church where injured men were being treated. Finally, Netts leaned against a wall and let out a long breath, before eyeing Maringdale suspiciously. He was almost brown from the filth of the explosion and the chase, but his shrewd eyes shone. He said, "Gonna introduce yourself?"

"Constans Maringdale," she replied hoarsely. "With the Purification. Investigating an attack on the Dread Corps in Cleave City."

"Aye," Netts nodded. "The Killsmith said. He didn't make it?"

Maringdale looked over her shoulder, to the memory, and left it at that.

"Right. Was Cleave hit by those same fucks hanging around Highscythe?"

"What happened in Highscythe?" Maringdale asked and Netts whistled.

"Whole communication line's broken down, hasn't it? Rumour was Stanclif had a man in Highscythe, asking about the Dread Corps. But that's as much as I know." Netts pushed off the wall, taking in the street. The town was filling with despairing, disparate soldiers, a sad aftermath to a bloody morning. "Well, this place is set to be a new front line while Foul manoeuvres around the other side of these piss-ants. No spies gonna come *here,* and if Cleave's done then Highscythe is next in line. It's my destination anyway. Come with and I'll get you passage on the Iron Canal."

Maringdale's head was spinning, one strange idea falling in after another – the Iron Canal conjured images of great, unusual machines. The height of industry, a world apart from fairy tales about waders and deadly chases through trees, men's heads exploding. Alive one second, full of promise. She shook off the image of Hill's one remaining eye – nothing left in it – and exhaled all of *that* to consider the next move. She had swapped one Dread soldier for another, much less impressive, but still had a job to do. She asked, "How far is Highscythe?"

"Good way west," Netts said. "Other side of the Broad River. Only a day's travel on the rails though, depending on when the next ride leaves. Interested?"

The other side of the Broad River meant the Western Front. Stanclif, the real war. And wouldn't it make sense, she told herself, that the bombers would keep going that way? The thoughts of waders faded from her mind. Hill hadn't died for bloody *waders*. Between Cleave City, rumours of spies in Highscythe and the fact

Ways' men never reached the Walton Nook, it had to be a more considerable threat. One with roots in Stanclif. One Maringdale herself would thwart. If she got to the Western Theatre before she reported back to the Purification, then they wouldn't have a choice but to support her. Then she'd make her mark where it mattered.

17

Popular thought on earth-touching is entirely tied to political favour. For proof, consider the pervading myths that corrupt "dirt-minding" can cause volcanic eruptions and earthquakes. Utter nonsense, but fears that survive as long as polite society frowns upon earth-touching. Meanwhile, it may interest you to know that in the 5th century it was commonly believed that witlacing caused cancers and even plagues. Now, with witlacers running academies and advising governments, no one would credit such blatant paranoia as having any basis in fact.

We the Mindless: a Brief History of Ostracised Magic, Lombardo, p. 5

Watching Sarge's body, bound in canvas, be lowered into the ground, Wild Wish longed to believe there was truth in the old ways, and that this woman, who had taken her under her wing, would see her spirit sprout back up through these trees, the grass, anything. That the worms would take a part of her and pass it on to eagles, and Sarge would see the world from up high. But while Wish could imagine a time when Sarge, and Loose, and the others might have joined her on a sunny day on a farm in Swelig, she couldn't quite imagine the Immortal existed, for all they'd seen. Better that it didn't, even, because the brutality of battle must've only fed it huge pain and hate. No. The world was simply what it was, not conscious. The spirit died with the body. Forever.

And they were gone. Sarge. Small. Wish's friends. No more.

With their farewells said, the scouts cooked the dead goblins and hunks of the hawk giant, to stock up on extra meat for their journey. Though the Vens' beliefs had faded away, some traditions lived on:

it remained a great insult to cook and eat the flesh of your enemies. If Fixit wasn't happy with the compromise of burying Sarge, she could take some solace in this. No one was quite sure how hawk giant would taste, though Four Skills said if it was anything like skalk giant they would regret it. She was right.

The scouts continued up the mountain to camp in the foothills, not at a way station as promised, but in the mouth of a cave, set back from an area of land left open by extensive logging. Around campfires, as night fell, they shared memories of Sarge. Wild Wish recalled taking her hand in the ruins of Cartwell, after two hours duelling a Har Coul sniper. Sarge had told her, "Your talents are wasted here."

No one said much about Small. The platoon would smile less without her.

Larkin came to take Wish away in the middle of a mug of wood wine – duty called, leaving the others on the precipice of intoxication. They went to a low fire at the edge of camp, where Brade was sitting on the ground, injured leg stretched out in front of him. Emi slunk up to join them, uninvited but ignored. Her presence made Wish's neck tingle.

"Lieutenant . . . Wild Wish?" Brade said.

"I'm not a lieutenant," Wish said, trying to get comfortable opposite him. She looked to Larkin with a frown. "Am I?" They didn't have much use for official ranks in the scouts, besides knowing the direction command flowed. Larkin's impassive face said she wasn't sure herself, but probably not.

"Either way," Brade moved on, "I'd like to share my condolences. It's never easy losing a friend, even less so a good commander, which everyone says she was."

"Much better than I'm likely to be!" Wish laughed, shrill with nerves.

Brade smiled. "What your captain said earlier is true: this is absolutely not in vain. Though it's likely we'll lose more before we get there."

"Oh it's a beautiful thing, to die for your country." Wish was grinning. Citing Stanish propaganda and grinning damn wide and how could she stop? It was a big joke, wasn't it, the war, everyone dead, all of it *for* something, no more meaningful than the weirdos eating flesh in old churches. Brade wasn't smiling now.

"It's a damn rotten thing and wasteful in the extreme. But what we're doing matters. More than thousands of fools marching across empty fields or them bombing fortified towns into the ground. We are going to make a difference."

Wish didn't speak but her bared teeth spoke for her, that dark grin she couldn't remove saying how little she believed that.

"Hear him out," Larkin said, hardly enthusiastic. "Believe me Wild, we've all wasted enough energy arguing against this."

"Where are you from, Wild Wish?" Brade asked, the old "if we're friends, you'll trust me" gambit.

"A village called Swelig," Wish said. "You won't have heard of it."

"Ah, lovely place." Brade returned a pleasant smile, making Wish laugh.

"No. No one knows Swelig."

"Thatched cottages on the River Dee? There's a working mill, and a Garret-era church with a bell tower and a unique rat-demon stained-glass window, if I recall?" At Wish's alarmed expression, he explained, "I wouldn't be much of an explorer if I hadn't travelled Stanclif before taking in the wider world, would I?"

Wish made a pathetic bleat. *No one* knew Swelig. It made all this easier, being so very separate from home, so she could imagine her picture-book village a dream untouched by the horrors of this reality. A pure place, waiting in refuge. If he knew the village, he might let it slip it wasn't worth going back to. Might convince the girls that it was an uninspiring country retreat, full of old people who couldn't hear well.

"It's perfect," Brade said, though. She narrowed her eyes suspiciously. "You must be fond of Swelig. You came to fight for your people, didn't you? To preserve our beautiful homeland. Even though the blasted war stands no chance of jumping the Stanclif Strait, the same way we'll never truly press north to the Arrow. We all know, in our hearts, that home is safe from the bombs and the bloodshed. As things stand."

Wild Wish stiffened, seeing he was building to whatever details he'd argued with Easter and Tate. Now, for some reason, it was worth trying to sway her.

"Imagine this," Brade went on. "The Drail are developing something so powerful, so very devastating, that its reach could stretch all the way to Stanclif. It could set those thatched roofs on fire. You'd see Swelig reduced to ashes."

"Something," Larkin interjected, "which we don't have any clear evidence for."

"I've seen enough to know what's going on in Low Slane," Brade said, with frustration. "I might not have the proof, but it's plainly evident. They're looking to –"

"Combine different schools of magic to raise the dead, or worse." Wish saved him the effort. "Yeah, I know, I had a chat with General Easter about it. We've only got a small graveyard in Swelig though, I don't think they'd be interested in that."

Brade and Larkin were both suitably stunned. Emi looked delighted. Wild Wish: not just a bumbling fool. However accidental it was she came upon that information.

"The general knows better than that," Brade said, collecting himself. "Command bring up necromancy because it's patently absurd and they'd rather not face the reality. But I'm fully convinced the Dread mages *are* combining magics. I've traced its nexus to a facility in southern Slane, not far from the Weeping Citadel. Deliberately removed from their main population. They've been redirecting resources, slaves, machinery and prisoners, as you saw in Blythe. A refugee fleeing for the Farne border reported screams and lights. Thousands of people missing, entire towns depopulated. Similar reports came from the east, where Garter meets the Mattin Mountains, confirmed by Khib scouts. There were rumours of Slanik mages in those areas. Possibly Dread companies."

"Lots of rumours and second-hand accounts," Emi said.

"Rumours I chased down myself," Brade replied readily. "The sigils we've turned up share familiarities with dirt-minding" – he nodded to Emi – "and *unfamiliar* concepts. They've moved into new territory."

"But not necromancy," Wish said, recalling Dollemore's response. "Some kind of chain-weapon?"

This impressed Brade. He nodded. "That's my theory. I met a contact in a pit-town called Null who said they had an accident where people died in an explicable, sudden way, far apart. At the same time. Witlacing can cause heart failure, brain aneurysms, instant death, through touch. Dirt-minding can spread power through the earth, even the air itself. Combine the two and you can kill people at a distance without apparently touching them."

Wish thought back again. "But Dollemore said it's costly for a witlacer to do something like that. You wouldn't have enough mages to make it worthwhile."

"Which is precisely what they're experimenting on, isn't it?" Brade said. "One witlacer with their touch is not an effective weapon in a war where thousands are dying. A witlacer's touch that can be spread through the world itself, though, spread out to hit many people at once . . ."

Wish blinked, getting the picture now. Dirt-minding had a broad and reckless reach. Spread a poison through it and a lot of people die. She was not sure what to do with that. She was tired, had lost friends and didn't appreciate Brade bringing Swelig into this. Everyone else was getting drunk in the only moment they were likely to get exclusively dedicated to mourning Sarge and Small, while she sat here. She said, "Respectfully, I'm just a sniper, sir. I don't need to know this. Just point me in the right direction and we'll take out the enemies that need taking out."

"Respectfully," Brade echoed, with his smile returning, "you're a leader now, and you need to know what you're leading everyone into. We can't afford doubt in our ranks."

"You don't need to worry about that," Wish insisted. "Whatever it turns out to be, the Blood Scouts are on it." She looked to Larkin, silently asking for a dismissal.

Larkin responded with mission details: "Tomorrow, we'll climb the low mountains. Captain Brade has a route. We'll slip through a gap in Drail defences at Mean Ridge, where we should be able to take the Cracked Trail through Har Coul to Edge Falls. Cross the river and it's barkman territory – the forest of Eardung, where they've no love for the Drail. We'll take a boat up to Heaven's Eye Lake, then follow Devil's River into Slane."

Wish's mind raced trying to picture it on a map. That route took them *way* out of their comfort zone, skirting the entire theatre of war, practically into the Valley of the Drail itself. It also relied on the charity of Eardung – a land that spurned human civilisation in general, not just the Drail. She said, "The barkmen aren't really known for their hospitality, Captain."

"They're fine. Sir Robert Smartwether spent a winter in Eardung and found them most accommodating." Brade said it like these well-spoken Stanclif boys regularly shared cigars and a joke with the elusive tree-people, but it was hardly reassuring considering Wish had no idea who Sir Robert Smartwether was.

Besides, that was the supposedly *safe* part of the journey. The Devil's River, if they made it that far, was named for a reason. Wish said, "Why not cross though the low mountains just behind their lines? Through Balnia, into Slane's southern farmland." Rolling green, peaceful landscapes. Probably.

"The Drail Empire has mobilised from here to Drail itself," Brade said. "Easy terrain is easily monitored. And we can *not* risk being stopped. This work is necessary, Wild Wish. *You* are necessary. There's no telling how much time we have, and we might be the only thing standing in the way of something truly catastrophic."

Wish felt that sarcastic smile come back. Fun. She said, "Hell, if we reach Slane, why not go all the way to the Valley of Drail itself. We could assassinate the Drail Patrain."

"Because that wouldn't stop what's going on in Slane," Brade answered seriously. "Trust me, it's where the biggest danger lies right now."

According to you, Wish didn't say.

But Larkin came in again, "Here's the sticker, Wish." *Good Castor!* There was worse news. "We're splitting up. Each squad to make their own way through Slane. Maximising opportunities, minimising the threat of mass casualties."

"No chance of helping each other," Wish said.

"Sarge already volunteered the northernmost route, skirting the Slanik swamps." Of course she did. "But we'll switch, give you a path further south."

"Okay," Wish said, because she wasn't sniffing at a break when her first command meant hustling everyone through the nastiest place in the world, alone. "How far is it, exactly?"

"Edge Falls is a five-day hike," Larkin said. "From there, another four days by barge to the lake. Four more days to the target, if we're lucky."

"No one ever got lucky in Slane," Emi reminded them all cheerfully.

"You'll do fine, Wild," Larkin said. "You've got a great team."

Wish looked over to her squad, joking around their fire. Pound and Dakoda were merrily oblivious, with one of Tate's new recruits, the redhead, awkwardly trying to join in their fun. Rue stared miserably into the flames, imagining death, and Fixit had her arms squeezed over morose knees. Newk managed to look separate from the rest, despite sitting in the circle, uninvolved and alone. One newbie, two in mourning and two unexceptional soldiers. Wish loved them, but there were better squads in the Blood Scouts. If only she could use her command to put together a dream squad, swap Pound for Four Skills, Fixit for Dollemore, swallow pride and bring in Oksy – and fuck it, trade Newk for Tate and give them a real leader. They could call it Wish Squad.

"Wild?" Larkin prompted, in the familiar tone of someone who had not been heard the first time.

"Yeah." Wish gave a mock salute – not something she'd usually do with Larkin, who was not easily amused, but these were desperate times. "All understood, *sir*. I'll break it to them softly." Maybe tomorrow. Or the next day. She pushed herself to her feet, dusting off her trousers. Brade watched her like he wouldn't be able to truly relax until everything was underway. Maybe the same uncertainty she felt? She said, "We wouldn't have been your first choice to do this, would we?"

"You're all Easter would give me," he admitted, but with a

crooked smile that suggested that wasn't entirely true. *Roguish* was the word for this man. Other women might be charmed, ones who were into that sort of thing. As Wish waited for more, he relented and said, "Truthfully, yes, I'd rather Easter threw everything he had at this. But only so I could avail the responsibility. As it stands, doing it this way, I don't think I could ask for a better platoon. I'd like to get there unexpected and secure rather than destroy what we find, including technology and prisoners. I trust your scouts can make that happen."

"Ah," Wish said. So they were destined to make life even harder with the burden of prisoners. Because Command considered the Blood Scouts the sort of soldiers who were more suited to keeping the enemy alive? From the sour look on Larkin's face, that was exactly it. And how wrong they were. How very wrong. Smiling again, because she couldn't stop, Wish said, "Well, we'll do our best, Captain, but I have to warn you, I'm starting to think I might be one of the most deadly people in this war." Brade looked at her with uncertain humour and her smile only broadened. Through her gritted teeth she added, "Seriously."

She turned away, before the thought of it could make her scream.

By the time Wild Wish had finished her mug of wine, her eyes were drooping. No amount of alcohol would keep her going. She'd balked at explaining the mission to the squad, preferring to quietly enjoy her own creeping dread, and everyone focused instead on Pound's boisterous account of a summer spent serving drinks in southern Garter. Dakoda took the lead in expressing disbelief over such details as the two-headed cave goat.

Wish chose a convenient break in the storytelling and laughter to advise the squad to turn in, ready for a full day's marching tomorrow. It was, after all, the responsible thing to do, and she led by example, standing unsteadily. The wine had screwed her balance. She looked at Newk. Disappointed that she was going? Wish said, "Before I retire, I should reassure our new recruits after today's events, yes? Responsible thing for a leader to do."

Newk froze under the attention of the whole squad.

"That was not an ordinary day," Wish said. "We only slay giants, what, once every three weeks?"

"Fortnightly, max," Pound said.

"Don't listen to them," Dakoda said, apparently more responsible than their leader. "Probably the first giant any of them ever saw up close."

"Not true," Pound said. "Big Reg in Huxleborn, you remember him?"

"He was an oaf, not a giant," Rue said, but amused. That had been a night.

Wish slipped away, giving Newk a sly nod to indicate she follow. Newk did so, more or less unnoticed as the others joked. Wish led her to their small tents.

"Seriously," Wish told her. "I'm here if you want to talk."

"About what?" Newk asked. Hard to read her expression in the dark.

Wish stirred uncomfortably. "You're used to that sort of thing? Killing giants? Friends dying?"

"I've seen enough of it."

"Uh-huh. But one of the benefits of being a Blood Scout and not, say, a Thunder Gunner, is that we're allowed to have feelings. And right now I'm prescribing" – Wish stepped back, making a show of assaying her charge – "at least one hug." She spread her arms and Newk's eyes opened with alarm. Slightly inebriated, tiredly numb, Wish managed to ignore the little voice warning her this was too forward. "We lost two good friends today."

Newk softened, silently accepting that this was more for Wish than her. She stepped into the embrace and Wish pulled her close, ready to sink into her, to let her support her, hold her, keep her. Resting her face in Newk's mass of locks, Wish inhaled and whispered, "Need to make the most of this. A few days' marching and we'll smell too bad to touch."

Newk extracted herself with a wry smile, beautiful and close – but over her shoulder Wish noticed the squad. Rue was looking their way.

Wish quickly stepped off, clearing her throat, and said, "Speaking of marching, how're the stamps holding up?"

Newk rotated her feet as though she hadn't realised what she was wearing, and a gentle realisation came over her. "When I marched with my people, it was with leather sandals or barefoot. These are better."

"But not great?" Wish frowned. "They're not a good fit? You'll give them to me, I'll take them in. Otherwise your feet will feel like lead and fire and your ankles will stab you. I insist, take them off right now."

It got a smile, maybe the first Newk had worn all day, and Wish felt her own face warm. Fuck Rue's glower from across camp, looking in Newk's eyes made Wish feel lighter, drunker than the wine. A long way from how uncomfortable things had got that morning with their supposed shooting practice. She certainly wouldn't bring that up again. But she did: "And any more non-humans want to talk to me, I'll listen, okay? It was just instinct. None of us are used to . . . mingling."

Newk's expression told Wish she wasn't quite there.

"I'm sorry. I'm an arsehole, okay? We all are. We just don't know better. I welcome being corrected, though. I want you to know that before . . . you know, I start bossing you around."

"Okay," Newk said. Neutral, hard to read. "Then I have some advice. Get some rest. You've had a tough day, too. You do not need to take off my boots. Yet."

She turned back to the squad, before Wish could react. Wish stood soaking it in. That was flirty, wasn't it?

Holding onto that warm thought, she settled into her two-berth tent. Sleep came easily, but she was woken when Rue came to join her. Wish pretended to be asleep and Rue pretended to believe it. Just the two of them tonight, with an empty space where Loose used to lie squeezed between them. Newk would be with Dakoda and Pound. Something should've been rearranged, Wish realised, so Fixit wasn't alone in the tent she shared with Sarge and Small. But she slipped back to sleep before that idea could go anywhere useful.

18

In the early 700s, much of the known world had been mapped, yet many territories remained hostile and inaccessible. While imperial adventurers raced to finish exploring Olon, Azir and the Emerging Isles, there were also untouched mysteries closer to home: Eardung and the Slanik swamps remained untamed, and the Winter Wilds were stuck in another time, to name but a few. The war interrupted all scientific study of such areas, and in some cases saw idle, classless soldiers being the first to encounter things typically reserved for only the most hardened explorer.

Empires of the Rocc, Xanthial, p. 578

For the first two days trailing the river north, the terrain of Har Coul reflected northern Farne, with rocky inclines and mountain passes broken up by great, sweeping fields of green. One by one, the squad had meandered closer to Wish during their marches, quietly asking for details of the mission. She alternated between playing it off as a joke or a serious undertaking, but the information basically came out the same, "Oh, we're just heading over Mean Ridge, then up through Eardung to a lake where we'll get passage down the Devil's River."

They invariably stared back without comment, the proposal too grand to question. Besides, it was hard to imagine those far off places as they rambled through peaceful territory.

The big change came on the third day, when the scouts reached a distinct line into Drail territory – a grassy field separated a cluster of trees and rocks from cliffs a hundred or two hundred feet high. The natural wall stretched in both directions, with slight rises and falls. There were outcrops that could be climbed, but it wasn't going to be easy, and there would be no cover. And the Drail were watching: almost straight ahead of the scouts, at the top of the cliff face, a squat concrete bunker stuck out, with sharp corners and thin black slits for viewing holes.

Wild Wish was whispered to the edge of the canopy of trees, a border of cover before the empty field. She found Tate investigating the cliffs through a looking glass, alongside Brade and Larkin. Brade, of course, had a leather-and-brass extending telescope. Wish settled in to look through her rifle scope.

Tate gave her summary first: "I see four gun nests."

"I make it five," Brade said. "Four on top, one halfway up, about two hundred yards left." Tate double-checked, as did Wish. She scanned the ridge again, ah, there was the cheeky extra one, a smaller bunker, only big enough for one man. It was overgrown with hanging ivy, but the vines were strategic, parted around the viewing slit. Well done Brade, they could make a spotter of him yet.

Four Skills joined them, having found her way up from the rear, and settled against a rock to make her own assessment. There was movement beyond their cover, as Oksy got into position at a different angle.

"You think they've got the line covered all the way along?" Larkin asked.

"We're not far from the Edge here," Brade said, talking about the area where the sheer drops of the Kleb mountains cut off Har Coul from Farne for a short distance before forming an enormous wall that stretched all the way to the sea. "Another mile or two west and it's completely impassable, drops of hundreds of metres. Two or three miles east and you've got the Flight Rapids, where the city of Aden sits on the river. Between there and the Edge? Four miles of this, tops. I'd say it's reasonable they've got it covered."

"Assuming all those bunkers are manned," Wish said.

"I got a Drail," Four Skills announced, rifle perfectly steady as she targeted the bunker dead ahead.

Wish checked through her own scope. Was there movement in the shadow of the dark, empty slit? Everyone waited, as though this simple confirmation, yes or no, could inform a whole plan of action. She bit her lip, rifle unmoving.

"Think they know we're here?" Brade asked.

"Maybe," Four Skills said. "But they'd see one or two guns from there, not the whole platoon. And they're not going to waste bullets unless we get closer. If all the bunkers are manned, it won't be with trained snipers. They'd be wasted here."

With a shift in the bunker's shadow, the sunlight caught the edge of something in the dark. A helmet? Wish said, "Yeah. There he is. What do we think, two hundred metres there, another fifty elevation?"

"You think you can hit him?" Brade exclaimed.

"Make him move, at least."

"Better get the full picture, first," Four Skills said.

"I spotted one other gun," Brade said, nodding towards the bunker to the right. Wish had seen it, a rather obvious long-barrelled machine gun sticking out. It would put the Reaper to shame, but at that height it had to have a limited downward arc.

Tate checked her wrist, a chunky time-piece there, and she grunted irritation. "We'll wait until nightfall. You two keep watch and I'll have the others run up and down the line, check for any better places to approach." She paused to give Brade an unimpressed look. Probably thinking that there was a reason no one was invading Drail this way, and it was a damned fool plan to bring them here.

With the sun setting, Tate came to Wild Wish in the cluster of bushes she'd settled into for the afternoon. The captain crouched and whispered, "We're going from here. On the next shift change. Between three and four, think we've got a path." She indicated the bunkers they'd numbered, counting up from the machine-gun one. "Unless you've got an update?"

"No," Wish said. "Shift change every three hours. Next one's in thirty minutes."

She'd kept an eye on the bunker they'd seen movement in, and noted two times when the men inside relaxed. They were amateurs, as Four Skills predicted: still for the most part, but once their time was up they gave each other companionable pats and wandered about ignoring the world beyond. No sign that they had any idea there was a platoon of scouts nearby. It also become clear that only every other bunker was manned, at best; no one had seen movement in the machine gun emplacement, and there had definitely been no one climbing up and down to the mid-point bunker. Likewise, the little one-man hut seemed abandoned – why would anyone hole up in there alone, after all, with more comfortable options available?

"I'm sending Sabre," Tate said. "With some additional support. You're good to provide cover?"

"Uh-huh," Wish said, though fairly sure she wouldn't hit much at this distance, in this light. It wasn't quite dark but it would quickly get worse.

"Watch the left and I'll keep Oksy on the right. Four Skills is going up. Take a break now, be ready. Who's your spotter?"

Wish considered that for a moment. Mostly, the three snipers worked together and spotted for each other. Failing that, Small had a keen eye, and kept well hidden. But damn. Small wasn't coming. Wish thought of the others, who else in the group – she could bring Newk, to lie close in the undergrowth. With the risk that she might make things go terribly wrong again. No, this was no time for playing about. She'd go with Dakoda.

Twenty minutes later, and Wish had stretched her legs, taken another piss, checked her rifle and settled back into position. She kept clear of the other scouts, back in the trees, feeling their tension even at this distance. They'd be stamping feet to release nervous energy, tightening each other's straps, checking ammo pouches and guns. Offering quiet words of assurance. She was better off out here alone. Better to let them think she was totally calm, ready to offer the best support.

Dakoda joined her with a scope, nestling into the little dug-out to get comfortable. Barest pleasantries. Wild Wish lay prone, trying to slow her breathing as they waited for it to begin. The moment those guards moved to change shifts. There was half a moon poking through moderate cloud cover, enough light to pick out contours in the cliffs.

"What's the mood?" Wish asked, for something to say.

"Like usual," Dakoda replied. "Glad it's not Boot, for once."

Wish hummed. It wasn't much assurance. If this went wrong, they'd all be screwed anyway, and if it went right, well, they'd get another go soon enough. But sure, she was happy not to run headlong into the dark unknown.

"Starting!" someone hissed, a short way down, and Wish tightened her grip on the rifle. Through the scope, she saw arm movements. Men turning their backs on the view. Good. Wish heard Sabre Squad rustling through the long grass. In seconds, they would be a cluster of dark shapes easily mistaken for animals, rolling weeds, anything but murderous women.

"Halfway," Dakoda whispered. No one on high had shouted or shot at them. The men in the bunker were chatting – a flash of light, someone sparking a cigarette. Wonderful.

"Almost there," Dakoda said, urging them on with her tone.

A gunshot popped, from the trees, and the men in Wish's sights turned, startled, towards the viewing slit. Wish fired and saw them dropping, no idea if she hit anyone or even hit the bunker.

"Hold fire, hold fire!" a voice ordered, someone running closer.

Wish kept her finger on the trigger, kept the scope over that viewing slit, as someone crept up behind them. She hissed, "What's going on?"

"Oksy fired for cover," Rue said – it was Rue. "Captain says keep still."

"They're clear," Dakoda announced. "Made the cliffs. Holding position." Then added, "Movement, left, bunker four."

Wish swept her gun over to it. The little hut; there was a barrel sticking out shoving at the ivy, to gain a better view. "That who Oksy shot at?"

"Probably," Rue said. "It was a distraction, didn't need another one. Why you always gotta make it about you, Wish?"

She ignored the comment to aim back at the first bunker. Gun barrels poked out, scanning below. They weren't firing, so they couldn't have seen where the shots came from. Wish shifted her scope to the base of the cliff. The silhouettes of her friends were just visible, pressed against the cliff wall. Four Skills among them. But she saw more movement, the same time her spotters did.

"What in holy fuck," Rue said.

Another figure was racing across the grass. Almost too dark to see, but a straight blade stuck out at her side. Newk? Bloody *Newk?* Wish quickly scanned the bunker. Still no retaliation, and no movement now – they hadn't spotted her.

"Down, down!" Dakoda said. "Light!"

As she said it, a beam of light shone out from Wish's target bunker, a great yellow circle falling on the grass and quickly moving towards them, away from Newk, who was almost at the cliff. The three women fell flat and quickly scrambled back through the leaves as the light swept overhead. It moved quickly, right over them and away. Then back, as they remained frozen on the ground. Over them again, not quite penetrating the trees, then off in the other direction. Searching the tree-line and the rocks. Very carefully, Wish pulled her rifle back to her eye and picked out the bunker again. The heart of the light was mounted on the lip of their viewing slit, a big electric bulb that must've been hidden inside during the day. It had to be a foot across, bright like a lighthouse.

"Another, a long way off," Dakoda whispered. "They've not got much cover there."

"I can put out that light," Wish said.

"Or you can let them get on with it," Rue told her. "If you're worried about your savage protege, she's the one put herself out there."

Wish adjusted her aim to check Sabre Squad. Hard to pick out their shadows now, but they were moving, Newk presumably with them. Scrambling over the rocks like a swarm of spiders, ten girls maybe, Larkin's team and a couple extra. Wish took a breath, checking the bunker again. The light was scanning over the field now, moving too fast to have spotted anything. With luck, they'd assume the shots came from a lone partisan venting frustrations, popping off random shots at their Drail overlords. It happened.

"First stop," Dakoda said. The shadows moved around the bunker midway up, blended into its shape and went still. Wish held her breath while the others caught up, then the shadows moved back out again. Continuing up a path, faster. It had to be narrow – the memory flashed back into Wish's head, Loose running into someone, *No* – She winced. Not Newk, too. But Sabre were off the path again, splitting up, moving in twos and threes over rocks. They efficiently lifted each other to the next level. Right beneath the bunkers now, splitting to send half under Wish's bunker and the others going for the little one. The light continued over the field and trees, the soldiers too busy looking out to check the cliffs.

Except no sooner had Wish thought that but the light swept quickly back and started up the cliff face, hunting for Sabre. Hell, one of them had got smart and they'd light up Newk any second. Wish trained her gun back on the bunker and fired. The light jerked, then turned, twisting back her way. She rolled her shoulders, relaxing into position, and fired again. The light went out.

Behind it, two rifles flashed, visible a split-second before the cracks of gunfire followed. A bullet hit the leaves far off to their right. They fired again, no sound of the bullet striking anywhere nearby, no way they had a clear idea of where to shoot. Wish carefully sighted the muzzle flashes. A shot popped to the right – Oksy – and Wish saw the bullet crack against the bunker. She fired herself, to keep the men down rather than expecting to hit them.

"They're up, they're up!" Dakoda reported.

Shouts came from the top of the cliff, the men panicking, raising an alarm to their nearest comrades. The next flash in the bunker came from inside it, further back, followed by another. Then stillness. Wish waited, but there was no more movement. Sabre Squad were in. Dakoda said, "The other one's secure."

Wish rushed a look the other way, checking the bunkers further afield. Nothing going on around the machine gun nest, and the next closest light was too far off to see in detail. The path was clear. Time to move. "Boot Squad. We're up."

***

At the peak of Mean Ridge, near breathless from the steep scramble, Wild Wish stumbled to a stop and took in big breaths of mountain air. Tinged with gun smoke – a bit of her own smell, too. She turned to find the rest of Boot Squad and a bunch of others panning out behind her as they clambered over the final rocks, all taking in the woodland ahead, the bunker to their right. Spyke was there with Captain Brade propped against the wall, watching Wish, waiting for her to do something. Wish gave them a smile.

"Look again," Spyke said, jerking a thumb over to the bunker, and Wish did, to see that what she'd taken for a body slumped in the entrance was actually just a head. Neatly severed.

"Oh."

"Your ringer is rather skilled," Brade said, somehow serving up both a compliment and a criticism. Wish kept quiet, not sure of the correct etiquette here.

Rue helped by sidling up and saying, "Fucking savage."

"She's kept things quiet for the most part, anyway," Brade said. "Nothing like a sword for stealth, with the rest of the world using guns."

"She's moving down the line with Sabre, making sure we're not followed," Spyke said. "Rock's in support, but the rest of us are pressing on. There's a path over there, should connect with the Cracked Trail."

Wish nodded and waved her squad on, though they'd heard and didn't need telling. The others adjusted their packs and continued into the dark. Rue lingered. Wish looked out across the land they'd crossed to get here. Moonlight picked out the tips of trees and jutting rocks as far as could be seen below, a gradually declining slope that looked gentle at this scale. Far off there were faint orange glows on the horizon, likely burning buildings. Here, it was peaceful, gunshots barely audible, little pops in the night. Maybe artillery, made pathetic by distance. However they'd done it, with Newk's irresponsible charge or not, they'd conquered a mountain.

The ridge was their throne, making them queens over a wide, rugged gap in the Drail's defences. Wish said, "With a little engineering, we could get the whole Stanclif Empire up through this back door."

"Hardly," Spyke said. A final couple of girls were huffing over the rocks with the Reaper carried between them. "Once we're up, we're all gone. This place is more than we can hold. Get on, Wild, I'll send your ringer after you when she's done collecting scalps."

Wish looked from her to the trees again, her friends already lost in the dark. Rue was about to say something, no doubt criticising Newk or Wish's management of Newk, but the bang of a rifle along the ridge broke that thought. Wish dropped her pack, leapt the few strides to the bunker and climbed onto the roof. She swung her rifle off her shoulder and looked to the next bunkers, following the curve of the cliffs to where lights bobbed along it. They were a long way off, but Drail reinforcements were coming. Shit. The attack hadn't been quiet enough after all.

A great explosive sound shook the world, followed by the immense crack of splitting rock. The bunker shifted beneath Wish and she leapt off. She hit a tree on the way down, a blow to her shoulder slowing the fall before she smacked dirt, rolling and coughing. The ground kept shuddering like jelly. Rue was suddenly next to her, a hand pulling her up. They ran together, arm in arm, away from the cliff edge, as the cliff gradually settled – but the sounds of distant rocks crumbling and earth moving persisted.

The pair staggered to a stop, looking in the direction of the riotous sound, but there was nothing to see through the trees and shadows. As the tumbling rocks grew quieter, Wish heard men shouting. Part of the cliff had collapsed? Cut off their advance? Wish listened for the sound of Emi cackling, but it didn't come. No, Emi had been with her squad, marching into the trees.

"Help me with this fucking guy," Spyke hissed, snapping her out of it.

Wish nodded, distractedly, but Rue beat her back to the bunker, which was still there, if cracked around the edges. Brade protested, saying he could move, but no one listened as Rue and Spyke each got under an arm. Together, they shunted him into the trees, moving fast, as other girls rushed in to join them from along the ridge.

A Sabre squad girl came from the direction of the blast, grinning broadly, and said, "You see that? Cade brought down half the mountain."

Wish smiled weakly. Well done, Cade. Now there was no doubt the scouts had been here, and the Drail would know Mean Ridge was vulnerable. Stanclif wouldn't get through here again. And they'd have a hard time coming back.

Newk came trotting out of the dark, then, sword at her side, with a Team Rock girl at her elbow, smiling like they'd just sneaked into a dance. Newk slowed down on seeing Wish, reading the concern on her face. She murmured for the Rock girl to keep going, and the scout – the red-haired girl again? – continued past, giving Wish a smirk.

"You left the squad without orders," Wish said, trying to be cold, stern.

"I came to help," Newk said, a weak excuse.

"You could've been killed. Could've given us away. You made *me* look bad."

Newk said nothing. The sword at her side said enough – a hard, brutal statement of purpose. She was here to kill, not take orders.

More scouts came trotting by, then – Fuse, Cade and Larkin. The officer slowed to let the sappers continue. She said, "What're you waiting for? We don't have much time."

Wish held Newk's gaze a second longer, just to make sure the message had settled in. Without knowing if it had, she flashed Larkin a smile. "Just making sure we've got everyone." With that, she turned to keep moving.

19

The Drail showed a flare for branding as they spread their machinery over the continent. For example, "iron" was a misnomer in reference to their rapidly expanding rail networks, reliant more on steel and other precious alloys. The rails themselves were specially developed touched metals, sunk deep into the ground to make them impervious to all but the most extreme conditions – and even then their magically charged nature would alert mages immediately to the location of any problems. But the "iron" label was used quite deliberately. It evoked raw, ancient power. To look upon Drail machinery was, after all, to see human mastery of the world's most resilient resources.

Engines, Chimney & Rails: How the Rocc was Industrialised, Yun, p. 54

Maringdale had never seen the Iron Barge before, but was sure not to let that show, lest she be associated with Donut as he gawked at it resting in Junker Station. She'd been ambivalent about him catching up to them, as the crooked clock-tower across the rails ticked closer to departure time, and was still undecided if his ability to lug all the gear from the Fever Crossing was balanced by how embarrassing his presence was. He practically slobbered, staring at the massive vehicle. Its linked carriages were each the size of a small factory, varying between two and three storeys high, curved and warped to look like a hundred upturned boat hulls fused together, painted black and dotted with slit windows, bulkhead loading doors and spherical gun turrets. It was a fortress on rails, driven by an enormous steam engine with armour-encased pistons and thick chimneys; perhaps the most powerful single machine in the world. If the war was confined to the immediate vicinity of the impenetrable rails of the Iron Canal, the Drail would dominate without question – the Farnish had only developed trains for speed, and Stanclif's luxurious cross-continental transports could never be converted to be quite as formidable as an engine designed top-to-bottom for war. As in most things, the Drail alone saw the railways' true potential.

"Wait till Ropert hears I got to ride the Iron Barge," Donut said.

"All that family money never bought you a train ticket?" Maringdale said.

"I've ridden *trains,*" Donut replied indignantly, "but this is the *Iron Barge*. It's a working engine, there's –"

"Saint's teeth, no one cares." Maringdale moved ahead, flashing Netts a warning look not to join in. She heard the bitterness in her own voice and felt the falter in Donut's pleasure. The soft sod. Fuck the pair of them, she'd had a bad day. People shooting at her, things exploding, coat dusty as sin and Hill dead as quick as he'd come. To top it all off, she now had two losers in her charge.

But, climbing the ramp to the Iron Barge, she couldn't help admitting, privately, that this was indeed more than a train. The carriage they entered was decked like a fine restaurant, carpeted in rich burgundy with wood-panelled walls and tiered balcony booths. It wasn't populated by society's best, though, just Drail officers in crisp uniform. They were in the higher echelons of the military, from their sleeve medals, but with some rough enough to be of lower class; sergeants who'd crept up the ranks through viciousness in the field. Maringdale gave one leering, stubble-faced man a wide berth as she navigated the packed space. Donut cooed over the light fixtures as he followed.

"I don't see my people here," Netts said. He took the lead, small enough to slip between the men unnoticed, where Maringdale had to grunt for them to step aside. "See any Dread uniforms, you let me know."

There weren't any. Dread soldiers had a habit of creating space and quietening rooms – even a carriage of officers would've steered well clear of them. Slight as Netts was, even his uniform caused conversations to falter. He hopped about from one level to another, checking all the faces just in case, asking rapid questions. No, no one had seen Battle Chief Gloven – who should've been riding the barge via Highscythe to Low Slane – or Kill Chief Crash with the rest of his men. Netts continued through a passage between carriages and Maringdale followed on.

As they moved down the train, whistles blew and the great machine stirred to life, chugging and coughing and creaking. The Iron Barge accelerated slowly and soldiers flocked to open doors and weapon slits to hoot and wave goodbye to anyone watching from the platforms.

The trio pushed their way through another extravagant dining carriage, then a sleeping quarters with a spiral staircase and two dozen booths, and another with booths dismantled to pass gun shells through, beds and benches removed for large-barrelled cannons. Men loitered chattering, smoking and drinking, watching Maringdale like they wanted to wink or make comments but sensing it would be a mistake.

They finally reached a seating carriage where the cushioned benches of the bottom level sat under walkways welded into the carriage walls, lined with gun-holes crowded by soldiers. Netts found a space and the three settled in. He huffed, "Once we're underway and people aren't moving so much, I'll find the others. They wouldn't have travelled by road, must be here."

Maringdale grunted dismissal and put her boots up, happy as long as they were moving. West. Closer to the *real* front. Probably better they were still alone, anyway – Netts was more likely to talk without his comrades holding him back. She said, "Out in the woods, and over at Highscythe Ward, is it the same as what they were doing in Cleave City?"

Netts narrowed his eyes. "What do you know about it?"

"What Hill and Battle Chief Ways told me. Is it true it could end the war?"

The soldier hesitated.

"You think the Purification wouldn't be informed?" Maringdale said.

"Yeah, no." Netts shifted his shoulders. "You're right, all part of the same project. We had good results in Fever, from what Gloven said, but not as good as Highscythe. Between them and Wick, looked like they'd got what Vorhale's after. Or close to."

"And no one outside the Dread Corps knows about this?" Maringdale asked carefully, noting that name, Vorhale.

"Well there'd have to be generals on the Arrow Council aware, ready to deploy gas, you know, developing air-drops or cannon shells for it or something. I mean, I dunno how that part works. And them in the Low Slane Court would have a hand in it. Wouldn't be surprised if Vorhale's friends with the Screaming Prince himself. Sorry" – Netts forced a smile – "but if you're looking for a leak, you've got a lot of ground to cover."

"Indeed," Maringdale agreed, and together with Ways' assertion that the enemy would target the Dread Corps anyway, identifying exactly how Stanclif or Khib had learnt of the project wasn't really viable. More important was understanding what details they might know. "Are there unique resources going into this that they could target, rather than go for Highscythe or elsewhere directly? The likelihood is they intercepted Ways' men on their way to Fever, so a supply-line attack seems reasonable to assume."

Netts almost laughed, but her expression made him stop. He couldn't suppress his slimy smile, though, as he tilted his head to try and figure her out. "You're serious?"

"Is it so absurd?"

"I mean, it's only *people,* so . . ." Netts trailed off, to give it some thought. "I guess they might go after the Dread mages? But that wouldn't be any easier, would it? The rest is – well, no. Make no sense to go after anything but the weapon itself."

"If it's like the Khib gases," Donut mused, evidently muddling through Netts' earlier allusions, "why wasn't there more harm done in Cleave? I heard they released poison gas on the southern trenches that caught a change of wind and spread two miles. Killed thousands on both sides."

"This isn't exactly something that catches on the wind, is it?" Netts said, but he lost his smile when he saw the confusion on

Donut's face. He huffed and folded his arms. "Ah hell, fuck you two. You've got no idea, do you? Shit, I should've known better." He stood abruptly.

Maringdale stood too, a head taller than him. "We're on the same side, Fearsmith Netts. You want us to help, we need honesty."

"No thanks, ma'am," Netts snorted. He rubbed his nose with the back of his forearm, a tick. "I ain't making that call. Already said enough. You want more, you find someone with enough stripes to take blame."

Maringdale drew back her coat to reveal her pistol, holding his eyes. She let her expression carry the warning: rank was not important to the Purification.

Netts eyed them both with renewed concern. He shook his head and said, "Bloody spooks. Screw it, I'll do you a deal. We don't find any Dread soldiers on this train, I'll tell you what I know."

She wasn't counting, but Maringdale imagined they had been walking for a couple of hours by the time the trio were satisfied that Netts' companions were not on board. In that time, they'd had a full tour of the train's double- and triple-tiered seating and dining areas, and complex carriages of machinery and gun emplacements. The Iron Barge exuded luxury, from the lavish carpeting and drapes to the polished casements around the artillery stations. It was also, between the larger entertainment areas, a warren of tight corridors and narrow stairwells, scattered with unpredictable turrets and side-passages. Almost all of it was packed with soldiers or supplies.

The trio finally settled into a cylindrical viewing tower that rose above one carriage near the rear, with a panoramic window. There were two soldiers there, smoking cigarettes which they offered over. Maringdale indulged for a minute before sending them back to their units, which they were reluctant to do. One mention of the Purification and they fled, after which Maringdale dispatched Donut to find supplies. The train would rattle on for another day at least before they reached Highscythe, and this was as good a place as any to camp.

"There's piped heating in the walls," Netts said, crouching as he felt under the bench. "Must be more wealth sunk in this train than in some cities." He sat and put an arm up on the side, twisting to look at the passing countryside. The sun was low, casting the plains of Garter in a rich orange glow. Hills and trees as far as could be seen, with occasional farmhouses and villages. "Hell of a thing rolling through here. You think they appreciate it, the civilisation we've spread across this damned continent?"

Maringdale remained standing, hands in her pockets, wondering the same thing. Fifteen years ago, Garter had been independent of Drail, and floundering. They had scant infrastructure, poor education. What foreigners failed to appreciate was that the Drail did not just bring armies when they crossed borders, they also brought communication, education and industry. The Iron Barge itself had been constructed in Garter, on the banks of the Broad River, and the deep-sunk touched rails, near impossible to break, were developed in Balnia; both would've been unthinkable without Drail coordination.

"My theory," Netts went on, "these savages don't *want* to improve because it means they gotta change. Gotta rethink all the idiot things they've been doing wrong. That's shameful – no one likes to admit mistakes."

That was oddly profound, Maringdale admitted to herself. She may have misjudged this one. She tested him, "Some would say they fear losing sovereignty. Paying tithes to the Arrow Council, losing control."

"Everyone's gotta have a master." Netts shrugged. "We always got that in Slane, y'know? Help your betters to help yourself. Screaming Prince bows to the Arrow Council, but he gets more than he puts in, no doubt. We got" – Netts counted on his fingers – "Drail scholars coming south. Better exports for our goods – not just to Drail, but worldwide. New railways, Har Coul furs, Camber plumbing, all the benefits. And the Arrow Council? Shit, they answer to someone too, anyway – they might rule, but the *Empire* is their master, right? If he ever went rogue, the Patrain would have to answer to the Purification same as anyone else."

Maringdale smiled. Part of this, she saw, was him talking himself into co-operating. Letting go of the Dread Corps secrets. She sat down across from him and said, "Indeed, it all works because we're working *together.*"

Netts gave her a last considering look, then nodded. "And I gotta say it's not right, not one of my people being on this train. I'd be lying to say I'm not worried. This project is everything, ma'am, like you said – whole war could count on it. Guess that makes you equally important. You'll have people can move faster, in different circles, to us. If we're under attack from enemies unknown, you gotta stop it."

"That's what I'm here for."

"Well I've heard stories, the sort of people might be after us. Thunder Guns, you know them? Bloody Stanclif shock troop been creeping behind Farnish lines hitting people from a mile away. Cowards with guns that'll take your torso in half, and you never see them coming. And there's the Bitch Squad, you know them?"

"Excuse me?"

"Women soldiers," Netts continued, disgusted. "Like – they lure guys into bed and cut their throats. A whole company of them. That's how desperate the Stanclif are, see? Got their women fighting dirty for them."

That one was news to Maringdale, but it only highlighted how much she'd missed, stationed on the Eastern Front. Such threats, unlikely as they sounded, chilled morale, while she'd been pottering about after worm-eyes. She said, "Have there been rumours of such units near here?"

"What? No. I didn't think we had a problem till you turned up. What I'm saying is, there's nasty forces out there. Sort that hit you where you sleep, make you doubt *women.* So, see, what we've been doing, it's fighting fire with fire." He paused long enough for Maringdale to grow wary of where this was going. It was a preamble to temper how deplorable this project was. Netts took a breath and said, "The Dread mages have been experimenting on people. Living people, taken from around the front line. With all the chaos, no one notices them missing, see? Whole towns are blown apart by Khib bombs, shit, what difference does a few more bodies make?"

"Go on."

"Right. So, I'd heard things. Dark stuff. And we had bodies to clear up, burnt or, like – dehydrated or something. Life sucked out of them. But then about four nights ago I saw something first hand. Gloven had me and a handful of boys come to a cave and watch these six Garter peasants, all walking stiff, upright, better posture than you ever see on a civilian. For a second I thought they might be dead and reanimated. There's rumours of that north of Singness, and back in Slanik lore."

"Rumours," Maringdale said, knowing full well it couldn't be necromancy. "Designed by Slanik clerics to build hope, or fear, that death is not the end. There's no evidence for it."

"Yeah. Of course it's not necromancy. Just looked like it. But whatever they'd done to put them in that state, that's not the point. The weapon itself, they tested that right in front of us. Gloven has us stand on one side of this cavern, prisoners lined up on the other, and then his Dread mage wheeled in this big engine of some sort, pipes and cables coming out, and honestly, I just tried not to watch. Better not to get interested, see? They told everyone to brace themselves and the mage activated it.

"There was a crack like lightning and this rotten smell like burnt hair. Blinding light. I couldn't see for a few seconds, but I heard things. People collapsing and groaning, and the mage swearing his head off. I was pushed out of the room, with other soldiers running in to clear up, and just got a little glimpse of what was left. Four of the prisoners were down on the floor, bleeding out of every hole, dead as you like. A fifth was rolling about screaming and the last one was just standing there, all confused. But two of my mates were dead, too, the same way."

He paused as if to let this sink in, but it was as much for his own benefit, struggling with the memory. He touched his hair and nose, in anxious gestures. Maringdale waited for a conclusion.

"It's not a gas, see," Netts went on, quietly. "I was just saying before that I dunno how they plan to deliver it. It sent something through the air itself, but it could go off like a bomb too, I dunno? My thinking is – the reason they had us in that room – they *hoped* it would hurt the prisoners and not us. Obviously didn't quite work. Anyway, Gloven decided to pull out shortly after, and like I said, I guess they made better progress elsewhere. But you can imagine the potential, whatever this is. Instant death through a flick of a switch? I figured if you set it off in a room with twice as many people, it'd do them all in. Drop it behind Khib lines and you might wipe out an army." Netts paused again, checking Maringdale's face. "Just not sure it's something everyone would approve of. That kind of power. And what they've been doing to create it."

It sounded as reckless as Captain Ogard had feared back in Cleave, with their own troops unwittingly killed in the testing. But sacrifices had to be made, in order to win. Whatever it took, Maringdale told herself. Slowly, she said, "It sounds to me . . . like progress."

Maringdale dwelt on the new weapon into the night, imagining the possibilities of establishing Drail dominance without ever needing to fight. Even the most ignorant nations would have to recognise the superiority of a race who would could kill without touch. And imagine *her* being responsible for helping make this happen, by thwarting those who would try to stop it. Yes, as she mulled over Netts' account, she decided this was an indication of something exceptional, something that *had* to be allowed to happen. You could not fight progress.

When the Iron Barge pulled into a station in the morning, Maringdale sought a radio station and sent a message back to the Purification. Avoiding any mention of Panderlair, she reported that her top priority now was to investigate movements around Highscythe Ward and potentially head further west to Wick, as the entire war effort could depend on protecting the Dread Corps' interests. The response was telegraphed back in under an hour while the Iron Barge still sat in station, and was thoroughly predictable: *produce evidence and the Purification will offer fitting support.* It was permission to pursue this further west, with the thinly-veiled counterpoint that without evidence she might find herself at sea.

Satisfied enough, Maringdale returned to the Iron Barge to regroup with Netts and travel onwards. She found the soldier's face downturned with worry.

He told her, "There was a quartermaster, in the second carriage, says he heard my company were expected on the train yesterday, for sure. They had more time than us, should've made it."

"So where are they?" Maringdale asked.

Netts shrugged. "Might be nothing. Last-minute change of plans and they went with Gloven instead? Then, they should've left word for me and Puls. Hate to think the alternative. Like, what if whoever intercepted your Cleave messengers got them, too?"

"Stopped a whole Dread company?" Donut exclaimed, and turned his shock to Maringdale. "Do you think we should go back? They'd have to be –"

"A very noticeable force," Maringdale cut in, damned if she was going back east to the revive rumours of waders. "No, there's likely a reasonable explanation. We'll send word back once we reach Highscythe. The pair of you, have some sense. If there was anyone dangerous enough to stop a Dread company, they would've stopped *us* from reaching Fever. Most likely the company got new orders – a quicker route or a short diversion. But you said yourself, Netts, Highscythe is the important one. I can't speak to your men, but that's where we need to be."

Highscythe Ward was an impressive sight; an ancient agricultural hub on a historically disputed border that had become a unique city. From a distance, the mesh of storehouses, homes and towers were combined into a great south-facing arch, like an enormous bump in the grassy plains that had been cut in two. The flat southern face was a stacked hive of openings, with artillery barrels poking out like a pine-lizard's spikes. The Iron Barge rattled parallel to it for a long time, the rails skirting tens of miles of empty land before the city, dotted with bombed vehicles, craters, abandoned trenches and ruined siege vehicles, testament to the futility of attacking Highscythe head-on. There were flags flying far off, where Comity forces were dug in, just outside the range of the Highscythe artillery, billets visible behind trenches lined with sharp barricades.

Before their final approach, the train was attacked by an enterprising company in Stanclif slate blue: armoured vehicles and men on horses charged from the rubble of a ruined outpost, firing rifles that pinged off the Iron Barge's shell. It was a desperate assault: a chancing brigade thinking they could harm this mighty vehicle, when they weren't even capable of damaging the rails it sat on. Shouts rose from within the train as men scrambled to the gun slits and fired back. The sporadic flurry of gradually building gunfire peppered the ground more than their enemies as the riflemen were thrown by the train's constant motion.

A boom tore through the chaos with a flash from the ruins and a shell hit the side of the train, three carriages behind Maringdale's bird's nest turret. She ducked, with Donut and Netts cursing, and the train rocked like it might topple. But it rocked back, and hadn't slowed. Another boom sounded, much closer – then another, and another, and finally the tremendous racket of a large machine gun, none of it swaying their carriage. Maringdale pulled herself back over the lip of their window to see the ruined buildings engulfed by a huge pillar of black smoke. The plain beyond was shredded in erupting clouts of earth. The train's mounted weapons had torn through the attackers.

Maringdale steadied herself, in awe of the vehicle's destructive power. There were only bits of vehicles and bodies out there now. The most complete, a twitching horse. And down the train, smoke peeled over the struck carriage with no signs of a break in the Iron Barge's shell.

They rolled on, unstoppable, and passed through a heavily armoured wall before turning towards the rear gates of the city.

From this angle, Highscythe looked more hill-like than ever, the north of the city blanketed by grass, only discernible as a settlement by occasional bulkhead doors sunk into the ground. One such door loomed large as the train came towards it, and as it opened to receive them, the scale of the immense hillock became clear. It would be a fittingly defiant place, Maringdale considered, to find glory in thwarting their enemies.

20

Har Coul is a fine place to visit if you enjoy physical hardship and limited amenities. Liberal dandies in Vasseer will call the Coulard stereotypes of vulgarity and stone-age sensibilities outdated and unfair, but my personal experience proved them to be true. Just try finding a Coulard tailor who doesn't exclusively trade in furs or a pastime that doesn't rely on contests of strength and you will see what I mean!

The Eclectic Traveller, Winimpal, p. 185

The terrain was tougher entering the Cracked Trail, where a series of mountainous paths earned the name. The rocks rose in monoliths and the slopes became a climb as the scouts delved deeper into Har Coul territory. Wish felt it could be described as *craggy*, if you were being cute. *Severe* was more accurate, as Har Coul was not cute. The stony inclines between walls of rock hid their advance, but often narrowed to shoulder-width, leading to a lot of bumps and torn clothing. Sound carried alarmingly well through the canyons of rock, so there was little room for conversation, and zero chance of marching songs, even with pairs of scouts moving far ahead to check for danger.

In snatched moments between marching, patrols and sleeping, Wish did, at least, manage to give Newk tips on the basics of how a rifle worked. Principally, she drove home that the sights needed to be set up properly. She made it so clear, in fact, that they had a rather tense moment, sat on the ground with Wish holding the rifle between them, when Newk said, "I shouldn't touch your gun, is that what you're saying?"

"No," Wish said, though it kind of was. "Just. You know, this is important. Basic rules that make a good sniper: always check your sights, never expose the scope or anything that might catch light, always wait rather than risk a mistake."

"But I'm *not* a sniper," Newk said. "You've trained for years –"

Wish gave a sharp laugh. "Months. At best. We were rushed through, all of us."

"But even so. Isn't it better to do what I'm already good at?"

The image of that severed head in the dark of the bunker popped back to Wish's mind. It warranted addressing, particularly as Rue kept giving her questioning looks. She'd planned a practical, rather than emotional, explanation for her concerns, and said, "You need a gun because we're not often within arms' reach of the enemy. I've maybe got that close to the green-coats once." The closest being that man on the cliff. Loose. *No –*

"Some of the girls were happy with how we handled Mean Ridge," Newk said.

"The ones that you didn't actively defy?" Wish shot back, a little of her genuine betrayal coming out, even if she tried to hide it with a smile to say it was a cheeky mistake. Not a lunatic move putting everyone at risk.

It was hard to stay mad at that face, though, and Wish only felt bad as Newk's features contorted guiltily. She leaned in closer, wanting to touch her, squeeze an arm, chuck her chin. A hundred entirely inappropriate things. Instead, Wish softened her voice and said, "It was very brave, and worked this time, but we have to trust each other. You can't make your own orders. You especially need to warn us if you're going to chop heads off. Some people need to be prepared before seeing that."

She meant that less seriously, to lighten the mood, but Newk's brow got heavier.

"How many heads are you up to, now?" Wish tried, for another way through.

"Eight."

"Including that goblin?"

Newk shook her head. This conversation was as dead as her victims.

"Call it a day, shall we?" Wish sighed. "How about a game of bones?"

Newk nodded, but she wasn't talkative when they rejoined the squad, and barely made eye contact.

After another two days of hard hiking, keeping ahead of patrols with minimal conversation and short breaks for sleep, the third night found the scouts camped across rocks at varying heights, with tent pegs squeezed into cracks or hammered into patches of dirt. A fierce wind beat the canvas despite the shelter of the nearby cliffs. Wild Wish had already given Newk the go ahead to join Fixit, so they had two people to a tent now, but she wondered if she should've invited Newk in with her and put Fixit with Pound and Dakoda. Economising on space. But there was a funk in the tent already, between Wish and Rue's rank clothing. Another day and they'd reach Edge Falls, where they could get clean and *then* Wish could ask.

"Your damn eyes are lighting up the tent," Rue grumbled from beside Wish, and rolled over to face the other way. "Get some sleep, *Captain.*"

Wish frowned. Between focusing on keeping quiet and alive, with fleeting thoughts of the Newk Problem, she'd barely spared a moment for the others. She whispered, "Rue. Are you okay with me being in charge?"

"Yes."

"Because I didn't ask –"

"You're the best one for it, Wild, just go to fucking sleep."

"I mean, if you did want to –"

"Wild." Rue swung back over, eyes just visible in the dark, inches from her face. "If I had a problem with you, you'd know it. I could squash you like a bug, no one's disputing that. But you're smarter than me and people like you. You belong in charge."

Wish smiled, not sure the last time she'd heard Rue say a nice thing about her. About anyone, really. Even if it came barbed with the image of Rue squashing her. "Thanks, Rue. That means a lot."

"It's only the truth. I would've busted Fixit's skull rather than listen to her stupid demands. And as for Newk . . . You're more . . . you know." Wish did not. "Restrained."

Ah, that. As if it was Wish's *restraint* that kept her from open conflict – or that kept her celibate – and not, say, misfortune and nerves. But Wish smirked. "Say, Rue, now I'm your superior, I guess I can order you about? Like, *let me test your biceps!*"

"That right?" Rue said, flat enough to make Wish regret saying it. Rue didn't always get jokes. But she went on, "Shit, Wish, that's just what I'm talking about. All you've ever had to do was *ask.*"

Damn. Was Rue leading her on or making a general comment? She swallowed and said, "I don't really – I mean, I value your friendship Rue, but –"

"But right now you'd rather bang that ringer, yeah?" Rue cut in. Just harsh enough to recall the judgemental look she gave Wish for trying to comfort Newk after the hawk giant. The sort of look that made Wish scum by association. Rue continued, though, "Funny. I reckon I'm warming to that girl just as you're starting to find her difficult. Larkin said she cut those Drail pricks down like some kind of ghost. Never thought I'd find a ringed woman impressive. And Loose would say it herself, you know, I oughta move on and take what opportunities come? Next day it could be you or me takes a bullet. Newk sure has a body, doesn't she?"

"I –" The words caught in Wish's throat.

"She's gotta be a *freak* for a lay," Rue went on, picking up speed. "Savages do things differently. Use tools, have rituals of the flesh."

"But –" Wish wasn't sure *but* what. But me? It was an idiot fancy, of course, that Newk would be interested in her after her blundering attempts at command, marching into some kind of hellscape, but it was nice to imagine and there wasn't room in that fantasy for Rue to overcome her bigotry with her unfailing woman-eating confidence.

"Relax," Rue whispered, breath suddenly right in Wish's ear, making her go rigid. "I'm messing with you. I would *not* go there. And I don't like seeing you do it either. But we *are* all likely to die, so maybe you oughta grow a spine and get on with it."

Rue shifted away and Wish felt a weight lifting, right before another settled. Something like shame. "Is it that obvious?"

"Only to anyone with eyes."

"But you don't think –"

"No Wild, I fucking don't. Who's got time for thinking in this war? Just go up to her tomorrow, once we're on the march, take her hand and walk with her. No need to keep thinking and planning and putting it into words and crap."

"So" – Wish hesitated – "you're done hating Newk?"

"I never hated her, Wild. Just don't fucking trust her. But whatever, she's your problem, isn't she?"

Wish almost liked that wording. *Her* problem. Except there was a problem. Insubordination. Clumsiness with rifles? But Rue was right. She had to take what she could get, if she could get it. It wasn't going to be much now, anyway. Maybe they could hold hands. Be close at night, as Loose had been when they all shared the tent.

If Newk wanted it, at all.

Rue's breath got heavier as she slipped towards sleep.

Before losing her, Wish quickly said, "I hate what happened, you know." Rue was silent, waiting. "With Loose. And with Sarge and Small and Colt and everyone. I hate it all, but especially Loose. I liked her."

Rue grunted. "Yeah, well. All we can do is get over it, huh? None of us came to war to make friends."

Wish hummed agreement. But she didn't entirely agree.

On the morning of the fourth day, with everyone eager to reach Edge Falls and take a boat, Wish told herself this was an important time to stay focused, so she did not take Newk's hand, but determined to do so soon. Instead, she offered her a smile as they were packing up, and Newk returned it, which felt like a win.

They hadn't been moving for long when the platoon's advance was slowed by two Sun Squad scouts reporting that a village bordered the trail ahead. As Boot Squad had had an easy ride for a few days, mostly relegated to rear guard duty, Tate decided it was their turn to investigate. Wild Wish gave this first real act as a commander a few minutes' thought, unsure who was best to send. Rue was competent but impulsive, not subtle; Pound was rarely quiet; Fixit was too valuable; Emi too unpredictable; Newk too likely to *cut off heads*. Wish caved and said she'd go herself, with dependable Dakoda. Safe bet. Tate didn't look pleased, but did not question her decision in front of everyone.

Traipsing over the rocks, getting to as high ground as was possible in a land of generally high ground, Wish stewed on the captain's look. Why had she disapproved? Because, as the leader, Wish was too important to go herself? Or did it show no confidence in the others? Or was it just because she wasn't the best scout? Well, it couldn't be that. She stopped as they crested another immense rock and found a wall of natural steps ahead. Dakoda moved to continue and Wish whispered, "Hold up."

Dakoda scanned ahead, seeming concerned she hadn't noticed any trouble. With rocks overhanging them, bald tree roots were their only company. "What is it?"

"Do you think Tate wanted me to send someone else?"

Dakoda looked suitably stunned. "I think we're about to –"

Movement above interrupted her thought. Both scouts pressed into the rock wall, rifles ready. Footsteps loosened small stones a tier above them. Getting closer, and too casual to be someone aware of their presence. The scouts met eyes, Dakoda expecting some kind of command, not entirely pleased about it. Wish gestured with a hand, pointing at her, off to the left, to herself, she'd go right. Creep up, get eyes on the stranger. Dakoda silently moved away as Wish climbed her own small incline. She listened for more movement, the footsteps passing.

Wish peered over the lip of the rock and thanked the stars that they'd stopped, regardless the daft reason for it. The next tier was the outermost perimeter of the village they were looking for: a rock path worn smooth by foot traffic, set before the first outlying homes that made up the community. Unmistakable Har Coul rock-houses; Wish had seen sketches, but never been close to one. The mountain-dwelling Coulards carved hollows into rocks for shelters, and these fine examples had round windows, broad-but-short doorways and patterned awnings, identifying the households within, all chiselled into an enormous rock face. Off to the right, where the stranger was walking, steps had been carved going up. Going by this person's back, it was not a village they wanted to pass through: he wore big furs, leather straps, a hammer bouncing against one thigh and an axe against the other. His shoulders would struggle to fit through the Cracked Trail.

Wish dropped back down as Dakoda returned and mouthed, "Houses that way."

"Here, too," Wish whispered. "We'll skirt them, figure out a way to avoid it." But as she was speaking, another movement caught her eye – someone in the clearing. She was moving before she realised it, rifle slack as she drew her blade and shoved the intruder back into the rock. Eye to eye, Wish froze with a hand over a little girl's mouth, covering most of her face, blade pressed into her neck. A second away from bleeding her like a lamb. Dakoda caught Wish's shoulder and she moved back, slightly. Shit was she really about to do that? Shit – didn't she still *have* to?

"Shh, shh," Dakoda whispered to the girl, crouching. She spoke in Coulard, words Wish guessed at: "Friends, we don't want trouble."

The girl was terrified, shaking, with thin arms poking out of a fur tunic, a little woven basket on the ground where she'd dropped it, mushrooms spilt out. Wild Wish lowered the blade but kept her hand on the child's mouth.

She looked slowly from the child's giant quaking eyes back to the blade.

"Wild?" Dakoda said, as a simple but also very complex question. What do we do?

Wish gave her a look, but quickly looked away. She didn't want to see Dakoda scared – not cool, collected Dakoda, eyes wide and trembling like she'd just been handed a live grenade. Let the child go and she'd raise an alarm. Take the child and the villagers would hunt for her. Kill the child and she'd *kill a child*. Wild Wish felt like she was going to start shaking too, any second. Vibrate into madness at the choice. What would Sarge do, what would Sarge say? Sarge would have said don't get seen, not ever. Dammit and dammit. Dakoda made a noise that warranted action and Wish snapped out of her thoughts.

"Okay. It's fine, we're fine. Tell her we're friends, we don't mean harm." She spoke rapidly, keeping her hand there on the petrified child, as she put away the blade and patted her pockets for her field bandages. "Only, we need to take her away, clear of the village. And we need to tie her up, especially her mouth, because actually it's pretty fucking obvious we're *not* friends. If we leave her close enough, they'll find her and will maybe limit their search. We'll be long gone by then. We'll be long gone, Dakoda. Come on and help me, so we can get the hell out of here."

Wild Wish was shaking in full by the time she got back to Captain Tate and the scouts started moving out. Many of them were giving her worried looks. Tate squeezed her shoulder, reassuringly, with a slight push that the others wouldn't have seen, to spur her on. The captain leaned in close to say, "I get it. Everyone gets it. But we're gone, okay? It's over."

It was only then that Wish realised that voice she kept hearing, repeating the same few frightened phrases over and over, was her own: "There was child. Just a child." She went quiet at last, and noticed Dakoda, a little way off, talking with Oksy – dammit don't confide in *Oksy* – but Dakoda looked as worried as Wish felt. Then Emi was on Wish, an arm around her shoulders, guiding her onto the path, falling in with the other girls. Someone had picked out another route while Wish was scouting, and Emi quietly asked, "There still *is* a child, right?"

"Didn't I say?" Wish looked up with alarm. "We left her there. We didn't hurt her."

"Sure," Emi said, and checked over both shoulders before leaning in a little closer. "That's what you *said.*"

The dirt-minder asked from a place of genuine concern, no trickery. Like there was something in Wish's manner that made things seem very bad indeed. Which they were, Wish realised, as she tripped along the path, trying hard not to simply fall flat on her face. She pulled away from Emi to scramble between a tight gap, scraping her hands in her haste to climb, and she slammed into another girl's butt above. Oksy, of all people – how'd she get here? – but Oksy held in her usual smugness and offered a hand instead, pulling Wish up before moving on. Frowning.

"It's okay, Wild." Emi had rejoined her, lightly moving on. "Whatever you did, you did good."

Wish nodded, telling herself that was true. They were clear – shaken but clear. Even if the villagers rallied in minutes, they'd have a hard time chasing down this platoon of seasoned hiders. She had done good. No one was hurt. No one needed to know that she *could* have killed that child. Even if they all definitely suspected it.

21

Words cannot quite convey what I found in Eardung. It is a land like no other, and describing it makes me nervous. Everything is where it belongs, and it is right that it be found nowhere else. It is right that neither man nor monster set eye on it, nor be able to discuss it in our plainly ignorant tongue. It is not for us, and I am not sure how far I can go in revealing to you, who cannot be there to feel it, exactly what those hallowed forests are.

Mountains of Wood, Smartwether, p. 88

The scouts heard the Edge Falls half an hour before seeing the river, which provided a distraction for Wild Wish from thoughts of child murder. She received sympathetic pats and nods throughout the day, but no one had anything to say. Emi kept close, and sober. Responsible Emi was more unsettling than her usual erratic self. The others kept their distance, perhaps put off by Wish's scowl. Wish spotted Newk falling back, walking with that new girl from Rock Squad. She asked Emi her name: Angles. A lean, sharp-faced woman with freckles and big curly hair. Nose like a triangle and eyes that bulged. No, that was unfair. Angles was pretty. They'd look good together. Had they bonded on Mean Ridge?

A gradually growing buzz made everyone refocus, the sound unusual until they realised it was the rush of water crashing over rocks. The scouts sped up to see one of the great sights of Boldarow: where the Step River's western off-shoot, Little Step, cascaded over the Edge for a drop of some two hundred feet. Wish's spirits lifted as they neared it, and she pushed Boot Squad to move faster, overtaking the others. She clambered over a large boulder and stopped, a big grin on her face. It was a perfect day for it, sky empty blue above and a fresh stillness in the air. The rocky terrain of Har Coul ran along the river's near edge, ragged and foreboding, but across a divide of half a kilometre, the far bank was smoother, more fertile, thick with trees.

The river moved with a steady, mesmerising flow, white peaks dashing into and over big rocks scattered between the banks before tipping over an incredible drop. Wish moved to the edge to look down, a dizzying height, to where the water landed thunderously below, before it snaked off through grassland towards the sea. The sea! She could see the distant sea from here, and it was humbling, immense, full of opportunity, empty of complications. Wish inhaled deeply, imagining she could taste salt water in the air, just as she enjoyed on the cliffs near Swelig.

"Wow," Fixit commented, the first to join Wish. Her glasses magnified the wonder in her eyes. "It's something."

Other girls climbed up and stalled at the sight, breathing it in, giving it reverence, until Larkin pushed through, businesslike, looking upriver. She pointed and said, "See the Twisted Bridge? Let's get across that before we stop to count our blessings."

"Can't we count a *couple* of blessings?" Wish said.

"Thought you already had?" Larkin shot back.

"We really need to hike to the bridge?" Pound asked, a little out of breath. "Plenty of rocks here to jump across."

It got a few sniggers, though she didn't seem to be joking. At first glance, the rocks looked like a welcoming set of stepping stones across the river, but in their deceptively large size, they obscured the gaps between them. Some were definitely not jumping distance, and there'd be no coming back from a little slip here.

"No?" Pound persisted. "Emi, couldn't you do something?"

Emi sidled up alongside her, hands deep in her pockets, and replied with a slow deliberation that suggested she was considering it a little too seriously: "I *could.*"

"I'd sooner trust my fate to the bridge," Larkin said. "No offence, Emi."

Emi shrugged like it was fair.

After a moment more to appreciate the view, they started to

move on, with Wish letting others take the lead as she snatched looks back towards the falls. They followed the bank as closely as the gaps in the rocks allowed, and as they gradually closed on the Twisted Bridge her attention turned forward. There was another marvel to experience yet – a sight rarer than the Falls, which were at least visible from Farne below. The Twisted Bridge connected Har Coul to the territory of the Eardung Forest, a domain technically under Drail control but home to the isolationist barkmen, a society of creatures seldom seen outside the Kleb Mountains. The Twisted Bridge was the best-known icon of their culture: a wooden structure that spanned Little Step, where the distance and current made its construction remarkable. If indeed it was constructed; the bridge, it was said, was grown rather than built. Artists' sketches made it look like the root of some giant tree.

The reality was even more impressive. The scouts slowed near it, impressed and nervous. They were going to have to cross this thing.

The Twisted Bridge swayed and groaned like the bough of a windswept tree. It was a system of roots – not one giant one, but a collection of hundreds or thousands of thick winding branches, weaving in and out of each other as they spread above the water, binding in pillars at regular intervals. As Wish got closer, she could hear it groaning loudly and saw how it swayed with the water, appearing ready to topple at any moment. Yet the uppermost roots, those not worn clean by the river, were gnarled and dark with age. Passing a prime viewing rock, Wish noticed Dollemore perched with a notepad, sketching.

"Good idea," Emi called up to her. "We'll never remember this."

"With the other memories from this war," Dollemore said, "don't count on it."

The fear-to-wonder ratio shifted closer to just fear as they got to the bridge's entrance and it became clear what crossing it would involve. It was rooted to the rocks ten metres above the bank, with grasping, snaking limbs, and a wide path ran down from it to the Cracked Trail. Wide enough for a couple of horses, maybe. The path joined the bridge where the roots were twined at their thickest, creating an almost flat, almost solid platform that went through a tunnel of branches. It was irregular, uneven and *constantly* moving. Not a simple sway from side to side, but a complex reaching and rotating movement, as if every branch that bound the bridge together had a life of its own.

Wish stared down the long tunnel, the exit at the other end variously coming in and out of visibility, and wondered if Pound's instinct to cross on the rocks had some merit. The full scout leadership gathered there: Captain Tate, Larkin, Spyke and Brade, along with Rock Squad's leader, Harmon. And Emi.

"Starting to feel like this wasn't designed for people," Harmon said dryly. She was a lithe woman with badly cropped blond hair, who made Wish uncomfortable because it was nearly impossible to tell when she was joking. Mostly, Wish thought she was, but couldn't recall ever seeing Harmon smile.

"Have you crossed this before?" Spyke asked Brade, accusingly.

"Me personally?" Brade replied. "No. But Sir Robert Smartwether gave a clear account. It's perfectly safe. I'd be the first across if not for this." He patted his leg. Right. He'd got up Mean Ridge well enough, and was taking regular sessions with Dollemore. Wish suspected he was fibbing.

"Emi, could you steady it?" Tate said.

Emi gave it some thought, then shook her head. "You wouldn't want me to. Right now it's working *with* the river; hold it still and they'll come to blows."

Tate huffed, not liking that. It was rare to see the captain nervous – Wish was not a fan. Or was it just rare that Wish was present for these discussions? During their dark history together, was Tate actually always shitting herself but they never saw it?

"I'll take Sabre across," Larkin said, surely aware it wasn't their turn.

"No." Tate said. "It's my place to lead. Captain Brade, you'll get your wish." Tate ignored his surprised look and placed a hand on the bridge's entrance arch. She took a breath like she was breathing in its energy, then stepped forward. Another step and she was clear of the rock. Another took her out over the water, already at a point where a fall could land her in the deadly current. The bridge shifted and she held her arms out to the sides to steady herself.

"Feels like it'll take a lot of weight, at least," she said. "But we'll tie ropes, one squad at a time. Spyke, Captain, if you'd join me."

Spyke and Brade looked united, for once, in their distaste. But Spyke swung her pack down and took out a thick rope. Larkin stepped in to help her unravel it, as Tate called out, "Sun Squad, up here!"

Wish watched, mesmerised by the captain rising and falling, bobbing on the bridge like a ship at sea. Tate was making herself visible, so the girls would see it was safe. Between them, they tied off a handful of ropes around their waists, from Tate back to Spyke, via Brade to the rest, and finally Sun Squad headed out tentatively after their captain. A chain of eight women and one man, each as worried as the next as they gingerly trod over the boughs, Brade had thankfully found his bad leg actually *was* okay now, saving Spyke a more difficult journey.

Tate called back advice from up front, pointing out tripping spots. Wish and the others watched wordlessly. Nervous laughter filtered back, as well as occasional quiet words of encouragement. About halfway across, the squad slowed down, but Brade's bravado picked up, as he shouted above the sound of the river, "It's remarkable, really – a bloody impressive structure! You're doing wonderfully, ladies!"

Then they were visible only in snatched glances between the moving branches, too far away to make out clearly, and Wish held her breath, silently praying to whatever might listen. Almost there, almost there. And finally a cheer went up, one at first, then all the voices joining in – the whole squad racing over the finish. The cheer was met by the girls down below, able to see to the other bank where Tate had plainly made it. Thank fuck. As the others laughed and uttered relief, Harmon, Larkin and Wish exchanged a look. Who next?

"Dammit, we'll go," Wish decided. Better get it out the way. Make sure the bridge didn't collapse in the meantime. She scrabbled in her pack for a rope before anyone could disagree, and shouted over her shoulder, "Boot! We're up!" Not looking up, to pretend the problem wasn't really there, she tied the rope round her waist and turned to the next in line. Which of course was Emi. The mage smiled wickedly and Wish handed over the rope saying, "Hell."

"I love you too, Wild," Emi chuckled, tying her waist off.

After her came Newk and then Rue. Wish watched distractedly for a moment as Rue helped tie the rope, probably tighter than necessary for Newk. But she was making sure it was done right. She nodded to Wish to say they were in this together. She'd look out for Wish by looking out for Newk. Newk, for her part, looked miffed, but muttered thanks.

Once the whole squad was ready, Wish turned to set out. Her first step landed on hard, solid wood – no different to a floorboard. Another step and the same, if you ignored the world moving around ahead. This would be fine. The next step and the bridge creaked under Wish, banking at one side, and she let out a yelp, putting a foot to the side and a hand up to steady herself. She grabbed a branch, snapped it, and fell. Someone cried her name and Emi shifted quickly to catch her, but Wish hit the side of the bridge, a wall of wood, and was stopped. She was still, as the bridge swayed the other way. She held up a hand for Emi to stay back, and beyond the mage she saw the expectant faces of her squad watching, ready to follow her into doom. Behind them, the audience included the other squad leaders and Oksy and Angles too, dammit.

"I'm okay, I'm okay," Wish assured, wishing they'd all look away. She shifted upright again and took another step, watching her feet, and below her boots a gap revealed churning water. "Oh fuck this place, fuck this place to hell."

She was shaking as much as she had been after encountering that kid. One unsteady step after another, hands up with cocked elbows. Stiffly continuing like an animate cactus.

"You're doing well, Wild Wish," Newk called out from a little way back.

Wish smiled. *That* attention she didn't mind.

"Oh we're so formal here," Emi countered it, though. "But the

Most Honourable *Miss* Wild Wish, if you will."

"I thought –" Newk said, a little thrown, but didn't finish that thought, as Wish took another abrupt step and pulled the squad with her. Once she was steady again, Newk asked, "I shouldn't use the full name?"

"Pretty sure *you* can call her whatever you like," Rue said from behind, far too loud for Wish's tastes. So Rue was going to replace prejudiced hostility with lewdness. Wish picked up her speed, to get them moving on from this bridge and the conversation alike. Her feet picked out the solid spots without looking, helping her to keep her eyes up and away from the water that roared a good two storeys below – the unstoppable, terrible water – hell – she moved faster.

"Easy!" Rue shouted. "You ain't dragging us across, Wild!"

"I won't have to if you keep up!" Wish called back, making good progress. Flashes of Tate came into view, waiting at the other end.

"Ah, ah!" one of the squad protested, unstable.

"Come on, girls!" Wish swelled. This was working; they could just *race* across, the bridge would take them, and – there was a cry behind, followed by another, then a tug as Wish was pulled sharply back, spinning to see Emi tugged, too, and down the line Fixit had fallen – halfway through the side of the bridge, arms flapping. The others scrambled for something to hold onto, pulling at each other. Wish hit her foot and banged a knee on a root. Emi bounced away, muttering something angry, trying to steady herself, but the struggling eased and Fixit was pulled back upright, into the middle of the bridge, Rue in front of her snarling a warning. They all froze, and Wish felt the entire platoon, either side of the river, was frozen too, staring in shock. The squad looked into each other's eyes – Rue in a half-crouch with an arm around Fixit's waist, Newk by them on her knees, Dakoda and Pound clutching the side of the bridge beyond Fixit, Emi with her hands clasped on the rope like she meant to toss it aside, Wish, herself, down in a crouch.

Wish said, slowly, "You see. Nothing to be afraid of."

It took a second, but they started laughing.

22

Dozens of fortresses lay claim to being historically unbreakable. The World Watcher Tower in northernmost Drail, Fulkaich Castle in eastern Farne, Bascane in Azir and the Slanik Weeping Citadel. Often it is untrue, if you look to a time when these locations were not at their prime. However, with regards the One War, it can be said of Highscythe Ward: though the city was not impenetrable, once the Drail settled in, they made quite certain it would not be taken.

Dueley's Comprehensive: The One War in 10 Volumes (Vol. 6), p. 130

Highscythe was a hive of stacked chambers under an enormous dome, with bare scraps of sunlight entering cracks above. The lattice of mostly vaulted rooms created a vertical city, lined up in uneven rows, and it was alive with activity, a bazaar of soldiers and weapons, with tents and vehicles set before the rigid stone buildings. Netts scuttled away while Donut mustered up some steaming broth, and by the time the chunky stew had cooled the Dread soldier was back with directions. He led Maringdale through the noisy crowds and up a maze of steep stairs without hesitation.

"You know this city well," Maringdale said, broadening her already long strides to keep up with the sprightly Netts. He gave her a cheeky look over his shoulder and she sensed his true feelings, that he was improvising but confident it'd work out.

After a series of muddling turns and ups and downs, they finally reached a tight tunnel that came to an oak door indistinguishable from a dozen others they had passed. Netts stepped back, taking in something that satisfied him. He wrapped his knuckles on the door, called out in Slanik, and the door was opened by a weary man in light Dread uniform. He gave Maringdale and Donut sceptical looks as Netts explained where they had come from, then he led them into a dark chamber. He had them sit at a wooden table lit by candles while he disappeared through another door to fetch the man in charge – Battle Chief Hark. The otherwise sparse brick chamber, with a small kitchenette, evidently connected to a much larger building beyond, because it took almost twenty minutes before the guard returned.

A bald, rapidly moving man in a stiff officer's jacket entered with him, bearing the same insignia as Battle Chief Ways. He had a thin, skeletal build and a narrow, hawkish bald head with eyes that stared intensely. Battle Chief Hark worked his gloved hands through one another, impatient to get back to his work, and Maringdale was quite sure she'd feel his hostility even without her gift.

Netts jumped to his feet and saluted, and Hark said, without introduction, "We got word from your company last night. They got waylaid and missed the train, but they'll reach us in two days."

"Sir?" Netts frowned.

"Came under fire on the road to Junker."

"Were there heavy losses?"

"Do I look like a bulletin service?" Hark waved a dismissive hand and turned to Maringdale. "I believe you are here to report to me. What did the Purification turn up?"

Maringdale held his gaze, considering that was presumptuous of him. "I'm Constans Maringdale, third class –"

"I know who you are," the officer snapped. "Presumably you have something more important to share than *that?*"

Maringdale felt something burning behind her eyes, but answered calmly, "We have reason to believe the Comity insurgents who infiltrated Cleave gained information about your other sites and are either targeting them themselves or have relayed that information to other interests. Chief Ways' men were intercepted on the way to warn Gloven at Fever. By the sounds of it, the insurgents may have ambushed Gloven's company, too."

Hark snorted, unimpressed. "Ways and Gloven were exposed. The sky will freeze before any Comity spies find their way into Highscythe."

"We came in on a train of thousands of people. Entering a city of over a million. Are you sure this location is secure?"

Hark eyed her with quiet disdain, not appreciating her show of strength like Ways. "Indeed, the enemy might come in the guise of Purification officers, mightn't they?"

Donut gave a squeak, and Maringdale clicked her tongue at him before locking her eyes back on the officer. "Or they might be working within the Dread Corps itself – that's the impression I get when someone does not cooperate." Dammit, that was Panderlair coming through, but she couldn't help it. "Battle Chief Hark, isn't it?"

"You accuse me?" Hark snapped. "I told Ways it was absurd, inviting the Purification in, and the Arrow Council agrees with me. You shouldn't have bothered coming. We're done here."

"You don't get to make that choice," Maringdale cut in hotly, letting that Panderlair energy flow now. "We're the Purification, not some low-rent constabulary – we're the one force that the Dread Corps cannot turn away. And believe it or not, we're here to help."

Hark glared hatefully. He wanted to hurt her. He had systems of torture, she could read it in his feelings – was considering how painfully he could dissect her. But he also had that slightest doubt – something Ways lacked. A concern that she really could make life complicated. He said, "Evidently I'm not being clear. We neither want nor need your help. Why would we?"

"You believe no one can get at you, for starters," Maringdale said.

His eyes brimmed with disdain, but he shifted tack as he saw authority alone wasn't driving her away. "Well I cannot stop you from scouting the city, if you please. Just do not presume to try and gain entry here. And do not disturb me again. Fearsmith –" He lowered his gaze to Netts.

"Netts, sir."

"Netts will be keeping an eye on you."

Maringdale ignored Netts' flaring disagreement to say, "You want me to go, first explain your operation here: who knows what, entrances and exits, resources coming in – any angle that might be used to gain access."

Hark paused. "That's a short conversation. This unit has a storage structure behind us. This entrance is the only one and I have a man watching it day and night. There's one other access point, an emergency roof hatch, which we've sealed, and the structure is packed in with concrete and earth. It's practically soundproof. There's a reason we're still active here while the others have pulled out. Highscythe will not fall. No one's getting in."

Maringdale digested that, accepting he honestly believed it. But his confidence didn't mean no one would try. She said, "I'll be the one to make sure of that."

Biting on the Dread officer's dismissive attitude, Maringdale stalked the tunnels of Highscythe with balled fists and an intense focus. She used that resentment for Hark to focus on feeling for something similar. She moved between halls, reaching out for surrounding moods and attitudes, letting it all flood in. Starting at the Dread company's hall, she found an absence of feeling there, and little around the place – and accordingly spiralled away from there. Netts and Donut trotted behind her, watching, jumping out of her way when she changed direction. Netts asked, "What the hell's she doing?"

"Shh," Donut warned. "She needs space."

"For what? Sniffing out threats like a squirrel after nuts?"

"Exactly," Donut hissed, with genuine concern they might throw her off.

They were barely blips on her radar, though, as she sifted through the other feelings, blanking out irrelevant patterns as easily as closing shutters on different windows. Fear of an imminent attack, gone. Fear of reprisal from superiors, gone. Longing for home, pain at lost loved ones, yearning for recognition – gone,

gone, *gone*. She blotted them out bit by bit and narrowed it down to those who were searching, anticipating, about to take action. Darting down tunnels to get closer to such feelings, she whittled them down, too – rushed into a mess hall and discovered a pair of snipers preparing to scout the city perimeter. Anxiety over an uncertain enemy – she found a quartermaster waiting by a radio for news on milk supplies. As she tuned these out, the pull got lighter. Still there was something more, someone to check.

She picked up her pace, running now, between the central locations of Highscythe. Past the vast chamber of a pillared church warren, through an open park area with more rusty old playground equipment than grass. As the search stretched out, they must've explored half the city before Maringdale finally honed in on something that felt right. Secretive, worried, important. Isolated – didn't belong here, afraid of exposure. Concerned by a particularly dangerous, uncertain enemy.

Maringdale stopped at the door of a terracotta brick chamber, one of the cheap, basic cells of the Highscythe hive. Beyond it, feelings bubbled hotter than one of Donut's broths. She said, under her breath, "This is it. This is where we want to be."

She took a step back, with Netts and Donut parting around her, and nodded at the door, the way Panderlair used to wordlessly indicate she go ahead. The two idiot men looked from the door back to her. Netts was questioning how in hell she had any idea what was in there, Donut was just stuck on what exactly she wanted him to do.

"Castor's sake," Maringdale hissed, then tried the handle herself. Locked, and her rattling it immediately sent a wave of panic through the people inside. A familiar fear: *they've found us*.

She whipped out her pistol and fired at the lock, the shot echoing down the boxed-in Highscythe street, drawing shrieks further away, then she heaved the door open and advanced on someone screaming in clumsy Drail: "Don't shoot, not in here!"

Feeling the severity of the feelings, Maringdale quickly lowered the revolver and drew her sword, crossing the threshold towards a man with a ragged striped top and long hair hanging out of a blue bandanna. Behind him was a table littered with paper and a pile of small wooden barrels. To the left, a set of bed rolls – and a woman, lifting a rifle.

"Dulcy, neun!" the man shouted a warning in Farnish, waving at the barrels. But the woman – same striped rags as him, dark complexion – didn't listen, desperate. Maringdale felt the intentions before the actions, aim and fire, and she swept into the room, putting the barrels between her and the gun. She sensed hesitation, then a new idea: use the gun as a club. The woman charged, swinging, but Maringdale's sword was already up, turning the rifle aside, scraping the metal under its barrel. Maringdale stepped back and the woman fell aside. But knew she couldn't stop, had to kill – Maringdale spun with a simple elegant feint and a stab.

The man cried and jumped forward to push them apart, and Maringdale ducked, slipping the sword out of the startled woman's gut and aiming it at him instead. He froze, terrified. Dark featured, too, a thin moustache, classic Farnish complexion.

"You were planning to bomb the Dread Corps?" Maringdale accused, and in his shocked internal response, she felt the truth. *How did they know?* Clear even before he started shaking his head.

Netts whistled, impressed, entering the room with his rifle half ready, as Donut hurriedly crouched over the woman. She gargled blood, twitched and was still. The Farnish man struggled to keep in his horror.

"Who're you working with?" Maringdale demanded, and he snapped his attention back to her. He steeled himself to resist at all costs, putting on a brave face. Only, unlucky for him, Maringdale knew his real feelings: terrified, unsure of his own mettle. She said, "I'm an intention mage from the Purification. I already know your secrets. It's just a matter of you admitting them."

In credit to the Farne, he resisted showing his shock, but she felt that, too. His eyes ran from her to Netts, taking in his uniform, and he said something in quiet Farnish. She didn't understand the word but got the meaning in his feelings: *how could she work with them?*

Then a quick decision – it didn't matter, he had one last hope – Maringdale lunged before he finished the thought, slicing down the back of his leg as he turned. To do what? Punch the kegs or tip them over in the hope of igniting them? Either way, he got nowhere near, crumpling with a scream. He rolled, clutching the wound, cursing her. Maringdale patted his cheek with the flat of her blade.

"You're a long way from home. Working for Khibba?" she asked, and beneath the pain sensed new hope, that she was off. "No. Partisans? Not this well-equipped. Stanclif sent you?"

He struggled to steel himself again, to lock his mind in the way those completely inexperienced with intention mages always did. It meant tensing physically, while flaring up the very emotions he wanted to hide.

Maringdale crouched and said, "Have you anything to do with waders?" *Surprise,* no. "Are you targeting other sites?" *Resisting –* trying not to think of them. "Ah, so you're not alone."

The Farnish man bit down on the pain and glared into her eyes. His defiance strengthened those emotions: confident that she was too late anyway. There was someone else, somewhere else, she would not reach. His senses weakened, though, as his eyes drooped. Blood was seeping from his leg over the floor, lots more than there should be. Shit. He'd lose consciousness soon. She clicked at Netts. "The other locations, tell me now." He mugged confusion. "Cleave, Fever, Highscythe – Ways said there were six, what are the others?"

"What? No way am I –"

"Give me those names before we lose this bastard!"

"Dudden, Null and Wick," Netts blurted out, and Maringdale focused back on the weakening man. She recited them and he made a clear effort not to listen, squeezing his eyes closed.

"Dudden?" Maringdale repeated loudly. "Wick? Nell?"

"Null," Netts corrected.

"Null?" There was something there. An unrest in the Farnish man, avoidance of the word. Willing her to move on. "That's the one. That's where his friends are." Maringdale stood as the man opened his eyes again, unable to hide the truth. She turned to Netts. "How far to Null?"

Maringdale sensed a desperate emotion: the man drew on all he had left and shoved forward. She sidestepped easily, casually, but

Netts, startled, fired. The Farnish man's chest burst open as he was thrown back. Donut gasped as Maringdale threw Netts an irritated look. Their lead was dead. Had he done it deliberately? She blocked Donut out to focus on the Dread soldier. Tetchy, gun still ready, apologetic. He hadn't meant to.

"It's fine," Maringdale murmured, stepping over the body to look at the papers on the table. Plans for the layout of Highscythe. Targets circled. "I got what I needed."

Once Maringdale had found an officer's billet with a telephone system, she reported back to the Purification that she needed to continue west to Null. She could unravel a murderous conspiracy in moments, but she felt impotent using this big black box rimmed with brass, a cable curling out to the pair of metal cones she held up, one to the ear and one to the mouth. The dry, distracted lady on the other end of line said they already had someone in Null, and Maringdale's power didn't stretch down these unnatural cables to give her any helpful insights in how to handle this. She explained that she would assist whoever was in Null, but wasn't sure if the woman was even listening, the line muffled by sounds of movement and chatter in the background.

"Your efforts are noted," the woman said, "and you will be given new orders accordingly."

"Accordingly?" Maringdale snapped. "What's that mean?"

"Officer Maringdale?" the operator checked, though she knew full well who she was. "I've got a note regarding the death of Sin Sight Panderlair. There are questions to be answered. You are to stay where you are until the matter is resolved. Please find lodgings and await instructions."

"Lodgings? Time is an issue here, and –"

"You have your orders, good day." Something clicked, cutting off the buzz of the connection.

Maringdale stared at the receiver, braced to smash it against the table, but restrained herself. Damn them. She turned to Netts, the weaselly man watching with his hands deep in his pockets. He was holding in a suggestion: it might've been premature to send Donut to secure the fastest transport to Null. Travelling now would trigger a hunt; there was no greater crime than defying the Purification. If it wasn't an arrogant officer holding her back, it was the self-righteous administrators in the Arrow. Never mind how important her work could be to the Dread Corps. Maringdale said, "Take me back to Hark."

Netts gave her a your-funeral shrug and moved ahead.

They got an equally frosty reception when they reached Hark's hideout, the man ready to shout them out before he even entered the room, but he paused when Maringdale informed him they'd killed two Farnish sappers. He listened in silence as she explained that they had explosives and his location marked on a map, and it wouldn't have mattered if no one could get in here – they would've buried the whole district. Hark's emotions were duelling between scolding Maringdale's cavalier approach and grim admission that a crisis had been averted. As she finished, he leaned towards the latter and said, "And you've come back looking for a thank you?"

"No, sir," Maringdale said, polite as possible. "Before the man died, he revealed they have accomplices in Null. I intend to hunt them down, but my superiors don't appreciate the urgency of the situation."

Hark eyed her. Resentment twisted to satisfaction as he correctly read her position. "You want the glory of the hunt but the Purification are nothing if not *practical* about such matters." He scoffed. "I suspect you already have people in Null."

"As do you. And you had people here, yet it was *me* who found those spies. Within hours of arriving."

"Assuming this is all true." Hark turned to Netts as though her word was not enough. "You can vouch for her, Fearsmith?"

"What's that?" Netts straightened up, his lack of full attention further irking Hark, which he quickly reacted to: "Um – absolutely, sir. Two Grade-A Farnish nut jobs, we found. Kegs of Azrian black powder."

"With more men in Null?"

"Seemed so, sir," Netts said.

"Seemed so?"

Netts gave Maringdale a look to rally his confidence. "No, it was clear. They were here for us, sir – could see it the way that prick looked at me." He curled his nose and looked like he wanted to spit in disgust, but resisted.

Netts' casual disrespect only combined with Maringdale's success to aggravate Hark. He held it in, to release later. He had a location in mind. Maybe a woman. Recognising that intention almost made Maringdale cringe. A weak man who'd punish a whore for his own frustrations. But she had to put those judgements aside.

Hark said, "Go to Null. I'll notify the Purification it's Dread Corps business and I will inform Dread Mage Starling. After all, you may be too slow to save the day there, too." He twisted that in, like he would enjoy it. "As this is a Dread Corps operation, Fearsmith Netts will continue to escort you. Your travel arrangements are your own problem."

"What?" Netts started, his attention arrested now. "But my company –"

"Thank you, Battle Chief," Maringdale said, eager to get on with it. With Hark's clearance, the rest was details. Donut was more than capable of finding them good transport, and she could get Netts in line along the way.

23

Precious few nations managed to stay completely out of the global conflict created by the One War. Those who refused to fight invariably still supported one side or another in a peripheral way, from the Jendig metal mines that supplied Drail shipyards to the Gonish diplomatic service who were instrumental in advancing Comity communications. Even the famously reclusive barkmen were drawn in, with various clashes seen on the Step River, though the exact manner of their involvement remains poorly documented.
Empires of the Rocc, Xanthial, p. 549

Most of the scouts had had a good chance to rest by the time Rock Squad crept over the bridge, last, moving slowly to protect the Reaper. The two carrying it, Cade and Fuse, got a round of cheers and jeers as they arrived. Cade, red-faced and huffing, looked like she might pass out, but Tate insisted they keep moving. By Brade's account, and a million popular legends, there was no way they wanted to be caught in Eardung after dark without an escort. They had to reach the nearest barkman commune and ingratiate themselves to the locals. Brade made that sound guaranteed, but Wish shared the girls' general uneasiness.

"Think any of us could name a single person, living or dead, known to have ingratiated themselves with barkmen?" Dakoda asked, walking through the trees alongside Wild and Newk.

"Sir Robert Smartwether," Wish said. "Although he might be made up."

"Might be mad, too," Dakoda said. "One of Brade's friends? You know their sort. Rich guys carving up the world from leather armchairs, drinking musk wine. They visit places like this for fun, and the forest lays down a carpet for them, doesn't it?"

"Is that not the Stanclif way?" Newk asked, genuinely, and Dakoda gave her a raised eyebrow. "I mean, the world opens its arms for your Civilisation. Your people."

"My people," Dakoda said, "ain't *his* people. We work every minute of sunlight, and wouldn't know about the world inviting anything, seeing as we got no time to get out there, let alone the money. Wish, you ever travel before the war?"

"I went to Eabd with my family."

"Just across the Strait? That's practically still Stanclif, shit. Half the people in this war, they're here because it got them a chance to travel!"

"Is that why you signed up?" Newk asked, unwittingly venturing into a favourite fireside game: what the hell are we all doing here anyway? She'd asked the wrong person, though, and Wish shifted to put herself between them, seeing Dakoda's eyes darken.

"I didn't," Dakoda said. Newk looked ready to ask more, but Wish gestured ahead.

"Ladies. We're in unfamiliar terrain, home to god-knows what. I think we oughta focus." They did so, leaving the chat unfinished, and Wish whispered an aside to Newk, "Later."

After another ten minutes walking, word came down the line for everyone to hold positions, keep quiet; they had contact. Dollemore hurried past to the front, to assist in whatever was going on, and Wish caught her sleeve, asking if she should come too, leadership team and all. Dollemore gave her a careful look and said, "No."

So Wish crouched to rest with her squad and smiled at Newk when the newbie gave her a concerned look. The wait dragged out, the woods darkening, until girls started to shift like they sensed trouble, hands resting on guns. Wish whispered, "Keep steady, sure everything's fine."

Rue gave her offensive eyes, ready for violence.

"It's good, all clear!" announced one of Sun Squad, rushing down the line. "Everyone come forward, we're in. You're not going to believe it." Her relief was tinged with just enough disbelief that Rue actually tightened her grip on her gun. Wish gave her a warning look, which further hardened her face. Great.

Slowly, the platoon continued through the trees to encounter a third marvel of the day. The Edge Falls, tick; Twisted Bridge, tick; a barkman commune? *No one* got to see that. And Wish felt her own skin tightening as they got closer, reaching a clearing.

"Lower your guns," Larkin hissed.

Wish pushed Rue's rifle barrel down, and held onto it as she took another step to properly take in the commune.

Most immediately apparent were the workbenches, which scouts were already standing between. The flat platforms were supported on multitudes of living branches like the pillars of the Twisted Bridge, positioned at varying, seemingly random, heights. On and around them, sometimes resting against trees, were long poles, some smooth but most knobbly with imperfections, all with unique tips, curved or pointed or otherwise fashioned to suit particular purposes. Around *them,* leaning against the trees or sometimes upright, were flat shavings of bark, big as a person and weirdly free-standing.

The indication that this was more than a mere gathering of scattered tools came from the trees themselves – most of those facing into this area had large areas of bare bark, skinned like potatoes. The patches were one or two feet wide, rising as much as six feet tall, at ground level and above. Wish followed some up and realised another curiosity: the branches were *organised.* It was especially clear higher up, where the trees had been woven together in unusual patterns, forming delicate weaves through the canopy – grown together, like the bridge. The purpose was unclear, but it looked amazing.

"Oh hell!" Pound gasped to the left, stepping back, and half a dozen others raised their guns.

Wish ordered, "Steady! Weapons down!" and her own voice sounded loud and vulgar in this special place. The squad eyed her fearfully. She looked to what had spooked Pound, though, and finally saw the barkmen.

They definitely warranted an *oh hell.*

Brade, Tate, Dollemore, and most of Sun Squad were scattered through the commune ahead watching her twitchy girls, and the barkmen stood alongside them, around them. One of the upright tree shavings turned towards Wish. It was alive – a flat, seven-foot-high stretch of tree bark standing alongside Captain Brade. It didn't have legs, but a mass of vine-like roots feeling around the ground to position it. Likewise, no arms but, now she looked, dozens of reaching twigs and branches stretching slightly from its edges. And once she spotted that one, she realised there were dozens more, natural, plank-like beings rotating on mobile roots, bending slightly at hinges in their bark, reminiscent of an insect's carapace.

The rest of Boot Squad joined Pound in their quiet cursing.

"Welcome to Heart Spot," Brade announced, wearing a big grin. "At least, that's what it translates to?" He turned to Dollemore for guidance on that and she nodded. "They've agreed to let us stay the night. Then on to Riverside in the morning, where this chap" – he indicated the living bark thing next to him – "has a brother with a boat."

No one said anything nor moved, all ogling the barkmen. Brade alone seemed unfazed by how damn weird this place was. But Wish considered his plan, and looked up to the sky, what little of the blue was visible through the canopy. She said, "At the risk of being unpopular –"

"Whoa, Wild Wish!" an unhelpful voice put in. "Facing your greatest fear!"

Wish turned to spot whoever had said it, and caught Cade sniggering alongside one of her squad. She forced an awkward smile. "Nevertheless, needs to be said. We've got an hour or two left of daylight, don't we? Why are we stopping?"

"Because an hour or two of daylight is *all* we've got," Tate answered. "Settle down, they've got clearings where we can rest and the means for providing warmth and light. Otherwise, as long as we're in their forest, there's to be no use of fire or combustibles –" Protests swept through the scouts, which Wish heard her own voice adding to. No fire meant no cooking, smoking, hot drinks – no *comforts*. But the captain went on, loudly, "That's their terms and we will not disobey them to so much as to light a match. Outside the commune, Eardung is a wilderness we can't hope to navigate. Am I understood?" Tate gave it only a second of disgruntled quiet. "Scouts, I can't hear you!"

"Sir, yes, sir!" the scouts chorused loudly, putting their frustration into the response.

The mysteries of Eardung kept unfolding into the night, as the scouts set up their tents. The density of the trees made night especially dark, and a chill crept in, until the barkmen did something and, high above and dotted over tree trunks, small green lights started to glow. It was a fungus of some kind, little orbs that hadn't been noticeable during the day, surrounding the scouts like friendly stars. It also got warmer, the forest a strangely comfortable temperature, though when they held their hands near the orbs the scouts found they were not giving off heat.

Wild Wish sat on the ground (oddly gently warm), close to Newk, the circle of her squad before her. They should've been gathered around a campfire, but instead had an empty space between them, ideal for tossing dice into. Emi leered as she took her turn. Wish watched Newk, smiling and starting to relax, actually joining in the jokes and quips. When she rolled her dice, and scored a terrible double three, the girls whooped at her poor luck. Pound said, "That deserves a forfeit, Newk! How about you tell us what the hell you're doing here?"

Newk paused as though expecting hostility with such a question, but the tone, and the other girls' expectant looks, showed it came from a place of genuine curiosity. After the week or two that they'd been trekking through enemy territory, Newk's mad conquest wasn't known yet. She dressed up the real answer by saying, "Your people and mine are very different, but we all trust that Stanclif stands for civilisation. The Drail would destroy that. That is why I'm here."

The circle gave that a moment's reverent thought, then they broke into laughter as one. Wish had difficulty stifling her own amusement. Newk's brow furrowed, though she was clearly finding it hard not to smile at the infectious humour.

"I'm sorry" – Pound held up a hand – "it's not – I mean – that's *noble*, right? But you could've stayed out of this, couldn't you?"

"With my nation burning under Drail rule? My family murdered?" Newk said. "No."

It quietened the circle, Pound's humour evaporating, so Wish tentatively came in, "Where she comes from, Fireti, they've been at war longer than us. Behind Newk's admirable ambitions, she also wants brutal revenge."

"Seems a hard thing to attain," Fixit said. "Against a whole empire?"

"I'll do my best," Newk said. "Is it so strange? Did none of you join to do the same?"

"Oh shit no," Pound cried. "I signed up because they let in my little brother, and the hell I was going to let *him* come back a hero and not me."

"I was promised steady pay," Fixit confided. "There was a certain demand for medical skills on the front, and not so much demand back home when the miners left to fight."

"Two pints of rum and a pack of cigarettes on signing, they said," Rue said. "That did it for me. Only they wanted to put me in a factory finishing bullets. I wasn't having that."

"Got more bone than brains in that skull, that's why," Dakoda said. "Weren't any factories to fill around my way. I was in a trench before they even questioned if it was a good idea arming women."

"You got lucky," Pound said, her laughter undercutting Dakoda's harsh tone. "They wanted me scrubbing laundry while shells fell around us, wouldn't even give me a knife to defend myself. Until the –"

"Bomb hit the officers' mess and you got up a rifle to hold back two green-coats single-handedly!" the squad completed the story in chorus, all familiar with Pound's tale. She swung a hand with mock irritation.

"And you?" Newk asked Wild Wish. "Why give up your nice village?"

Wish bit her lip. Of course, *everyone* knew Swelig was lovely. It was the Hall of Heroes to which they would all return, if she had her way. Green expanses, clear summer days, wild flowers swaying in the breeze before the cliff-top views of the sea. People were ridiculously friendly and everyone knew everyone. It was also a village locked in traditions two centuries old, though, where everyone *judged* everyone.

Wish bit her lip. The other scouts knew she'd believed the war would open her horizons to travel, naive of the dangers ahead. That she had a lame sister and poor parents that a soldier's salary could help support. But really her father made good enough money mending boots, and so could she, and she had scarcely travelled Stanclif, so those were feeble excuses. With Newk asking, her keen eyes watching, Wish felt an urge to reveal the truth of it. She said, "Swelig is perfect in itself. But I had to come to war because none of *you* were there."

It got a round of laughter and Pound mimicked vomiting, finger in her mouth, but Newk didn't look satisfied. Wish smiled and diverted, "But my peasant background's the least interesting; we've got a hero in our midst – tell them *your* deal, Emi."

"Me?" Emi grinned, dragging her knees up under her chin. "You know me. I've always been here." It got less sniggers, no one ever quite sure how to interpret her.

Wish told Newk, "Emi was a Farnish battle mage before the war began."

"Not true!" Emi raised a finger. "I was a *court* mage, consulting on mining contracts. The negotiations just turned violent a lot. But if you want war stories" – she pointed at Tate, talking sombrely with Dollemore and Brade – *"she* killed thirty Khib spiders at the Battle of the Bald. Last woman standing."

"Only woman there in the first place, most likely," Dakoda said.

"I heard she was awarded the Saint Cross for taking out a machine gun in the Azrian campaign," Pound said.

"There were no machine guns in Azir," Dakoda countered that, too.

"Well something like it, whatever! She kicked arse. She's kicked arse in every continent, hasn't she?"

"That's what I heard," Fixit said, quietly. "Captain Tate is famous. And I don't think it's so silly, wanting to fight for the Empire. I'd as soon leave the Drail alone, if they'd leave us alone, but they won't. Bly knows we've seen enough people buried over it."

"Buried at best," Dakoda agreed.

Rue huffed, about to be objectionable. "Well, I could do without being *here*, anyway. They should've given us warning, whole night without a smoke. Would've filled my lungs on the way in."

"It'll do you good," Fixit pointed out. "Help you run faster."

"Think we'll need to make a quick getaway?" Pound said, smiling but with a hint of genuine concern. The barkmen were, after all, still looming. They didn't come close, but they were everywhere, leaning around the trees, watching without eyes. The way they moved was unnatural, with a tap of roots against the foliage.

"I don't know how the Captain trusts them," Rue said, not quite done. "You know they can suck people dry. Smother them and drain them of blood."

"Where'd you hear that?" Emi asked, picking up the dice. "No one's ever had much to do with this area."

"Except Sir Robert Smartwether," Wish reminded them.

"Fuck Sir Robert Smartwether," Rue said. "I bet *he* smoked out here."

"How much?" Emi replied, eyes lighting up. "Ten bob says he didn't."

Rue glared like she knew it was a bad bet, but spat on her hand and held it out. "You're on."

The mage grinned as she shook, then twisted and yelled through the trees, "Captain Brade – did you know we wouldn't be able to smoke here?"

The man's uncertain response was too quiet to hear, from across the camp where he stood with Tate and their bark friend. He stood, making apologies, and came over, leaning on a tall stick. "What's that?"

"You knew we couldn't smoke here? No fire allowed?"

Brade's smile didn't falter, though he looked like he suspected a trap. He said, "Sir Robert Smartwether's account mentioned it, yes. It gave him some trouble." Rue punched the ground, and fumbled in her pockets for coins while the others jeered. Brade tilted his head to one side. "My apologies, I forgot how you ladies enjoyed your vices."

"We *enjoy* getting laid and swearing," Rue growled, "but we *need* to smoke."

Brade kept smiling, fondly taking in the camp of grubby, battle-worn women. They must've been a long way from what he was used to, with their smell, untidy hair, shabbily adjusted men's clothes and filth-darkened skin. He said, "Respectfully, where we're going, it's probably a good thing you're not wasting your supply now."

It quietened the circle. This dashing, erudite man, whose presence alone should've cheered up some of the girls, had to come and remind them of the death-mission ahead.

Wish tried to find a positive and nodded to Brade's leg. "You're walking, Captain. So I guess our odds are improving."

"What? Oh yes." He held up the stick he was using for support, a smoothly finished cane that the barkmen must've provided. "Dollemore had been doing a wonderful job. I'll be fit to walk freely soon enough, I imagine." He twirled the stick with practised grace.

"Then you're gonna help us fight the horrors of Low Slane?" Pound asked.

"Well it has been said, by some, that I'm the third best swordsman in the world."

"Third?" Wish immediately cried, to a backing of incredulous agreement. "Not even second?"

"Barely on the podium!"

"That's second loser!"

From Brade's smile, he was getting exactly the response he'd expected, lightening the mood, and Wish appreciated that. But Rue came in venomously, being Rue: *"Respectfully,* Captain, we were doing fine before you came along. None of us asked for a male chaperone."

Brade held Rue's gaze for a moment, face hardened but not unkind. "Well I won't tell your girlfriends back home if you don't, Corporal Rue. But you'll be thanking me before we're through. For now, by all means, I'll give you my leave. Ladies."

With that, Brade walked back to Tate, almost swaggering as he limped, leaning on that stick. Wish jumped in just before Rue could make another nasty comment: "On that joyful note, I reckon it's time to turn in. We'll need our wits tomorrow."

It almost sounded authoritative.

Wild Wish wandered into the trees to relieve herself. She couldn't go far for risk of losing the light of the commune, but wasn't sure where was safe to pee. The barkmen had started sliding onto those bare patches on the trees and kind of fusing with them, like peeled off wallpaper loosely slapped back into place. The trees were apparently their homes, where their little root feelers dug in and took sustenance or whatever. It made it unclear if Wish was pissing on someone's doorstep, or even on *someone*, so it wasn't the most relaxed experience, and when Captain Tate whispered to announce her presence it made Wish jump with a yelp.

"Wish, a quick word."

Rapidly retying her belt, Wish gave Tate the eye to question if she'd been watching, but the captain was looking back into the commune. Wish asked, "I'm allowed to pee here, aren't I?"

"Damned if I know. I'm holding it in until I can see what I'm doing." Possibly serious. "Wish. How are you coping?"

"Me? I'm fine. Why wouldn't I be?"

"We all felt it, what you went through today. This morning, and the bridge."

"What I went through?" Wish's voice pitched higher, with a little laugh. "It got us all didn't it? Quite a day, sure. But I'm fine."

"Sure," Tate said. "It weighs on all our shoulders. But it was in your hands."

Wish merely grinned back, not sure what the captain wanted her to say. Some deep reflection on the hardships required to complete their mission? An admission that her nerves were fraying day by day, especially since seeing Loose – *No* – and then Sarge, Small. And how many men had she killed on Green Rise? Was some sagely heart-to-heart coming? *You know why I chose you?* Or *we've all done terrible things . . .* Maybe a story about the Khib spiders.

"I'm sending Brade with you," Tate said, though, and Wish's gut clenched. "When we get to Devil's River. You'll have the safest route, and I have faith in you. Also, he likes you."

"You meaning *me* or . . ."

"You meaning you, Wish. Play your cards right, you might come out of this war with more than that farm to go back to."

"I don't *own* a farm. Yet."

"Exactly. He's a very capable soldier, by all accounts. Well respected."

"Third-best swordsman in the world, I heard."

"Only third?" Tate sounded disappointed. "Anyway. I thought it might help to know. Once we split, you won't be alone going into Slane."

"Ah ha," Wish said. Between Brade and Emi she'd have the command of Boot Squad pretty well sewn up. So she'd failed the test today, whatever the test was. Tate paused, something else to add. Did she want Wish to apologise? Ask if she was upset over the choice over killing a child, or, in truth, over how *easily* she could've done it? Confirm that she was in control on that bridge and it was no big deal? Wonder exactly how much it hurt that she'd recently seen three friends die badly? And hell, Colt was gone too, no one even *mentioned* her.

But Tate said something else altogether: "You didn't want to sit on the Reaper." A statement, saying she saw *that* as the problem. Wish frowned. "You think anything would've been different if I'd put Cade on it? Oksy? Taken the gun myself? It needed doing and it needed doing well. The rest is unimportant. The time to question it, any of it, is once we survive, and only then. But accept this, at least: you killed those men so no one else had to." Tate's gaze lingered on Wish a second, sadness in her usually stony expression.

It was almost certainly something she kept telling herself, and she gave a slight nod that said she knew that this was not enough. But it was something. With that, the captain walked away.

Wish recalled the churning, dismembering brutality of the bullets tearing the – she physically turned away from the thought, squeezing her eyes shut. Tate was right. If not her, someone else would've done it. Or if they hadn't, the Drail might've overrun their people and be swarming towards Swelig, burning fields and chaining necks. That's why all those men had to die and Loose whimpered *no*. And if they could keep fighting, putting one atrocity behind another until the final peace was accomplished, hell, Tate thought Wish might marry a swashbuckling toff met on the battlefield.

And the scouts thought *her* dreams were wild.

24

Hep Hattrik's efforts to normalise witlacing simultaneously involved preaching the dangers of earth-touchers. Both spread their powers through touch, he said, but witlacers touched life where "dirt-minders" touched death. A misleading and simplistic stance: while witlacers do indeed manipulate human life, earth-touchers more accurately manipulate non-human life, through contact with the elements. The elements, surely, carry more life than any one person.

Hattrik's message was simple and evocative, though, creating a dichotomy whose prejudices survive to this day: on the one hand, the magic of humanity and life, on the other, the magic of the inhuman and death.

We the Mindless: a Brief History of
Ostracised Magic, Lombardo, p. 45

The sounds of low talking and spoons in pots stirred Wild Wish; apparently she'd been tardy in waking. She yawned and stretched and gently prodded Rue with a foot. Her companion growled the warning of an angry dog and, as was her tradition, Wish crawled out of the tent to let her rise on her own terms.

The forest of Eardung made for a dark morning, though hints of blue sky and sunlight were visible through the thick canopy. A few tents down, Oksy was preparing beans, the redheaded newbie, Angles, sitting beside her with sleep-smothered patience. Trust Oksy to endear a new recruit. There was no fire to cook by, so Oksy was merely stirring spices into a pan, but it smelt good. Wish casually slipped on her stamps, took her mug and wandered over, making like she just happened to be in the area.

"You want in you'll contribute," Oksy warned without looking up.

"Next time I've got a tin simmering, I promise," Wish said, crouching. Ordinarily, she'd raise her hands to warm them on Oksy's (now absent) miniature stove, but she realised she wasn't actually cold. She breathed out and couldn't see her breath. Despite their travelling north, the temperature had been comfortable through the night.

"They control the climate." Oksy guessed Wish's thoughts. "This whole forest is like one big living, breathing –"

"House," Wish said.

"I was going to say organism," Oksy finished. She gave the beans a final stir and started serving. Angles stooped forward eagerly, metal mug in hand, and Wish was quick to join her, seeing others starting to emerge from tents.

Wolfing down spoonfuls of beans, Wish noticed Oksy was eyeing the surroundings carefully. The morning shade made it hard to pick out the barkmen, but some were clearly lingering at the edges of camp, like sheaves of wheat, watching them. Wish said, "You don't trust them, Oks?"

"They're strange. I didn't get the best night's sleep."

"Well, the next stop's Low Slane, sure you'll sleep easier there."

"We've got a way before that. But at least that's enemy territory, where we know what we're dealing with. No idea what this lot are thinking." Oksy didn't make an effort to lower her voice or hide it, the comment coming out as typical Oksy fact. Barkmen equals untrustworthy.

A nearby tent opened and Newk come out, bleary-eyed, tangle-haired and a pillar of natural beauty. She was in just her shirt and pants, not yet bothering to cover up, showing off long legs, taut, muscular – she waved and Wish quickly turned her bulging eyes back to the beans, swearing under her breath.

Oksy kept muttering, lost in her own concerns. "There are creatures out here we've got no conception of, you know. Barkmen are the start of it – they herd massive beetles out west, and there are snakes bigger than horses, close to the Horns."

"No one's going near the Horns," Wish said, head down as Newk came closer. She bit her lip to steady her nerves.

"That smells wonderful," Newk said, voice husky from sleep, not helping.

"Sure Wish'll share," Oksy said distractedly. "You all heard the noises at night, didn't you? Flesh-eating birds and monkeys up here."

Wish ignored her to stand before Newk. She held her mug forward in both hands as an offering and Newk looked at it uncertainly. "You're sure?"

"Sharing is caring," Wish said, and held up her spoon. She watched tensely as her friend helped herself, lips touching where her lips had touched. She took another mouthful and made a pleased noise – Wish laughed, "Don't hog it."

Newk looked confused, but Wish took the spoon back for another helping herself, quick, *by Bly* sharing the spoon that'd just been in Newk's mouth. She took another spoonful then offered the mug again. "All right, you can finish it."

The confusion turned to amusement as Newk took the mug again and helped herself to the scant remains. Holding Wish's gaze as she ate. This was *definitely* flirting, Wish decided.

Heavy footfalls on dry leaves interrupted them before Wish could ruin it, as Tate marched through camp, announcing, "Ladies, it's past dawn and we're wanted by the river. Hustle fast, move!"

There was a flurry of movement within tents, girls startled awake, lunging for gear. Oksy rolled her shoulders and said, "Thank Castor. Sooner we go the better."

It was a pleasant two-hour hike between the commune of Heart Spot and the harbour, Riverside. The forest air was invigorating and the paths through the trees mostly flat, with sounds of unusual wildlife keeping the scouts company. At first they were quiet themselves, watching out for barkmen that lingered in the trees, either escorting them or just watching them. They rarely seemed to move. But conversation gradually filtered through the platoon as the girls realised they were safe.

With girls laughing ahead, and Pound chattering with Dakoda behind, Wish fell into step alongside Newk. Not saying anything, just enjoying the proximity. Newk gave her a knowing sideways glance, not quite smiling but not speaking either. Walking close, because the path was tight?

The sound of rushing water announced they were nearing the river again, then they passed through Riverside itself, with trees shaved for barkmen resting spots but no other indication it was a community. Then the trees gave way and the scouts saw the barkman port – a jetty similar to the Twisted Bridge, with tools and barkmen gathered along the bank, and a boat unlike any Wish had imagined before. It was thirty metres long, made up of panels of seemingly unworked wood, overlapping like scales of a vast sculpted dragon, but less orderly. There was little elegant about it – no cabins, no particular shaping to the bow, nor any sign of sails, masts or controls. If it were smaller, it could've passed for a massive cluster of random driftwood. But at the end of the jetty, with barkmen purposefully positioned around and on it, it was clearly a transport.

"What are these freaks doing going up and down the river anyway?" Rue grumbled, taking the strangeness as a personal affront.

Wish frowned, Newk's presence reminding her of the trunk in Blythe, and said, "Out here, Rue, *we're* the freaks." She flashed Newk a look and got a blank expression for her efforts. Not enough?

"I'd say –"

"Don't, Rue," Wish snapped, startling herself. "At least not as long as we're in their territory, counting on their help." All the scouts in hearing distance were stilled by the warning, and Wish didn't dare turn to see what Rue's face was doing. But dammit she was in charge, wasn't she? If they were about to rely on a pile of scrap wood manned by sticks, they couldn't piss anyone off. Realising she had to cement her position, Wish added, "Is that a problem, Rue?"

"No, ma'am," Rue said, not concealing the bitterness.

She's going to cut my throat in my sleep, isn't she? Wish fought against letting the fear show and walked on. "Good. Let's go, then."

The scouts took the jetty onto the boat, boarding with great care but finding it was stable in the water, hardly moving under their weight. There was plenty of space, between stacks of piled logs, twigs and leaves, and collected flowers and berries. Wish studied the foliage being transported by these unusual people – people was fair, wasn't it? – and saw they really were a civilisation of gardeners, trading in forest cuttings for mysterious purposes. Taking rarer plant life from one region to bolster another?

Once the scouts were settled in, with dice games and Larkin strumming on her little lute, the boat set out. Wish wandered to its edge, where there was no barrier, to find some clue as to how it moved. Going by the barkmen's little root tendrils, she suspected the underside was a remarkable network of dangling vines and flaps. Clusters of the barkmen pressed against shaved patches of the boat appeared to be controlling it, connected as they had been in Heart Spot overnight.

Clear of the tree canopy, the sun shone down on the scouts, a beautiful day to be on the river, and Wish sneaked glances at Newk, bathed in the sunlight, sitting with one knee up, breathing in the air and the view. Wish left a game of shake-bone to join her, abandoning the new girl, Angles', attempts to outdo Pound with an unlikely pre-war story of an aristocrat she'd met on a cruise ship.

Wish stood over Newk, making her squint into the sunlight, and said, "About those beans earlier . . ."

"Huh?" Newk said and Wish immediately regretted her admittedly ill-conceived conversation starter. "What was wrong with –"

A scout at the boat's bow shouted a warning that saved Wish from thinking: "Drail gunship!"

In an instant, games were discarded, rifles were whipped up and the scouts were rushing to the boat's edges, elbowing to look ahead. Wish was further forward than most, her Long 0.48 up and ready. The ship was a dark floating trapezoid with a barrel pointing out the top, a long way upriver, where the banks got wider apart and water stretched to the right.

"What the hell is this?" Spyke shouted furiously at the barkmen.

Concerned Rue would take that a step further, Wish threw her a look and found her fellow scout wore a grim, ready expression. But the barkmen were scuttling quickly over the boat, to the front, seeming to shield the scouts.

"It's not supposed to be here!" Dollemore shouted over the commotion. "They say the river's been clear for weeks, south of the Little Step turning!"

"So that ship's come for *us,*" Spyke responded angrily.

"It wasn't the barkmen!" Dollemore insisted. "They've got ties to the whole forest – they would *know* if we'd been betrayed – there's no individualism in their society!"

The wooden boat slowed as the Drail ship started turning in the water, clearly aware that they were there. Wish called out, for anyone who couldn't see, "They're coming."

"Dollemore, tell them to take us to the bank," Tate commanded. "Emi, what can you do?"

"With that cannon?" Emi said. "We'll be in their range before they're in mine."

The wooden boat drifted sideways as the barkmen moved busily between the scouts, but the bank was approaching painfully slowly, compared to the Drail advancing quickly down the river – and Emi was right, whatever weapon was mounted on top of their ship, it looked like it could shoot a long way. Wish tracked the gun through her scope, but Four Skills noted its movement first: "They're taking aim!"

"Everyone back!" Tate roared, and as one the scouts fled the front of the boat. "Grab your packs – ready to jump if we need to!"

Wish skidded down to her own pack and swept it up onto her shoulders. Swimming was a rich idea with this weight to drag her down, but the others were doing the same, gathering all they could – a cluster of Rock Squad girls even fussed over the Reaper.

"Get down!" Four Skills yelled, and they all flattened themselves as the report of the far-off cannon sounded, a boom that rumbled gently louder as the blast approached.

There was an explosive sound and the boat rocked heavily. Girls shouted in fear, but the boat splashed back into place and someone announced, "Missed us! Barely!"

"They won't again," Tate warned. "Can't we go any faster?"

"Let me," Emi said, hurrying to the starboard side and holding up her hands. Barkmen moved towards her, as though in protest, and she patted them away with snarls.

"To the left," Tate kept on. "Be ready!"

"Boot, over here!" Wish shouted, spotting a patch of empty deck on the left-hand side. Her group gathered around her, throwing glances upriver to the impending doomship. Their boat suddenly listed again, without a blast, as though hit by a tremendous wave – Angles wailed as she tripped over the edge, towards the water. Rue jumped forward, catching the cuff of her sleeve, and Pound came a second behind to wrap an arm around Rue's waist. They all heaved backwards and fell onto the deck. The boat was moving fast, banking at a sharp angle, as scouts braced themselves against the woodwork people, shrieking in fear. Someone screamed, falling off without being caught – and beneath that, against the sound of churning water, Emi was laughing.

"For fuck's sake, someone stop her!" Harmon roared, but they were being pushed too fast towards land for anyone to risk moving. When the gunship boomed again Wish watched its projectile fly into the river.

"Stop!" other girls added to the yelling, the bank and the trees coming dangerously quickly. Barkmen raced over the deck, some launching off the boat. Wish pressed one hand down hard into the wood, trying to dig her nails in, and reached another to grab whoever was closest. Newk. She pulled Newk close to her side and screamed as the boat slammed into land.

The collision came with a terrible crack, tossing Wild Wish skyward. Unable to keep hold of Newk, she flew into the trees. Branches smacked her face and stabbed her limbs as the weight of her pack pulled her heavily down. She landed with a hard smack. It rained scouts and barkmen, as the fractured wall of the boat split over the rocky earth behind them, before it jarred to a halt.

Wild Wish sat up gasping, alive, amazingly still mobile. On the wreckage of the boat, those who'd managed to keep hold were jumping down, some onto land and others into the water. Four Skills was on board dragging Emi back, the dirt-minder cackling now, arms twitching at her sides, and there were barkmen gathered around them both, like a moving wall, more ominous than protective. Wish patted the ground around her, searching for her rifle. There – down on the ground, metres away. She scrambled upright, took a few steps and practically fell on it, then turned back to the boat. Four Skills and Emi were almost off, but the barkmen were getting closer.

Wish fired a warning shot, over the top of the cluster, and the barkmen flinched back. Enough distraction for Four Skills to twist Emi away from them and shove her down, so they could both fall clumsily to the bank. As they hit dirt, the gunship's cannon sounded again, its boom closer now, and a second later the centre of the wooden boat exploded into a cloud of black smoke and shattered wood. Wish held up an arm to protect her face as the blast threw her back and peppered the forest with splinters.

"Up, up!" Fixit's voice came in Wish's ear, an arm suddenly looped through hers and pulling her back. "You hurt?"

"Probably," Wish said, distractedly, searching the tree-line with her eyes. The other scouts were helping each other, many dazed and bloody. Someone's mumbler rifle sat broken in two on the bank. A pack had been discarded, tins spilt out the top. Wish asked, "Have you seen Newk? I was with Newk?"

"Everyone's pushing into the trees," Fixit replied.

Wish went with her, arm in arm, realising the hum in her ears wasn't just the ringing from the gunboat's blast: its engine was rumbling near the bank. Then she heard the shouts of Drail soldiers. To her right, girls were screaming about the Reaper, someone wanting to set it up, someone else calling her an idiot, *keep moving!* The movers won out, and the scouts were sprinting through the trees together. Wish sprinted with them, for minutes just running, breath heavy, and she fought the urge to collapse. She could've kissed Fixit when the medic gave out first, wheezing that she had to stop.

They fell against a tree together and turned back to watch others following, scouts slowing down, alone or in pairs, many with rifles ready. Rue and Angles, Pound with Cade, Oksy. Further along, Tate and Dollemore, more Sun girls, Dakoda – where was Newk? Wish felt emotion colliding with exhaustion. They'd been at the edge of the boat, thrown furthest. She was lucky her back wasn't broken. How easy it was to lose someone, how quick – Loose looking that man in the face – *no*.

There was another crack of cannon fire, but the shot went wide, tearing through trees off to the right. The gunboat must have lost track of where the scouts had disappeared into the trees. As other scouts shouted to guide companions further in, Wish croaked, "Newk? Anyone seen Newk?"

The Drail were shouting too, far off. They were frustrated, not yet following the scouts into the woods. Afraid? But there was other movement: Wish noticed the creeping advance of barkmen, flanking them. The scouts slowed down, grouping together in a wider cluster. An icy giggle cut through the trees, met with a curse from Four Skills, almost losing her cool as she pulled Emi along to join the survivors.

"Newk!" Wish shouted, pushing off from the tree and stumbling. "Anyone –"

"Here," Newk said, and Wish spun. There she was, suddenly right behind her, one hand raised. Pack on one shoulder, sword in her other hand. She gave a faint smile and Wish almost jumped on her but caught herself at the last moment. Merely exhaled relief.

She took another breath and called out, "Boot Squad, we're all here?"

A series of ayes greeted her, the scouts closing in. Tate shoved through, scanning faces. She said, "We lost Graves from Sun. Sabre?"

Larkin called out from a way off, "I saw Baston and Cold go under. Otherwise all here."

"Rock?"

"Ill Dog," Cade volunteered, voice cracking as she looked imploringly to one of her squad-mates. "The – the Reaper –" She indicated her head, patting it, leaving the disaster open to interpretation. The machine gun, nowhere in sight now, likely smashed her friend's skull in the crash.

"Otherwise all here," Harmon said, miserably.

Everyone looked at Emi, the mage huddled up at the edge of the large group, stifling sniggers as she met their eyes. Someone grumbled curses at her, Harmon snarled, "Fucking lunatic." Others started agreeing. Someone added that old slur: "Bloody mindless."

Wild Wish snapped, "Did you see what they did to our boat? We wouldn't have made the bank without her help!" A half-dozen hands suddenly held her back, faces pressed close to hers warning her to be cool, leave it, and Wish realised she was lashing towards whoever had spoken.

"That's enough, ladies!" Tate shouted. She was looking back, alert, to the sounds of the Drail, voices less aggressive now as they got organised.

"They won't enter the forest," Dollemore interpreted, likely just guessing. "But they're giving the barkmen an ultimatum."

"What kind of ultimatum?" Larkin asked, as if it wasn't obvious.

"We're moving," Tate announced.

"Moving where? Not into the woods –"

"To the Horns." Tate looked to the edge of their gathering where Captain Brade was leaning against a tree, watching carefully. They had evidently been sitting on a backup plan already. "We'll press on through Eardung to the Horns, get to the lake that way." A wave of disbelief swept through the scouts – everyone knew going deeper into this forest was mad, let alone approaching whatever the Horns had in store for them. Tate wouldn't hear it, raising her voice. "There's no telling what else is waiting on that river. The Horns will take us an extra two days, max, if we move fast." She adjusted her pack, ready to go. But Wish followed her gaze to the nearby barkmen. The upright shards of wood were spread through the trees, keeping their distance, seeming less friendly now. Tate added, "We *have* to move fast."

With that, she started marching. The scouts fell in, throwing backwards glances to the river. Larkin pulled away, up to Wild Wish, and whispered, "It'd make a hard trek easier knowing we don't have that boatload of green-coats on our backs. Your squad can handle that."

Wish frowned, not following until she realised Larkin was watching Emi. Four Skills held the mage's shoulders, looking her in the eye to bring her back to reality, as Emi swayed, grinning madly. The fallout from using her magic made her look like she belonged in an asylum. Wish replied slowly, "Sounded like we already had our orders."

"Yeah," Larkin scoffed, not happy about it, "but as squad leaders we're allowed some initiative. That boat could send word back to base as to where we're headed. You've got the resources and the command, Wild. Tate's busy leading, this is on us."

Wish looked from Larkin to the backs of the girls stalking off ahead, many distracted by the barkmen nearby. All of Boot Squad lingered near Wish, so they were apparently forming the rear guard. Meaning the gunboat had become their problem by default, anyway.

"If Emi was still in Sabre," Larkin said, leaning closer, "I'd do it in a heartbeat." With that, she jogged off to regroup with her own squad.

The other girls surrounded Wish, variously afraid or defiant. She caught Four Skills' eye as the sniper backed off from Emi. The Sabre Squad sniper was staying with them for now, at least, which was some form of approval. Wish called out, "What do we say? Worth securing our butts?"

25

I preferred the bloody pits of Null and no doubt, Jinni. We had sixteen hours underground with scant light, little food or water, and the constant threat of collapse, explosion or suffocation. But the work made sense, and we had professional standards. On the front line, we're not going deep enough to hit hard ground or escape flooding. The tremors from artillery can bring things down in a second. We've not got materials nor time to shore the shafts and no one has a bloody clue what they're doing. The chances of surviving long enough to tunnel under the enemy are so slim we might as well be back in Null, digging up more metal to armour our tanks.

This just feels like we're digging ourselves a path to hell.

**Extract from the Letters of
Major K. Tyne, Elmn, 720**

In an age of colossal mechanical trains, steamboats and gasoline-fuelled road vehicles, Donut had outdone himself by securing one of the least comfortable and most erratic forms of transport: a wyrling sire. Alleged kin of ancient mythical dragons, wyrling females were giant armour-scaled lizards that flowed gracefully through the sky, capable of tearing metal with their enormous jaws and teeth like axe-heads. They were rare, elegant warrior mounts, three metres long and bonded to trained lancers from noble families. The male sires, however, were opposite in almost every way: their jaws and teeth were dull and blunt, their bodies fat and sluggish, and their movements slow and imprecise. Though they could easily cover great distances from the sky, they were notoriously difficult to get going, unintelligent, and food-obsessed. Maringdale wondered if that affinity was what drove Donut to choose such a mount.

Her aide stood proudly by it, in a stable otherwise housing fine horses and imperious giant pack beetles. Donut's rotund wyrling was lying down breathing slow, weary breaths. It looked old, with wispy manes of hair around its snout and in patches on its scratched, scaled flesh. A murky green shade, with milky eyes, and an utterly disinterested air. Its only saving grace were the hide saddles and travelling furs that Donut had already fastened to the mount.

"Nuh," Netts said, shaking his head. "Not going on that."

"What kind of Dread soldier are you?" Maringdale said, hiding her own reservations.

"Sort that'd rather not fall to his death," Netts answered readily. "Hasn't been any good reason for man to risk them monsters since as long as we had horses."

"But we'll get there in half a day, flying," Donut said, sounding hurt. "I'm told this one's particularly obedient. He's called Gulvar."

"His name's irrelevant and they would say that. Make sure you take it off their hands. Listen, pack beetles go over rocks like it's nothing; they're fine for the mountains. Probably only take a little longer."

"A day more at least. And the beetles are all taken – the 3rd Cavalry are doing manoeuvres every evening."

"Then here's another thought – we wait. Maybe join a truck convoy. We need rest anyway. And there's the Iron Barge? Maybe that'll continue west once it gets going again."

"It's heading north," Donut said. "Up into the Valley, before coming back this way and east." He gave Maringdale a worried look, as Netts' anxiety deflated his clearly well-researched plan. "I really do think this is our best option. I've ridden before – it is safe and fast. Even if not everyone thinks a wyrling sire is dignified."

Maringdale didn't especially like it herself, but hell, whatever Donut lacked, she trusted his sense for logistics. She said, "No, you did well, Donut. Netts would just rather we stall so his chief can catch up and stop him from coming with us."

"That's not it –" Netts said, pointing at the beast.

"Doesn't matter," Maringdale cut in. "We're not delaying. Mount up."

Maringdale had to give Donut credit: he controlled the wyrling calmly, and had made the ride comfortable with the seats, leather-framed goggles and fur hats he'd acquired. They rose out of a tunnel into dusk light, banking over the hillock of Highscythe and aiming towards the setting sun. The vistas of hills and forests had a quiet grace from high up, despite the patchwork grass, pockmarks of craters and debris. But Maringdale appreciated Netts' concerns, as the smaller man cursed behind her, clinging to his saddle. The lift in her stomach and the dizziness of this immense height were not natural nor welcome. Maringdale closed her eyes, took a breath, looked again. They were even higher, the world like a rich-man's game board below. Netts' cursing got quieter.

"We're steady now!" Donut shouted over his shoulder, fighting against the rush of wind. He rummaged in his great coat, brought out a sweet bun and offered it to Maringdale. She let her look tell him no. An absurd time to eat. He explained, "We'll have a few hours, nice and steady."

"You have somewhere picked out for the night?" Maringdale shouted, and he gave her a confused look.

"Null," he replied loudly. "It's a few hours to Null."

Maringdale felt for his feelings, for a lie, but Donut wouldn't dare. They could genuinely travel that fast? She said, "But that's close to the Farnish border?"

"That's right. In Willoke."

"Hundreds of miles away?"

"I told you this is the fastest way to get there!" Donut gave a big smile, proud that for once he might've impressed her. Maringdale looked, alarmed, from him down to the landscape below, drifting by totally removed from them. If they could move so fast, it was a wonder wyrling mounts had never become a popular form of transport. But then Netts heaved, leaning to the side and snarling even louder, and she got some idea why.

The circle of Null fit its name, Maringdale saw, as Donut directed their wyrling over it, picking out a gaslit camp on the outskirts. It was a pit town, with its wooden and stone huts, mills and halls, taverns and towers, all built around and inside a giant mining pit. In the night, the yellow lights of the community glittered along the edges of the earth's maw, surrounding an enormous hole of pitch darkness at the community's centre.

As the wyrling drifted lower, Maringdale's stomach rose and Netts almost shrieked. The military encampments became clearer. To the south, unlit, abandoned for the evening, were rows of huge trucks with canvas covers, and between them and the town were military tents – big ones, for command meetings, infirmaries and storage. There was movement coming out of town, as the wyrling's approach drew attention, and dozens of soldiers hurried out to meet them, rifles up. Maringdale felt the rush of their emotions as they got closer – men unprepared, not expecting trouble.

The wyrling made an untidy landing, lumbering across the ground and rearing uncertainly, away from the dim lampposts that marked the closest street. It gave a low rumbling sound, a little too lazy for a roar, and turned away from the shouting soldiers. Donut pulled at its reins, calling at it for calm. He bounced in his seat as the creature jolted. Maringdale and Netts joined the shouting for him to get it under control. It kept padding, immense clawed feet churning the ground, and Donut called at everyone to make space. But the soldiers piled in, raising their rifles like sticks to herd it, and together they drove the animal away from the buildings, barely avoiding a truck that it almost swiped, until it broke free and paced off onto a patch of empty grass, where it finally slowed.

Donut chuckled, announcing, "There we go. That wasn't so bad."

"To hell with you!" Netts snapped, wrenching at his belt buckles.

He leapt off the beast's back, botched his landing and quickly staggered away. The absurdity of it all drew relieved laughs from their audience.

Maringdale instructed Donut to take care of Gulvar before jumping down and following Netts. The crowd kept their distance, just inside the light of the town's gas lamps, maybe two dozen soldiers and civilians lined up. At the centre was a dressed-down officer, shirt untucked, cap askew, likely interrupted from some unseemly activity. Maringdale looked past him to a more important looking man so tall he had a humped, self-conscious stoop. His long features were framed by overlarge studded-leather pauldrons holding a heavy black cloak decorated with jagged bones. Behind him, two or three soldiers wore similar Dread markings.

"Constans Maringdale!" a booming, jovial voice drew Maringdale to the right where a big man in mountain furs was pushing through the crowd. He had a thick beard, with poorly combed hair up top, and the swollen, blotchy face of an alcoholic. A large metal pendant hung around his neck, similar to Panderlair's. "You come to relieve me?"

"Pale Taik?" Maringdale suggested, guessing his size and furs marked him from Har Coul. Taik was the only Coulard Purification officer she knew of.

He was a foot taller than her and twice as wide. He held out a huge hand and grinned, teeth crooked between bristly whiskers. "The very same. Where on earth did you get a wyrling? I've been asking the Purification to give me one for years."

"Highscythe," Maringdale said, as he gave her hand a surprisingly gentle shake. "I'm not sure I'd recommend the experience yet."

"That's because you've got a transporter," a nearby soldier contributed. "Best used for freight. Difficult to control and not good with people."

Maringdale watched Donut guiding the monster, patting its nose, offering it food. It hadn't seemed bad until that landing. But what did she know. Or care. She turned to Taik. "You were expecting us?"

"Not so much me." He nodded to the tall man in a cloak, who stood waiting like a sinister scarecrow. Taik put a heavy hand on Maringdale's shoulder and boomed, "Come, we'll discuss it inside. Nothing left to see here, folks!"

Murmurs of disappointment swept out, the wyrling's havoc the most entertainment they'd likely seen for a long time. Taik didn't wait for them to disperse, guiding Maringdale with one hand and shoving his way towards the buildings with the other. She tensed against his touch, thinking to push him off, but sensed he was nervous rather than bold. A concern too curious for her to jump on right away.

Taik led Maringdale along a street that curved around the dark space at the town's centre and up to a top-heavy tavern that leaned out over the pit's edge, its swinging sign naming it The Overhang. The big man joked, "It's safer than it looks. The miners are engineers – their lives depend on good architecture."

Maringdale only half listened, keeping part of her attention on the tall cloaked man who walked a few paces behind them, not quite looking at them. Netts was similarly giving him uncertain looks.

The tavern was a tight, heady space, decked in timber and smoky from a large fireplace. The ceiling was slanted in a way that gave doubt to Taik's claims it was safe. As men in dusty uniforms watched, Taik ordered drinks and continued to a stairwell he barely fit up. On the next floor, they entered a private booth with a warped window looking out at darkness, the lights of town dropping sharply below with only a few visible around the opposite edges of the pit, like stars lost in the night. Taik slapped a mug of frothy ale down and said, "Ah but it's good to see an ally! Where's old Sin Sight? You were under his crusty wing, were you not?"

Maringdale twisted on her seat. Netts hovered with his hands in his pockets. He looked worried, the wyrling ride having further convinced him he didn't want to be involved in this, and the tall man had put him more on edge. The man had silently slunk in after them, eyes strangely averted. His Dread soldiers had not followed.

"Panderlair is dead," Maringdale told Taik, watching for his reaction.

"They got him?" Taik boomed back, scarcely surprised. "Shame, he was a stick but he got the job done. That it, then – they've assigned you a new mentor?"

Though outwardly hidden by his jolly manner, she registered more worry. Last thing he needed. A hard-drinking man in a backwater like this, no doubt he wanted to be left alone to not do his job. Maringdale said, "I'm following the threads of my own investigation. Which you can probably guess at."

"Here?" Taik said, his worries rising a little more. "We've had no cause for concern."

"I have." Maringdale finally addressed the cloaked man, seeing as he wasn't going to introduce himself: "Has Battle Chief Hark been in touch?"

"He has," the man answered with a surprisingly deep, loud voice, considering his timid demeanour. His head tilted down, he looked at her from under his brow. "I'm well aware what's been happening at the other sites, but, like Officer Taik, I'm not sure why Hark sent you."

"Are you in charge here?" Maringdale asked.

He nodded.

"Dread Mage Starling."

"Hark wasn't sure why I was needed there, either, until I stopped a couple of sappers from bringing half of Highscythe down on his head."

Starling raised an eyebrow. "You misunderstand. I don't doubt this site needs protection, but we already have a Purification officer here."

Maringdale gave Taik another look as the big man swigged heavily on his ale. He put the mug down and smiled again, to say, *see, I'm taking care of things*. His feelings implored her to believe it, don't rock the boat.

"I believe," Maringdale said, "that there's a network of insurgents targeting your sites, and if they're moving east to west then this location is next. I have skills you might be lacking. I'm a third-class intention mage, and –"

Taik spurted foam across the table, coughing on his surprise. He quickly wiped a big forearm over his mouth with a laugh to cover it up. "Heavens, sorry – I'm impressed, that's all. Thought the military had snatched up all our mages. Good on the Purification." Again, his feelings spoke differently, muddled with anxiety. Afraid his shoddy work would come into question, or something worse?

Maringdale gave him a dismissive smile and said, "When did you get here, Officer Taik? Was it in relation to the bombing out of Cleave City?"

"Heavens no." Taik shook his head. "I've been here maybe three weeks – investigating rumours of Stanclif spies. I found little evidence of such activity, but since I was already here, they made a watchdog of me."

"The Dread Corps?"

"Dreads and Purification both. I'm not complaining. We're a hundred miles from the front line and you might not think it to look at him" – Taik gave another laugh – "but Starling is good company when he wants to be!"

"But as you see," Starling said, humourless, "I mean no offence to your talents, Miss Maringdale, I'm just not sure what we need an intention mage for."

Maringdale gave him a smile, too, showing her gold teeth. Though looking at him, she blocked out his simple feelings – merely inquisitive – to focus on Taik's. Severely worried about her, more than he had a right to be. She said, "We'll find out, I suppose. Give me a day, I'll see if there's anything I can do to help. If not, I'll move on. I won't get in your way."

"Well, can't argue fairer than that!" Taik said. "Drink to it, shall we? We'll have some food brought up, arrange quarters. Be merry, rest, and tomorrow we get to work."

Maringdale raised her mug to him.

With a cheer, Taik led them in drinking, and quickly changed the subject: "Now forget work. Let me tell you about the brothels of Null, for here it is an art form – the finest partners for one of the Empire's strongest mines."

He proceeded to ramble on about the town, where honest men and convicts were digging up fantrit, the most sought-after metal in the world, as the easiest substance to reinforce with dirt-minding.

The town itself was now sparsely populated, as labourers spent days or even weeks underground, working overtime for the war effort. They were rewarded with the finest entertainment money could buy. Prostitutes from exotic lands with unimaginable skills – male and female. As he slipped into these accounts, Maringdale felt Taik's worries fade, and alcohol softened his fears, too, when she occasionally tried to ask if he had any concerns about the alleged Stanclif spies. No, was the basic answer. There may have been some Farnes who didn't belong here, but they disappeared when Taik arrived. If they ever existed.

Maringdale let him talk without stirring, similarly giving Netts a chance to drink and relax. Starling scarcely joined the conversation but drank comfortably. Donut finally entered with apologies, wet with spilt drink, having been waylaid by soldiers who insisted on buying him beer. Taik took the interruption as an opportunity to excuse himself for a comfort break.

Once he was gone, Maringdale turned to Starling and asked, "Have you been satisfied with his work?"

Starling raised an eyebrow. "It's been quiet here. And he did manage to quash rumours of the Gentleman."

"The what?"

"A Stanclif spy. You're not aware of him?"

"We've been working in the Eastern Theatre, Stanclif's agents aren't my forte."

"Yes? He is someone everyone's been out to get, out west, and we briefly thought he might be targeting us. But this adds to my curiosity as to what led you here, if it wasn't the Stanclif angle that concerned you."

"I'm an intention mage –"

"Third class, with the Purification. Yes. I suspect you're not one of our most valuable mages, or you'd be in a rather different position."

"That has more to do with my gender than my talents," Maringdale replied irritably, before she could stop herself. Starling did not reply. His feelings remained neutral: he wasn't accusing, or testing her, his concerns were genuine. She softened her tone and said, "I can demonstrate my value. Taik has your confidence because he is outwardly confident himself. Fun to be around. But he's doing a bad job –"

"He's done what I needed," Starling said. "His presence alone does the job, no matter his talents. What spy would dare operate in a town with a Purification Officer present?"

"Then why's he so worried about me?"

Starling paused. "Is he? He seemed nothing but welcoming to me."

Maringdale believed him; whatever Taik was worried about, the Dread mage did not share his concerns. The loud slob was up to something, she was sure of it.

Taik re-entered with an armful of beers, shouting, "All right, who's ready for more?"

"What happened with the Gentleman, Taik?" Maringdale asked sharply.

He handled it brilliantly on the surface, not losing his stride as he came over laughing. "Ah, you've been talking shop again! Don't worry about that, I drove him off. Or drove off the rumours, anyway." But his senses raged. The same feelings as the Farnish spies in Highscythe: confounded at how she could know about this.

Dammit, she'd chanced upon a huge breach and she wasn't wasting any more time. Maringdale drew her pistol and stood. "Officer Taik. I'm arresting you in the name of the Purification."

For just a second, a smile twitched on Taik's lips. He watched her, unsure how big a threat she was. But she felt his attitude shift – considering attack – and Maringdale lifted her pistol as he whipped a hand down to his belt. Before she could fire, Taik was thrown aside as though hit by an invisible force. He smashed into the wall, hard enough to crack it. Netts jumped up, rifle swinging round fast to target Taik, but the man was done, groaning weakly on the floor.

Maringdale looked from Taik back to Starling, and found the Dread mage standing with his arms down, lightly shaking. He was a parse mage, she realised – a witlacer who could move bodies. He spoke with a wavering voice, "One of you go down and get my men. Secure the traitor."

26

The divergent 3rd-century trajectories of witlacing and earth-touching can be attributed to two key individuals who emerged when persecution of mages was at its peak. Lord Hep Hattrik of Ernth, a noble whose son was born gifted with witlacing abilities, and Fin "the Biter" Baston, a Khib rebel who radicalised earth-touchers. The former made it his life's work to normalise attitudes towards witlacing, using his influence to establish an academic discourse around mortal magic. The latter did his utmost to threaten the status quo, prophesying that mages would inherit the Rocc. Their goals, strategies and characters were vastly different, but both men had in common, at least, that they were fiercely competitive, and incredibly dangerous.

We the Mindless: a Brief History of Ostracised Magic, Lombardo, p. 32

Wish had started to wonder if separating from the others was a mistake. It was just her, Emi and Four Skills perched by a rock, with Rue, Pound and Angles (somehow) spread out in the trees to support them, the rest of Boot Squad having moved on ahead. Ordinarily she trusted that between herself and Four Skills they'd have no trouble catching up to the Blood Scouts, but who was to say if trails worked the same in Eardung. They might have worms that rubbed out footprints, or worse. But she tried to stay focused on the task at hand, studying the ugly Drail ship. It floated away from the bank and the wreckage of the barkmen's boat, presumably too large to get much closer to land. Barkmen were gathered around their own vessel, tending to debris and their fallen comrades – which, frankly, looked the same. Only a handful of Drail soldiers had come to shore, clustered around a rowboat, two in green coats, one in a crisper uniform with a flat, important hat, and one in a cloak – a witlacer, most likely, brought to communicate with the barkmen.

A single barkman kept lurking nearby, distracting Wish like a watching dog, very judgemental for a plank of wood. Wish murmured, "How do we know he's not sending tree-vibes to his mates over there right now, warning them about us?"

"There'd be commotion if he did," Four Skills said.

Wish shifted, checking again to see if there were more of them, or any Drail soldiers sneaking about to flank them, but Four Skills was right: they were safe, for now. She took a breath and eyed Emi. The mage had calmed to a point of near-normality, but her pupils were big as plates and her smile hung somewhat sickly open. "Emi. You sure you want to do this, so soon after?"

"Please, Wish," Emi said. "I could throw down all day, it's just riding a high. You're the ones who don't like what it does to me."

"She'll be worse, second time round," Four Skills warned more soberly. "But she's right to a degree. Worry about her when we're safe. You ready? I make it a hundred thirty feet, here to the bank."

Wish scanned the boat and the soldiers through her scope one more time, impressed by the men's arrogance. There were guys on deck smoking, chatting, scarcely anyone watching the trees, with no fear that the scouts might double back on them. But they had reason for confidence, considering their boat was metal-plated with a cannon big enough to obliterate small villages. What kind of madwomen would have the gall to take *that* on?

"Once I start," Emi said, "that mage is going to notice. But there's no sense shooting him first, giving ourselves away. Just watch and wait for him to connect the dots."

"You got him, Four?" Wish asked, and the sniper nodded, done talking now she had the man in her sights. "I'll take the officer."

Emi inhaled deeply. "Let's have some fun." She exhaled, hard, pushing her hands into the ground, and Wish felt a small wave of energy pass through her. She imagined the air shimmer across the ground, a pulse that swept down into the water and took Emi's power through the river to the boat. With her cross-hairs on the officer, Wish saw in her periphery that the mage moved, expression shifting. Emi let out a tiny snigger, and the mage's eyes snapped sideways, looking their way. Four Skills fired and Wild Wish pulled her trigger the same time. Both the mage and the officer went down, and the two green-coats dived for cover, down behind the startled barkmen. Shouts came from the boat, everyone moving. Wish ran her sights over the deck looking for any stray head, arm or knee.

Caught a helmet poking up, fired and saw it drop.

"Here we go, here we go," Emi hissed fiercely and winced as she did something.

The boat wrenched from Wish's sights and she had to look over the scope to take it in. Water frothed around its edges and a sound of twisting, screeching metal rose from under the river. The gunboat folded inward. It was creaking together like crumpling paper, hull cracking and complaining as the soldiers screamed and fled. A few men leapt over the edge, a twenty- or thirty-foot drop, as the vessel twisted. Four Skills kept shooting, methodically, a steady shot, bolt slide, shot, like a machine. Wild Wish merely stared, marvelling at the war machine's weakness.

Emi slid forward, down onto her elbows, cackling at the world's maddest joke, and the boat rocked, slowing its implosion but beyond repair now. It was going down, fast, no longer buoyant with this new, warped shape. The cannon on top moved, trying to find one last victim for its dying breath, but it rotated one way then another, like the men below were fighting over the controls. A series of pops sounded on the boat, rivets exploding? No, there were flashes – gunfire. Were the men turning on each other? Wish couldn't focus for an answer, though, as Emi's laughter worsened.

"Come on," Wish said, scooting back and grabbing the mage's shoulder. "We need to move before she gives us away."

Four Skills lowered her rifle to help, and together they pulled Emi back, the mage trying to shake them off with shuddering laughter. Wish had never seen her this bad, in the throes of a magic attack, and it was chilling, how wide her eyes and that wicked smile had grown, how taut her clawing fingers were and how her head moved in jerking, erratic motions, flicking saliva like a dog. She pulled free of them both suddenly and slammed her hands back into the ground, snarling, "No! More!" The boat gave a new, roaring complaint as they pulled her away again amid howling laughter. Four Skills clamped a hand over her mouth, cursing. Emi screamed as they dragged her down. Wild Wish's foot hit something hard and she tripped to a knee, half twisting to see their watching barkman looming over them. Trying to block their path?

No time to think, Wish shouldered into where she imagined the thing's crotch would be, and it folded, falling back – an obstacle with little substance now she put her weight into it. She grabbed Emi's arm again and ordered, "Time to go!"

The sounds of the sinking boat and its screaming occupants followed Wish's squad into the forest. They haunted her even after they'd gone quiet. Men knowing they were being dragged under, fighting each other for a chance at a lifeboat or what, she didn't know. Some would escape, and maybe find the barkmen on the shore hospitable until help could arrive. Assuming anyone knew where they were. Most would've been trapped in that crumpled ball of metal, though, drowned if not crushed. Others might have been swept away in the current, towards an inevitable plunge over the Edge Falls, if they kept their heads above water long enough. Wish could see them flying over the cliffs, crying out one last time, swimming through the sky.

Probably had families back in Drail. Little farms of their own. Maybe children and wives. Maybe woke up this morning enjoying the sunshine and thanking their saints that they'd been given a patrol on the unassuming Little Step River. As safe as anywhere this terrible war could offer.

Sorry, guys.

It didn't help that Emi kept laughing, not watching where her feet fell so Wish and Four Skills had to keep pulling her back up when she tripped. An annoying distraction while they were trying to pick out the signs of where the rest of the scouts had gone – they'd caught up to the other Boot Squad members, but the Blood Scouts at large were far ahead. Then, Emi's cackling subsided and she suddenly snapped upright, swatting off their hands, and she wiped her leaking nose on a sleeve before saying, with vague dignity, "That went rather well, don't you think?"

"Can you be quiet now?" Wish replied.

As they continued deeper into Eardung, the forest grew darker. The trees were thick, dense with untamed branches and leaves, which was stifling but made it easier to follow the path of the girls who had pushed through before. After a couple of hours, they had not caught up to the main scout group. Tate was driving them to move fast, evident in the wide strides of the tracks and the force with which the undergrowth had been broken. Wish spurred her girls on in turn, but they could only go so fast while maintaining the correct route.

Fortunately, they were going slow enough for Four Skills to stop them when she noticed something ahead. The trees looked too square and regular. Not trees – they stopped around six feet high. Close together, like a wall. A regiment of barkmen? Now Wish considered it, there hadn't been any sign of them for some time. Had they raced ahead to block them off?

Her team fanned out behind her, taking in the obstruction with similar wariness. Angles whispered, "These creepy fuckers – what do we do?"

Wish flashed her a look, seeing the young soldier had her finger on the trigger, ready to shoot the tree people that had so recently hosted them. Of all the soldiers to have with her, how had Angles ended up here? At least Oksy was only annoying in a highly competent way. Granted, the barkmen *were* creepy, silently blocking their path, but they were also basically bits of tree, how dangerous could they be? Wish cleared her throat and asked Emi, "Can you communicate with them somehow?"

"You've got the wrong mage for that."

"Where exactly are we supposed to shoot barkmen?" Rue asked.

"They don't even have heads. Do they have hearts?"

"Who said anything about shooting barkmen," Wish said. "They might want to help."

"Lined up like a barrier?" Emi said.

"Shit." Wish imagined the threat – these creatures slowly closing around her friends, smothering them against trees, worming their little tendrils into –

She snarled at her own imagination and looked at her companions. Pound had their most powerful gun, the Rik 56 Repeater. That would blow a barkman in two. The rest of them might merely put holes through them. But these things had put them up last night, helped them out. They weren't attacking, exactly. Wish took a breath and said, "Emi. You're good for fire, aren't you?"

"Give me a couple of sticks and I'll make them burn."

"They'll see it as an act of aggression," Fixit warned.

"We won't light them unless we need to," Wish assured, already searching the undergrowth. She picked up a broken log and held it up. "This do?"

"For sure." Emi took it. Rue came from the other side, holding up another. The mage held them both up, chunks of wood almost too thick to grip, and she grinned like she could do untold damage with these innocuous instruments.

Wish pointed at her, severely, *"Only* if we need to. I'm going ahead, the rest of you back me up, okay?"

They all nodded, readying their weapons, and Wish marched on. Bloody Tate, putting her in charge, could've been any of the others taking the lead. But no. She had no choice. Four Skills matched her pace, a little aside. They crept forward through the trees, and Wish noticed that the barkmen's line was at least a couple deep, and stretched to the sides. Now she looked, there were more along their flanks. She suspected others had crept up behind them.

"Ready, Emi?" Rue grumbled.

"Give Wild a chance," Fixit hissed.

Yeah. A chance to do what? Wish approached the nearest barkman slowly. It was an upright lump of wood, only evidently alive by the occasional twitching of the roots that hung down along its sides. No eyes to look in or mouth for speech. The scouts might squeeze between the gaps, but not without a tussle. She tried diplomacy: "You know we don't mean you harm, right? That was all the Drail. They fired on you and didn't give us a chance."

The barkman was motionless, along with its ranks of friends.

"All we want –" Wish faltered. All she'd wanted for a long time was to go home, really. This was the opposite of what she wanted. But hell. "All we want's another way through your land. To get north? We want to help, truly. To end this war."

Silence.

"Wild?" Rue demanded an update.

"I don't know," Wish called back. "They're just standing there. Do you think they understand Stanish?"

"If they're not doing anything," Four Skills said, "I'd say keep going."

"Um." Wild Wish looked at the piece of wood in front of her. "We took care of the ship. You're safe from that, at least?"

Great, impassive silence. She was talking to an upturned bench.

"We'd just like to get back to our friends?" That came out like a squeak.

The barkman's reaching roots moved along its flanks, twitching and rotating like idle fingers at work. Then it pivoted, moving back, and its closest companion did the same, the pair parting like opening doors. Inviting Wish to continue. She eyed them warily, until the barkman's tendrils on the left side grouped together, about halfway up, and moved as one towards Wish's waist – pointing. The barkmen had created a pathway, leading on into the dark. Wild Wish hesitated. "Girls? They want me to go somewhere. Come with?"

The squad edged up to join her, shoulder to shoulder, all aiming their rifles out. Rue had her hatchet up under the barrel of her gun, for extra protection. Emi hovered in the middle, logs raised.

"No need to panic," Wish told them, unconvincingly. "They're our allies."

"They're technically Drail," Pound said.

"Well. Let's just see where this takes us."

Wish followed the path, slowing continuing through the trees, watching the barkmen. Their trail veered around, and down a slope, to where some dark mass blocked the view ahead. A rock formation? No. Roots. Thick, tangled roots, wide as a house, piled up higher than two people, curved like a bee's hive. A huge nest of some sort. Pacing closer, wide-eyed, Wish dreaded what sort of creature might live there.

"Holy shit," Angles gasped. "What *is* that?"

It was sealed, with no sign of an entrance, or any way to let light through. And it stretched too far back to see an end.

"I can burn it," Emi volunteered. "Along with whatever's inside."

"Along with our chances of getting anywhere safely," Four Skills said.

"No one's burning anything," Wish said, and turned to the nearest barkman. Identical to the first one she'd addressed. Had they moved with them, leap-frogging to form the path? "What do you want, exactly?"

"Wild Wish?" a muffled voice came from inside the root nest. "Is that you?"

Rue swore as she moved ahead, but Wish put up a hand, holding her and her axe back. There was movement behind the roots, just visible in the slight gaps. People in there already?

"Hell," Wish uttered. "Captain?" She turned on the barkmen. "What the fuck?"

But with a creak of twisting wood, the nest shifted. The squad stepped back, watching the roots peel open, revealing the dark of the hollow nest. Captain Tate came hurriedly out, throwing a distrusting look at the structure. Close behind her came Dollemore, holding a hand back as if warning others not to move.

"Where've you been?" Tate demanded.

Dollemore added, "What did you say to them?"

"Huh?" Wish answered.

"Come inside." Tate gestured, then looked to Dollemore. "It's safe now?"

Dollemore nodded and Wish hung uncomfortably on that *now*. Still, she did as she was told, and the squad followed cautiously. Through the opening of roots, they found an arched chamber, stretching into the dark, with the rest of the scouts gathered in a space big enough to make them seem small.

"What *is* this place?" Wish asked. "We weren't sure –"

"You were right to doubt it," Tate said. "It happened fast, them leading us here, promising shelter. Before we knew it, we were trapped. They were considering handing us to the Drail, but Dollemore's been negotiating with them."

"Through the roots," the mage explained. "But you seem to have swayed them, Wild."

"I only said we wanted to find you," Wish said.

"That's all?" Tate replied with a heavy frown.

"Um. I guess I told them we sunk the ship, too?"

"You did *what?*"

"We spoke with actions," Emi offered, giving Dollemore a triumphant smile. "The best kind of negotiation."

27

And so we see witlacing divided into four rough disciplines, wherein some practitioners crossover but most are limited to one. In order of commonality, these are:

1) Intention magic: the ability to sense others' feelings (i.e. understand)

2) Will magic: the ability to influence others (i.e. command)

3) Parse magic: the ability to influence energy between people (i.e. move)

4) Flesh magic: the ability to influence the physical body (i.e. change)

Generally speaking, the less common the magic, the closer in proximity the practitioner must be; an intention mage might pick up feelings through walls, whilst a flesh mage requires physical contact to do their work.

Essential Witlacing Theory, Kilmack, p. 3

Pale Taik started out as they all did, insisting they were making a mistake. He grew louder, making threats, and Maringdale let him fume. Starling said nothing as the big man shook his wrist and ankle restraints. It was just the three of them in the stone cellar, built into the immense wall of the mine pit, a breeze from the empty abyss whistling through a tiny window near the ceiling.

Maringdale finally interrupted Taik to say, "You're wondering how hard it would be to steal the wyrling. Getting ahead of yourself because you can't see a way out of this room."

Taik was momentarily silenced by her prescience, but recovered quickly to address Starling: "She's not even a fully-fledged inquisitor – who even knows where her mentor is? Sin Sight

Panderlair never would've let this happen. You honestly believe she can read *minds*?"

"No, that would be absurd," Starling said, flat enough to give Maringdale concern. But he continued, "Intention mages merely read emotion. The thoughts, then, are extrapolated. It's not a talent I possess myself, but I *can* tell when it's being used."

Taik held the mage's stare icily. "But you can't tell if it's being used correctly. Come on, Starling, how many times have we dined together!"

"Enough to know you've been more friendly and helpful than I'd expect a Purification officer to be."

"You're going to hold that against me?" Taik laughed, recovering his jocular persona. "Not even you are that cold, Starling. I'm telling you she's an impostor. A quick call to the Purification would confirm it."

"Because you outrank me?" Maringdale read his feelings out loud. "They're bound to back your word against mine? A *woman?*" She narrowed her eyes. "You'd hope to buy some time, at least."

Taik spat aside. "You've got all the answers, huh? And now I'm thinking, you didn't actually say what happened to Panderlair, did you?"

"His throat was cut, by insurgents who targeted Cleave City, Fever, Highscythe, and apparently here." Maringdale read his reaction carefully: hope, a chink. She'd said something wrong. She continued carefully, "Perhaps you don't know about the other sites. You're just concerned with this one, working separately. If they could get a Purification officer on board, after all, they might've turned a Dread soldier in Cleave."

"You see how absurd this is?" Taik asked Starling. "Traitors in the Dread Corps?"

"Why don't we start from the top," Maringdale said. "Explain what you've done here. Convince me your investigation is valid."

"Go back to bloody Purity School," Taik snapped. "You upstart bloody amateur, I'm ten years your senior –"

"No man, regardless rank and position, is above the authority of the Purification," Maringdale quoted quickly, channelling old

Panderlair. "Believe me, I'd interrogate the Screaming Prince himself if he gave off your guilty energy."

"Then we can all see the kind of base heretic you are!"

"Taik," Starling came in. He tapped a thoughtful finger against his chin, standing straighter in this dark, private space, though the ceiling was too low for him. "Let's all accept where we are now. You stand accused by a gifted peer, and your opinion of her is irrelevant. This is serious. Indulge us. Why were you first sent here?"

Taik laughed again. "Starling, be –"

"Indulge us," Starling repeated, firmly.

"Fine. I came here after hanging a troop of bloody Arrow Shock Troops, shall we start there? I found evidence they'd let Khib prisoners go. The Purification appreciated I was up to dealing with the hardest of hard men, so they specifically asked for me when they discovered Stanclif had agents targeting the Dread Corps."

"Lie," Maringdale reported. She felt Starling's surprise at her quick ability.

Taik's eyes were steely with defiance, but she felt his fear. "Why would I invent that?"

"You tell me. You're the one with something to hide."

"Ask the Purification. They gave me the task. They wanted their best man to secure the Dread Corps. You tell me" – he raised his voice – "where's the lie in that!"

Maringdale ignored the outward show of emotion. No, there was no lie this time – meaning he'd either worded it very carefully or omitted an erroneous detail second time around. She went back through his words. *They wanted their best man*, in his mind true, but first time he said *they specifically asked for me*. Maringdale said, "Who brought the rumours to the Purification to begin with?"

"I don't know, I was only told to come here!"

He had spoken too quickly, gone right into a clear lie, wilful to move her on, and Maringdale sensed his regret the moment he finished. She said, "You approached them with it, didn't you? They didn't ask for you, you asked to be sent here. Did you invent the Stanclif spy to get close to the Dread Corps operation?"

"No," Taik said through gritted teeth, choosing his words carefully now. "He exists and he was here. I turned the town over looking for him. You know this, Starling."

"Yes, you had a lot of access," Starling admitted.

Taik paused, a moment of shock. His doubts created a wall as he realised his own words were betraying him.

Maringdale addressed Starling. "Tell me more about the Gentleman."

"Supposedly Stanclif nobility," Starling said. "Debonair, a man of fine coats, sharp swords and thin moustaches, if you believe the stories. An audacious kind of spy, the sort who hides by standing out. The sort Stanclif want us to believe in to keep our boys scared."

"Opposite of me in every way," Taik said. "Before you suggest I could pull that off, *miss*."

"I'm not suggesting you're him," Maringdale said.

"No, we have a reasonable candidate already," Starling said. "An explorer named Captain Rikard A. Brade, of the Brade Iron family. He famously infiltrated dangerous cultures even before the war. Allegedly once joined the scale-covered Lizk on a pilgrimage. Suspected of many activities behind our lines, as far north as the southern Slane border. Some believe he sabotaged the Gutterbane Bombship and organised the escape of two Lomish platoons at Ponted Bay. The collapse of the Vax Bridge was certainly him, at any rate. Given his prolific nature, I believed it plausible he had been here and equally plausible that he had moved on."

Maringdale's heart warmed at the possibility. A man that capable was exactly the sort of person who could strike multiple Dread Company sites. This was the difference between the west and the ugly wastelands of the Eastern Front, with vile Khib creatures and their clumsy schemes, and rumours of wretched *waders*. And where Taik had failed to find this man, or had even helped him, she could thwart this plot. She said, "What evidence was there of him being here?"

"Locals spotted someone lurking," Taik said. "A shadow at night. White enough to be Stanish, moustached. He left before I got here. I found an old degrebus hutch on the other side of the pit, abandoned, with no evidence of what messages might've been sent from it."

"He passed this on to you?" Maringdale asked Starling.

"Yes, and I did not see it as hard proof of a spy," Starling said.

"He's real," Taik insisted again. "He was here. I kept him away."

There were those lines again, spoken firmly, something he'd decided he could say confidently. It was a mistake. Maringdale said, "You seem absolutely certain of that. What evidence specifically indicated it was the Gentleman?"

"I pieced what I had together! Because I'm good at my job!"

"No. You're certain – not from a deduction. You'd have to have seen him yourself. Had contact with him. Did you meet him here?"

"Oh fuck off!" Taik shouted. She had struck on the truth. "You're living in a dreamworld. There's a Stanclif spy out there but you're creating fantasies of a Purification hero turned rogue! Might as well be hunting Rocardian tunnellers or Cantalesian bandit dogs. Dragon-sooths from the Sil mountains!"

"Gonish assassins?" Maringdale suggested, looking for another chink, but Taik's anger didn't shift. No sign of recognition for the waders. "Or that Stanclif Bitch Squad?"

"Don't be so fucking facetious," Taik said.

"Sorry, I thought that was the game," Maringdale snapped. "Making shit up to avoid the question. When did you meet the Gentleman?"

"Starling" – Taik rolled his head to the mage – "she's mad. You cannot possibly entertain this nonsense."

Starling was silent and Maringdale sensed he was unmoved.

She pressed her conclusions: "I'm sure the Gentleman isn't here because *you* are, Taik. I'm guessing he laid some groundwork and you followed on, pretending to drive him away to remove yourself from suspicion. After all, who would suspect a spy hunter?"

"Shove it up your arse."

"What have you done since? How much did you share with the enemy?"

"Nothing. I've done nothing." Truth. Confident but bitter. He had missed the opportunity.

"You hadn't got round to it, yet," Maringdale interpreted.

"Were you waiting for a signal to attack?" Starling asked. The big man's face cast with alarm, seeing the mage commit to his guilt. "Compiling a report to take with you when you left? You know we'll find whatever you left behind."

"You'll find fuck all," Taik said. Not denying it now, defying them.

"Your role here doesn't matter anyway, now," Maringdale said. "It's over. What's important is what comes next. What you can do for us. Where can we find the Gentleman?"

Taik glared. He was aware that he'd entered territory where any word could cost him dearly, but still didn't appreciate how much his feelings gave away. He had some confidence yet, sure they weren't going to catch his accomplice. If he could just stay quiet.

The conviction gave Maringdale pause. Taik was still prepared to suffer for his mission. She said, "Why did you join them? How did they sway a Purification officer?"

Taik turned away with a sharp, derisive laugh. There was deep bitterness there, hatred even, for the Purification.

"Our people hurt you?" Maringdale said. "Let you down. What happened? Someone you cared for got purged?"

He met her eyes coldly. "Are you joking? Has anyone *not* lost someone they cared about to the Purification? It's what we do, woman. It's *all* we do. Rewarding ourselves for punishing the smallest deviations. Punishing others so we are not punished ourselves. A mantra writ especially large by this war. Or do you honestly believe we're making the world better?"

"Do you believe Stanclif are?" Maringdale answered. "They kill, and plunder, worse than us. You'd exchange an honest fight for *your people* with a fight for someone else's?"

"Stanclif," Taik said, leaning as far forward as his restraints allowed, "do not burn their own children."

Maringdale felt his rage. A deep and terrible truth there, something he had seen. Years of similar events, loathed. Panderlair used to say only the strongest could stomach the work of the Purification. It had broken Taik, so badly he was willing to die to see them fail.

"Shall we get back on track," Starling said, sounding bored, somehow not surprised nor interested in Taik's fall from grace. "Where will we find the Gentleman?"

"Dudden's the next closest site, isn't it?" Maringdale suggested.

"Dudden has already been shut down."

"So that leaves Wick? Near Stanclif lines?" Maringdale clarified, unfamiliar with the Western Front. Starling nodded. She asked Taik, "Were you planning to head there to regroup? Hit Cleave, Fever, Highscythe, then finish up around Wick with a short jump to safety?"

"I got no idea what you're talking about," Taik said. "Never heard of these places."

Maringdale frowned. There was truth in that confusion, Taik perhaps not privy to the complete plan. "But you do have some way to contact him? Somewhere to go?"

He shut his mouth, a familiar feeling coming back: resistance, a will to stay silent. She waited, and Starling remained completely still, too, until Taik looked down, swallowed, and finally said, "Go to hell."

"That's enough," Starling said calmly. "Listen. Officer Maringdale is clearly an accomplished intention mage. She can ask you questions, probe for the answers, and you will give away all that you know, faster and more reliably than we could achieve with torture. It would save me bringing in my painsmiths, but if we have to do that, you will meet the painsmiths anyway, for wasting our time. Make this easy on yourself and confess, Taik. We'll get our answers, one way or another. The Dread Corps always does."

When they were finished with Pale Taik, he had given up the name of a meeting point, The Dripping Cauldron in Wick's Fifth Ward. They would find the Gentleman somewhere in that area, and Taik would be executed for treason at dawn.

Starling led Maringdale outside to a bench that overlooked Null's pit, with its canyon of a mine forming an abyss. They breathed in the night air, to cleanse the reek of sweat and fear from the cellar. He said, "I can't say this was an especially welcome development. But Battle Chief Ways was right about you."

"Ways?" Maringdale replied with surprise.

Starling nodded. "We do talk, you know. He said to give you a chance."

"And Battle Chief Hark?"

The Dread mage smirked. "I have not heard from him. I can imagine what he would have said, though." Disapproving. So it wasn't just her that disliked him. "I won't lie, I thought we had the Purification in our pocket with Taik. He didn't stir trouble. Which was apparently a problem."

"I'm to sorry to say," Maringdale said, "that as long this war lasts, anyone who's not knee-deep in trouble is not doing their part."

This drew another thin, regretful smile from Starling. "True. We've been complacent, not least because we have relatively little to hide here. I merely organise resources for our efforts at the front."

Maringdale read between the lines. The resources the Dread Corps were experimenting on, as Netts had described, were people. Was Starling taking prisoners from the mines to send for use in the other Dread stations' tests?

"It's almost easy to forget what it's all for, out here," Starling continued. "That there are threats everywhere. We got very lucky today. I'll need to withdraw. We're almost there, anyway."

He went quiet and Maringdale felt his emotions coming stronger than before, inviting her to question him. She realised then that he had been masking his feelings before, and the understanding startled her. She felt people's intentions in different strengths, but to encounter someone who could actively block her was rare. He was now demonstrating he trusted her. She said, "You want me to ask exactly what you're doing?"

Starling met her eye to say she'd have to confirm that herself.

"From what I understand," she said, "you're combining magics, to chain a psychic attack. Though the strain on the mages involved must be considerable, and the range limited, so I'm not clear on the exact outcome desired."

"The desired outcome," Starling said, "is to win the war."

"Of course."

"Do not worry about the details. You are already playing a part in realising it. An intention mage of your calibre is exactly what we need to keep vigilant, and you're plainly wasted in the Purification. Would you be willing to travel to Wick?"

Maringdale was thankful that the dark would hide the pleasure that flushed to her face. She replied, "I was going to suggest it myself."

28

Nightly, I am treated to an otherworldly orchestra. Aficionados of the great Fillani music scene could not conceive of the sounds of Eardung. How can I describe the calls of creatures for which our language has not been trained? Ah, but you must hear it for yourself!
Mountains of Wood, Smartwether, p. 95

"I'm just surprised there was any worry," Emi said, as the scout leadership walked together with her and Dollemore through the tunnel of tree roots. "Saint Dollemore should've been able to part those roots with her infinite skill and wisdom."

"The barkmen, I can communicate with," Dollemore said, irritably. "But there's not enough that resembles life in their root systems for me to manipulate. *Your* people are the ones useful for shifting dead weights."

Wild Wish was happy to see the mages biting at each other, drawing attention away from her drastic decision to sink a ship. But Tate interrupted, "Whether or not we could've got out wasn't the issue. It was whether or not we would be permitted to continue. The barkmen went quiet on us."

"And they're still reticent," Dollemore said. "This could lead us off a cliff or even back to the Drail, for all we know."

"We're heading in the right direction," Captain Brade said. He was walking quite well, now, his injury having all but healed. "Trust me, the compass doesn't lie."

"Unless the mindless make it," Emi volunteered.

"Or you hold it near a magnet," Dollemore said. They found common ground, at least, in contradicting him. The captain gave them a submissive smile.

"The right direction for the Horns?" Larkin confirmed, with scepticism. Since Boot Squad had caught up and they'd walked into the tunnel of roots, rather than turning back to the now-safer river, she'd taken on a grumpy, disappointed air. Wish understood that the lieutenant's encouragement over sinking the ship had been less to do with covering their tracks than hoping they wouldn't be forced deeper into the woods. "Remind me again what dangers lie between here and there?"

"The beasts of Eardung?" Brade replied, perking up at another opportunity to share his knowledge. "Some say they're larger and stranger than even the Dread creatures of Slane. They've only ever been the subject of speculation, though. Sir Robert Smartwether reported hearsay of them, when he made this journey, but even he never claimed to encounter anything stranger than the six-legged stag of Westerbane."

"Yet the barkmen gave us this shelter."

"For protection from people," Dollemore said. "It'll last a couple more miles, before we're clear of any possible Drail scouts."

"And if we go a couple more miles and the roots don't open again?"

"Then we die in here and get consumed by the forest," Dollemore answered flatly. "What do you want, a written contract? They constructed this tunnel *for us*, why bother unless to help?"

"To lead us to the lair of a monster?" Wish suggested, almost under her breath.

"Shall we stop trying to second-guess the barkmen?" Tate said. "We'll deal with it either way, but as we're alive right now, they appear to have thrown in their lot with us. That Drail ship cost them lives, too – the war has come to Eardung and they've made a choice."

"It might represent an opportunity for the Empire," Brade said. "If we could get a message back to Command. Mean Ridge alone represents a small chink in Drail's western flank, but if Eardung granted safe passage, that could create a wide opening."

"Good luck dragging artillery through the trees," Tate replied, then turned to Wish. "Explain properly, Wild Wish, what were you thinking going back to the river?"

Wish cringed. In the brief flurry of discussion before they'd started marching, Larkin had jumped on the fact that the river was empty as a justification to go back, but Tate said no, there was no question of risking it. The little disagreement had distracted everyone from holding Wish properly responsible, and she had hoped it would simply never come up again.

Not wanting to make Larkin any more upset, Wish said, "I wanted to make sure the Drail didn't follow us."

"An idea you came up with all on your own?"

Tate knew, Wish was sure of it. Knew that Larkin had planted seeds and the lieutenant wasn't owning up to it. There were Power Politics going on here, the sort played by commanders, which Wish was not equipped for. So she said, "Yup."

"And you killed every last one of them?"

"Um."

"We dealt with enough of them," Emi said. "Including, you'll be pleased to know" – she leered Dollemore's way – "a witlacer."

"You did?" Brade asked Wish, impressed.

"Yes," Wish said. "Emi broke the ship, we covered her. Four Skills shot the mage."

"Well isn't that something. Of course, now they'll definitely throw all they've got at us. But still, bravo."

"They sent a gunboat," Tate said. "It doesn't get much more serious than that. Well, Wish. I'm not sure it was wise, but I expect we can credit it for swaying the barkmen towards helping us. Either way, with the gunboat gone and the potential aid of the barkmen, we might get through this yet."

"They *are* helping," Dollemore insisted.

"We don't have a capable enough guide right here, I guess?" Larkin said, folding her arms as she stared at Brade. He cocked his head to one side, half smiling at her audacity.

"Don't tell me you're afraid of the wilderness," Brade said. "An infantry unit that's taken down a gunboat, broken Mean Ridge and killed a hawk giant all in the space of a week? As well as put the thorn in the side of 8th Division at Green Rise." He looked particularly at Wish as he said this, and she felt herself reddening.

"Indeed," Tate said. She moved a few steps ahead of the column of scouts and turned back to shout. "Listen up, any of you who weren't already eavesdropping. We're hiking to the Horns, assuming the help of the barkmen for now, but be on your guard. Expect the worst. We're in the fire, but together we'll get through." She stood tall, chest up to give everyone an eyeful of what a leader looks like. "Scouts, we just survived a Drail gunboat. We can survive all the way to the heart of Hell, I have no doubt about it. Boorah!" She repeated it louder, seriously. "Boorah!"

A couple of girls half-heartedly joined in.

"I can't hear you! Are we going to kick this forest in the arse or what?"

"Boorah!" they shouted back, jolted into a proper response.

"Are we going to march into Slane and *fuck* the Screaming Prince from behind?"

"Boorah!"

Wish joined in and twisted back to watch her fellow scouts. Newk was getting into it, putting her all into the chant. They were in this together, and that made all the difference. They had each other's backs. They had the righteous fight. They *had* to survive this and win. Wish jumped on the spot, punching a fist in the air, shouting, "Boorah!"

And the girls were laughing then – only half serious, knowing this was the men's chant, this was the mad posturing of soldiers who puffed themselves up to avoid facing the reality of what sat before them. Fooling themselves because it was easier than the truth. But *half* serious, because a good shout could inspire and light a fire, to give them the guts to face whatever this forest held, and distract them from why the Drail had a damn gunship waiting for them anyway, and how in hell any of them were ever getting home.

The root tunnel eventually parted, spitting the scouts back out into the impossibly dense wilderness. Thick with trees, occasionally beset by large creatures making strange noises nearby, Eardung only got more difficult to traverse as it became increasingly uneven. The scouts had to hike up and down again, up further, through valleys, around the edge of cliffs, only occasionally able to see beyond the trees when the slopes rose high enough to look back over blankets of canopy. It was incredible to see how densely packed it remained for so far, a nation reportedly as wide as Stanclif itself.

Tensions remained high for the first day, after the attack on the river, but calmed after a restful night; the next day was easier, given that the higher they climbed the cooler the weather became and the more apparently distant they got from civilisation. The chances of running into the Drail were almost non-existent, and with a little care and guidance from the occasional barkman it was easy enough to steer clear of the wilder threats of Eardung. Despite their initial fears, it seemed the fauna wasn't comparable to the Dread creatures of Low Slane. Wild Wish only spotted animals that looked a little like too-tall deer (with four legs), and kept noticing small squirrel-like creatures jumping between the branches. Charming rather than threatening.

That was all just as well, because a lot of the girls got their blood around that time. Perfect timing, away from the fighting, as it brought tired, cranky pain for Wish, and it made her too irritable to talk. Conversation was already sparse as the march was tough and no one had much energy, so it fed into a general silence. Wish tried, a couple of times, to engage Newk, but she struggled to come up with natural conversation and received only minimal answers. She was jealous of the couple of girls in the squad who found the war stopped them bleeding. A result of stress or terrible diets or all the exercise, who knew. It sounded like a blessing. It might indicate serious long-term medical issues, but who was going to live long term, anyway.

Wish was also getting tense about Angles lingering around their group, mostly getting into nonsensical conversation with Pound but also flashing Newk lots of knowing little smiles. Pound and Angles kept jabbering about their past lives, much of which Wish was certain was invented. She was used to it from Pound, a boisterous girl whose bar work had given her all sorts of tall tales to tell, but dubious about Angles, who claimed to have worked a year as a hairdresser on a cruise liner that travelled the world. She had been to three dozen ports and seen everything, to believe her.

On the third day, Wish heard laughter down the ranks, as concerns for keeping quiet faded. To tackle their waning supplies, they took a diversion to a creek where they stocked up on water and washed their underwear. Four Skills volunteered to hunt animals for meat, which Tate allowed only after Dollemore conferred with a barkman. After an afternoon's rest, they marched on. Brade claimed confidently they were going the right way, but he continually checked his compass and his map. His bigger worry, Emi suggested to Wish, was that they were taking too long. Every day marching was another day the Drail had to finish their weapon.

"Maybe they've used it already," Wish said. "Out here, away from it all, how would we know? What difference would it make?"

"Kind of peaceful here, isn't it?" Dakoda said, walking alongside them "Maybe a better place for a farm than Stanclif."

"Ha," Wish said. "With no running water, no city?"

"No war."

"No risking our necks on some fool's mission," Rue grumbled.

"We'd go crazy," Emi said. "Without other people, we'd only have each other to blame for our everyday frustrations. We'd end up eating each other."

"Fixit would be happy, I guess," Rue said.

"What's that?" the medic, further back, called out.

"Said you're slowing us down!" Rue shouted, and on they marched.

On the fourth night, when Brade suggested they might make the Horns the next day, the scouts cracked out the booze. Some started singing. Wish determined it was the time to properly connect with Newk. She marched through the clustered girls and froze as she spotted Newk, sitting on a log the other side of camp, leaning over Angles. The pair were close, feel-the-breath-in-your-hair close, and Newk was smiling – *laughing*. Wish stared wide-eyed as Newk pushed Angles' shoulder. The flirt.

"Wild, a word," a man's voice snapped Wish out of staring, startling her enough to yelp. She turned on Captain Brade who looked entirely not bothered by her reaction. "I need to go over what'll be expected of you tomorrow."

"Of me?" Wish bleated, trying to keep one eye on Newk.

"You know what it'll be like, going through the Horns?"

"Huh?"

"Miss Wish!" Brade's uncharacteristic assertive tone snapped her to attention. He looked harried. He'd been walking without aid for two days now and appeared as run-down as when he'd first made it to Blythe. His fine uniform was frayed, muddied and tired, his stubble uneven and his moustache bristly. He said, "We're days behind, this is . . . not easy for me."

Wild tried to push Newk out of her mind, to focus. "You're used to moving without baggage, huh?"

"No," Brade said. "You're all doing fine. Admirable in fact. What I'm used to, though, is *winning*. I can't allow those bastards back in Drail . . ." He trailed off. "I just want us to succeed. Hence we're taking the Horns. This is going to be dangerous, Wild Wish. I've discussed it with Tate and your sniper friend –"

"Four Skills?"

"Other one."

"*Oksy?*" Wish exclaimed. "Why would you –"

"She's been mountaineering in Mattin, has some experience with these things. What do you know about the Horns?"

"They're noisy," Wish said. That's what they taught in school. The Horns of Heaven were a system of caves running through the mountains that formed a natural border between the Heaven's Eye Lakelands and Eardung. The mountains climbed into the clouds, they said. The Horns themselves warned strangers off, with deafening trumpet sounds caused by the wind. Wish added, "Loud enough to explode heads."

"Doubtful," Brade said. "The bigger danger is the strength of the wind once we're inside. They channel air at great speeds – it's thought that's how they were formed, where small tunnels picked up wind currents that smoothed them out, creating wider caves."

"Did Oksy tell you this? Because I'm not always sure where she gets her information. She claims to have studied at Farroway University, but I haven't seen her papers."

Brade stared, nonplussed. "No, what Oksy shared with me was some good practices for mountain climbing and rappelling. It might not be easy to navigate the tunnels and we're not going to have much light, if any. Our key goal is to always move into the wind. That'll eventually take us through to the lake side."

"Got it," Wish said. "Walk into the wind." She gave a mock salute and went to turn away, but Brade's hand was suddenly on her arm, pulling her back.

"I'm counting on you to take your squad through intact. I'm not going to lose anyone to some bloody wind, you understand?"

Wish frowned, not exactly surprised that his affable charm so far might have been a front for a more forceful, typical man underneath, but not liking that the outburst was directed at her. She said, "Okay, I don't intend to –"

"Drink tonight? Stay up too late? Get distracted by who likes who around the campfire? Good." Brade held her gaze, his hand still on her arm. "They can enjoy themselves. They need to – it'll help everyone if they're relaxed. You can't. You're going to be awake early. You're going to be focused. You need to be their foundation, not their friend."

Wild Wish paused, trying to stir up exactly the kind of *fuck you* this warranted, but the look on her face must've been enough, because he went on: "The girls need strong leadership. Tate, Spyke, Larkin, Harmon, Dollemore, Emi and *you*, Wild Wish. We'll have our heads so the rest don't have to. Understand?"

Wish kept staring. What right did he have –

"Captain Tate won't say it because she thinks you'll do better without pressure. I disagree. I don't want you hungover tomorrow, Wild. I *can't* have you hungover." There was just enough desperation in his voice to say his concern was genuine. Not a madman trying to control her, but a fool who thought their survival depended on this. Wish looked from him back to Newk. She was giggling with Angles. Rue, Dakoda and Fixit were rolling dice on the ground. A couple of Rock Squad girls were warbling along to Larkin's lute.

How was Wish supposed to enjoy any of this now? Thinking about her responsibility and the possibility of them all dying because she couldn't keep her head. Brade should have listened to Tate; she didn't want to hear this, and tried to get rid of him: "It's fine. Whatever you say. I'll be a good girl."

"Thank you," Brade said. "I'll make it up to you when this is over."

Wish eyed him. "I bet you've been saying that to everyone."

He smiled, finally a crack in his tension. "Funny." He paused. "You know, being the only man in a troop of formidable young ladies might sound enticing, but it's deathly intimidating."

"Oh I know. For it to be a dream, they have to all *like* you."

"Indeed." Brade laughed.

"But I can offer some tips on who you shouldn't lose sleep over trying to impress. Myself included." The second point just came out, and Wish felt a pang at the thought of Tate thinking she could string this wealthy captain along. She didn't want to. But he didn't even seem to notice.

"Ah, it wouldn't do to be distracted by such feelings out here. I have the utmost respect for all of you, that is all."

"*All* of us?" Wish said. "Because honestly, Emi is a bit of a –" Wish stopped. Rue was now with Newk. Angles had gone to get drinks or something and Rue was smiling. Rue only smiled when she was about to do something bad. Or was this worse? Rue driving Angles off to claim Newk as her own. "Oh no."

"Ah but she is fascinating, isn't she?" Brade mused, following her gaze. "Do you know quite how *different* her people are? They live on back-towns, built on the shells of enormous beasts. Often moving, fluidly joining and parting from other communities as they go. They are true nomads, so different to us. There's so much we can learn from them, yet we treat them like lesser races. It's good to see how easily your platoon has accepted her."

Wish bit her lip, having not prepared herself for Rue's specific acceptance there. And not sure exactly why Brade was telling her this, either. To drive home that she shouldn't get too close to someone so different?

"I'll let you get back to your team," Brade said rather than elaborate. He gave Wish a pat, very gentle in contrast to grabbing her before. "Just keep what I said in mind."

That brought her out of her current concerns. What had he said? Don't have fun, don't get cosy with the girls. Wish frowned at the spot he'd touched, recalling again Tate's encouragement to seduce Brade. Get a husband out of the war. Had he understood she wasn't interested? She said, "Captain. You're not . . ." He held her gaze with kind eyes. Silently acknowledging that the question didn't need asking.

Brade offered a tired smile. "I'm not an idiot. Just . . . be responsible."

He winked and walked away and Wish stared uncertainly. Responsible. She hated being responsible. She would rather be anything but responsible, for her actions, for making friendships messy, for keeping her friends alive, for all those men dead in the river, all those men dead on the battlefield, all those men dead –

Wish shuddered. She didn't need any of this. She wandered quickly through the camp, deflated, and interrupted Rue to bid them all good night. They booed and jeered as she said, "It's gonna be tough tomorrow. I'm turning in so I'll be ready to take care of you all. Enjoy yourselves."

She gave Newk a little extra smile and offered Rue a questioning glance, who gave her a blank look in return. Well, she'd done what she could. Wish clambered into the tent and stared at nothing, ignoring the muffled sounds outside. She clung onto the little smile Newk had returned her. Sleep didn't come. Brade's words wormed into her brain like the sort of grubs they feared lurked in Eardung. This was their last chance to relax before diving tit-deep into the Drail quagmire. She was supposed to relax and leave the likes of Tate and Larkin to worry. The way she used to, passing off concerns to Sarge. But she'd taken that role, and by hell – was that what it would be like in Swelig, on *her* farm? They would frolic in fields and giggle by the fire while she worried about taxes. Was it a bad plan?

Behind her worries, Wild Wish noticed a change of tenor outside the tent. Voices lowered. The rest of the scouts started turning in. Early. Rue came through the tent flaps, crawling carelessly over Wish's legs, and Wish eloquently asked, "Whu?"

"Ruined it for everyone, didn't you," Rue grumbled, making a show of shuffling into the ground, getting comfortable. "If *Wild* can be responsible, the hell does it say about the rest of us?"

"You've got it backward," Wish told her. "I'm taking a night off so you don't have to. That's an officer's job."

"Give me a break. You ever see Sarge turn in earlier than us?"

Wish frowned. Sarge *did* like to drink, even if she was seldom fun. Had Brade tricked her into making an example? *Why?* She squeezed her eyes closed, too many questions. "Whatever. It's probably for the best."

"Too right for the best," Rue said, as though she hated the best. "Nights like these are numbered, you know? There'll be no talking and drinking once we're surrounded by greens."

"That's why —"

"I don't need telling. Shut up and get some sleep, if we're gonna."

Wish lay still, eyes open, a warm feeling growing in her chest. It *was* sensible. They'd be rested. And she had split up whatever was happening with Rue and Newk. She said, "You seem to be getting on with Newk, after all?"

"The ringer?" Rue said, sounding half asleep already. "She's all right."

"Think you'll . . ." Wish didn't want to ask. Didn't want to imagine a new mess like sharing a tent with Rue and Loose. Enjoying a relationship by proxy, imagining one day it might be her. Rue and Newk. That wasn't a natural match, but the whole war was unnatural, wasn't it? She instead said, "Do you know they live on the backs of giant animals, down in Fireti? The creatures must be huge. The biggest thing I've ever seen was probably that hawk giant."

And I killed it. Her thoughts ran on without her. The most impressive creature most of them had ever seen, most likely, and they slaughtered it. Ate its flesh.

Rue didn't respond. A throaty snore suggested she didn't even hear.

29

The Horns of Heavens, a cave system that separates Heaven's Eye from Eardung, have never been successfully navigated by people. The winds, one of the most unusual and impressive natural phenomenons of the Rocc, are strong enough to damage the brain and the tunnels are too narrow to walk down.

**Geography of Boldarow, Atkins, p. 72
[School textbook, discontinued in 721]**

Tikan Mythology held that Prince Orfus walked the Horns with rags stuffed in his ears, to bring back his beloved Jupion. He heard the word of the Saints, which guided him on the right path. He returned without Jupion, but blessed with new knowledge, to become a Priest of the Saints. To this day, the people of Lakelands leave offerings to the Saints around the Horn openings, and make pilgrimages into the caves seeking spiritual guidance.

Legends of the Kleb Range, Brade, p. 120

Early morning, the scouts heard the first notes from the Horns of Heaven. The sound was both gentle and arresting, its far-off tenor more than a whistle on the wind. From the front of their marching platoon, picking up speed and new enthusiasm, Brade called back to the girls, "Robert Smartwether never came this close – he recounted second-hand stories of the Horns, but never heard them for himself. He was a day's walk away, still, when his companion, Jon Saye, was afflicted by a terrible malady."

"He got attacked by a duck?" Emi said.

"An illness," Fixit explained, "not a mallard." Emi mugged to be absolutely clear that she was being a dick.

"It wasn't an illness, was it?" Oksy came in. "Jon Saye was injured."

Brade gave her a backwards glance that said he wasn't planning to divulge the details, but he smiled and elaborated. "Yes. I suppose we're almost out now, so it won't hurt to share. Burrowing beetles came into Saye's tent at night. By the time they woke him, some had already crawled into his ear. He only managed to drive them out by melting candle wax onto them." Gasps of shock and disgust ran through the platoon, with those towards the back spreading the tale quickly for anyone that hadn't heard.

"I bloody knew it," Wild Wish whispered, close to Newk.

"That's behind us," Brade insisted over the hubbub. "Things will be a simpler on the other side of these mountains."

"Yeah," Spyke grumbled. "Over there, no one's pretending we're safe."

"Long as we have each other's backs," Tate said, gruffly, "we'll take on all comers."

It sent a ripple of half-hearted bravado through the scouts.

Getting closer, the Horns sounded occasionally, like piped chimes from a music hall. Chatter increased nearer the rising mountains, as the sound became louder and the scouts sought distraction. The melody was becoming something closer to the dramatic warning of ship horns, notes designed to be heard over storms. Where the trees thinned, the craggy inclines became apparent ahead, along with the great cave entrances that were producing the trumpeting. At the base of the mountains proper, the scouts marvelled at rushes of air that came from the vast tunnels.

The scouts followed Brade and Tate's instructions to tie off together, not as squads but as one platoon, two-abreast, to crawl through the caves like a giant human caterpillar. Sun Squad took the lead, Tate at the front with Brade just behind, his courage up now he was able to move properly, ready to outdo Smartwether.

Dakoda said, "Bet you twenty bob he writes a book about this and bags a fortune off our slaving."

"Bet you he's already written one," Pound replied. "His lot don't wait to actually do stuff before selling stories about it."

"Pound's right," Oksy offered, helpfully, because of course she knew. "He told me he's published three books already, including one about Eardung mythology."

"Well, he'll have to update it," Dakoda said. "Seeing as we're about to become a part of it."

"Think we'd best focus now, don't you all?" Wish suggested, before anyone could lower the tone some more. It was a relatively lame effort at command, but it did enough to redirect attentions to securing the knots around their waists. The girls checked one another's work, tugging at the straps of bags and rifles, and gave each other reassuring pats before starting their ascent. The nearest cave entrance blew out a low, sad note, and was met a moment later by a series of higher, longer chimes far above.

Brade called out advice for climbing, securing handholds, lifting with your feet, bolstered by titbits from Oksy who insisted they were going to keep secure by frequently digging in their axes and picks. There were only a dozen picks between them, if that, but they'd pass them along the line. The pair sounded confident, but Wish wondered if they had any clue what was really in store.

It took another hour before they reached the entrance to the closest cave, high above the trees so they could enjoy another sweeping view of leafy canopy, stretching as far as the horizon. Wish squinted against the morning sun to try and make out a slither of sea far off, but couldn't.

The scouts waited outside the cave for everyone to regroup, taking food and water, and listened for the wind blasts. It sounded planned, the harmony of enormous notes that boomed above, gusts of air visible only with the occasional rocky debris propelled out of the caves at tremendous speed, with the power of a cannon.

When the cave next to them blasted its note, everyone pressed back to the rocks and each other. Wish squeezed Newk's hand. They were tied together, at Boot's front, in behind Oksy and Angles at Rock's rear. In this case, Wish was happy to follow Oksy, she being one of the few people with some idea of how they'd get through this, her arse less likely than others to distract her. But Oksy let out an unfiltered curse at the speed and volume of the air rushing out of the cave.

"Think we can run through between blasts?" Angles shouted.

"They're two-minute intervals and we're walking through an entire mountain range!" Rue shouted back. "How long you think that's gonna take us?"

"Emi, could you do something?" Larkin yelled.

"And risk collapsing the system?" Emi shouted back. "I'm not *touching* this shit."

But the argument was moot; they had their plan. The blasting air died down and Tate yelled her orders, "Everyone in and move fast! Dig in when the first wind comes!"

They piled in together as one rapidly marching troop, boots drumming against smooth stone, and once they were round the corner of the cave their pace picked up further. A short way inside, the floor became smoother, and when someone near the front slipped, a word of warning swept back. Wish dogged Oksy's heels, taking small steps to make sure she kept her own balance, watching for light ahead. They had only a few electric lamps between them, climbing into a stone beast's gullet.

The cave slanted, its incline getting steeper the further they descended, and the light from outside got dimmer behind them. Wish looked back, the opening small now, like the monster's mouth was closing.

"We're tiny snacks," she whispered.

"Until it spits us out," Newk replied.

A few steps more and the first panic came from up front – a wind blast was coming. Oksy shouted at the top of her voice, instructing everyone to secure their picks or hold on to what they could. The breeze teased at their hair as the picks sparked into place – then the great gust suddenly burst over them. Girls cried out up and down the line, locking their legs into place, fighting against the wind. It lashed at Wish's face, making her turn away, hair flattened across her eyes. She gritted her teeth as a stronger whoosh of air caught her chest, slid her boot back across the stone, to collide with Rue behind her, who pushed back. Someone yelped, a helmet came loose and spiralled through the air, making everyone else duck. The girls cursed and cursed as the wind's sound rolled around them, a rumbling crescendo, then it left the cave mouth.

As quick as it came, the wind was gone, and the girls were still. Just for a moment, before they all started laughing, helping to steady each other. Tate wasted no time, ordering them on, and they continued, checking again that their equipment was tied securely.

They moved quickly, deeper into the cave, and stopped every few minutes to dig themselves in as the wind rushed over them. After three or four blasts, when it became clear they weren't all going to get blown away, they got braver and started moving through the wind, digging the picks into a wall but pulling themselves along them, the scouts at the rear passing the last picks forward. It wasn't gaining them much ground, but it kept them going without breaks.

Soon, commentary came back that the tunnel was getting narrower, and when the walls were barely more than shoulder-width apart Wish started worrying they'd find their passage blocked. But there was another problem: where the cave was tighter, the wind pushed harder, and the first blast in this confined space caught them by surprise. Angles was knocked off her feet and almost went tumbling back, caught only by the quick intervention of the girls of Sabre squad. Worse, someone lost their grip on a pickaxe and it came free, flying overhead. They all ducked, the tool clattering into the walls and then off down the tunnel behind them. Gone. They continued more soberly after that, taking care to brace themselves in the tighter patches. But when the tunnel widened again, the winds grew less oppressive.

The march through the dark lasted forever, repetitive, with no features to pass, no hint they were getting closer to an exit. The tunnel dipped down, down, and then up again. It curved one way then another, and they started to pass alternative passages. Circular holes connected offshoots like tracks in an ants' nest. Brade insisted they always stick to the largest path, the channels the others fed, and assured them repeatedly they were going the right way, but the further they went, the more tired they got from the thumping winds, the more doubt crept in. Shouts escalated: "We've been here forever! We're lost!"

"We're going the right way!" was all Brade yelled back. But he'd told them no one had gone through these tunnels, hadn't he? The caves might never leave the mountain again.

He'd also told Wish they needed to be brave, strong, steady. She dug deep, knowing something was required of her. "Next person to complain is sleeping in the bloody barn when we get to the farm!"

It got a ripple of laughs, but it wasn't enough: one of Sabre squad called out, "We might not bloody *get* back!"

"Not if you keep whining about a windy tunnel. Suck it up!"

"Come on, Pound's done farts worse than this!" Rue shouted, to help.

The next blast almost took one of Wish's legs away, though, and she wished she could just curse and complain too. She soldiered on, head down, fearing the winds were getting stronger, like they were entering the central heart of this mountain's fearsome force. Others sensed it too, because murmurs ran through them. With all her effort to keep positive, Wish shouted, "Nearly there, everyone!"

Larkin took over, thank hell, and started a classic call and response, "Where are we going!"

The closest girls sniggered before a couple gave the response, "Off to the war!"

"What are we going to do?"

"Even the bloody score!" more girls joined in.

"Where are we going?"

"Off to the war!"

"Why are we going there?"

"Who fucking knows what for!" A cacophony of hoots and whistles met the amended end to the traditional jingo, and as the girls laughed, Larkin started it again. The girls joined in louder, improvising other lines. After a couple more rounds, Wish caught Newk joining in, wholeheartedly, looking like she belonged. Wish was beaming, imagining their song echoing through the whole mountain, carried out through a hundred exits, the scouts serenading Eardung and the world beyond. This was their stage, little parasites that had taken over the beast that swallowed them.

Once Larkin finished, Dollemore broke into song, her voice more melodious than most in the platoon, with a tune of loss and sorrow. Made irreverent by the similarly amended lines of crude, cynical soldiers:

Where are you now my Jimmy?
Come back to me a hero,
Or don't come back at all.
Where are you now my Jimmy?
Come apart in pieces,
We'll flush you down the stall.

It helped. Song always helped in long marches and dark nights and even as the winds beat down on them and the tunnels only got darker and one of the damn girls dropped a torch, they could still sing, together, loudly, defiantly. Words meant to keep them in line and bolster the Empire, but changed into words that said they knew. They knew it was all a lie, that everything was wrong with this war, but they'd keep fighting. They'd survive.

They sung through the Horns of Heaven, songs they hadn't sung for weeks – even months – not since before Green Rise and Blythe and Loose fell and Sarge died. Back when they could still *see* the war and Wild Wish hadn't yet killed a thousand people. They sung and Wish sung louder than most, with a wide smile as she did, not caring for the looks she got, even as the others joined in. She sung and the mountain itself, with its roaring winds, sung with them.

30

Much can be said of Wick, but it is perhaps best summarised by the work of military historian Edmin Pinster, who painstakingly studied records of every war in modern Farnish territory on record, deducing exactly how long the city, in all its forms, was considered part of an active conflict. Pinster concluded that Wick is likely the single most besieged site, quantitatively speaking, in the entire Rocc.

Dueley's Comprehensive: The One War in 10 Volumes (Vol. 6), p. 261

Wick exuded tension and violence as it drifted into view. An immense fortress city surrounded by high walls dotted with anti-airship harpoons and ground cannons, its stone-carved, tower-riddled streets combined into a single massive entity with one purpose: war. As the wyrling brought that into perspective, Maringdale took in the surrounding theatre: a wide river twisted behind the city and rocky, tree-spattered hills rose either side. It was green to the north of the river, the lands the Drail controlled. South, where the terrain opened up, the ground was craters and black-brown churned mud. There was more movement than around Highscythe, as trucks drove down from the north and sporadic groups of soldiers, the size of ants from here, raced towards the city. Donut brought their ride lower and Maringdale noticed war machines moving through the trees, hulking metal vehicles too far away to properly make out.

The Drail guns lining Wick's walls started firing – huge cannons, with bases the size of houses. Their booms echoed through the terrain and their rounds flew impossible distances before exploding with puffs that had to be immense at ground level. Distracted by the drama, Donut circled Gulvar around the city before descending to a landing bay, an area of elevated wooden platforms with men in padded hats waving flags. A small airship was at rest to one side and airmen gathered to see the flying lizard come in. Maringdale cringed, imagining the spectacle they'd make, but Donut brought the beast in steadily, with quiet commands, and it trotted only a small distance before steadying. He'd apparently mastered it since last time.

It didn't stop Netts cursing. He jumped down from the wyrling the moment it was safe, complaining about the flight, the fact that he'd had to come at all, and the truly screwed situation this city was in.

"Who you with?" a burly, overworked man in greasy overalls demanded, striding over. "Didn't get word of wyrlings needing taken care of. Got two more airships coming down from the 21st Division, don't have space for this."

"He'll go in any good-size stable," Donut said. "He's no worse than two horses."

"That's not what I bloody asked!" the man fumed.

"We're with the Purification," Maringdale told him – a flat promise of trouble that stopped him in his tracks. "You will find space for it. What's the situation report?"

"Situation?" the bay attendant replied, coy now from saying whatever belligerent thing he wanted to. He ran one hand through the other and shook his head. "City'll hold. Like I said, 21st Division's coming down to reinforce us, 13th already have a strong hold here, and what's left of 8th are piling in. We've got artillery can out-blast anything Stanclif have and parsers warding the walls like you wouldn't believe."

"What's left of the 8th?" Maringdale echoed. She didn't know the divisions for their different numbers, but she did know that each number represented a sizeable force.

The bay attendant nodded gravely. "Guess you were in the air when it happened, huh? Green Rise. The Comity fucked us up."

"Shit." Maringdale quickly started shedding her riding clothes. "Do you know where we can find the Dread Corps?"

"Dread Corps?" the man startled, wanting no part of that. But her fierce look made him answer. "Yeah, they took Riker Cathedral. Head for the centre and look for the bell tower with the Saint blade, can't miss it."

"Donut, meet us there when you're done. Netts, with me." Maringdale marched down the stairs to the city proper. Beyond the city, the Comity forces were pressing closer, with bomb blasts shaking the walls, and the Drail's own big guns replied explosively.

"Bloody hell, we're not gonna wanna stay long," Netts said, trotting to keep up. "Straight to this rendezvous point and away, what do you say?"

"By nightfall this city will be locked down," Maringdale replied irritably. "He'd be mad to have stayed a moment longer than necessary. *Shit.*" She clenched her fists, feeling this falling away from her. So close to cornering a major Stanclif agent and the damned wider war had to interfere. And with the chaos around her, she'd never pick up dissenting feelings, even if the spy was still here. Striding down a street bustling with soldiers, she called out for directions to the cathedral and got vague pointers. Soon, the bell tower showed between Wick's tall buildings – a military-strength turret with the jagged, dull metal symbol of the Cane Saints, a hand-blade meant for reaping crop that was also alleged to have gutted the prophet Venzus. A crowded path through alleys and narrow streets brought them to the base of the great cathedral, a slate-and-stone brick structure with narrow, metal-latticed windows and a foreboding iron door. Maringdale tried it. Locked. After knocking loudly with no response, she went around the side of the building and found a smaller side-door, this one open. It led into an unlit antechamber lined with empty boxes and shelves, where two Dread soldiers were leaning against a wall, idling. They didn't move, but one took in Netts' uniform and asked, "Where've you come in from?"

"Null," Netts replied.

The soldiers frowned and a moment later realised there was also a *woman* present. One of the men made a belated protest as Maringdale continued to the next chamber. The ceiling rose away to vast height, partly lost in shadow, the cathedral interior a pillared space decorated with sharp-edged carvings, more elaborate and intricate than the exterior suggested. The benches had been cleared away and a great number of Dread soldiers were gathered amongst weapons, supply packs and bed rolls. Maringdale's eyes fell on a grekkel squad amongst the soldiers, by a dais reserved for the Cane worshippers' stone-bleeding pool. The four hunched grekkels, likely seven feet tall if they stood up straight, had curled, taloned hands and canine snouts. Like upright wolves with the spiky skin of a thorned lizard. Maringdale felt the emotions of those surrounding her falling away, dominated by the feral, bloodthirsty attitude seeping out of that squad. It made her cringe and that somehow caught their attention. One turned its head towards her and its long jaws stretched to a nasty slit of a smile.

"I'd guess the Battle Chief's that way," Netts said. "Something wrong?"

Maringdale shook herself out of the grekkel's gaze and turned to follow Netts' gesture to a vestibule door. She tried to refocus. But Drail society was better than this. Why did the Dread Corps have grekkels in their ranks? Wearing their ill-fitted *uniforms?* As she slipped between the watching soldiers, she said to Netts, "I thought your people were elite. Exclusively human."

"Elite, sure," Netts said. "Human? Nah. How could we be the best if we didn't take in grekkels? Seen how fast those bastards run? And they're strong as you like."

"But erratic, irrational."

"If you say so." Netts shrugged, not bothered either way.

They got through the cathedral to the vestibule door, where a grim-faced officer eyed their approach. He didn't have any rankings on him, but had an air of authority, presumably the Battle Chief himself. But as they got close, he nodded over a shoulder without a word, instructing them to continue, and through they went to another dark chamber, where men were gathered over a table talking.

"– because they're not built for that kind of traffic," one man complained.

"They're not *built* at all," someone else hissed, a sinister sibilance to his voice. "That's what makes it's an opportunity."

Maringdale cleared her throat. A bearded older officer looked up from the other side of the table, alongside a humourless, gaunt man in the robes of a Dread mage. Opposite them, with his back to the newcomers, a lanky figure straightened up. He kept rising, taller than Maringdale expected, until his head almost touched the ceiling, arms angling out sharply at the elbows. A canine head turned a chilling look over his shoulder.

"Ah, guests," the grekkel hissed – the sibilant speaker revealed. His eyes glinted invitingly, glassy pale-blue beads, and his curled jaw, bearing sharp teeth, had a sly, untrustworthy smile. "You must be the intention mage." His feelings jumped at Maringdale's intention senses, so sharp she could practically hear them as words – *kill, kill!* – and she flinched back, drawing a frown. "What is it?"

"Must we play this game every time," the bearded officer said. "Yes, miss, the Battle Chief is a grekkel. No, he won't eat your liver. And yes, you're interrupting something important."

Maringdale scanned the men anew and realised now that the grekkel wore the same Dread uniform as Ways, though the cuffs were short around his sharply hinged ankles and rode high on his prickly forearms. He had the same officer's insignias, and a big square pistol holstered low on his narrow hips. The bearded man, however, wore the starched green uniform of a regular Drail officer, gold bars over his heart labelling him a colonel.

"Give us a minute, please," the grekkel asked, civil despite the nasty lisp.

Maringdale nodded and wordlessly backed out of the room. The man who'd gestured her in was smiling, enjoying having sent her in unprepared.

"Probably should've warned you about Battle Chief Baron," Netts murmured, amused too. "Realise that now."

Maringdale stared daggers at him – of course the little shit knew. But thank hell she hadn't said anything too loudly about her disdain for the non-humans. She closed her eyes and tried to calm herself. It wasn't important; even if the city was falling apart and there was a freak in charge here, she was still only a few steps away from thwarting this Stanclif plot and securing a place for herself with the Dread Corps.

She felt for what was going on back in the command room, but could only pick up on the colonel. The grekkel, Baron, was laying out a plan and the colonel both doubted it and worried the plan would work. He would look bad if these aberrant Dread soldiers succeeded where he had failed. Was there a way he could take credit? As the cathedral shuddered under distant artillery fire, the colonel became resigned to letting it be.

"We can talk now." Baron startled Maringdale, poking his animal face through the doorway. She forced a smile as his dead eyes looked through her, then followed him into the room, leaving Netts outside. The colonel was gone, though the Dread mage remained. Maringdale tested to sense the grekkel again, again picking up feral needs – *blood, rending, blood!* Maringdale squeezed the feelings out, hiding her shock. Baron looked perfectly calm, giving no external hint of such murderous thoughts, and spoke smoothly, "Forgive the delay. You're no doubt aware of the developments here. 8th Division gave up a great deal of land and lost countless men, thanks to General Amalric. It's only Castor's mercy that we weren't drawn into that catastrophe. But we've an opportunity for a counter offensive, if the Arrow Council sees fit to let us use rock-worm tunnels. Will you have some root wine?"

"Thanks," Maringdale said, accepting a chalice from the Dread mage while she tried to cleave the battle chief's educated tone with his frightening appearance. The cup, presumably from the cathedral's collection, was full of a thick burgundy liquid that smelt of smoke and dried leaves. A sip warmed her throat.

"What was your read on him?" Baron asked, and Maringdale looked up uncertainly. "The colonel. Don't tell me you weren't working your magic while you waited. *Can* you switch it off?"

"Not exactly," Maringdale said. "Only focus it in particular ways."

"Something of an affinity with the mindless," the Dread mage commented, pouring himself a glass of wine. "Most mortal mages pay a price in energy, but intention mages use this skill as a point of course. Their price is in the maddening, ever-present thoughts of others."

"Feelings, not thoughts," Maringdale corrected. The mage's expressionless face said he didn't care. "And the cost of the magic's neither here nor there – we interact with life energy, mindful creatures, which is the *only* defining factor of a witlacer, versus the scrappy, ugly art of dirt-minding, concerned only with warping things that have no conscious agency."

The Dread mage remained completely impassive, which further irked her, but Baron was smiling again – an unpleasant sight. The grekkel said, "I believe she may know more about it than you, Artemus. I *hope* she does, otherwise why would she be here."

"As far as that's concerned," Maringdale said, happy to get straight to business, "the issue might already have been forced. I was hoping to secure the Fifth Ward of the city. In particular, a tavern called The Dripping Cauldron."

"Starling did wire ahead, yes," Baron replied. "But I'm afraid we have, indeed, been rather busy. You imagined the Gentleman was there?"

"I didn't imagine anything. The man we interrogated in Null said it was their meeting point. He's been spying on you for at least a week."

"Trying to, perhaps," Artemus said. "It's unlikely he saw anything. Our experiments are being conducted a hundred feet under the rock. The catacombs of this cathedral are a fortress within a fortress."

"What about your operations in the field? Are they as well hidden?"

The men exchanged a look, Artemus concerned and Baron slyly impressed.

"It's no coincidence you've got sites near the front," Maringdale said, revealing her conclusions, "so I assume what you're doing here isn't restricted to just *here*."

The sooner she could get out of this room, away from the grekkel, the better. But he was in no hurry and answered with lazy pleasure, "Oh you are as sharp as Ways said."

"Yet for someone so clued-in, you don't know we've already

withdrawn from Blythe," Artemus scoffed, a small victory. Maringdale sensed little malice, though. He wanted to leave, too, to attend something more important. Whatever was in the catacombs.

"Would our spy know that?" Maringdale said. "Because if there's one thing these people seem to have no trouble with, it's finding *where* you are. And if he hasn't given up, with this city coming under siege, I guess we'll find our man on the road to the next easiest target."

"The news of the battle is still fresh," Baron said. "He might not have left the city yet."

"So we let him. He'll be easier to find outside."

"Except" – spittle hissed through his grekkel's teeth – "we've got to assume Blythe is *lost*. It's the wrong side of the river, now, and the 8th Division thoroughly abandoned that land."

"Indeed," Artemus agreed, "we'll be lucky if the last of our fearsmiths make it back."

"Again, would *he* know that?" Maringdale said. "Blythe's still his most attractive target, isn't it?"

Baron considered this. "It's a reasonable assumption."

"I came on a wyrling. How are the airways? I could do a flyover."

"Nonsense," Baron scoffed, rolling a claw. "You've earned a rest, Officer Maringdale. I have cirga that can patrol that road as fast as a wyrling and degrebus that can see twice as far. If he's out there, we'll drag him back screaming. Then you can have your way with him."

Maringdale tried, with effort, to hold his glassy eyes. He would put her chase in the hands of the violent, chitinous cirga and the mentally deficient degrebus. She tried, peripherally, to read how he might react to resistance. Vicious ideas cut at her – *stab, tear!* It was no use, grekkels were on a different wavelength.

He wore a knowing expression and said, "You'll understand by now this is bigger than the Purification. Time to let us go to work for you."

Maringdale nodded, conceding. Cirga were, after all, practically unstoppable.

31

It might pain you to hear it, Betan, but I cannot imagine a situation where I will ever find closer bonds than I have in my brothers-at-arms. We share the same space, the same air, comfortable as pack animals that share a den. We fight and die for each other, and, yes, I truthfully and deeply love my brothers in a way I cannot imagine repeated. It is not like our love, Betan, which is eternal. This is a love of coexistence and shared survival. We are as one body, as it were. Even in the stench and dirt, and the arguments and trespasses, even ███████████████████████ ███████*, our bond is intimate and real.*

**Extract from the Letters of
Corporal T. Sander, Balnia, 719**

The climb out of the Horns was the hardest push yet, with no sunlight or fresh air to aim for, only the dark absence of a ceiling in a tunnel that kept going up. The wind flowed in, unceasing, like the scouts were climbing up a pipe while pushed down by flushing water. Wish imagined them emerging into a giant's sink, to be captured by an overworked maid. If giants had sinks, or were civilised enough to wash things, their captor might be mild-mannered enough to make pets of them – it'd be one way out of the war. They'd been underground so long, pressing so hard, they could have crossed to another world where that was possible. Not this world, where Wish's experience of giants brought the memory of Sarge. Bones crunching in that evil grip.

She shook herself out of it, to focus on the hard task at hand. Sarge wouldn't be lost in thought, she would be leading. Wish tried to evoke that energy and shouted at the top of her voice, "Almost there, girls! Just a little further!"

They cheered each other on, pushing up jagged rocks for twenty, thirty feet, before the exit. Then someone got out and shouted back it was over, they'd made it (not into a giant's sink), and they started pulling each other up.

When it came to Wild Wish's turn, she found herself under Oksy, pushing up with her cheek pressing into her arse, wondering how she was in this situation *again* when there were so many other arses she'd more happily get acquainted with. On the plus side, Rue was beneath her, and Rue was *strong*, practically carrying Wish up with no opportunity to slow down. Rue growled as she lifted, a storming bull, and Wish yelped, she was moving already!

Oksy suddenly disappeared and more wind barrelled into Wish's face, almost knocking her off the wall, but she caught hold of the rocks and clawed herself up, tugged by her rope as others heaved her over the lip of the tunnel and out of the way. They were in a cavern, a massive rock funnel that caught wind and pushed it down the little escape hole Wish had emerged from, one side open to the world. She shouted to the sky in celebration, falling onto solid earth and seeing, far above, pricks of shining starlight.

"Not done yet!" someone snapped, maybe Spyke? And Wild Wish was on her feet again, pulling at the rope, helping the others up.

At last, with the wind howling through the wide cavern behind them, the scouts were finally all free, congratulating each other and checking for injuries. Plenty of cuts and scrapes, boots worn and torn, a lost helmet or two, but otherwise they'd made it intact, together.

Wild Wish put an arm around Newk's shoulders, guiding her to look outside. She caught Pound's shoulders with the other arm, and swung herself between them looking down on their prize. There was scant moonlight coming through the clouds, but the enormity of the landscape was apparent. Beyond rocks and treetops that sloped down from their position, a vast black expanse stretched out like an immeasurable hole in the earth. It filled the horizon, the great lake of Heaven's Eye. And at its edge were dotted yellow lights of small settlements, glowing like the decorations of a Relight tree. Far off to the right, one site glowed brighter than the rest, silhouetting towers and ships in a bay, tiny at this distance.

"All right, all right!" Pound squirmed out from Wish's weight, laughing. "By Bly, I'm aching enough already, Wild."

"Hey" – Wish pointed – "you're my minions now, I'll ride you into battle if I want."

"Ah, who'd predict that Wild would go mad with power?" Pound replied with a wicked smile. "Apart from everyone. Dammit, Captain, what were you thinking."

"She's got you this far." Captain Tate appeared at their side. "I'd say she's done all right." Pound tensed with surprise, about to stutter an apology, it was just a joke, but Tate continued, "That was a hell of journey, everyone. See that city? Most likely Dask, the westernmost city in the Lakelands. The chances are we're not running into military out here, but we're a long way from where we want to be." Others gathered behind them, listening. "We'll need to cross the lake tomorrow. Dollemore, Four Skills, can you take whoever you need and get us a boat? Everyone else, take a well-deserved rest."

Wish woke to find herself pinned by an arm, bent at the elbow with a hand on her chest. She went rigid. The fingers were callused and dry, nails cracked, a dead weight not actually holding her, just lying there. Wish lifted the wrist with the care of relocating a stab-spider and gently placed the arm on the ground. It belonged to Dakoda – Boot's most cynical member had rolled into an unconscious cuddle while they slept. Wish couldn't help smiling as she sat up. She was surrounded by the others, the exhausted scouts having clustered for warmth rather than bothering to put up tents. They were spread across a cliff-edge in a blanket of scruffy-uniformed bodies, draped over each other, snuffling, snoring, and collectively smelling like rotten laundry. Pound was on Wish's other side, and beyond her was Newk. So close, maybe she could slip around to lie there instead –

Wish swallowed a shuddering breath. Inappropriate. She wriggled out from between the girls and stood, careful not to wake them. The view was even more impressive in the morning light. The lake, immense as a sea, was deep blue, under a pale, almost cloudless sky. The villages were collections of brightly painted little houses, blues and yellows, pinks and reds, square things with thatched roofs. A steepled church, quaint and untouched by war. Idyllic.

Until you looked right. The port city of Dask breathed out the thick smoke of industry, the workers off to an early start, and the jetties were crowded with hulking, inelegant warships. There was a long tanker, cornered with gun turrets, a handful of small battle boats similar to the one that had blocked the Little Step, and two wider, uglier ships with artillery cannons at their fronts. Practically a fleet, surrounded by cargo vessels and trawlers.

An agreeing hum announced Wish was not alone in her observations. She twisted around to spot Captain Brade perched on a rock above, one hand on a raised knee, holding his telescope. Though his pallor had improved, his shabby suit, messy hair and growing stubble made him look like he'd fallen down the mountain to get there.

Wish whispered excuse-mes to tread through the mass of scouts. Newk and Dakoda stirred but slipped back into slumber as she tried not to step on anyone. Once free, she pulled herself up the rock to sit next to Brade, rubbed her hands and commented, "Good to see you didn't freeze to death."

"We had a small fire," he replied, quietly. "But I'm always impressed soldiers can get any sleep sprawled on top of each other like gather-rats." He gave Wish a look as if she was of particular interest. "The other girls know you're . . . you know?"

Wish held his gaze rigidly. That was a rather direct assault on her nature for so early in the morning. And of course everyone knew she was *you know*. If they didn't, they'd never leave her behind when they went gunning for hook-ups every time they brushed shoulders with the men. You didn't waste time when you might die any minute. Unless you were Wild Wish.

Wish said, "No one cares. And it's not just me."

"Yes?" Brade said, more curious than critical. "The same situation in a regular platoon would make men very uncomfortable."

"Maybe because men confuse sex and violence," Wish said. "Or power, I don't know. No one here is *scared* of me."

Brade gave her a sceptical look she didn't exactly appreciate. Why would they be scared? The worst she could do was make a hug last too long and go to sleep imagining it lasting forever. The captain said, "I hope you'll forgive my questions. I take a keen interest in anthropology. It fascinates me how people fit together. Your platoon is . . . inspiring."

"Ha!" Wish exclaimed. "Well I had to come to war to find friends like that."

"I suppose you would. Rural Stanclif, unfortunately, has great open spaces filled with very closed minds."

It was Wish's turn to give him a look, suspecting he had not thought that up on the spot. She shuffled a little closer, against the chill of the morning air, and said, "Do you speak from experience, Captain?"

"Only from what I've studied," Brade said. "My reputation, justly or not, rather goes too far the other way." The other way, Wish suspected, meaning he was the archetypal ladies' man. "Which is perhaps why my experiments in other cultures, and papers on them, have not been taken too seriously in Stanclif society."

"What experiments?" Wish asked. Did he own a cellar filled with jars of gender-fused mutants?

"Cultural experiments," he shattered that illusion. "Living as others do. High Society considers it a dalliance, really. But the war is a catalyst. Things will change, when it's over. Technologies, cultures, power structures, they'll all be reimagined."

"Women will get to vote and run the country?"

"Possibly."

"And countries like Fireti will be free and respected?"

He went quiet, not so quick to validate that.

"They've fought for us," Wish said. "Upheld the ideals of Imperial Civilisation."

"Yes," Brade said. "But do you understand what we're fighting for?"

Wish frowned. "To stop the Drail taking over the world."

"Not quite. More accurately, to stop the Drail taking the world from *us*." He didn't look especially happy about it. "If we're to help the colonies, it will be in building something new, not rebuilding what they had. Nomads like the Fireti folk don't have secure territories to lay the roots of civilisation. No industry, no advanced agriculture. They're one example in hundreds of less developed cultures who Stanclif would radically change, to adapt to our concept of civilisation. Because we, supposedly, can show them how to do things *better*."

Wish brought her knees up under her chin, as more girls woke, sitting up, yawning and rubbing their eyes. Brade must've been up for a while, mulling over such thoughts. She felt a pang of guilt for waking with hugs on her mind. She said, "It's not fair, though. That's just because we got there first. That doesn't mean our way is better."

"The world isn't fair," Brade said. A familiar answer.

"Do you think the same of us?" she countered with a sudden thought. "Women, I mean. Men lead our country the way Stanclif leads the world, right?"

Brade gave her an uncertain sideways look.

"Like, men travel and talk with other countries," Wish went on. "Men have been fighting our wars for centuries and they don't even imagine that women could do it. But now anyone can pull a trigger and actually we can shoot even better because we've had to train harder just to get given a chance." A smile crept onto her face – not a pretty one, she was sure, but a mad one, as an alternative to getting angry at what she was saying. The closest scouts were looking up, listening. "And, you know, maybe if I'd had sword lessons when I grew up, I could be the second-best swordsman in the world, too?"

"Third," one of the nearby Sun Squad girls mumbled.

"Or third," Wish agreed. "Couldn't I? If I grew up in a rich family with the right training and people who actually thought I could do something?"

Brade kept quiet, impassive, and she expected she'd overstepped her boundaries. He was a captain, after all. He could have her chained in a town square for insubordination. But he nodded. "Perhaps. And maybe once we get through this there are things that could be done to make the world more aware of that."

"What sort of things?" Wish asked, slowing down as she realised he was, impossibly, in broad agreement. Was this another kind of trap – as dangerous as him wanting to seduce her? He might want to use her another way. Parades in the city? Speeches to parliament? Activities that were a long way from relaxing on a farm.

"It can wait, I'm sure," Brade said, with a little shrug that said he appreciated her discomfort. He nodded towards the horizon. "It's not worth worrying about when we've still got that ahead."

The warships sat ominously in the immense body of water.

32

No less than sixty major classifications of warship were utilised by the Drail and the Comity during the war, not including the countless merchant-class ships that were modified for military use. It brought floating armour and deck-mounted artillery into a new era, from intercontinental behemoths to lithe bank-thumpers that duelled for river supremacy.
Great War Machines of the Modern Era,
Little & Ganimese, p. 356

Shortly after the scouts started moving down towards the lake, a boat drifted out from Dask's port, a small metal steamer painted Drail green. Oksy spotted Four Skills' glinting scope signalling from the deck. In the time it took the boat to steer their way, the scouts hurried to refill their water and wash what they could in the lake. When the boat arrived, Tate shouted at them all to get moving, chasing some girls out of the water half naked.

They gathered on the lake shore, below an unpaved road that connected the villages along the waterfront, staring at the boat a hundred metres out. Two wooden dinghies were lowered and rowed over by thick-muscled men stained with soot and grease. The men barely acknowledged the scouts clambering into their boats, grunting acceptance, and obediently rowed back out.

When it came Wish's turn, she waded through the icy water and tossed her pack, boots and rifle in before flopping messily into the boat. She sat with Newk pressed in next to her, Rue further down. Emi and Fixit took the bench behind the rower. He deftly turned the dinghy and powerfully rowed back, ignoring Wish's attempts to talk. "Nice day for it?"

Grunt.

"Don't suppose you ferry female soldiers out here often?"

Grunt.

"It's good of you to help, anyway."

Grunt.

Wish noticed Emi's face was twisting into her usual leer that said the mage knew something she didn't, so she gave up. They reached the big boat, a shabby vessel with cracked paintwork and the dents and scrapes of an either incapable or uncaring crew. They climbed a rope ladder to join the other scouts on deck, where Four Skills greeted them and explained it was best if everyone went down into the hold – there was plenty of space and food. More crewmen were gathered around, including two smoking near the stern and a fierce-looking chap in a striped top watching from a wheel-house.

"How exactly did you persuade these guys to help?" Wish whispered to Four Skills, as the others went inside.

"We didn't," Four Skills replied. "Dollemore's got the skipper in a mind fog. He thinks we're Har Coul refugees. And that she's a Drail officer arranging our passage."

Wish cooed. That explained the unpleasant welcome: the men resenting the military for requisitioning them. Though it raised another question: "Can she keep that up until we get all the way across?"

"Guess we'll find out."

With that reassurance, Wild Wish carried on into the hold. Almost as dark as the bowels of the Horn tunnels, with the added benefits of being damp and smelling like old fish. And there was *barely* space for all of them, which, okay, meant Wish had to squeeze in close to Newk, but her other thigh was pressed against a crab cage and when the rest of the scouts came down Cade ended up pushed in close, too. It got decidedly less comfortable when the engines chugged to life and the boat swayed as it moved, throwing unprepared scouts off-balance and pitching them into an ungentle rise and fall that didn't settle down. Wish occupied herself with thoughts over why the journey was so rough, given that the lake had looked so calm, and decided it was because the men piloting the boat were thugs.

The scouts stayed hidden for the journey, only Dollemore and Four Skills keeping watch up top, with girls occasionally climbing the ladder to race to the sides and vomit. When Cade started looking green, Wish urged her to leave fast, with a shove, but the rotund sapper only made it to a bucket metres away. So now they had that smell to contend with, too. They didn't dare move the bucket, as she looked like she might not be finished.

"Anyone feeling bad you want to put your head up top!" Angles shouted, flouting her seafaring past. "Get a sight of the horizon, that'll settle you! And lime. We got any lime? If you suck on a lime, that helps too."

Wish wasn't sure how accurate that advice was, and wondered if the swell would eventually claim her, too. But she'd sailed over the Stanclif Strait without incident, hadn't she? Maybe she was a natural. She found Newk's face in the dark, watching the others like they might explode. They met eyes and Wish gave her an encouraging smile.

Sometime into their passage, when the worst affected were starting to settle, besides one or two who couldn't keep from groaning and retching, the scouts resumed chatter and games. Pound found a space to roll bones and Larkin got enough room to start plucking at her lute. Wish rifled through the many ideas in her head looking for one that would make a good conversation topic to share with Newk. In the drama of what they'd been through, between the marching and the shared meals, she still didn't know much about the Fireti woman or anything they might have in common. Spurred by the motion of the boat, Wish asked, "Have you ever seen a sea dragon? Like, the Bay Creek Monster?"

"Like, a mythical being?" Dakoda interjected, uninvited, such was the danger of sparking conversation in a room crammed with people.

"No, there's been actual sightings of the Bay Creek Monster," Wish said. "They think it's an old sea dragon. I'd love to swim with something like that, can you imagine? Two hundred feet long."

"Big enough to swat you dead without even noticing," Dakoda said.

"Yeah, but imagine the rush." Wish turned her smile to Newk. The ringed woman merely stared, amused or pitying? Hard to tell.

"You didn't get enough of that rush with the hawk giant?" Fixit said, a few heads back from Dakoda, and Wish went quiet. Another reminder of that huge thing, which definitely wasn't pleasant. Sarge and Small crushed. Fixit's expression told her to think before she spoke again.

"I actually saw one once," Angles said. "At least, the shadow of something that big, passing under our boat outside Kinessa. We were –"

A clamour on the deck interrupted her, quickly building to something that sounded like general alarm. Men shouted, boots stomped. The hold hatch swung open and Four Skills ducked her head in. "There's a patrol ship. Everyone keep quiet."

"Should we get up there?" someone suggested.

"I can help," Emi said.

"No," Four Skills said. "We've got this."

With that, the hatch slammed shut. The commotion on deck settled and the rigid, still silence of the hold allowed the rumble of a second engine to be heard. It got closer and more shouting followed. The scouts were deathly still, waiting, all eyes on the ceiling as if they could see through the rusted metal and wood. There was more movement, clomping about. Was someone coming aboard? Shouting again, not hostile, but it was hard to tell with sailors. Then the engine started again. The patrol pulled away. Silence as the hatch remained closed. Their engine chugged and the boat began moving. Wish stared at the hatch, imagining Four Skills dragged away, offered up as sacrifice?

But it creaked open and the sniper's head reappeared. She spoke in a hush this time, conveying danger, "It's fine, turned them away. But the captain's getting itchy. Trying to keep him focused." She left it at that, closing the hatch with the suggestion that everyone keep quiet, so the crew might forget they were there.

The little calm and fun that had crept in was gone, leaving the scouts tense, willing the journey to be over. Dakoda muttered, "Could take us two days, crossing this lake. Maybe more."

"Make life easier if we just took the boat for ourselves," Rue said. "Shouldn't be hiding down here like rats."

"They never tell you, do they?" Newk said, almost a whisper, a private thought.

"What's that?" Wish prompted, equally quiet.

"About the waiting. They never tell you how war includes so much waiting. We're halfway around the world and we're still *waiting*." The thought had taken Newk, aggravated her, and she turned Rue's way to say, "It would be better with our own ship. At least then we would say when something happens, instead of waiting."

"Shit, Newk," Dakoda said, "you should've met us when were stuck in the trenches. They had us playing watchdog eighty per cent of the time."

"I'd happily go back to that," Fixit said. "It was safe, mostly."

Wish laughed. "What's not safe about floating in this rusty tin?" No one else laughed and she regretted saying it. But kept going. "Don't worry, we'll be through the Lakelands soon and into Slane, and from there, a skip and a jump to ending the mission and going back to hiding in fox-holes. Can't be more than a couple more man-eating monsters between us and there!"

"Way more than a couple," Fixit grumbled again, adamant in her misery. "Without even knowing what's at the end of this road."

"We've left the roads behind," Dakoda reminded them. "You can count on that, too."

As Dakoda suggested, it took two full days to cross the lake, but after an achingly uncomfortable ride and unpleasant toilet breaks in buckets and over deck rails, with more than a few stomachs' worth of food lost, the scouts finally disembarked. It was nighttime when they were rowed ashore, the moon breaking through thin cloud cover to give an idea of the terrain ahead. The trees were tall but thinner here, like ill cousins of the woodland on the other side. The lake shore was split by a wide opening, a river running off, inevitably, to Low Slane.

Was this the Devil's River? Or did it join that notorious beast later?

Wish distracted herself by trying to make conversation with the same sailor from before, as he rowed her and half the squad in. She thanked him for their efforts and asked his name and he kept gruntingly quiet. Right until they all jumped out to splash through the water, at which point he snarled an insult in Lakish that sounded close to the worst words in Stanclif. Wish stood in the ankle-deep water watching him row away, wondering what his problem was.

It was a matter for another life, though, she decided, as the steamboat turned away at last, to disappear back into the great watery unknown, taking their shit and vomit with it. Rue sloshed up next to Wish and said, "I think we ruined women for them."

"Ah," Wish replied. That was probably it.

33

Women were commonly known to hold the fort, as it were, keeping domestic interests running while the men were fighting, but less publicised were the instances of women engaging in combat. This varied depending on the nation: Khibba women, having always enjoyed more autonomy in the Khib family dynamic, were more readily seen on the front, while female soldiers were begrudgingly accepted into Stanclif ranks. The staunchly patriarchal Drail Empire were the slowest to adapt to such needs, but even they allowed the odd woman warrior; indeed, the most famous female soldier of the war, legendary artillery captain Ver "Load'em" Flarrank, came from Arrow City.
Dueley's Comprehensive: The One War in 10 Volumes (Vol. 8), p. 209

"Hold her steady!" Netts shouted from the rear of the wyrling, as if Donut could actually control Gulvar. Maringdale held onto her saddle bar tighter as they buffeted through the sky, Donut pushing the beast to its top speed, drawing disgruntled noises and heavy breaths from its big jaws. Netts' rifle appeared alongside her head and Maringdale flinched. She loosed one hand to cover her ear and was about to shout at him when the gun went off.

They were a long way from the enemy serpents, a pair of sharp and slender shapes gliding through the air, armoured soldiers mounted on them. There was zero chance of Netts hitting them and Maringdale, ear ringing, screamed, "Do that again and I'll cut your fucking throat out!"

"They're gaining on them!" Netts yelled, as if she couldn't see the two cirga charging over the open field below. Another hundred metres or more between the shell-plated centaurs and the bridge.

"Take us down!" Maringdale ordered. "Put us between them, at least!"

Donut wordlessly complied and Gulvar banked suddenly. Netts yelped as he struggled to keep his gun up. Maringdale kept one eye on the enemy, holding onto her rising gut, gritting her teeth against a scream. The riders pierced towards the earth like javelins. One of the cirga pushed ahead as the riders aimed their rifles. The long, lance-like things bucked with pops barely audible behind the rush of air. Earth erupted around the rear cirga, causing it to sway, but it kept going. Impossible to aim from the backs of these flying monsters.

Gulvar hit the ground hard and bounced, gathering its footing, dozens of metres from the front cirga. As they steadied, the enemy wyrlings caught up to the rear cirga. One of them fell on it with reaching, terrible claws, like a bird on a mouse. Donut shouted dismay as it ripped at the unfortunate beast, but Maringdale focused on the closer one, drawing her pistol.

"Now, Netts, if you will!" she shouted, and Netts steadied himself again.

The front cirga pounded towards them with everything it had, its insectile face somehow managing to look frightened. The second wyrling was right behind it, claws stretching, its rider braced at the reins. Netts fired and Maringdale joined in, one shot after another. The cirga ducked under the barrage, and one of the shots hit home, as the wyrling twisted sideways with a screech. The cirga thundered past them, straight for the bridge.

The Stanclif wyrling rose out of range and started circling, ready for another attack. The other one hopped off its kill, shaking blood and gore from its talons. Netts fired at it, too, and it retreated at a run.

"Back, Donut, back!" Maringdale instructed, and he steered Gulvar to take big sideways steps towards the bridge. The flying enemy speared down again and Netts struggled to keep steady, trying to keep him in sight. Maringdale flashed a look across the bridge, seeing the cirga pass between buildings, a small town lined with barbed wire and big metal barricades designed to keep vehicles out. There were green-coats coming out of the buildings now.

As the enemy wyrling quickly approached, a bigger, more powerful gun fired from the buildings, with a flash in one of the upper-storey windows, and the creature banked suddenly. Maringdale watched it turn away, accelerating fast to get out of range. The gun fired again. Again. The wyrling was a dark shape in the sky once more, its companion fleeing closer to the land. Maringdale exhaled relief as their own wyrling padded to a standstill, marking the bridge secure.

"Yeah!" Netts vented emotion, waving the rifle overhead. "You better run!"

Behind them, their allies cheered. Small victory, Maringdale grimly thought. There was no sign of the cirga having stopped the spy.

Battle Chief Baron was furious, but on a grekkel, especially one with his erudite manners, it came across only in a wider, pointy smile and an ominous drawl. Maringdale's news of saving the cirga was predictably a weak consolation, as his people had now decided it was highly possible the Gentleman, with his previous presence confirmed, might have gained access to their documents. Not the cathedral itself, no, but if he knew the Dread Corps were in the city, he could've checked shipping manifestos and got an idea of where they were moving to and from. Baron paced the short space of the cathedral's vestibule growling, "He not only reached Blythe, but will have the ear of Stanclif Command itself. We should've moved faster. Damn General Amalric for overreaching – another day, *one more day* and we would've had him."

"The cirga's account was confused," Maringdale reported. The riverside platoon's comms officer had only a broken understanding of the monster's language, and she had difficulty reading its non-human emotions. "It suggested Blythe was in the hands of female soldiers. They had a dirt-minder."

"Female soldiers?" Baron reeled, like that was the worst news that could've been added to this catastrophe. "The Blood Scouts?"

"You think it's true?" Maringdale said.

"Of course it's true. They were at Green Rise. Flanked 8th Division with a machine gun – if you believe Amalric, that cost him the day. As though it wasn't lost the moment he chose to advance. Gave up a position of strength, spread his troops too thin – lost Blythe. There was enough there, along with whatever this Gentleman's turned up, that they might make us a priority."

The grekkel paused to catch his angry breath, giving Maringdale a moment to try and come up with a solution. She'd hounded the insurgents to the very front, where the mastermind behind the attacks had slipped from her grasp. At the trail's end, all that was left was to account to the Purification over why two of her superiors were now dead and she was a long way from where they had assigned her. Damned if she was going to let this end with the failure of a handful of insectile horsemen or rumours of women soldiers. As if trudging after worm-men and the suggestion of waders hadn't been insult enough.

Baron turned to his table, with all his maps, muttering to himself as the Dread mage Artemus stepped forward. Ready to dismiss her. Maringdale hurriedly said, "If they're going to mount any kind of covert attack, I will see them coming."

The grekkel looked over his shoulder at her. "Wick is about to become the most secure fortress in the whole theatre of war. I'm not worried about us being attacked. I'm concerned we've lost the element of surprise."

It fed into what Starling had shared in Null. Whatever the Dread Corps were doing would change the war, all the more so if Stanclif could not see it coming. She asked, with little hope, "Were there any further potential targets in the information the Gentleman might've obtained? You said he might have an idea of your supply routes –"

"Between here and Low Slane," Baron said. "We'll divert them in future, to avoid any ambushes."

Maringdale frowned, realising the locations involved had all been along the front line until now. "What's in Low Slane? Would they consider going directly there?"

Baron didn't answer straightaway, and though his emotions betrayed nothing useful – *rip them down, rip them up!* – she could tell she'd hit on something. He shook his head. "Impossible. No one could reach us there."

"Respectfully" – Maringdale shifted slightly closer, ignoring how the grekkel made her skin crawl – "Battle Chief Hark said the same of Highscythe."

"This is different," Baron said. "No. I appreciate you want to help, Officer Maringdale, and you have done enough to warrant recommendation, but it's time to step back. We'll clear up matters with the Purification for you, and in the meantime you'll have our hospitality. A billet somewhere nice in town."

She wanted to say more, but his glassy eyes said not to. She was dismissed.

Thwarted as she felt, Maringdale told herself she'd made progress, given the townhouse that the Dread Corps secured for her, even if it was shared with Donut and Netts. They had separate rooms, with luxurious four-poster beds and gold-framed mirrors and paintings. A valet brought them supplies of fresh meat and cooked vegetables, which Donut promptly set about rationing. Netts quickly lost his own insecurities when he discovered the drinks cabinet filled with unlabelled crystal decanters of fine liquor; after a few glasses, he gave up any idea of discovering what his next post would be.

Maringdale held off reporting back to the Purification. They would catch up to her themselves, eventually, and for all they knew she was still in the employ of the Dread Corps. She settled into enjoying the scant reward of this requisitioned apartment, and put her boots up on the mahogany table, to rest at last.

Two days passed, split between brainstorming some plan or other for getting back into the Dread Corps' graces and wandering Wick inspecting the fortifications, making herself look like she belonged. Donut gathered increasingly luxurious foods and resupplied them with ammunition and fresh laundry, and otherwise tended to the wyrling he'd become oddly attached to. Netts mingled with fellow soldiers and drank, checking in once a day at Riker Cathedral for orders. He was instructed to stay with Maringdale until she was reassigned – no pretence in the fact she was being monitored. But Netts was hardly a threat; she read nothing of malice in his intentions, he was merely taking advantage of a chance to relax. She regretted, though, that chance had set her on a long journey with this self-serving rat while Hill had been so cruelly cut down. For all the city of grubby, eager soldiers, she was yet to see another man who appealed to her as Hill had.

On the third day, their break was shaken when Netts returned from Riker Cathedral, eager to share news. He went straight for the drinks cabinet, as had become his tradition, and pointed across the room to Maringdale, slumped in her armchair. "Here, you'll be interested in this. Reports of an elite force heading north, west of the war zone."

"And?"

"We got a line of gun encampments on cliffs, they blew a hole in it. We've secured it again, but they did a fair whack of damage. Punched through. What's that suggest to you?"

Maringdale sat up. "An infiltration. Where would it lead them?"

"That's the funny thing," Netts said, perching on the footstool in front of her, a sick smile saying he knew exactly what this would mean to her. "Nothing but rocks up there, no way to move any serious troops around, and we've got men crawling all over Har Coul from here to the Valley of the Drail. At best, they'd have to stick to the far flank all the way to the Lakelands before they could cut east again. Might be assassins hoping to make a break for the Arrow Council itself, or to bomb the factories up there, but that'd be a hell of a journey for something stupid like that."

"You've got another idea?"

"Need me to say it?"

Maringdale chewed on it, liking his sharpness and wondering now if Hill would've picked up on this himself, being less of a sneak. "They could go north far enough to find a way into Low Slane. Did you mention this to Baron?"

"Did I fuck." Netts leaned back. "No one with more than two stripes on their chest's gonna listen to me. Besides, the boys in the cathedral say he's got his hands full, him and that Dread mage working overtime at finishing whatever they've got in the cellars. Resources are thin, ma'am. Take someone more of your stature to sway him."

But why bother swaying him, Maringdale considered silently. If the insurgents had already moved north, she had no reason to stay here.

34

Nestled between the industrially booming Valley of the Drail and the rapidly advancing nations of Har Coul and Balnia, Low Slane remained an anomaly well into the 8th century, as a haven of untouched lands. It was not that Slanik society were particularly protective of nature and indigenous species. They did not develop the feral swamplands, and let monsters thrive that had elsewhere been hunted or exterminated, because the land was, frankly, vastly inhospitable.

Empires of the Rocc, Xanthial, p. 579

The scouts moved with care through the peripheries of the Lakeland territory, where the denser population of industrial towns proved dangerous. Huge brick warehouses lined the banks of the Devil's River, fed by roads busy with trucks carrying arms and equipment. The river itself was crowded by heavily laden barges with military escorts and the towns had large Drail flags hanging from windows and sandbags surrounding important buildings. It was good to see they feared aerial assault even this far north, though Wild Wish doubted wyrling riders and short-distance ladder-wing planes, notoriously lightweight and flammable, had any real chance of getting here. It was only the Drail who had airships capable of crossing whole continents. If you believed them.

After another day of splitting into small groups and stalking through forest and hills, often pulling far away from the river, the scouts reached the border into Low Slane, marked by a hydro-city that put Farnish pool towns like Blythe to shame. This was a factory-rich walled settlement that crossed the river, built up with bridges and chunky brick structures that channelled the water through power generators. Even from the distance of a hill vantage point, Wish could hear the noise of industry, with great wheels turning, boat engines chugging and men shouting. Studying the place through her scope, she picked out huge gun shells, bigger than a man, being loaded by crane onto the beds of flat boats, and she spotted an intricately layered water-wheel fed by a canal to supply a building big enough to house giants.

And ah, there *was* a giant, way over on the other side of the river. A skalk giant, beige-skinned and craggy. It was just visible over the rooftops and between the factories, helping to carry large crates. There were other unusual creatures that side of the river, she saw now: massive carrion bats sat on the tops of buildings, wings wrapped close so they looked like spikes, and pack beetles moved through the streets, bigger than any Wish had seen before.

"If we laid charges at every factory between here and the lake, we could put a real dent in the Drail's infrastructure," Wish mused, lowering her scope and looking back up the river, to more barges and dots of towns.

"A minor dent," Dakoda said, disagreeably. It was just her, Wish and Rue up here, checking the terrain so everyone could move on safely. "There's regions like this up and down the Drail Empire. The Lakelands are nothing. I heard they've converted practically the whole of Maurania into a munitions workhouse."

"With everyone fighting," Rue said, "how is anyone left to work there?"

"Women, I suppose," Wish said. "For every million dead on the battlefield, there's a million women back home supporting them. The war would end quicker if *all* of us came to the front."

"The war and the whole human race," Dakoda said.

"More than that," Rue said. "They put lesser races into battle first."

With that cheery reminder, the girls went quiet and took in the city again. Despite the munitions being made, and the flags and uniforms visible, there was something refreshing about seeing a place at work, without everyone hiding, looking for the next bullet, listening for sirens. They soaked it up in silence for a minute, until

Wish said, "It's all so small from up here. We're like gods looking down."

"About to sneak into Low Slane?" Dakoda replied. "Nah, Wild. I feel more like an idiot bug."

"On the plus side," Rue said, "at least we'll learn some new ways to die."

With the hydro-city behind them, Tate gathered the scouts at the edge of an abandoned farm and gave her final instructions. She rearranged the squads slightly, lending Dollemore to Sabre but confirming, then, that Brade would join Boot Squad. He had prepared maps of Low Slane, each showing a different route, and at the next crossroads they would split up. Boot and Rock were set to cross a bridge a short way downriver, and from there take different routes through skalk woods – clear of giants, Brade assured, since they'd been put to work in factories. He couldn't guarantee what else might be there, though. Sun and Sabre would travel along the north bank of the river, taking less obvious and more difficult terrain through the swampland. The full details weren't shared between the squads, in case of capture.

The ultimate destination was now revealed, though: they had four days to reach Reeve Abbey, a large, repurposed religious estate. It was a distance of a little over a hundred miles, Brade said, which shouldn't be heavily patrolled, given the Slanik territories had little industry worth targeting. And because there were so many natural threats out there. On the morning of the fifth day, they would move in to sabotage the operation in the abbey. It would a be a first-come-first-attack operation, with stragglers to assist as they arrived.

Once inside, the orders were disconcertingly simple: destroy the Slanik project through whatever means necessary and capture those responsible alive. Tate added that they should choose prisoners carefully; they couldn't cart a whole company home.

That brought up the question of how to get home. Brade had

another point marked on their maps for when it was all over. A town that served the Iron Canal, where they'd be able to gain disguises and take the train south. The Drail would be much less wary over movements going to the front, rather than penetrating their land, especially once the scouts shed their military gear, no longer necessary after attacking the abbey. It sounded like a shitty plan, but he was confident, claiming he'd crossed the front line enough times to know it was easier coming back. Wish had experience herself, though, and knew "easy" in war was about synonymous with "messy".

No explanation was offered for why Captain Brade would travel with Boot. Most clearly accepted it as being because Wish was the least experienced leader. She grinned and bore it like a good girl, still not sure if he'd be a distraction or a boon. Trying not to over-think it, she gestured for him to lead the way.

Boot and Rock travelled over the promised bridge, a quiet single-lane road arch, and left civilisation behind again to pass into the increasingly twisted trees of Slane, following unpaved roads. The river turned away from them, to where Brade said it would eventually become vicious rapids over a set of cliffs before coming back their way. The ground dipped to a steep decline, the scouts now travelling down the huge height they'd climbed back in Eardung. Rock peeled off, taking a northern route, and Boot Squad spread out to cover a wider area, watching for whatever horrors this land held.

The Slanik forest was a huge contrast to the majestic lands of Eardung. Here, the trees were almost black, spiky and clawed as though warning you not to come close. The ground was increasingly soggy and Wish's boots kept sticking in the mud. Wind whistled through the branches like mocking laughter, and despite their moving to a lower height it seemed to be getting colder. Worse than all that, the further they walked the more strange sounds came through the woodland. Clicks and whines of unseen creatures, and calls of unfamiliar birds. Occasionally, an animal moved through the undergrowth, seen only as a dark shape disappearing between tree trunks. *Big* dark shapes.

With night coming, Wish tried to channel Sarge's efficient management skills to set up camp. The squad would find a defensible space to sleep and set up sentries, with Pound and Dakoda moving out to establish a perimeter. They found a nice dip in the land where rocks provided a natural wall on two flanks, which would also hide a small fire. Wish wanted to call the day a general success, but was vaguely aware the nasties always came out at night. Sure enough, before the scouts could even take all their packs off, Dakoda came trotting into the camp, almost out of breath, to say, "There's trouble. Think it's Rock."

"What?" Wish exclaimed.

Dakoda threw her pack down and said, "I heard sounds! Come on, we need to move fast!"

Wish shed her own gear, down to just her rifle and blade, as the others did the same. Without thinking, she ordered, "Fixit, stay and watch our gear, everyone else —"

"What if they need medical help?" Fixit said.

"Okay, you come – Rue?" Wish hesitated, not wanting to leave their toughest fighter behind either. Or Emi. Pound was already out on patrol and Newk was too new. Who was she supposed to leave?

Rue patted her arm and said, "Go quick, shout if you need me."

Wish caught Brade's eye then and wondered if he should've been the one to stay. But he had his pistol out in one hand and his thin sword in the other, more ready than anyone. For a moment, Wish expected him to tell her to stand down, let Rock Squad be. They were moving separately for a reason. But he gave her an assenting nod, and she ordered, "Okay girls let's go!"

They followed Dakoda as she raced through the grim trees. She explained, "I found a pack, and there's webbing everywhere, didn't want to continue alone."

"They're much closer than they should be," Brade said, running as though he'd never been injured. "Something must've diverted them."

"Hey! Hey!" Pound's voice came from behind as she struggled to catch up. "What's happening?"

"Don't know," Wish replied. "Rescue mission."

It was further than Wish expected, the winding route taking them through the forest with light fading by the second. Wish was torn between being impressed that Dakoda remembered the way and being distraught at the distance, diminishing her hope for whatever webbed terror their friends had fallen into.

Finally, Dakoda stumbled to a halt and Wish almost crashed into her. The others bunched up behind them as she pointed. Webbing, as she'd said, thick, but translucent, running between the trees in strands that might be missed if you didn't tilt your head and let them catch the light the right way. It stretched in both directions, marking new territory.

"Look, there." Fixit pointed with her rifle. A pack lay sunk in the foliage near a tree ahead, hastily discarded. Clearly one of theirs.

"Yeah," Dakoda said. "And there." Another pack.

Whatever made this webbing had descended on Rock Squad. The scouts stood still in that knowledge. Brade suggested, "Could be wild spidroms, but it'd be unusual for them to attack people. Maybe chigrakes, if you believe the tales."

"Cirga that fire webs?" Pound replied fearfully. "Great."

"Not exactly. Different breed entirely, actually. But either way, we've got to advance to find out."

"Can you feel for whatever it is?" Wish asked Emi. "Get us some warning?"

"I'm not a mortal mage," Emi reminded her. "But as we established in Eardung, I can be more useful than that." She searched the forest floor for a moment, stopped, disappointed, and jumped up to tear a branch from a tree. It came away with a loud crack, then she split it in two over a knee, forming two batons of wood.

"Shh, listen!" Dakoda said, waving a hand.

A muffled sound of protest up ahead. Someone alive.

The two logs in Emi's hands snapped to life with a pop and a little giggle from the mage, fire rising in a whoosh of heat and light. It calmed slightly, until she held two flaming torches, grinning, and Wish was quite sure no one had ever looked more madly threatening holding two sticks. Thank Bly she was on their side.

"Okay," Wish said. "Okay, but take it easy, everyone be careful. Spread out."

She took one wary step after another, dreading what the trees hid.

More sounds came: groans, urgent but almost inaudible, muffled. Then the patter of something heavy but delicate. Tapping against string. Wish bent side to side to get a better view, but the webbing formed a white haze.

Fixit seized up down the line with a gasp. Wish came to her side and got an angle between tree trunks to see movement. A great shape moved off between the trees to reveal a wide opening, no tree trunks beyond. This was it, a clearing ahead. Wish waved to let the others know it was there. With Emi's torches blazing just behind, they moved on together, parting around a tree to see what lay ahead.

Wild Wish trod carefully, avoiding any web near the ground, stepping between dry leaves, and stopped where the trees grew further apart. The forest floor fell away into a rocky chasm, circular and wide open, with webbing stretched from the trees into it. Just below the drop, the webbing was interwoven like a net, and within it were a handful of human-sized cocoons, together with more discarded packs and rifles, bobbing on the elastic. Around them and above them, large dark creatures were moving – one group rearranging a cocoon as another gathered on the far side of the chasm. Immense, many-legged insects, plated with armour-like shells the colour of rust, jointed at least three or four times in their long bodies, with clawed arms and mandibles. Wish stared in horror as she saw what the far group were doing: an arm flopped from between one of their sets of mandibles, the fabric of a slate blue sleeve still evident on the wrist.

Wish aimed at the feasting monster and fired.

35

I wish I could say you get used to it, but the front always finds new ways to surprise you. New weapons with unexpected results. New creatures you never imagined enlisted in battle. And the new comrades, always the new comrades you hope this time will last. I've seen such terrible things, but the war keeps finding ways to show me more.

**Extract from the Letters of
Major K. Tyne, Elmn, 720**

For their fearsome size and sinister, angular appearance, the creatures' plating proved brittle. Wild Wish and Brade fired a series of shots into the group that exploded their carapaces apart and sent them twitching and tumbling to earth. Equally surprising as their frailty, however, was the agility of the cumbersome beasts. They moved with unnatural jerking motions, sharp-angled limbs clicking in and out with a rapid, jerky patter more mechanical than muscular. They swarmed across the chasm and out of it, some slinking between the trees as the others stampeded ahead.

"Stand your ground!" Wish shouted, taking a step back. She kept her rifle steady and shot the closest creature between a snatching set of mandibles. At her side, Brade shot another, equally steady and effective with his pistol. Both creatures went down, the tops of their shells shattering like gunky eggs. Mumbler rifles and Pound's 56 cracked around Wish's peripheries, covering the sides – running would be suicide now, and everyone remained stoic in the advance.

A creature launched over the lip of the chasm, having crept closer unseen, as tall as a rearing horse. Its otherworldly underside, cross-knit with gleaming black ribs, froze Wish, but tremendous heat swept over her head, blowing her hair across her eyes. She squinted as flames shrunk the monster like singed paper. When the fire cleared, an instant later, only ash remained, twisting in the breeze. Emi made a noise like she was trying not to laugh as she moved past, twirling her flaming torches. She threw fire again, this time sweeping it onto the nearest webbing. The blaze spread rapidly and Wish yelped in a moment's fear that the entire nest would go up – but the mage knew her craft, and the fire danced across the webbing with direction and purpose, snaking out towards the creatures. One was about to break into the trees, lunging towards Fixit, as the fire caught it, jumping from the web onto its thin legs. The limbs lit with a matchstick flare and it dropped and rolled, quickly engulfed. Fixit fired into it for good measure.

Wish swung her gun around, searching for her next target, and found Newk dodging the reaching claws of one beast, stabbing her sword between its top two carapaces. It was too big for her to drive the blade all the way through, but Brade reached her, pistol down as he brought his own sword up, and expertly pierced between the thing's eyes. He and Newk moved fast, with grace, to slide their swords out of the beast and turn back-to-back to invite more.

The remaining beasts were gone. The others stopped firing, watching the last monstrous carcasses shrivel up in death throes. Breathing in relief, unable to blink, Wish turned to the nearest face to share their triumph. Dakoda met her eye, scowling. Together, they looked back out over the chasm to where one of their fellow scouts had been torn apart.

"Quickly, get them out!" Wish instructed, running to the edge of chasm and dropping her rifle to draw her short-blade. She tested a boot on the webbing, and though it was strong, and would bear her weight, it was sticky. She tugged herself free again.

Brade pulled her back, saying, "We're not getting them out by getting ourselves stuck. We need branches, something to reach –"

"I've got it," Emi said, chuckling unnaturally as she knelt and placed a hand on the web. Her laugh deepened into a cackle, head shaking and eyes rolling. She threw her head back and howled and the webbing split across the chasm. It twanged up like giant, broken guitar strings, and the cocooned scouts were tossed free, writhing like maggots. As Emi slid to the ground laughing, Wish raced to the nearest cocoon and cut at the web, cursing, *please, Oksy, please –* Cade's face gasped out, gagging for air, eyes too sticky to open.

Wish stood, scanning the destroyed nest, littered with bits of the giant creatures and scraps of scout equipment. A shredded pack, a rifle bent out of shape. The monsters had torn through the squad – it was a miracle any of them were left. Wish relented, feeling her eyes well with tears, not her friend –

"Got Oksy," Dakoda announced from another cocoon and Wish whipped her head around to her, seeing the sniper struggling out from the confines of webbing. Wish's heart lifted. Yes, the sniper was okay. Now they just needed Harmon, she'd know what to do. Pound and Newk pulled another cocoon open, revealing Angles. Then at the next cocoon, Fixit quickly backed off, aghast. No saving that one.

Boot Squad hurried the survivors out of the monster nest, leaving Emi to torch what was left, including the remains of those who had fallen. Fixit gave the barest bleats of protest which Wish immediately shut down, shouting that they absolutely were not staying in the area nor leaving their friends' bodies to be eaten. They ran back, Dakoda finding the way with one of Emi's torches, the others half carrying Oksy, Cade and Angles between them as the scouts groggily tried to regain their senses, weakened by venom in the webbing. Pound straggled behind, gathering whatever of Rock's gear she could carry, under Wish's frantic urging.

Finally, they returned to the campsite where Rue was waiting, rifle ready, a fire going. The scouts set up a quick perimeter, Pound on one side, Dakoda on another, as Wish helped wipe goo from their rescued friends. Cade was rattling with nerves, tearful as she whimpered, "What happened to Fuse? What happened to Fuse?" Her horrified tone said she knew exactly what had happened to Fuse.

"We safe here?" Rue asked.

"There wasn't much left of those things," Wish said. "And the nest was a long way off. So maybe?"

"What *things*, exactly? Where's the rest of Rock Squad?"

"They came from behind," Oksy explained, hoarsely. She was hunched over, sat on a rock, face drained of colour except around the eyes, where her lower lids were sickly red. She untangled web from her long hair as she continued, "We ran, but they were herding us, right into their lair. They knocked us in. It happened so fast."

"You're miles off course," Brade said.

"What course?" Angles rasped. "There wasn't any cover, any path. Swampland."

Brade cursed and Wish shot him a look demanding an explanation. He said, "We're going by best-guesses out here. What worked for explorers in the past might not now. That was always a risk. These regions aren't well understood by even the Slanik scholars."

"They fucking ate Fuse," Cade spat, trying to push herself up. "You understand *that?*" Fixit eased her back down but the sapper continued, "Could've gone a million other ways, but you led us right into a pit of bugs!"

"You weren't supposed to be there," Brade replied testily. "And any other routes we took would be just as dangerous, if not more so."

"As dangerous as getting –"

"That's enough," Wish cut in, as firm as she dared. She felt the pressure of the others watching her. Fixit, Rue, Newk even, *needing* their leader, even if she wasn't bloody Sarge. Wish took a breath. "We all knew the risks coming here. And there's another three days of it to go, at least. We can't fall apart now." She winced, regretting the phrasing. "We've got two choices – continue or turn back. If we turn back then everyone's died for nothing. If we continue, then Captain Brade knows this place better than the rest of us combined."

She particularly focused on Cade, the sapper's face puffy with anger and sorrow.

"I don't think anyone wants to give up," Fixit murmured. "But maybe we do need to rethink our approach."

"The Devil's Wetlands stretch a hundred miles north and south of the river," Brade said. "South of that, there's the Dust Plains, which are the domain of lava crabs. They don't die as easily as whatever those things were back there. This *is* the safest way to Reeve Abbey. We just need to be careful."

"Starting with surviving tonight," Wish said. "Are we safe here or do we press on?"

Angles made a worried sound, not ready to stand, let alone face the forest at night.

"Okay we stay, but we keep a constant watch and move at first light. We'll scout ahead *and* behind. We've got the numbers, we'll look out for each other, we can do this."

"Did anyone get my rifle?" Oksy asked, with little hope. The scouts exchanged looks, and their eyes fell to the scant provisions Pound had recovered. A spare mumbler rifle and two packs, one of them with holes through the fabric.

"That was Fuse's," Cade said, with a sniff. "It's got explosives in it."

"And probably not much food," Fixit said.

"We'll worry about that later," Wish said. "Look. We've been through a nightmare and I'm damn sorry for those we've lost, but *we* are safe. And we're going to keep going, aren't we, Cade? We're going to show these bastards hell?"

Cade met her eye again, and slowly nodded. She whispered, "We'll keep going."

Wish smiled, uncomfortable, inappropriate maybe, but she could hardly not. She walked by, patting Cade's arm, and looked to Brade again. He didn't look so hot himself, as shaken by any of them by those giant bugs, so Wish gave him a forceful glare, one she hoped said *just keep it together*. He nodded back.

∗∗∗

Without especially thinking about setting up comfortable pairings for watches, Wild Wish found herself sharing a log with Oksy in the middle of the night, watching the dark before splitting to their separate vantage points. Her fellow sniper was almost as quiet as the others sleeping by the smouldering fire (not counting Pound's snores), lost in thoughts or memories Wish didn't want to guess at. She wouldn't have wished what they'd been through on anyone, even Oksy.

Wish whispered, "You'd didn't need to take a watch."

"Wouldn't be sleeping anyway," Oksy replied vacantly.

"Yeah. It took a lot of alcohol to put me to sleep after Green Rise."

That drew a hooded eye Wish's way.

"I didn't ever think . . ." Oksy trailed off to reconsider what it was she hadn't ever thought. "Signing up, how could any of us know it'd be like this?"

Wish bobbed her head in rough agreement. No one could've predicted the way this whole war would go, and their latest venture was a new lesson in how messed up it could get. She said, "It's given us friends and taken them away."

Oksy frowned, not appreciating that thought.

"Sorry," Wish sighed. "I never had many friends back in Swelig. Not like here. It's been a real . . . confusing time. Without the war I never would've known you guys."

"Yeah," Oksy agreed. "They're a special bunch. Cade and Fuse . . . they were kindred spirits. Engineers, you know? They were thrown down the mines together, digging tunnels under the enemy lines. And the pair of them – I never met a girl who'd fart in front of a man before. Then suddenly I knew two of them."

Wish almost laughed. Oksy smiled and went on, "Thing is . . . they were my squad, my girls, sure. But none of them really liked me." She took in a big breath and let it out. "You're probably the only one in the platoon who really does like me, Wish. I've never got on great with other women. But that squad, I was still closer to them than most."

As Oksy trailed off again, into deep, dark sadness, Wish found her mouth open in a startled O. She couldn't hold in her question, *"I'm* the only one who likes you?"

Oksy gave her a sideways smile, some of that smug knowingness creeping back in. "For what it's worth, Wish, if I *was* into girls –"

"I do *not* –" Wish cut in, incredulous, but she was halfway to standing and heard her voice rise, through the deathly horrible forest, and stopped. Sitting back down she continued in a harsh whisper, "What makes you think I *like* you?"

Oksy eyed her nonplussed, as if trying to figure out a joke, then said, "Look, whatever. The point is no one *else* does, and that doesn't make what I saw today a damn bit easier."

Wish froze, brought back down to earth, to the grim reality of this conversation. She raised a hand. Hesitated. Patted Oksy's leg. "They definitely liked you, Oksy. What's not to like?"

She placed her hand on top of Wish's, releasing a little shudder of emotion. "How do you do it, Wish? Lost Sarge, Small, Loose – how do you keep smiling?"

"Something wrong with me, I guess," Wish replied apologetically.

"Still think you'll make it back to your farm?"

"Not just me," Wish said, picturing it herself. Fuse and Cade might've operated a steam engine together, taking turns in the cab, playing pranks over slab sandwiches. Now it'd just be Cade, half complete. But Oksy, too. "You'll be there. You're gonna be the brains of the operation. Tell me about the history of farms and workloads of pulleys and stuff."

That drew a sad smile. "See. That's what I'm talking about. For what it's worth, I'm happy it was you who picked us out of there. Not Sun or Sabre."

"And I'm happy it's you we picked out," Wish told her. "I'm sorry about the others. Sorry about everyone we've lost. But I don't know. I . . . . couldn't have stood losing you, too?" It came out a question, squeaked.

Oksy didn't really register it, just nodded along. "Captain Brade's taken us into territory no one is supposed to tread. Facing new horrors when there were already enough back there in the war.

Do you think it's all worth it, Wild?"

Wish considered it for a moment, then said, "It makes more sense for us to be here than anywhere else, to me. He's convinced this is going to change the war, and that could make us the most important people in the world right now. It's easy to believe, looking at the girls we're marching with. And it makes more sense to die on the way to do a big thing than to drown in mud because too many people crammed into a field to shoot each other. That's messed up. Loose thrown from a cliff because her gun jammed? By a guy who was running away from the fighting? What was that even for?"

Oksy was back to staring distantly, and Wish figured that was probably the worst pep talk ever. Oksy said, "I think one's as bad as the other. I don't know what any of this was ever for. How's anything ever going to go back to normal?"

"It will," Wish gave her leg a light squeeze, another pat, and smiled brightly. Oksy returned a sceptical look, so she insisted, "We're going to have peace, Oksy, I promise you. You and me and the others, we're going to *make* it happen."

"However many must die to get there?"

Wish held her grave look, and behind the loss she saw something much worse in Oksy's expression. The empty sorrow of abandoned hope. So Wish said, "Yeah. Whatever it takes."

"Wild. You seriously think any of us will make it out alive?"

"I bloody hope so," Wish replied. She sighed and tried again. A leader needs to lead, after all. "We have to. We've got something to go back to, worth fighting for, and I want you all there to enjoy it with me. Especially you."

Oksy faintly smiled back at last, buying it at least a little. And Wish wondered how much she bought it, herself. How thin a line was she treading, with her smiles and laughter and happy thoughts holding back a complete and utter despairing collapse? It was best not to think about it. Best not to dwell on all the deaths, or keep a tally, or look forward to more. She'd have her whole life to resolve those emotions. Right now, they just needed to stay positive and survive.

36

These women were nasty, understand? They didn't take any quarter, didn't hold back, because they had that much more to prove than all these other soldiers just out there trying to survive. They were deadlier than deadly and meaner than mean. Just look at the way the Drail reported rumours of them (or didn't; most times they were too scared to keep notes).

The Blood Scouts had them scared rotten.

Languid's Everyman Guide to Fierce Women of The One War (Issue 4: The Blood Scouts), p. 48

"A woman?" Maringdale replied to the soldier's account, not quite believing it. The man was twitchy, with his right shoulder pressed forward, not quite making eye contact with her. But at least he was talking, unlike his heavy-set companion who only mumbled quiet monosyllables. It was typical: of a whole battalion stationed across Mean Ridge, these two idiots were the only ones to see the insurgents. Though considering the battalion had let them through, perhaps they were all idiots up here. It was glorified guard duty, after all – a phalanx of machine-gun nests that no one ever expected to see action.

Maringdale had got a good view sweeping in on the wyrling, of both the rift of rock and rubble the attackers had caused and the expanse of inhospitable mountain terrain that sat behind it. There was no question in her mind that anyone climbing these cliffs was looking to sneak a small force further north; there was no strategic value to securing a passage through such difficult terrain. And now it came with rumours of women, scarcely better than rumours of waders. Except Baron had confirmed the so-called Bitch Squad, the

Blood Scouts, actually existed.

"Only saying what I saw." The man shrugged his forward-pushed shoulder. "There were two short ones, little bit fat, that's how I could tell they were women. They had on uniforms, but the curves showed. And we heard their voices, didn't we?"

"Two women?"

"Three, at least. Had those two throwing down charges while another was shooting at us. Maybe more than one."

"It was dark," Maringdale said. "You were under fire and they dropped in and out of sight before exploding half the mountainside. It could've been anyone."

"No ma'am," the soldier said. "We give good watch and I know what I saw. What I heard."

"Women," Maringdale said it again. "In light-infantry armour."

The man nodded obstinately.

Maringdale left them to go back down the narrow path along the ridge, Netts hopping along behind her. She said, "This is like a nightmare where you're terrified of the big evil and it turns out to be a fluff-bear with a moustache."

"On account of it not being this dashing gentleman spy you're after?"

"Only because it screams *distraction*. It's the main event we're after."

"Wouldn't think you'd be so quick to dismiss them, of all people," Netts said. "I mean, I reckon enough people have underestimated *you,* after all."

She slowed down. The weasel might be right. She imagined another possibility. What if there were people like her, on the other side of the line? With everything to prove, everything to gain, those women might be dangerous. They had won the day at Green Rise, by some accounts.

Yes, this *was* different to the suggestion of waders. Maringdale led Netts on, more briskly, to where the rocks gave way to the rear camp and a pair of wooden huts, one large one for billeting soldiers and a small comms building, a fire pit between them. It was probably a holiday camp before the Drail military took charge.

Donut sat at the fire nursing a mug of steaming soup that smelt like meat, the sort they promised was as hearty as a meal. She pushed him as she passed and he clumsily rose to follow.

Maringdale entered the small hut, where a network of plugs and cables covered a wall. A spotty girl chattered into a receiver with two officers standing behind her, drinking the same vile liquid Donut had. The room stank of it.

The older officer, gaunt with the rough leathery skin of a Har Coul mountain man, said, "Got what you came for? Like I said, *women* scouts." He said *women* like the crack of a whip, not believing it himself. "Ever since word came up about Green Rise, everyone and his dog's seen fighting women in the shadows, like damned spectres. We haven't found a trace of them though, not like you'd expect from their sort."

Maringdale didn't want to know what that meant, but shared a knowing look with Netts. He was right, it was wrong to think the Bitch Squad were a negligible threat. She said, "You have men blocking their progress further up, though?"

"Near as we can. The Cracked Trail isn't a single path, there's a dozen routes, some heading up towards the city of Snow, others peeling off to the Falls, take you outside Har Coul itself."

"That's where they'll be going."

"No shit. And we're not able to get there any quicker than they are, so we can't cut them off. You might fly over with that lizard of yours, but good luck seeing anything between the rocks. Only hope would be if Amalric would spare us our own scouts from the front, but he's got his hands tied. Still, least we've got you."

Maringdale curled her nose at his sarcasm, but didn't waste energy on him. She turned to the girl at the telecoms machine and asked her to get hold of Battle Chief Baron. She switched plugs about, talking rapidly into a free-standing microphone.

"We going after them, or what?" Netts asked, quiet enough to indicate privacy from the officers. The men retreated to slip back into inane talk.

"How well do you know these mountains?" Maringdale said.

"These ones right here?" Netts said. "I know *of* them. I grew up in the Sand Basin, I got shit-all business being here."

"I'm from Pace. Spent a lot of time outdoors, in terrain not unlike this, and I know for sure we've got no chance tracking soldiers through the Cracked Trail. What we need to do is cut them off."

"I have him," the girl at the machine said, scooting to the side and holding up a hand for Maringdale to take her place. She crouched at the machine and took the offered headset, a heavy pair of wire-framed earphones.

"Battle Chief Baron? Can you send any scouts from Wick?"

"Really?" The long-distance line added a metallic crackle to Baron's hiss, impossibly making him sound even more sinister. "I hoped you would prove an able tracker yourself."

"There's only so much ground I can cover. If you can spare –"

"Absolutely not. But there's been developments, regardless. Prognane Salter, head of the 21st Division, has plans of his own that look like they'll feed into ours, misguided as they are."

"Misguided?" Maringdale echoed.

"He was responsible for defending Har Coul. He's not taking the attack on Mean Ridge seriously, but is using it to muster resources for himself. Do you believe it was the Blood Scouts out there?"

"*They* certainly believe it. I'm" – Maringdale eyed Netts, considering his point – "open to the idea. Whoever they were, they broke through without much trouble, and are likely to be a significant problem somewhere. But the reports are limited; I wouldn't be surprised if the threat of these women soldiers has been exaggerated."

"Quite so," Baron hissed. "Salter is pushing the line that they are destined for the industrial sites of Lakeland. Carrying bombs, escorting magic-users, plotting subversion. He's recalling parts of the Sacred Fleet from along the Step. Assuming our enemies will have to come up the river at some point. There will be barricades at the Little Step and a stronger presence at Heaven's Eye."

"But it could just be a gang of spies. A show of force might only better indicate our defences."

Baron breathed in, a sound as chilling as his speech. "Yes, and it rather assumes their destination to be the places Salter wants defended. Perhaps you can better predict their route, though, Officer Maringdale?"

Maringdale hesitated, hearing a hint of accusation in his voice. That she had come here to investigate was proof enough she suspected where the insurgents were heading.

"They cannot be allowed to reach Low Slane," Baron came back in, firmly. "Do you understand?"

The ridge officer was right about how little there was to see from the sky, with the rocks overhanging each other, making the trails hard to pick out. The wyrling could cover a lot of ground, offering excellent visibility, but not in this wretchedly inhospitable hovel. They spent the better part of two mornings circling, moving further north, then west, wasting time landing, with difficulty, to question people in the small mountain villages.

Returning from a futile trip to Edge Falls, which convinced Maringdale there was no way the Stanclif soldiers could've travelled so far on foot so quickly, they finally spotted two men charging down the mountainside, axes in hand. Donut landed as near to them as he could, tentatively putting the wyrling down on a nearby rock, and Maringdale and Netts hurried to intercept them. They spoke in rough, urgent Coulard, which Maringdale had a hard time translating. The gist was clear, though: invaders in their village.

They followed the men back up to find a frightened child being questioned, tearful, claiming to have seen two people. Women. Definitely women. A local with a scrappy grasp of Drail, better than Maringdale's Coulard, explained that they'd tied the child up to torture and threatened to cut her to pieces, before getting startled and disappearing back into the mountains. What few men were left in the village, too old or lame to join the army, had failed to find the mystery women after half a day of searching.

Maringdale and Netts jumped back on the wyrling and Donut steered them out over the rocks for their own search. Another half-day went by, and they found nothing by nightfall. The scouts were either very good or very lucky. But Maringdale had just three sets of eyes trying to spot as few as three women in a whole mountain range.

They set out again at first light, going north to join Salter's patrol at the river bend. The captain of a military steamship insisted no one was coming this way. While they spoke on the deck, Maringdale scanned the heavily forested far bank of the Little Step and wondered, "Could they travel through Eardung?"

The captain gave a light laugh, thumbs looped in his belt. "If they do, good luck to them. Nothing gets by the barkmen – they're connected to the trees themselves. Your friends from Stanclif wouldn't get two feet without getting tangled in carnivorous roots."

"Okay," Maringdale replied, "but say they *do* find a way, considering we don't have people there ourselves, where can we expect them to next cross our lines?"

"We do have people," the captain said. "Right here. There's nowhere else they can get by." He slapped his mortal mage companion on the back. "Besides which, we've got Frederick here. Intention mage *first class,* got more experience than most of this crew put together."

Maringdale gave the mage a polite smile. He nodded back modestly, and said, "He's too kind. I'm a legal prosecutor by trade. *Was,* before all this. Certainly not up to the standards of a Purification mage, but I do what I can. Nothing human will escape my notice."

It added a strange and unexpected positive to Maringdale's day, as the military mage deferred to her. They invited her to stay for dinner, and she found the pair to be wholly genuine in the respect they showed her. The captain was amiable, in light spirits for the relief of being repositioned at this quieter post, while Frederick pleasantly asked Maringdale's advice on improving as a witlacer, somehow deciding she knew better than him despite their imbalanced ranks. He asked about books she'd read, good practices for daily meditation, and how she felt about combining schools of witlacing. He aspired to develop some will magic, and she wished him luck in complicating his life. It was a pleasant diversion, though, and for a moment she felt appreciated.

Maringdale left to keep patrolling, though, realising pleasant company was not helping her track the enemy. The only alternative was for the scouts to press through mountainous Har Coul, crossing the Step at Bale Bridge. Donut flew them that way and they found the bridge fortified with Coulard homeguard armed with blades and bows. The trio settled there for the night and Maringdale let herself believe that one way or another they would stop these scouts. She improved her mood further by winning a game of cards against soldiers who refused to accept she was an intention mage, but they refused to pay up. She'd have stabbed them if Netts wasn't there to change their minds, with his Dread uniform, rifle and gender.

Mid-morning the next day, after another patrol of the sky, they set down at Bale and were told the guards had lost contact with the steamship at the bend. There had been reports of cannon fire. They flew back down the river, beyond a gathering of three smaller search boats, to a heavily damaged wooden barge on the shore. It was covered with creepy barkmen that Maringdale wanted nothing to do with. She had no idea how to communicate with barkmen, nor if it was safe to try, so they just circled the site until Netts spotted debris further downriver. They swept low without stopping as barkmen watched. A metal support stood jaggedly out of the riverbank, likely part of the missing ship.

Maringdale was sure the rest was gone, the crew dead. The captain and Frederick with them.

"You'd expect bodies," Netts shouted over the wind as they flew off. "Some sign where they fell."

"Those wooden shits are working with Stanclif," Maringdale shouted back. "They must've been riding that boat and ran into our boys. They've covered it up." She looked out over the trees, the canopy impenetrable from the sky. Somewhere out there was a group of very dangerous people who were threatening children and slaughtering good men. "Back north, Donut. We'll have them at the next crossing."

But there were no bridges connecting Eardung to northern Har

Coul. The only option would be for the scouts to cross at the river mouth itself, where ferries and one very tall arched bridge connected the city of Dask with the eastern Lakelands. The trio set down just outside the port and Maringdale stalked the streets feeling for intentions while she sent Netts to report to the Dread Corps. He came back saying Baron wasn't happy. The scouts had travelled further north than he expected, and that suggested threatening competence. With General Easter establishing a strong position outside Wick and Stanclif's River Armada pressing up the Step, their timing was going to be tight. No mistakes could be permitted now.

Maringdale realised, then, that they were wasting their time, as there were a thousand routes that might be taken but only one place where the insurgents were bound to be found. Over a platter of spread ribs, she told her men that they would head for Low Slane in the morning and find the man at the bottom of this. It was time for her to speak to the Vorhale Netts had once mentioned.

37

We can illustrate the relative danger for different combatants with a series of dehumanising numbers. The average life expectancy of a cavalry rider at the front was two months. A Drail airman, six weeks, and a ladder-plane pilot, four. Khib bursters had the dubious honour of the lowest life expectancy: these explosive shock troops fully expected to die – and indeed typically did so within a week of completing training. Regular infantry enjoyed a relatively longer expectancy of an average five months (for non-officers). This is hardly remarkable, however, when we consider that they spent an average two months stationary in trenches and seven weeks marching. If we considered their life expectancy during periods of actual fighting, it might be counted in seconds.

The Great Ebb and Flow: Reflections on Modern Trench Warfare, Sommer, p. 64

Watching for movement and listening for sounds, Boot Squad managed to avoid any hint of life as they trekked deeper into Low Slane. Deeper, too, into the mud, which became almost knee high. Three days to their destination seemed an impossible dream as each step came slow and heavy. They aimed for mossy patches, rocks and roots for stable ground, but there were often spaces of bog with nothing but skeletal tree trunks far apart, requiring a surge through the mud, trusting it wasn't deep enough to drown in. Following their caution from the Horns, Wish had the girls tie off, roped in pairs in case someone sank.

Despite the hardship, she felt lucky as the first day passed without any signs of monstrous life. The mud even started to get thinner, only ankle deep at worst, and the bare trees let more light in from the grey sky. Tied to Brade herself, responsibly leading the pack, she wanted to make conversation, with some light, witty remark. It was too quiet, though, and she became eerily aware of that. There was nothing in the air, not the breeze or distant call of birds, no rustling leaves or even small creatures. Just the trudge of their vulgar squelching boots.

Wild Wish slowed down and Brade drew alongside her. Behind them, she could almost hear the question in the silence of the rest of the squad. She studied the bog ahead, with wide spaces between the trees opening up the view. Endlessly the same, sentinels of black trunks and bulging mud. Then she saw a tree move, far ahead. A tall, narrow shape, that appeared to drift sideways. Wish swung her rifle down from her shoulder and aimed through the scope. Alongside her, Brade drew his eyeglass. She asked, "Do they have barkmen here?"

Fixing the creature in her sights, she saw it was far taller than the barkmen, and humanoid. Long, straight limbs, hanging from an impossibly narrow frame, with a top-heavy appearance as its head sat the size and shape of a roughly dug tree stump.

"Almost like a grekkel," Wish murmured – creatures she only knew from books, wolf-like, tall and sharp. But this was too thin. It moved again, with erratic strides, the same lifelessly mechanical motions as the giant bugs.

"That's no grekkel," Brade said.

"I said *like* a grekkel."

"We should move quickly. As far from that thing as possible."

Wish lowered her rifle to check if his expression matched the worried tone. "You know what it is?"

"I could be wrong." He kept following it with his eyeglass. "But best be cautious. For now, we need to stay well out of its range. And be careful, they can move fast."

"Will there be more?"

Brade shook his head. "No. We're unlikely to find anything at all within half a mile of a sorber."

"I could hit it from here."

"But you might not kill it. I'm not even sure how to kill one. No, we can't risk alerting it to our presence, let alone angering it."

Wish watched him, rather than the creature, hoping for some hint that it was a joke, a bit of fun after a long, dull morning's march. He looked pale, though, genuinely concerned in a way she hadn't seen him before. She took another look at the stick-creature but found it was gone. It took a moment to pick it out again, a lot further to the left than she expected. So, Brade definitely wasn't joking. She flapped an arm back to the squad. Time to move, fast.

The scouts' next break came after a steep incline that brought them to an area of thinning trees, which began to slope back down again. Wild Wish leaned against a trunk, considering that this place, at least, was similar to the overgrown gullies of Stanclif. Brade excused himself, politely murmuring that nature was calling, and took out a flask as he unbuttoned his trousers, moving around some bushes. Wish frowned at his back as Newk and Dakoda approached her.

"Relief break," Wish said, then gestured down the slope. "Reminds me of Ashvale Dyke, near Swelig. When the rains came, and the ground got slick enough, we could slide down the slopes between the trees."

"Try that here you'd probably fall into a giant frog's mouth," Dakoda said.

"It's nothing like Fireti," Newk said. "It rains and rains, but the land stays solid. And the trees are never naked and raw. I do wonder which of our nations is truly most bountiful."

"Obviously yours," Dakoda scoffed. "Otherwise why would we invade it? Slanik, Drail, Stanish – we all live in shitholes, it's driven us to find something better."

Newk stared like she wasn't sure if she was serious. Wish wasn't either. They didn't get to unravel it, as an urgent rustle came from Brade's direction, and they found the captain hurrying back through the trees, struggling with his belt.

"Can't stop, not here, not anytime soon," he said.

"What is it?" Wild Wish said, hand going to her rifle. Newk's was on her sword hilt.

"Either we're not out of its territory yet or it's following us."

Wish stared blankly for the second it took to register what he was talking about. The same fear from an hour or more earlier. "The somber?"

"Sorber. There's no time, come on."

Needing nothing more than that, Wish pushed past Newk and looked down to the rest of the straggling squad, climbing the hill. She almost shouted, but stopped herself, realising that would be a bad idea. Instead she waved, caught Rue's eye leading the others and gestured with quick hand movements for them to hurry. She told Brade, "Take them on, quickly, I'll let the others know."

The squad filed past as Wish patted them on the shoulders, saying, "Something's got Brade spooked, we need to keep ahead of it." With looks of fright or confusion but no back-chatter, everyone pressed professionally on. All except Emi, who dawdled at the back, not so much walking as swaying from one foot to the other.

"Get a move on, Emi!" Wish hissed. "There's a sober out there."

Emi gave her a quizzical look, further slowing. "That *is* a rare thing."

"Or whatever it's called." Wish hurried to take her sleeve and pull her along. She gave the mage a light push and Emi dug her heels in, suddenly glaring. "Fine, stay! Let it eat you or turn you inside out or whatever these things do." Wish strode ahead. There was no sound of the mage moving, apparently calling her bluff, and after a dozen hurried paces Wish turned back. She almost shrieked, fumbling for her rifle, and Emi followed her alarmed look back over her shoulder.

Looking even taller and gnarled than it had at a distance, the sorber was a short way back along the path, arms curved up at its sides as it twisted on the spot, scanning the air. Emi backtracked quickly and bumped into Wish, the pair tripping together and struggling to stay upright. When they steadied themselves, the sorber was gone.

"Should I –" Emi started.

"No – if there's any chance it hasn't seen us yet, we keep moving, stay hidden."

Wish pulled Emi's sleeve more forcibly then, all but dragging her up the hill.

A low crooning sound came from a rock formation far off in the trees, like a troll on a woodwind instrument. Wild Wish wasn't sure that was so far from the truth, and they kept studiously away from the rocks. As they continued, similar sounds came from other directions. At least two or three of the creatures, maybe more, depending on how the sounds echoed through the woods. Whatever they were, they sounded big, unhappy, and unreasonable, but at least the forest sounded alive again. There were things moving through leaves. Birds, not exactly tweeting, more scratching the air with their calls. Oksy named them, with reverent quiet: "Deviljack crow. Flesh raven. Actually mostly eats fish, so we can't be too far from the river."

After their late-night chat and the revelation that perfect Oksy was nursing insecurities, Wish decided she wasn't really *that* annoying. Just a girl trying to share something she found interesting. Wish flashed her an appreciative smile and Oksy smirked back smugly. Pitying Wish's affection?

The annoyance returned.

As Boot Squad pressed on, Wish continually looked back for fear of the sorber, the close encounter having chilled her enough to last days. That feeling drove them on at a pace that made up for the bog trudge of the morning, and by nightfall Brade promised they were making good time. He laid out his map, now ragged and grubby from being tussled throughout the day, and pointed. The girls leaned in to look, gathered by a small fire in another enclosure of large rocks, everyone but Rue, who was out keeping watch.

"I expect us to hit this peak tomorrow morning," Brade said. "From there, we'll have eyes south to Daggertooth Yard, one of the biggest lumber operations in central Boldarow. It's the northernmost facility this side of the river, so it doubles as a station warning against anyone fool enough to venture into the Dread Forest."

"But you took us through the back entrance to avoid that warning?" Dakoda said.

"To avoid them warning us, shooting us, feeding us through a sawmill, yes."

"Is anyone going to explain exactly what we're in for here?" Angles asked, huddled extra close to the fire as she shook with nerves and cold. "We were running all afternoon, weren't we? What were we running from?"

The captain sat back and said, "Sometimes it's better not to know."

"Would've helped knowing there were giant spider-slug nests out here," Cade said, harshly, but he returned a look that asked: *would it really?* The sapper lost her bottle and looked away.

"Were those siren trolls, in the caves?" Oksy asked.

"Possibly," Brade said, "but more likely graspers. Troll-like creatures attracted to deep, dark places, which grow very rapidly once they hit maturity. They become too large to leave their cave, so they sit luring animals in with their sad song, a call to help."

"What animal responds to *that* call for help?" Dakoda asked.

"You'd be surprised. Anyway, we're past them now."

"But they *weren't* what we were running from," Angles pointed out.

"No." Brade still hesitated. "I wasn't sure at first, but with the way it moved after us, I'm confident it was a sorber. A mixed blessing: no other creatures live near one, hence we had safe passage for much of the day. But they have a power not unlike the will schools of witlacing. They can directly affect the mind. Something in their –" He tapped his head. "It's said they can paralyse anything within a certain radius. Absolutely anything, rendered motionless, but retaining all its senses. They feed on internal energy as much as on flesh itself, once they attach to a prey."

"Oh, great," Cade laughed, uneasily. "More things that can devour us. Just great! What do we meet tomorrow, serpents that suck out our eyes?"

Brade kept quiet. Probably because such serpents existed.

Seeing her squad's jitters, recalling her need to comfort even Oksy, Wild Wish had to be an example. Lead, lead, lead. She said, "Doesn't matter, we survived it, and the worst things are behind us now, right? Just a mill ahead, and that's people. We know how to deal with people." She waited a beat, and saw a lot of expectant faces, so suggested, "We avoid them?"

"It's not just a mill though, is it?" Angles snapped. "Past there it'll be something else, then something else. We're where the worst bloody creatures imaginable are, while the rest of the world's fighting over things that matter? What're the Blood Scouts good for – this wasn't what I was –"

"Pretty sure they'd be good for burying you, speak out of line like that again," Rue said, voice shunting in like a hammer as she came out from the trees, returning from patrol. The circle was quiet as she and Angles exchanged glares, Rue daring her to say something more. When Angles was quiet long enough, Rue went on, "Wild Wish is our commander, and Captain Brade hers. Know your place. Unless you think you can do a better job?"

Angles didn't have the nerve to say more, and broke off her glare to look to the others. She particularly appealed to Newk, Wish saw – her fellow newbie and chuckling companion. But Newk added a scolding look of her own to Rue's. The others were no better, looking awkwardly away.

Angles pushed herself to her feet. "Well fuck you all, then."

She turned to storm off, but Newk rose with her, and in a flash had her sword out at her side and a fist clenched on Angles' shirt. She said, "You should be thanking them for keeping you alive this long. You'd rather walk out here alone?"

"Get your black claws off me, ringer," Angles growled, sending a gasp of surprise through the camp and cementing the malicious look on Newk's face.

"She looks more a Blood Scout than you right now," Rue said – this was moving fast, with allegiances shifting before Wish's eyes. About to come to blows.

Wish shot to her feet and called out, "Angles, enough. Newk – let her go." She held up a hand for clemency. Really hoping Newk wasn't about to decapitate anyone. "We're a team. Everyone's scared, but we can't go back, whatever you think of going forward. The only way we're surviving is together, so let's all take a damn moment."

"I don't gotta like it," Angles snarled sideways. "I don't gotta like any of you. Fucking ridiculous – Dakoda runs her mouth all day and you never have your ape threaten her –"

Out of nowhere, Rue struck Angles' jaw with the butt of her rifle, and she went down with a cry. As the other scouts jumped up, Angles crawled across the dirt and Rue put a boot on her back. Wish was locked in horror as Rue pushed her down and crouched in close to say, "Difference is we complain without undermining command. And no one *ever* insults our friends."

Angles whimpered into the ground, pathetic enough that Wish felt sorry for her, but she couldn't stop this, torn between helping and a kind of pride at Rue standing up for her. She shot Brade a look, and found the man had backed off, watching with interest.

"You gonna play ball?" Rue demanded. "Or you want to walk home alone?"

"I'm sorry, okay?" Angles cried, desperate enough it might be true. "Sorry!"

Rue let off her weight and stepped back. She held out a hand. Angles looked at it sceptically, so Rue bent and grabbed her, pulled her to her feet. Pulled her close and whispered in her ear. Private this time. Angles nodded, then hung her head, abashed, and Rue put an arm around her, to signal all was well.

Wish stared for another moment, unsure now if she needed to intervene at all. She cleared her throat to say something, anything, but Captain Brade beat her to it.

"Probably seems facile to say now," he said, casual as though their little drama had meant nothing, "but this is exactly what I thought would happen once we started discussing the details of the Dread Forest."

Wish glared at him. Blood Scouts *never* fought, not like this. She said, "Well now it's happened, I think it's time you told us everything."

38

*With wartime deaths being counted in the millions, there
are great gaps in accountability; many events that might
have become historically notorious during peacetime went
entirely unrecorded during the wartime era. We may never
know the full details of the Pace Alley Murders, claiming
twenty-seven lives in 719, or exactly what happened to the
dozens who were killed or went missing in the village of
Pray, the mountain community of Luddok, or at
Daggertooth Yard.*

**Dueley's Comprehensive: The One War in
10 Volumes (Vol. 10), p. 173**

Armed with Brade's tales of tusked wild pigs, venomous rat-
snakes, and a host of other delights that they might encounter in the
Dread Forest, Wild Wish found sleep elusive. She also had a
niggling sense of unease over how she'd handled Angles' outburst.
She'd lost a chance to prove herself a leader, let her girls come to
violence.

After listening for the next change of watch, Wish stuck her head
out and saw Newk sullenly moving into the dark as Fixit returned
to her tent. Wish shoved on her boots and tip-toed out to follow.
She crept up behind Newk as she settled onto a log overlooking tree
trunks and shadows. Newk looked up with eyes narrow from
tiredness.

"Came to keep you company," Wish said and Newk obediently
shifted to make room. Wish sat next to her and they stared into the
darkness together before she got up the nerve to say, "Angles
shouldn't have said those things. I'll see she's properly
reprimanded."

"She was hit in the face," Newk said. "She's been punished. And I've heard worse."

"But you shouldn't do here. Among friends. Under my command."

Newk gave a noncommittal grunt. Wish hung her head, staring between her knees. Fuck it, they might die in terrible ways here, she might as well say it: "It should've been me that knocked her down. I should've said what Rue did."

Newk looked up to meet Wish's eye. Thinking Wish was an idiot, pathetic, too little too late? Something more positive, happy she cared?

"I'm glad to have you on the team," Wish mumbled. "That's what I really want to say. And I want to do better for you."

"I can handle myself," Newk replied.

"But that's –" Wish stopped, took a breath. She'd made Newk defensive and this wasn't helping. Too tired for sharp thinking. And Brade's words came back to her from before the Horns: *it wouldn't do to be distracted*. She said, "I just hope we can be friends."

Newk's eyebrows squeezed together. "Aren't we friends?"

Wish knew she couldn't explain right now. Not friends like casually connected through the scouts. Friends like they might be together even if they weren't battling Big Evils. Friends like they could forgive each other for weaknesses and misunderstanding. Friends like they might think of each other in quiet moments. Over-the-top, unreasonable dreams that could all be lost in a second. *No* – It wasn't real, was it? Wish didn't know Newk. Had she really known Loose? She felt Newk watch her with concern, and said, "Can you tell me something about yourself? Something meaningful."

Newk hesitated, giving it too much thought. It felt like a shared acknowledgement that this was futile when they could so quickly die out here. Wish was about to get up and leave when Newk said, "I miss Anlia. My menafis."

Wish tried to recall what that even meant. Newk's tattoos marked her as a magic conduit and the menafis was her wielder, right? "What's . . . was she like your partner?"

Newk nodded. "I was capable of so much more, with her."

"I feel that way about the scouts," Wish whispered, a truth she was worried to admit. Because what if she lost all of them, the way she'd already lost so many. They'd given her strength ever since Sarge had saved her from sniping alone in Cartwell.

She sat in silence for a time, inches from touching Newk, the rest of a possible conversation going unspoken but easily imagined. Anlia and Newk had been close, but she had met a terrible fate. Wish could make promises about the scouts replacing her, but it was not, and never could be, the same. And it was temporary. One way or another.

Finally, Wish stood and said, "I'll do my best, anyway. While it lasts."

Newk held in whatever response she had. Wish walked back to camp trying to get a grip, not sure if she'd been trying to reassure Newk or herself. But yes. She would do better. Keep them alive and end this war. Put silly thoughts aside.

Her mind wasn't quite blank when she lay back down, but it wasn't far off as she stared unblinking into the darkness of her tent. At some point she fell asleep, and was woken by the others clattering about getting ready to go. When they started marching, she caught Newk's eye and gave her a friendly grin. Newk smiled back, but cautiously. Great, Wish told herself. Made things weird.

The squad's trepidation as they started marching thankfully replaced those thoughts, as everyone watched the shapes that surrounded them with new paranoia. Wild Wish wondered if Captain Brade was right, and they were better off not knowing what the forest contained. In the light of day, seeing how far the monotonous woods stretched, Wish couldn't dispel her own worry. The sorber was still out there, for starters, and could be hiding behind the next tree. Every next tree. Brade was shady on the details of that one; he couldn't say how it hunted, so maybe it took pleasure in the chase, and would leap out later – surprise! Welcome to painful death.

Much as Wish hated to admit it, Angles had a point. Back in the trenches, the bloody violence at least led somewhere. Kill enough

Drail and Stanclif would secure more land, after all. They had a destination, here, but exactly how useful was it fighting random monsters? But she couldn't say that.

Then, she was drawn from such thoughts by almost stumbling upon the enemy.

Oksy returned from scouting ahead, calling her to come see, and Wish joined her with Brade to climb a hill overlooking his promised lumber mill. Daggertooth Yard was even scrappier than its name suggested, visible beyond miles and miles of felled trees. The buildings looked like iron cathedrals, lined with tall chimneys. There were wagons out front, on tall, spiked wheels, dragged by carapaced creatures that made pack beetles look delicate. The noise of huge machines churned through the woods, and scores of workers moved in and around the buildings' enormous open entrances. This place was to the mill in Farne what a city like Vasseer was to piddling Swelig.

"Are they making furniture for giants?" Wish whispered.

"Prefab building materials," Oksy said. "They've got a perimeter of some sort over this way, but that's not to say there's not some of them spread through the woods."

"All right. Can you go ahead, find us a safe way round? Alone?"

"Sure." Oksy set down her pack and lifted her rifle. "Wait here."

Wish watched her move quickly into the woods. The great Oksy, doing Wish's bidding. Even if it come out as a rather meek request. Was this what power felt like? Cracking twigs drew her attention to the rest of the scouts, further back in the woods, and she asked Brade, "Can you tell them to stay hidden while we assess this?"

Brade regarded her with a mix of humour and mild resistance. Shit, he was a captain, she'd gone too far giving him an order. But he nodded and went in the other direction, leaving Wild Wish to watch the lumber mill alone. It was so busy, this tree-churning complex, bordering on the Hell Woods and a long way from anything she might understand. Who *were* these people? Did they ride into the mill each morning from civilised towns or did they live in a thousand small huts tucked between the trees?

A truck reversed up to one of the buildings and men called out to one another as a crane arm swung out from the huge doors, dangling huge beams of wood. The men guided the load onto the bed, strapped it in place, and the vehicle drove away, engine shuddering as it strained against the weight. No sooner had it left, another near-identical truck pulled in.

Brade crept back alongside her and Wish said, "How many vehicles like that do the Drail have? Enough to switch places every five minutes, all day long?"

"Probably. As do we."

"But we've got like . . . five tanks in a battalion? Mostly people on horses."

"For now," Brade said. "That'll change. Though we'll never lose the personal touch, I expect. Tanks can't take cities. Or sneak around enemy lines. And they cost an awful lot more than people."

"While not being all that much harder to kill?" Wish suggested.

Brade nodded grimly. "For those who know how."

They were interrupted as Oksy came back with a stooped, hurried gait; something was wrong. Wish said, "You couldn't have got round that quickly?"

Shaking her head, Oksy moved in close, confidentially. Her studiously neutral expression was more troubling than any worried one could be. "It's here. Ahead of us."

"What *it?*" Wish asked.

"The sorber."

Wish darted a look to Brade, found him frowning. He asked, "You saw it?"

"About two hundred yards out from the yard's perimeter," Oksy said. "We might slip between it and the mill, but we'd need to move slow and it could change direction and come towards us at any time. Leaving us nowhere to run."

"Shit," Wish said. "We can't even shoot it now, we'd have every lumberjack in Low Slane on our arses."

"You wouldn't want to risk shooting at it anyway," Brade reminded her. "The thing must be tracking us unwittingly, if it's here but hasn't struck. Maybe we just disrupted its usual hunting patterns, crossing through its territory. But it must've been following *us,* for it to have come this far —" He stopped in a way that said an idea was gripping him. Not necessarily a good one. No, from the set of his mouth it was a really unpleasant one. "It must've sensed *people* nearby. If the locals know to keep their distance, whatever trace of us it picked up on must've presented a rare prey. A special lure. But if it is following us, we can stray a little closer, lead it off."

"Lead it off where?" Oksy said, but the answer was obvious even without Brade glancing towards the mill. Give it other people to chase? As it dawned on Oksy, she actually looked afraid and met Wish's eye for support. "Not knowing what this thing is capable of?"

"It's capable of killing all of us," Brade said. "I can guarantee that. Them?" He gave the yard a cursory glance. "They might be able to handle it."

"Except if they could wouldn't they have done it by now?" Wish said, and wondered why she had to make things difficult. Because it was true – the power of this thing was unmistakable in the silence that surrounded it, and the locals surely knew about it. They must've warned their children exactly where not to go – *don't disturb the sorber, and everything will be fine.* No one expected some gang of ignorant scouts would cross its path and set it hunting.

"We can go back," Wish suggested. "Then cut north, right until we reach the river, as wide a berth as we can give it."

"We'd lose a day, at least," Brade said. "To say nothing of what we'd face up there. We have what we need right here, ladies – a distraction that will let us press on fast. Otherwise there's no telling how long the sorber will hound us or when it might finally strike."

Oksy went quiet. She was logical if nothing else, and even if she didn't like it, Brade made sense. And besides, it wasn't her call, made perfectly clear by the way they both watched Wish expectantly. Another grim choice – risk the lives of noncombatants to help win the war. One step closer to Swelig. *However many must die . . .* She said, quietly, "They're not soldiers. This isn't the battlefield."

"They're fuelling the war effort," Brade replied readily.

"Everyone from the Ice Sea to the Arrow is a part of this. However it might look, it remains us or them."

Wish searched Oksy's face, hoping to see another choice, or confirmation they should just pack it in and go home, all they'd discussed two nights ago having arrived at this unattainable head. They'd done their best, got in too heavy. But sights came back to Wish, sounds, words. Loose falling, *No* – and so many more would die if Drail swarmed Stanclif soil. Sarge, crushed. Tate telling her the time to question it was when they survived.

"It's the only choice," Brade said, with a slight edge as her hesitation concerned him. He'd pull rank if he had to. Make the choice for her. But if he did that, the other girls might rebel, and then they'd get nowhere. Tate's other missive came clear: she must do it so no one else had to.

"Did you tell the others the sorber was ahead, Oksy?" Wish asked.

"No."

"Don't. Better they not know. We'll move ahead, linger until we see it start to move, then we'll double back, move up and around it as it comes this way. Tell the girls we're circling Drail scouts or something, anything – I don't want this resting on them."

Oksy nodded. That was that, then. Wish took a deep breath, took off her pack and gestured for her friend to lead the way. Off through the trees, keeping one eye watching the yard in case guards actually did show, another eye out for where Oksy last saw the monster. Finally, Oksy put a hand back, slowing Wish down, and they watched through their scopes as the sorber crept around the far-off trees. They ducked, hidden in a ditch, and waited silently. Wish's mind screamed that it wasn't too late. She didn't have to do this. But then, it might be okay, the thing might not even move, maybe it was happy where it was.

It picked up something from them, though, clear as it twisted to face their way. Then slowly, deliberately, it took strides towards them. Almost as if it could see them, but there was no way. Oksy nudged Wish to say they'd done enough, and Wish agreed, nodding to retreat. They kept low, back along the ditch, pulling closer to the edge of the yard, so their scent might mix with the mill's. Moving faster than they had before. Soon, they found Brade waiting with their packs.

"Looked like it worked," Wish said, shouldering her bag. "You two go, move the girls on, and I'll catch up."

"I don't think –" Brade started, but she cut him off.

"No way I'm leaving this to chance."

The captain hesitated. "I'll stay, too. Reliable observations of the sorber are incredibly rare – it'd be something worth reporting back to the Empire."

Wish hated how cold it sounded coming from him, while her insides were knotting with doubt and guilt. An almost academic proposition. But it was a proposition – he was asking, knowing this meant something to her. She nodded assent. With one last unhappy look, Oksy darted through the trees to get the squad moving, and Wish and Brade turned their attention back to the clearing.

They had little time to spare. The baiting must've encouraged the sorber, that or it was spurred on by picking up on the mill full of people, as it swept out from the tree-line, three hundred yards from their position. Aiming for the nearest massive building. Out in the open, moving with an angular, stalking stride, it looked more alien than ever, a set of crooked dark lines that shouldn't be alive. There was a good empty distance of tree stumps between it and the mill, and once it was about halfway across the workers started to stop and take notice. Those at the fringes, in the midst of loading another truck, turned towards it and slowed what they were doing. Calmly, curiously. One, a little further back, moved fearfully from the truck and shouted something. More men came running outside and the driver of the truck started panicking in the cab, waving at them to finish tying off so he could leave.

With each stride the sorber took, more workers went calm, as though put in a trance. The nearest men stood stock still, and then those around the truck, hurrying to untie the logs or climb off it, paused too, erect like the barkmen. Men were caught mid-run, those around the big doors twisting to sprint back inside but seized by the same energy, jolting to a standstill. Only a few more strides and the sounds of men were quiet, though the machines kept whirring inside. Everyone in sight was frozen like a garden of living statues – the truck driver sat rigidly looking out the windshield.

"How's it doing that?" Wish gasped. "Its range is – why didn't it get us?"

"Waiting for the right moment, I'd say," Brade replied. "Until we were all together, or it had us all in its sights. I don't know. By the Saints, it's even more powerful than I thought."

Wish shakily followed the sorber through her scope as it kept moving forward, aiming at the closest man with jagged arms out at its sides, preparing a welcoming embrace. She found the man's face, hoping the zoom would reveal something passive, sent to sleep with no idea what was coming. His eyes were wide. She could see the whites around his irises, and felt his fear through the scope as he watched this thing bearing down on him. She tracked back, sights over the monsters' log-like head, knowing she could hit it from here. To do what? Kill it and alert Slane to their presence? Miss and send it their way?

It reached the man and lifted its skeletal limbs, the ends stretching into pointy fingers that wrapped around him like a bird's talons, almost tenderly. It lowered its head towards him and touched it to him, and fed without spark or sound. The man shrivelled slowly, shrank into the monster's embrace, as though it was sucking his blood through a straw. Except it took so much more than that; Wish could see it somehow, in the way his body withered. She looked away before it could reduce him to a simple sack of skin, and she saw the ranks upon ranks of labourers standing pivoted towards the creature, not a single one able to resist its entrancing power.

The sorber stepped away from its first victim, leaving a pile of empty clothes, and started towards the next, only a few paces on, a man who would be screaming through his eyes. Something rose suddenly in Wish's gut, threatening to burst out her mouth, and she gagged, turning away. Covering her mouth, she swallowed hard, desperate to keep it down and not make a sound.

Brade put a hand on her shoulder, his lips close to her ear, and said, "We can go. It's definitely distracted enough."

Wish gave him a hateful look, to say this was his fault and it wasn't a good thing, and it wasn't a distraction, it was murder of the worst and most horrible kind. But his face was pale, too, and her hate faltered, because he looked exactly how she felt.

39

Soldiers gave everything nicknames, including people, places, events and weapons. The names were often so obviously simple that outsiders invented more creative origins for them. For example, Drail's Section 28 shock troops were popularly called the Punchers, not because they "punched through the enemy lines at Florid" or because they "punched so many enemy tickets", but because they got in tremendous drunken fist-fights during their downtime. For a parallel in Stanclif, see the Blood Scouts, whose name was not due to their violent nature but a derisive nod towards their gender (see Vol. 4).

Dueley's Comprehensive: The One War in 10 Volumes (Vol. 2), p. 148

Maringdale could say one thing for the Dread Corps, she decided as she arrived at Reeve Abbey: they had a penchant for the dramatic. They had chosen the most unsettling locations for their secret work. The abbey's central church loomed tall over the surroundings with stone arches, angular buttresses and overly realistic carvings of monsters. It was an opposite to Riker Cathedral's huge but practical design; this architect had a restless mind, and used sharp angles and frescoes to ensure every inch of the property screamed something unpleasant. The aged stone added to the effect, cracked and blackened as though attacked by barbarians and fire-breathers. It was everything Maringdale would expect from Low Slane.

The church's wrought iron doors stood tall enough to accommodate a giant, with an almost comical human-sized door open at the base, which Maringdale's trio entered through. They craned their heads as they walked over marble slabs into the central nave, the vaulted ceiling an impossible height above them, trimmed with twisting, reptilian supports and slit skylights paned with green glass. The open central space of the church had been repurposed with tall metal walls and walkways welded into place to form a cluster of stacked cells, sealed by bulkhead doors.

A group of three mages in black robes looked down from one of the chambers, while a cluster of four soldiers sitting around a table barely acknowledged the spy hunters' entrance. Maringdale ignored both groups to focus on Battle Chief Ways, the big, armoured man standing on a walkway two storeys up with a man whose identity she could guess. He was a head shorter than Ways, with big mechanical devices in place of arms, like he was wearing engine parts for sleeves.

"Maringdale!" Ways boomed at her, his voice echoing with the power of a god's. "Come up here. Just you."

Maringdale glanced at Netts and Donut, the former's expression saying better her than him, Donut still too busy gawking at the building. She strode off, jumped up clanking metal steps and worked her way along the walkway to another set of stairs. She slowed passing one of the cells, seeing movement through a circular glass panel. A man inside, skeletal with undernourishment, clutching his shaved head as though in pain. He looked up suddenly, darted towards the door and smashed his face into the glass. It made Maringdale flinch, but he was knocked back. He screamed, mouth wide, but no sound came out. And she felt nothing of his pain or anger. Then she realised there were more people in other cells. Not just people: a trunk in one, a water-walker in another. Equally distraught and ill as the first man, but none giving her senses a hint of their feelings. Unsettled, Maringdale continued to the next tier and Ways.

He was waiting with his arms out, a cheery look on his face, an uncle pleased to see his wayward kin. In better spirits than in Cleave, for sure, and apparently now warm to her. Instead of offering an embrace, he grasped her hand in a grip that swallowed it and shook vigorously. "So good to have you join us, Officer

Maringdale. I've been singing your praises to the entire team, you know."

"Rather a smaller team than I expected," she said. Rather an awkward reply, too.

"We've everyone we need," the other man, surely Vorhale himself, said, his back to her as he studied a panel of vibrating needles, reporting measurements of the chamber they stood next to. He was shorter than she had thought, about her height, but was made formidable by the great mottled metal blocks jutting out from his shoulders, framing his head. They divided into blocky false arms, each joint a foot square, at least, powered by pistons and cables and ending in three-fingered hands. He turned to her, at last, with a studious look, partly hidden behind dark, round glasses, and a metal plate covering the lower-right side of his jaw. The arm mechanisms whirred, and she saw then, through the cable-threaded gaps between joints, that there was no space inside for muscle – the blocky artificial limbs were all the arms he had. His narrowed eyes suggested she was equally unusual to him, though he said, "Everyone we need now you're here, that is."

"Forgive my ignorance," Maringdale said carefully, "but I thought you'd have some defences already. There were only two men I saw stationed outside, and your guards scarcely look ready for an attack."

"Oh, pish," Vorhale said, semi-mechanical mouth struggling to smile. He didn't look used to such expressions. "I continue to doubt Stanclif can make it this far into our territory."

"As did Battle Chief Hark."

"But even if they did," Vorhale continued sharply, "we have better defences than *men* can offer. You won't have noticed, dropping from the sky, but the grid system of Reeve Abbey itself is a ward. This was an unholy site, once, a long time ago. Every inch of it devised to raise devils, did you know? Fitting." He sniggered, and she sensed no doubt in him; their security was guaranteed. He flexed his metal arms in front of him and added with a proud afterthought, "You're standing in a land of rich history. The heroes of our past knew how to tame monsters."

Maringdale frowned, reading clearly enough that he somehow associated the outstretched arm contraptions with those heroes – perhaps he'd had them constructed in honour of one such person. He expected her to ask for more details, so she turned to address Ways instead, and said, "And if the enemy come in by sky, too?"

"They won't," Ways said. "And from your ability to track this fiasco so far, I expect you're well aware of that. In fact, it was my assumption that by the time you arrived you'd have a good idea of exactly where to head off any potential attack, so we might start withdrawing out troops."

"The troops that already aren't here?" Maringdale replied uncertainly.

"My company is just over the next hill. Ready to defend Reeve, despite Vorhale's assuredness. But they're not coming close, for now. I'd rather move straight to Wick. Find a way to guarantee this site's safety and I'd like you to come with us."

"Wick? I've got no –"

"The mind chain is almost ready," Vorhale cut in. "We will send Bomb 64 to Wick, to use it in the field, and we would *all* rather it be escorted with full protection than anyone stay trying to babysit *me*."

Maringdale took that in and read the part of his mind that was open to her – a technical, simplistic focus on something that he sincerely believed to be both incredible and inevitable. He had no doubt and very little capacity for distraction. Rarely had she felt a man so driven. And he would rather she help deliver the weapon than complete her task here. She said, "Much as I appreciate the confidence, I've been tracking a serious threat."

"Which we'll deal with presently," Ways said. "Frankly, none of us expect them to make it here, but there's no way to enter this valley undetected, if they do. There's a reason my own men aren't stationed here."

"Part of it," Vorhale said, "is to avoid distraction. The other part, destruction." His face crinkled at his own joke, and Maringdale suspected that he had little experience talking to people.

"Walk with me," Ways instructed, reading the look on her face. "Let's leave the doctor to his work."

"Indeed, indeed," Vorhale agreed, turning back to his dials.

Ways moved with creaking steps, too heavy for the walkways. He led Maringdale deeper into the complex of cells. "I've been keeping an eye on your efforts. Excellent work in Highscythe and Null."

"Not so great in Fever. Or Wick."

"You chased the goblin from that hen house, at least. Bought us enough time to complete this project. Gloven has already set out to help reinforce Highscythe, and we will be ready to move south and rejoin Baron within days."

"Stanclif could've reached Lakeland by now; you might not have days."

"Women playing solider and a mindless mage do not concern me. The fact that we had any breaches in Cleave and Highscythe, Fever and Wick – *that* troubles me. Enough to doubt the Dread Corps can defend this weapon alone. Hence, you are here."

Funny, Maringdale thought, hadn't it been her idea to come to Slane?

"Why I *allowed* you here," Ways clarified, her thinking apparently obvious. "Your skills at intention magic are better than I feel anyone has given you credit for. You'll provide a warning beacon better than a hundred guards. And before we set out, you can help me with some enquiries into the state of my own house."

"You're thinking Pale Taik wasn't the only traitor?"

"That's for you to decide." Ways clapped a big hand on her back, nearly knocking the wind out of her. She tensed, refusing to stumble, but had to catch her breath. She made the pause look thoughtful, like she'd stopped to give the chamber a fresh scan. Magic-dampening cells, filled with people.

"Can I ask what exactly is going on here?"

"Better not to, don't you think?" Ways said, recalling the not-overly-subtle hint of a threat she'd first sensed from him back in Cleave. It was easy to accept now; this wasn't a place she wanted any large part in. "But feel free to ask Vorhale about his arms. He imagines he's channelling a great Slanik monster hunter of centuries past, some thug who wielded similar contraptions to bring down a terrible giant. Only he has higher hopes. He sees the monster as our enemy's entire empire."

The men in and around the nearby village gave an aura quite unlike any Maringdale had encountered. She had been in violent crowds, when the Ulkfactors marched in Pace, and she had run gauntlets of emotion mingling with soldiers on or near to the front line, but she had never felt something quite like the raw, unified energy that Ways' company exuded. She felt it before they arrived, riding in a motor car with Ways and his driver. The feeling crested on her as clearly as the slate-sided buildings, a cluster of dark and jagged Slanik homes thrumming with malice and hostility. Maringdale tried to sift through it, to focus on individual feelings or particular sources for the mean emotions, but there was a collective, unified rage to it.

The men looked the part, staring as the car drove towards the centre of the village. The black, bone-lined metal plates of their Dread Corps armour was battered and faded. Their faces, even the young ones, were leathery and lined with scars, hair coarse and brittle, eyes deadly hollow. Each man exuded the same feelings: threatening, murderous, eager for the kill. Almost as stark as the feral emotions that fogged Battle Chief Baron and the grekkels. The dark aura was all around them.

Ways smiled at Maringdale as they pulled up, satisfied by her expression. He said, "These are the 1st Wavecutters, the Dread Corps' shock troopers. Typically, we spread shocksmiths out to support other companies, but we've gathered all we could here."

Through a gap in the houses sat a tank, a black lump of metal only given contours by its dents and scratches. The gun mounted on top was enormous, with a metal plate behind it to protect the gunner. This was, collectively, the best escort Vorhale could ask for. But it steeled Maringdale in her resolve: stronger security would only make them more complacent.

Leaving the car behind, Ways guided Maringdale towards a

market square, where men gathered around supply crates, all the eyes in the world on her. The weight of their feeling pressed down, angry, hateful, aggressive. She tried to resist, but it made her cringe.

Ways asked, "What's wrong?"

"How've you done this?" Maringdale responded quietly.

Ways waited for her to continue. She steeled herself and focused on the youngest soldier nearby, a skinny man not long out of adolescence, lower lip curled by a scar, with a mop of black hair and armour too big for his frame. He met her eye then looked away, but while his body suggested nerves, his intentions came out strong: violent anticipation, a fire burning chaotically, something ready to stab out. To explode. It prickled at her all over just sensing it.

"Come, I'll give you a tour." Ways put a hand on Maringdale's shoulder.

She ducked out from him, shaking her head, and his brow knitted. Maringdale hurriedly explained, "I can already see your men are fortified against witlacing. I don't need more of a demonstration."

"You're here for my benefit, not the other way around," Ways reminded her.

"With respect, Battle Chief, even if there is a spy here, ousting them won't help us stop the insurgents who are already in motion. *If* I could get around the mind defences here. I'll happily do whatever I can, whatever you say, but I honestly believe the best use of my skills right now remains in stopping these scouts before they get close to you."

Ways regarded her with mild distaste, but she recalled their first meeting, when he'd shown respect for her willingness to challenge him. Getting this far, after all, had all been about thinking for herself. He said, "What do you propose?"

He was actually asking, and at last Maringdale felt listened to, after however far this long journey had taken her. She said, "The Gentleman and his soldiers are always a step ahead: the fact that they headed off your men before Fever *and* got a spy into Null should be proof enough of their ability. They've travelled through Eardung, Battle Chief. Taking a long and careful route to be sure they're not spotted. These are dedicated, highly competent people. If they to come to Reeve Abbey, then they'll approach it with extreme caution. But I think I can predict their caution. Give me maps of the area, all the possible approaches from the west, and I'll figure out where we're likely to meet them – *before* they get here."

40

**Extract from the Letters of
Corporal T. Sander, Balnia, 719**

"Here's what you can do," Rue said, gruffly, as she drew up next to Wild Wish at the front of their procession. "Tell me what the fuck happened at that lumber yard, privately, and word'll naturally spread to the others. You can pretend like you were just confiding in a friend, while actually letting us all in on it."

Wish cocked an eyebrow to her, feigning ignorance.

"Don't. Plain as a beige hide something bad went down."

"Yeah?" Wish replied. Since leaving Daggertooth Yard behind, there had been almost no talk between the scouts, not during their rapid advance through the rest of the day nor once they set up camp that night. A rigid tension set across them all, especially when Wish lay beside Rue in their tent not sleeping. Through the morning, things had been little better, with worried looks thrown Wish's way even when Pound tried to lighten the mood with jokes about a Khib baker. And finally, a full day's quiet and tension later, Rue was brashly demanding the explanation. Wish told her quietly, "You'd get it, I think. But I'm not sure about the others."

"Get what? How much worse can it be than every other fucking thing we've seen and done? You torch the place, cut some throats, what?"

Wish shook her head, trying not to picture those men served up to the sorber. What was left of the first victim, and how the same fate would've reached the rest by now. She said, "This one's better left unsaid."

"The fuck did I say about how that works? You shoulder this shit and it weighs on us. Better we know the load we're *all* carrying."

Wish looked her firmly in the eye, stopping dead. "It's not, I promise."

"Well, it's not helping any leaving everyone wondering. You said the same shit to Brade not two days ago!"

"Whatever you guess," Wish said, "I'm pretty sure that'll do the job."

Rue glared. "A *lot* of men dead, then?"

"A lot."

"In a horrible way."

"The most horrible way."

"What's the difference?" Rue shrugged, though her heart wasn't fully in the dismissal. Even she wasn't that callous, and respected that the mill was full of civilians, not soldiers. And considering they hadn't charged it shooting their rifles, everyone knew that whatever happened was close and personal. Most likely, Rue had assumed cut throats. That would do.

Seeing she wasn't getting any more than that, Rue turned off with a snort. "Fine then, you eat it. But get over it, right? Because there's more where that came from, isn't here?"

"Probably."

"But we're almost at the end, aren't we?"

Another day out, yes. No great threats after the sorber, and a final stretch that Brade promised would be more about avoiding people than forest dangers. Another day and they'd reach the abbey, and whatever was waiting there. Something more terrible, Wish suspected. It had to be, didn't it? Because that was how war worked. It didn't get *less* terrible.

Wish forced a bright smile, a grin even, and patted Rue's arm. "Onwards and upwards!" And with a spring in her step, she fell back into marching, trying to let her body suggest things were okay, now this talk was over. Because her mind couldn't agree.

Rue let it drop, and must've spread that message through the others, because the tension faded as the day drew on, partly helped by the appearance of villages through the trees. Where there were villages, there weren't monsters.

The scouts crept along the tops of hills, marvelling at the quaint thatched roofs and smoking chimneys in a green valley, not unlike parts of Stanclif, and a world apart from the thorny woodland they still had a foot in. The scouts salivated over the settlements, imagining darting enterprises to steal chickens, booze, bread – anything for a break from the rocks of hardbread they'd been living off. The lack of alcohol over the past few days had everyone notably crankier and edgier than usual, and they were all hungry. But Wish had to forbid the distraction, as she knew Tate or Sarge would've, with all that open ground to cover and the possibility of alerting locals. Luxuries like fresh food were for after the war, she told them. Hating herself as much as they probably did.

Brade's spirits were higher than anyone else's as they camped that night, having regained his composure quickly after Daggertooth Yard. He promised they'd see Reeve Abbey tomorrow, ready to strike the following day, as planned, and then they'd be home free. With the end in sight, he gave in to their demands and told stories around the fire of his travels, before the war. They were modestly framed, remarkable stories of a well-travelled man who had faced every challenge and yet remained unsatisfied. His account of searching for the lair of a hydra in east Sil was laced with a bitterness for the Imperial Geographical Association that became apparent throughout all his accounts. His stories were less of the monsters he had seen, or incredible cultures he'd uncovered, and more about the people who thwarted him back home – Lord Ulster tried to ban him from the Club House, Lord Ealing attempted to censor his publications. They hated him because he lacked their parentage. Not that his parents weren't of notable stock – Lord Brade had sponsored Statesman Dowel himself – but the Brades were still recovering from a shame two hundred years old. Something he didn't explain.

Wish could've done without the entertainment, however much she appreciated some insight into this man who'd ruined their lives. She would've preferred to get him alone, the only other person who had seen what the sorber could do, so she could share that single memory with shocked phrases like, "Did you see – wasn't it horrible?"

But she could see how his shared stories were an escape that let him cope with the horror his own way, and she felt selfish for wanting to take that away from him. Instead, she listened for a polite amount of time, before announcing that she was going to be responsible and turn in early, *again*, but they should stay up. For once, they didn't give the customary round of jeers, for whatever reason, and as she snuggled into her sleeping bag their voices dropped to quiet whispers, not to disturb her.

After a few minutes, the tent rustled with an intruder. Wild Wish prepared to scold Rue for following her again, but the head that poked through wasn't Rue's. Newk crawled down next to Wish, and whispered, "I asked Rue to switch tonight. So she can stay up later without disturbing you."

"Really?" Wish was thrown. "I'm used to Rue waking me, it's no problem."

Newk paused, crouched over Wish. Filling up the tent with shadow and a sweet mixed scent of sweat, alcohol and smoke. Her eyes and the bone lines on her flesh shone white in the dark, luminescent in a way Wish felt *had* to be some kind of magic, even without her menafis fuelling it. Newk said, "Reaching the abbey's going to be bad, isn't it?"

"Yeah?" Wish replied hesitantly. "So you wanted to be extra rested yourself?"

"I wanted to be extra sure . . ." Newk trailed off, eyes fixed on her for a second before flitting away. She chewed her lip as Wish clutched tightly to her sleeping bag with anticipation. But Newk didn't continue.

"I'm glad you came," Wish admitted, quietly. Too quiet to hear? Newk shot her another look. Her expression shifted. Something like a smile?

"I didn't want – it's not –" Newk paused, trying to think this through. Another look back to the tent flaps, an awareness that things were only getting quieter outside. Newk shifted, down onto an elbow, beside Wish. Breath on her face. She whispered, confiding, "I didn't want anyone thinking I'm just trying to please an officer. But I also didn't want to wait. We might all die tomorrow."

"That keeps being true," Wish said, holding in the other comments that cried to be said: she wasn't an officer, as far as she knew, and *please an officer* how?

"Do you mind if . . ."

Wish waited, but Newk didn't finish again. Just stared at her, at the same time both impossibly close and impossibly far. Shit, this was too much. Wish sprang forward to kiss her. Their lips touched and she shot back again. Staring horrified into Newk's eyes. Newk looked surprised. Why wasn't she expecting it – was that not what this was? Was it just a really bad kiss? Wish blurted out, "I don't normally kiss like a bird."

"How do you normally kiss?" Newk asked, sounding nervous too.

"Good question," Wish replied, hoping that sounded smooth, suave, rather than honestly unsure. Potential answers involved mirrors, hands, and curses. Newk was waiting, though, inches away, lips slightly apart. Not wanting a spoken answer. Shit, guess it was time to find out.

Wish ran a hand up the side of Newk's neck, slowly, steadying her, before approaching even slower. Letting their lips just touch, gently. She breathed softly, drinking in some of Newk's breath, then squeezed their faces together, searching, savouring, hungry. Newk slid down onto her and their hands were roving, clutching, pulling, like if they held on tight enough they might merge. Wish struggled quickly out of her sleeping bag and they rolled to the side, intertwined their legs, trying desperately not to separate, to keep this kiss going.

But Wish pulled back, to catch her breath, far enough apart to look into Newk's eyes. They were both smiling, chests heaving. And in the space between them Wish could see a future, where they might be together with the morning sun spilling through windows of a country cottage to wake them. The call of gentle fields and sea breezes promising the rewarding, simple life of a place without fear, without war, without death. Days of labour to bring in food and maintain a home, build something that would last, make their own bread, make love, make a family – and Wish's throat closed, her vision blurring. She was shaking in Newk's arms, unstable even lying on the ground, and a noise was fighting to escape her. Her efforts to hold it down only made it sound more pathetic, and she tried to apologise with her eyes. The surprise in Newk's face softened to sympathy. She held her closer, and somewhere behind the sound of Wish's muted sobs, there was a gentle whisper, "It's okay, it's going to be okay."

At least for tonight, Wish told herself. At least for tonight.

And she let herself cry.

41

It's impossible to accurately consider the impact of friendly fire, with battlefield death counts so high that specific causes of death were rarely verified. It's further complicated by inconsistency in what might be considered a "friendly" casualty; within the allied forces there were divides between nations and races, and, for example, a Khib general might consider it a bonus to lose a certain number of Stanclif soldiers during a joint effort.

The Great Ebb and Flow: Reflections on Modern Trench Warfare, Sommer, p. 244

Marching at last to Reeve Abbey, Newk's hand brushed the back of Wish's mid-stride. They shared a smile. It was a pleasant morning walk in the woods, the air thin and fresh. They'd woken close together and Newk had said nothing of the night, only stayed close to show she wasn't leaving. No one had said anything about Wish crying, either, though the others must've heard it. Oksy gave an understanding look while they were getting ready to leave. That was all. They'd all been caught crying at some point and Oksy at least knew how dark the reason, this time.

Rue, alone, asked Wish, "Have a good night?" But she looked pleased with herself, referring more to pairing her with Newk than her breakdown.

Wish smiled. "Thanks, Rue. I didn't know you cared."

"You shitting me?" Rue said. "You made us drag a ringer all this way and still hadn't got with her, right up to the point where we're all gonna die. Fuck that."

Again, Wish felt the best she could do was smile. Rue leaned closer, lowering her voice. "She's all right, Wild. You'll do well together."

"Thanks," Wish repeated, and again felt the load lifting. This *was* a good day.

Nothing about the Slane countryside suggested otherwise, with the woodland taking on more colour, green leaves on the trees, grass and moss underfoot. Blue in the sky, even, as the eternal cloud parted. The girls broke for lunch by a creek of crystal-clear water, did some washing and relished the drink. They closed on Reeve Abbey in better spirits, a little refreshed and a long way from the horrors of the woods. Even jittery Cade walked with a lighter step alongside Pound, the pair sharing jokes.

But the day got darker and the weather shifted by the time they reached the abbey itself, rain starting to pour down. Shortly after passing an abandoned, overgrown cloister building, the scouts took shelter in the trees at the top of a small slope that overlooked what Brade said was likely the rear of their destination, the south entrance. They had a limited view of the abbey, at last, as a foreboding spectacle in the half-light.

It wasn't, as Wish had expected, a grand church with a few guards, but a village of mausoleums, with dozens of carved stone structures scattered through a patchy grass valley, surrounding an enormous central building with flying buttresses like the legs of a great insect, decorated with infernal gargoyles. At the front rose a ribbed tower with a top-heavy bulge, presumably a bell chamber, with a peaked top that finished in a barbed spike. It was unclear what this place was dedicated to worship, with no symbols like the Blades of Cane or the Venerate Fork, but its scale and grandeur unmistakably marked it as a place of worship. Nothing about it was welcoming or comfortable, for one.

There were no signs of life below, but definite indications that they were going to have trouble getting closer. The valley sat in a strange orb visible only through the way it affected the downpour, rain distorting as it passed a huge perimeter above and around the buildings, shimmering like an enormous snow globe.

With the other scouts gathered behind and around her, Wish tilted her head to one side to better make sense of it, and Emi said, "It's old magic. The sort left over from the Sunless Age." The mage squinted, feeling for whatever it was. "Just an aura, though. It's not dangerous, it just hangs over the place."

"Not dangerous?" Wish questioned, hardly believing something so strange wasn't worth worrying about.

"It won't *hurt* us," Emi said, "but it could be used as an alarm system. A minder trained in the old arts would be able to sense disturbances in something like this. Sitting in the middle of that building like a spider in its web."

"Bloody great," Rue huffed.

"Can't you" – Pound flapped a hand – "magic it away or something?"

Emi gave her a mean leer. "I am *not* trained in the old arts. You'd be worried if I was – that kind of work really takes something away." She tapped her temple. "Up here. Bigger, scarier results, bigger, scarier costs."

"Heaven forbid Emi should get madder," Dakoda said.

"Well," Wish said, "presumably we're in the right place."

"I believe so," Brade said.

Yet the abbey was unlit, with no signs of life throughout its many buildings. Though it was big enough to house an army, there didn't appear to be one present. In fact, it looked abandoned. The empty windows of the nearest cluster of buildings, a trio of low stone huts, revealed nothing inside but shadow. The sky thundered, a great, echoing boom that sounded far too close. The scouts watched the clouds as though something might come out of them – an artillery shell or a tank or whatever. But more rain fell and the sky grumbled loudly again.

"Let's fall back" – Wish indicated over her shoulder – "and take shelter in that building we passed coming up. A couple of us can search the perimeter for a way in, or some sign of the others." She scanned the faces around her, uncertain which of them to send into the unknown.

Oksy said, "Might as well be me. I can see further than anyone."

"In that case *I* should go," Wish said.

"Can't do everything," Dakoda said, with a look that invited her to remember Har Coul. Her doubts as to a leader's place in it all.

"I'll go," Brade said. "I know the Dread Corps best."

"No offence, but scouting is our job," Rue said.

"And exploring is mine," Brade replied. "You didn't know what I was along for. Now you get to see."

"It's a lot of ground to cover," Wish said. "I wonder –"

"I can go the other way," Dakoda volunteered, impatiently. "Rue, you up for a walk? Meet them the other side, cover the place in half the time."

Twice the risk of losing scouts, Wish didn't say. The squad were apparently organising themselves, so she let them. That was the end of the discussion, Brade and Oksy ready to move one way, Dakoda and Rue the other.

The rest took up their kit between them and ambled back down the hill towards the cloister, a horseshoe-shaped building in a clearing between trees. Its long structures had pillared fronts, with windows dark and no sign of movement, a growth of moss spread over one corner suggesting it had been a long time since anyone had been here. The rain was loud enough they could run without fear of being heard, unlikely that anyone watching would even see them through the downpour. They piled into an empty stone chamber, dry and chilly with rain thundering on its roof. Though unlit, it was possible to make out the corridor stretching away, half a dozen doorways running off the side.

The squad shed their gear, shaking off water like a pack of wet dogs, and Wild Wish gave them jobs: Angles and Cade to make camp, unpack whatever hardbread was left, with Newk keeping watch; Fixit and Emi to cut across the courtyard, sweep the far side of the building. Wish concluded, "Pound, you and me will take this wing."

Newk's face said she'd rather come patrolling, but Wish gave her a smile to say it didn't matter, this building was empty anyway and she was giving her a break. Wish readied her rifle and Pound set down the Rik Repeater, excessively big in these quarters, to draw her stubby short sword. They shared a brief nod and pressed on down the corridor. Their left flank was exposed to the weather, through pillars, the rain only getting stronger.

"Got here just in time, didn't we?" Wish said. It would've been hell enduring this weather in the woods; the bogs would be impassable after this.

"Yeah, I'm definitely looking forward to a night in this creepy place," Pound replied, beaming.

Wish approached the first door on the right and pushed it open as Pound continued down the hall. Dark inside, an empty room. Satisfied, she ducked out and moved to the next one. Empty, too, not even stone slabs for beds. If this was a cloister, it hadn't been used in a long time. As Wish left the second room, Pound ambled up to a doorway at the end of the hall. She called back, "There's some steps."

Pound carried on without waiting, as Wish popped in and out of another empty room. Cobwebs in a corner, for variety. So far so good.

There was a loud grunt from the end of the corridor, snapping Wish's attention to Pound's doorway. Another sound echoed out of it – a struggle. Wish raced down the hall as thunder boomed overhead. Hidden in its tail end, she heard a shout. Pound in trouble.

"Boot, on me!" Wish shouted over her shoulder, before skidding around the doorway. She looked down steps that twisted into a room. Sounds of the struggle bounced up the stairs: heavy footfalls, Pound grunting as though caught in a grip. Wish leapt down the steps and slipped, hitting the wall with her shoulder before stumbling into the room. Pound was in the centre, pressed against a stone font, arms flapping at her neck and eyes wide. Mouth open, gargling. She slid forward, reaching limply towards her back, and as her face hit the floor Wish saw a small figure riding her shoulders. Holding onto a pole sticking out of Pound's neck.

Wish fired her rifle from the hip and the attacker ducked to half its height, missed. She jumped towards Pound and swung a desperate kick, but slipped on Pound's blood, as the attacker dodged, so her boot connected only a glancing blow. It was enough to fling the small man across the room, though. He hit the wall and fell to the floor. It *was* a man? Barely a foot tall? Wish stumbled to a standstill next to Pound. Thick blood pooled around her throat as she gagged, eyes big and frightened and quickly losing life.

"Out the way, out the way!" Fixit was there, pushing Wish, a medical bag out and materials falling around her. She cursed as Wish regained her senses to charge across the room after the attacker. He was down on all fours, coughing to catch his breath. She lifted an angry boot to stomp him as he raised an arm, hand spread for mercy.

"Wild!" Emi's voice, of all people, cut through with warning, and Wish froze.

The man under her hovering boot was young, terrified, and so small – a wader. His utterly hopeless expression, together with the sheer surprise of *Emi* calling for reason, gave Wish pause. She looked up, checking the room to see what the others saw.

Fixit sat back on her haunches, away from Pound, giving up already. In the doorway behind her, Newk and Emi were staring with alarm. Pound was dead. So much blood. But it wasn't just hers – there was a body the other side of Fixit, another small man, crumpled in a corner, at the bottom of an arc of blood spread across the wall. Another wader. Pound had fought them hard, killed one of theirs, and it was incredible that one had managed to bring her down. With a small spear, not a gun. These weren't soldiers, they were tiny people – surprised into battle by Pound barging in?

Wish turned and spotted a third one, the other side of the font, propped up on his elbows. He had a couple of little packs next to him, bandages around his arm and head, injured before this began. He looked just as fragile as the one Wish was about to squash.

Nothing about this was right. The Drail had nothing to do with waders, waders weren't a threat – they definitely weren't with the Dread Corps. Wish lowered her foot and brought her rifle around, excessively large before him.

The little man's eyes shimmered with tears and he spoke a Drail word she'd understand in any language: "Please."

"Wild Wish," Emi said, "they're Gonish."

"I see that," Wish said, holding the little man's eyes. He had close-cropped hair that'd grown out into a messy nest, like most of the scouts. There was fuzz around his chin, a beard he wasn't old enough to grow. They were almost human, the waders, with mouse-like ears and wider noses, but the same limbs, the same hands, even similar clothes. They might not be properly armed but they did have uniforms – a khaki camouflage. Khib. The murderer could've been any of the million innocent young men Wish had seen cowering in the trenches. He swallowed and tried to speak, in quiet, hoarse Drail.

"What's he saying?" Wish demanded.

"Can't hear," Emi said, moving closer. She replied to the man in Drail and he looked from Wish to her, only growing more afraid. He couldn't muster a reply.

"What did *you* say?"

"Asked if he meant to kill our friend."

Wish gave Fixit another look and the medic shook her head. Yes, Pound was gone.

Gritting her teeth, Wish saw one of Fixit's bags that'd come loose in her attempt to help Pound. She grabbed it and tipped out the contents. As she turned back to the wader, he pushed up against the wall, rallying his last energy. He got halfway to his feet before Wish grabbed him around the waist, then she tossed him into the bag. The injured one started to crawl, making frightened sounds just before she snatched him up. He gave a pained cry as she put him in the bag, too, but she muffled their complaints by bundling it closed. They kicked like trapped rats, weighing about the same, as Wish turned her attention to Pound.

"Didn't stand a chance, a wound like that," Fixit said, still kneeling, unable to look away from their dead friend.

With an angry snarl, Wish swung the bag against the font, making the other scouts wince at the flat thump of bodies hitting stone. The men inside went still. Without another word, Wish strode past Newk and back up the stairs. Back along the corridor, with Cade and Angles watching from the far end. How was Wish going to explain to them, and the rest, that waders had killed Pound?

They were supposed to be on the same side.

42

*Stories emphasise heroics, with moments of great courage
or valour leading to victory. In reality, the field is most
often won by he who prepares best.*

Winning War, Takata, p. 54

Maringdale gave herself no room for doubt as she waited with a
squad of shocksmith soldiers. It was cold and dreary and they had
been outside for hours, but they were in the right place. They had
to be in the right place. She had analysed the options carefully, and
while there were a thousand possible routes through the Dread
Forest, there were a handful of choke points that had to be crossed
to reach Reeve Abbey itself. To safely travel far outside the forest
would take too long, and with Vorhale's weapon practically ready
to go, the enemy would not risk such a delay. They were also
unlikely to travel on the river itself, which was precarious at best
and would leave them exposed. That left a series of paths south of
the woodland, where the going was dotted by villages, or north,
which was sparsely populated but had more treacherous terrain and
creatures to avoid.

North, Maringdale decided, would best fit the Gentleman and his
women soldiers. They were daring and would sooner face physical
hardship than risk discovery. Their biggest weapon, after all, was
remaining hidden.

And so Maringdale pinned down a specific pass, with the help
of Ways' cartographers, that she was convinced the scouts would
travel through. Two miles northwest of Reeve Abbey, a dyke
formed a funnel of trees and rocks. It was innocuous, utterly
removed from civilisation, and the last place anyone would expect
to see a Drail patrol. To ensure it still appeared that way,

Maringdale brought only a small squad of Ways' men and kept them well hidden, under foliage, far back, while she sat in meditation waiting to sense the coming enemy.

She had a humourless captain for company, who said nothing but exuded the Dread mentality, giving her practice blocking out their savage intentions. When she finally felt movement, people approaching, he immediately wanted his men to advance.

Maringdale put a firm hand on his arm to stay him. "Not yet. We wait and watch."

Seeing the soldiers emerge between trees was how Maringdale imagined a hunter would feel spotting a majestic goldstag. The unreal had become real: a person in murky grey-blue uniform, rifle down, sneaking between the trees. Off to the side, she felt the intention before spotting a second one: wariness, caution, knowing this was a perfect place for an ambush. Impressive; these scouts were wide apart, exploring away from the path and the choke point, fully alert. Were they this vigilant for the whole journey?

The scouts didn't notice the shocksmiths though, well hidden. They stalked around the dyke and finally descended into it. Two of them. Women, Maringdale could just about tell from their hips, though only because she already knew it. They carried themselves like men. One had a short mess of greasy blonde hair and a scarred grimace of a face, mean as any soldier in the Dread Corps.

The pair converged on a central point where rocks and trees clustered to tighten the path. They whispered to each other and Maringdale picked up their conclusion: *safe to this point.*

"Easy targets," the captain told Maringdale in a low whisper. "Could shoot them both myself."

"No," Maringdale said. "There has to be more of them."

At least one more. Hopefully the Gentleman, too.

The blonde scout sent the other back down the path and leaned against the rocks, gun relaxing as she took out a cigarette. She stared through the trees as she smoked, watching for danger even now. Maringdale peered carefully at her, scanning her feelings: resentment, hating the creepy damn woods, eager for this to be over.

"More coming," the captain told Maringdale, and she saw he was reading hand signals from one of his men, off through the trees. Maringdale refocused to up the path. Yes. The anticipation of more soldiers, similarly eager to get clear of the woods. One hungry. One tired, wanting to stop. One stern, hard-headed. Holding on, just a little longer. Half a dozen at least? Even better than Maringdale had imagined.

A few minutes more and they came into view, a trail of similarly-dressed, fully-equipped soldiers passing through the woodland, some more at ease but all ready for trouble. Maringdale picked out the sternest feeling one, stiff-backed with dark hair, at the head of the troop. That was their leader. They were all together now, passing between the rocks below, exactly as Maringdale predicted.

"I want them alive –" she started, but caught a flash of emotion to her left, a moment before sounds confirmed it. *Enemy!* And a gunshot, followed by a shout. Maringdale saw a flash of light from another gun going off, a yell in Stanish cut off – one of the scouts had continued along the top of the dyke, but she'd been shot down. The shocksmiths were all suddenly moving in, firing, shouting.

The scouts in the pass scrambled with startling effectiveness – the blonde one ducked a shot that sparked off a rock and she dived behind a tree. The others split in six different directions. One caught a bullet in the chest and went down. The Dread captain joined his men in the charge, yelling orders to slaughter them all, and Maringdale's senses were flooded by a surge of rage from the Dread soldiers – *kill, kill, no mercy, die!*

The scouts returned fire from quickly found defensive positions, leaning around rocks and trees, as the shocksmiths descended from higher ground, from all angles. The women were hit in the flanks, yelling high pain as bullets knocked them out of cover. One made a break for it, running back up the path, obscured by the rocks, and two shocksmiths broke from the advance to chase after her, firing as they ran.

"Alive!" Maringdale yelled over the barrage, skipping down the slope to follow the captain. "Get them alive!"

But she could barely hear her own words over the guns and the Dread drive for murder, the scouts' terror. It was over in seconds, a short, brutal battle that saw the whole squad dead or dying on the forest floor as the shocksmiths ran over them, scanning for more. The captain reached the pass ahead of Maringdale, where a scout was crawling feebly, coughing blood. He fired a single shot into her back.

Maringdale pulled him around to face her, snarling, "I said I wanted prisoners!"

He returned a dead-eyed, disengaged look that chilled her to a standstill. His feelings seeped out like a bad stench: no mercy, only hate. Maringdale took a step back to steady herself, and the captain continued, communicating with his men in more growls than words. They stalked between the downed scouts, rolling them over and patting them down. The blonde one was slumped back against a tree, eyes open and glassy with death, half her forehead blown off.

The leader was at the centre of the path, already flecked with mud and leaves the Dread soldiers had kicked up going past her. She'd been the first one shot, Maringdale realised. Never stood a chance. Maringdale studied her hard-lined face, caught in a flash of pain where she'd died. The arrogance of Stanclif lay bare in this deathly dyke. Sending women to thwart the Drail's greatest weapon. Able women, she would grant them that – and women who might've made it all the way if not for Maringdale.

But this was pathetic. If Maringdale had been given free reign from the start, this farce never would've even got close. She spat at the insurgents' leader.

"There were eight of them, in total," Maringdale reported to Ways, the big man looking up with interest from a meal of charred rock-hen. He had barely stalled his eating when she entered his chamber in the church. "A bigger force than we imagined. But no Gentleman."

"Did there need to be?" Ways said, stuffing his mouth with a fist of meat and bone. He ate like an ogre, fitting to his appearance.

"Taik confirmed he was working with him. If he wasn't out here –"

"Then he's probably warming his feet back in Vasseer," Ways said. "I know his sort. All game for sneaking about until there's real work needs doing, then they're palming it off to cannon fodder. Women, even? Shameful."

"They put up a fight," Maringdale replied, feeling a need to defend the scouts, even if his words echoed her own thoughts. The Dread soldiers had lost two men in the skirmish, despite their insurmountable advantage.

Ways crunched bones between his teeth. When he'd finished chewing, he said, "It's still shameful. If this place's existence wasn't at stake, we'd send news of this to the front. Stanclif hiding behind women soldiers. Pah. But it's over now, yes?"

"I'd have liked to question the insurgents," Maringdale said. "To be sure of that."

"Why? They took a shot and failed. You got them, Maringdale. Pat yourself on the back and take a break. Now you're free to come south."

"Thank you, sir," Maringdale replied, not as convinced. There were things she still wanted answered: who else did the Gentleman have involved, considering their efforts at Fever? And where *was* the mastermind himself? And a subtler niggle: which of those women had been their magic user? They surely had one, to have escaped the steamboat on the Little Step, but whoever it was hadn't helped here. Was it the leader herself, cut down too soon to put up a fight?

They were not questions Ways cared for, made clear as he finished eating and stood, using his bulk to indicate it was time to move on. He said, "It always feels like an anti-climax, to find your enemies weaker than you imagined. We'll make up for that. You'll get front-row seats for Stanclif's curtain call, soon enough."

He walked her back through to the main chamber, explaining that they were shortly to leave, with the weapon ready and the abbey secure. Maringdale tried to take his words to heart, wondering if her disquiet was merely the disappointment of a success that came too easily.

She wandered through the church and found Donut and Netts in a back room, where the pair were sat cross-legged on the floor between thin-framed camping cots. Though she'd left them for the better part of a day, they still ignored her for a moment, engrossed in slapping down worn cards with muttered words of challenge. It was a welcome contrast to the Dread company's impersonal, simmering danger, and her body responded to the normalcy with a tremble at all she'd been through. Maringdale forced her hands still, no time for this weakness.

Donut scored a trump and Netts swore, fist clenching like he might lash out. He caught that emotion and Donut wasn't troubled, only feeling guilty for winning.

Forcing lightness into her tone, Maringdale asked, "Since when did you pricks become friends?"

"About the time I apparently joined the Purification, I guess?" Netts said.

"You're welcome to walk any time."

He gave her a look, genuinely considering the option, then kicked up from the ground with a scoff at Donut. "Enjoy the chocolates you bloody cheat."

"I didn't –"

"How you been, then?" Netts breezed over the complaint, as Donut tried to push himself up as well. He did it much less gracefully, rocking from side to side before finally using his momentum to rise. He smiled as though it was something to be proud of. "Hobnobbing with the big and powerful? Plotting and scheming?"

"I've been with the 1st Wavecutters. We stopped the insurgents."

Netts' face glazed over, mouth slightly open. "They've got shocksmiths here?"

"Yeah. All of them. Over the hill, stationed in the nearest village."

"Shit," Netts said. "And – wait, you caught them scouts? Without us?"

"Yes," Maringdale said. "Just this morning. I saw no need to interrupt your rest."

Netts was caught halfway between laughter and disbelief. He

settled on the latter, "Wait, you're serious?"

Maringdale nodded. "Shot down a full squad."

"Well, shit!" Netts slapped his thigh in triumph. "That's brilliant! You handed those Stanclif bitches their shit? We oughta crack open a bottle – Donut, bring us your best."

"Think there's some silk-wine," Donut suggested, but he sounded wary and Maringdale sensed why. She didn't exude happiness herself.

"You two have a drink, I'm tired," she said. "Didn't expect to finish this so soon, I suppose it's crept up on me."

"Sure," Netts laughed. "War doesn't care for satisfying endings, does it? Happened to me once, back in Manz. We were caught pinned down by a machine gun nest for three days, scheming all sorts of tricks and traps to take them down. Finally had a plan to distract and flank them and you know what happened? They'd abandoned the post, retreated, and a wyrling rider cut them down from the sky. Shot them in the backs, a mile down the road."

Maringdale barely listened. She was tired, that was true. After resting, she could reflect on the result more favourably. It *was* over, no matter the blunt method. Ways appreciated her and wanted her to stay with them, to see this project through to its dramatic end. She'd have a place in the Dread Corps for sure, damn the Purification, and this had all been worth it. Panderlair, Taik, defying the Purification to head west. But she'd felt the Dread Corps' elite's emotions, seen how ruthless they were, and she wasn't sure it was exactly where she wanted to be.

She drew herself out of those thoughts and told her men, "We've got a new responsibility, anyway. We'll be helping move the weapon to the front. Shipping out on the Iron Barge again, save flying."

Donut looked aghast. "What about Gulvar?"

"Piss off, let that lizard rot!" Netts said. "We can keep our feet on the ground for once. Brushing shoulders with *shock*smiths, no less. When this is through, you gonna put a word in for me? It'll be promotions all around, won't it?"

"Probably," Maringdale said. "From what Ways says, it might

even end the war. And you can buy all the wyrlings you want once we're done, Donut."

Netts whooped and Donut tried to smile. Maringdale heard the flatness in her own voice that he must've recognised. It didn't matter. For now, she was just going to lie down and not think about what was to come.

43

The Gonish enjoyed a unique collision of luck, tenacity and courage when the empires came to colonise the Emerging Isles. Their nation stood as an exception that proved the rule that no one was safe from the imperial advances of the 6th century: it was perhaps because of their diminutive stature, rather than despite it, that Gonish diplomats were not met with open hostility, and in turn gained big concessions from Stanclif rule.

Empires of the Rocc, Xanthial, p. 562

More time than seemed healthy had passed before Wild Wish reengaged her thoughts, beyond petty rage and despair and words like *unfair*. The squad kept careful watch in case any Drail were alerted by Wish's gunshot, but their surroundings remained empty. It was unlikely anyone had heard them over the storm, even if someone was nearby. They left Pound covered, downstairs, nothing they could do for her. Fixit didn't suggest any burial rites, though Wish knew she wanted to. There must've been something in Wish's expression, as she sat with her knees up, back against the wall, bag of waders in one hand, because no one said anything for the longest time. She stared at nothing at all.

The bag shifted, the men inside moving, reminding her they were alive. She gave it a light shake, not sure she wanted to see them again. She could toss them out in the rain, drown them in a puddle, not even have to look at them.

"Bastards," Cade broke the silence, at last. "Ought to finish them right now." Emi made a thoughtful sound that suggested caution. Cade glared. "What? You got something to say? They killed Pound. What're you waiting for, Wild?"

Wish didn't know, so didn't say.

"The Gonish aren't our enemies," Emi said. It was the unspoken fact that'd been troubling all of them; the reason the mage had stopped Wish from stomping on someone. They all knew – same as Wish knew. The Gonish weren't fighters and they certainly wouldn't have joined the Drail. Whatever had cost Pound's life, the most likely cause was a misunderstanding.

"Then what're they doing defending this place?" Cade spat, the one person refusing to see it. Taking her turn to snap, just as Angles had a few nights ago. Angles was keeping quiet, probably still remembering her reprimand, but Cade had been growing close to Pound. Finding a way to move on from Fuse.

"Guess it's time we talked," Wish said, quietly. She opened the bag and found two worried faces looking up. They did their best to look brave, but they had to be even younger than the scouts, and they were huddled together like children. Wish asked, "Why did you do it?"

They hesitated in fear that anything they could say might make her kill them. Wish worried about that, too. But the one who'd killed Pound managed to speak. "You ain't Drail?"

Wish frowned.

"Fuck them," Cade continued grumbling. "Why even talk? Break their necks, put them in the fire. We can roast them. About time we ate something proper."

"What?" Newk said. "Are you a barbarian?"

"What's barbaric?" Cade said. "They're rats on two legs. Soft-boned."

"Rats can't talk," Emi pointed out. "Or run a government that's successfully formed an alliance with the Stanclif Empire."

"That wasn't *these* ones. These ones killed our friend. All I'm saying is we return the favour. You get it, right, Fixit? We can put that meat to good use."

Fixit folded her arms guiltily over her stomach, hungry like the rest of them, but kept quiet. Emi said, "I think it's been considered poor taste, eating the Gonish, for a few centuries now."

Angles moved into the doorway and looked outside as if in the hope that someone would come to save them from the rising tension. Brade or Oksy, even Rue, might better handle it. Where had they got to that *Emi* was the voice of reason?

It gave Wish her cue to move. She reached in and grabbed the murderer then lowered the bag with the other one to the floor. The man panicked, kicking and pushing at her fingers with quiet complaints, "No, stop!" But she lifted him and held him steady, and he went still, meeting her gaze. He looked frail and painfully ordinary in her grip, and the fear in his eyes brought back memories of Sarge. The hawk giant. These waders, hiding in the dark, intruded upon by Pound, no one thinking straight. The little people must've fought hard, trying to survive. Pound had killed one of them before they took her down. Who were the real monsters here?

But Pound was dead, so maybe Wish had every right to be a monster now. She said, "Why are you here?"

The man hesitated. He spoke in rough, clipped Stanish: "Promise you ain't gonna eat us."

"Why would I promise you anything?"

"You ain't Drail! We can help, long as you ain't eat us."

"We're not Drail." Wish tugged the fabric of her top demonstratively. Showing the faded blue-grey material, which in this light could've been anything. The wader twisted to take in the others. He focused on their guns resting against the wall. Wish said, "But that doesn't make us friends. You killed Pound."

"She came at us stomping big," the wader insisted. His Stanish was clear and surprisingly fluent, but he spoke with a particular Gonish roughness. "It's like – we ain't expected a patrol and it got Robards startled – he was defending us." He looked around, desperate for them to believe him. "I dint want to – ain't even think I could! But you're Stanclif, gotta be here for the same reason as us. General Kettal dint send support did he?"

The room was quiet. The mention of Kettal, the southern theatre's man in charge, only added sourness on confirming that they really were allies.

"He'd say anything to save his skin," Cade said. "Pound would never have –"

"Shut *up*, Cade," Wish said. "It's plain to everyone but you that this was a mistake." She rolled her eyes back, groaning. "The whole war's just full of senseless killing."

"Then what's one more dead? They're fucking rats."

"Stop." Wish met her eye with fierceness she wasn't aware she had – because Cade froze in her tracks, mid-step towards her.

"Step outside," Emi intervened. Quietly, calmly, and fully acknowledging things could easily get worse. She gestured to the corridor. Cade twitched like she wanted to argue – a heavy girl, if not tall, and the sort that could scrap. But if she might've dared cross Wish, she wasn't about to test Emi. Cade huffed and stomped out and Emi slunk silently after her with an *I've got this* wink.

The others were perfectly still, waiting on Wish to make this all better. Even the man in her hand watched her with worried hope. He said, "You gonna put me down?"

He had blood on his face. On his uniform, sprayed off Pound. It distracted Wish enough to ignore the question, and she asked her own: "Why are you here?"

"Same as you?" he said. "Account of what the Dread Corps are building? Or built. That and they took my brother. *Our* brother." He pointed to the bag. "Charl's and me. Ain't no one else gonna come. No one else believed us. But someone got word to you?" He scanned the room again. "Who *are* you? What are you doing here? You're *women?*"

"What's that supposed to mean?"

"Nothing – I mean –" He stopped himself. "Not getting rude, but why's Stanclif sending women for a job this ugly?"

"We're the best," Wish said, flatly. "General Easter himself sent us. Without, as far as I'm aware, any input from General Kettal."

"No. We dint get word to him. I only hoped *someone* had." The wader sped up, confidence growing now they were talking. "See, we was in Garter, trying to get back to Gonland, when we got overrun. My brother got taken – him and a few others – and when we figured *why*, those of us that could, we knew we had to come hard and stop this."

"On behalf of the Comity?" Wish said, to be sure.

The wader hesitated again. He shifted, to get more comfortable in her grip. "Not officially. They wouldn't have us. Dint listen. We took some supplies and went after Finton – my brother – on our own. After what we saw in Cleave, knew it was bigger than us."

"That wouldn't be hard," Wish murmured, not meaning to joke. Just fact. The wader gave her an uncertain look. She moved on, "What did you see?"

"Magic," the wader said. "Dark magic, being used on people. Lights, screams, and discarded bodies. Drained. They piled them up – bodies from all over, different races, human, trunk, kefir. Ain't had obvious wounds, though, except blood about their orifices – ears, mouths, noses. Like their minds melted."

The same sick experiments conducted in Blythe. Newk's potential fate. Wish said, "They just killed them?"

"*Just* killed them?" the wader echoed.

"Didn't manipulate the bodies?" Fixit clarified, recalling details they'd ignored since Brade took them on this journey. "To use them for energy or . . . bring them back to life?"

The wader frowned. "No, ain't seen anything like that. I mean – have you seen something like that? Necromantics ain't real, is it?"

"Doesn't sound like it," Wish said. "But Captain Brade has been investigating the Dread Corps for months without any more to show than what you're saying."

"Months? Then why'd they never listen –" The wader took a breath. "Well, we found their locations. All along the front. Figured *this* was the place it was all feeding back to. You did, too, dint you? I wouldn't never have hurt your friend if I'd known who you were! I'm sorry, I am – I swear!"

"Shit," Wish said. "Shit on all this." She looked up for contributions from the others, but Angles, Fixit and Newk held the awkward silence of knowing there would be no justice here, not for Pound. Worse than that – the wader was suggesting Brade and the officers in the Western Theatre could've had better intelligence if they'd given these waders a chance. They could've moved out sooner, been more careful. Wish asked, "What else did you see? Tell me everything."

The wader nodded, exhaling. "Right on. Yes, ma'am. But do you have to –" He looked down, indicating his discomfort at being held up by her. Wish glared, to affirm that no she still wasn't letting him go, and he swallowed the complaint to continue. "Right. Well, I'm Colm Hightower – that's not a joke, our family came from a hill settlement – pleased to meet you." He held a hand up for Wish to shake and she stared. He dropped it sheepishly and continued, "So, we Hightowers settled in Garter decades ago. Had a jewellery business. But our town was bombed and we moved out with a refugee caravan, headed for Elmn. Slanik troops ambushed us one night, killed half the caravan. They captured the rest. Only a handful of us escaped."

"They attacked a civilian caravan?" Fixit asked with shock.

Colm Hightower nodded. "They wanted to take people alive. Anyway, we headed straight for the Stanclif line, to get help, but we were told ain't nothing they could do. So it was down to me and Charl, Robards, Killion and Banther. We followed rumours of Slanik troops near the Mattin Mountains, until we found this battalion in Cleave City. Slanik, with a Dread Corps company there. That's where we saw these experiments. No sign of Finton, but they had machines and documents, maps. There were bodies, too, and a big mechanical thing which we figured did all the killing. It had pipes, weird lights, a sort of metal dish up top? Whatever it was, we ain't about to leave it there, so we took what files we could carry and set charges – the blast was like nothing you've seen. And I know blasts, we worked the mines. It should've been more controlled, but like I said, there was magic in it."

Hightower took a breath, then continued more slowly. "It was Killion who figured out the other locations were all along the front line. Doing experiments where no one was gonna notice people missing, weren't they?"

"Yeah," Wish murmured. It seemed so long ago that they'd pondered over the same fears in Blythe.

"We cut off some Dread soldiers on the way to Fever Forest, and we –" Hightower paused, an awkward memory. "We got one to talk. He told us any test subjects not killed outright would get sent here. But he took the piss, said we were screwed anyway and ain't never gonna reach Slane alive. We didn't see any sense trying to convince Stanclif again, so we did what we had to. Travelled through Garter, then Slane. And that Dread bastard was partly right, we ain't all made it." He crossed his arms in the Blade of Cane, muttering, "Rest their souls."

Wish allowed him a moment. They'd been through a similar hellish journey to the scouts; no question they were kindred spirits in this, however much easier it would've been if they weren't. How much she wished they could just get revenge, take out the injustice on someone, something. But no. She slackened her fingers and nodded to the bag, where Charl hadn't stirred. "How did your brother get hurt? This one, I mean."

"Wolves," Hightower said simply.

"By Bly. Does he need help? Fixit? Maybe there's something you can do."

Fixit looked startled.

"It shouldn't have been like this," Wish said, voice softening. "You're right, we're here for the same reason. We could've worked together. Instead of . . ."

Hightower swallowed, regretfully. "But we can work together now? We might not look like much but we're more use than a good meal, guaranteed." He gave a nervous laugh. Wish wasn't quite up to smiling back, so he continued, "We've been here for three days, looking for a way in. You do *not* want to go in unprepared."

"We realised. So what's the situation?"

"Good news is there's only a skeleton crew of guards," Hightower said. "Mostly left security to a couple of grekkels who come as far as here twice a day. But they ain't thorough. Bad news is the place is sunk in magic. There's a way around that barrier, but I dunno what we'll find inside. Definitely Dread mages of some sort."

"What's your way in?" Wish asked.

"Pipes," Hightower said. "Found one that runs under and between these buildings – for drainage, but you might fit. They go below the barrier. We were gonna go in, find Finton, set some charges. If it's anything like Cleave, this place will blow like a Azrian gas pig. We were just waiting on Charl to recover. But with your help, we could do it fast."

Wish let the proposition settle between them. Should she trust him, now, after everything?

"I'm not smart enough to make all this up," Hightower promised.

"I believe him," Newk said.

"Me too," Fixit murmured. "I think."

"I *want* to," Wish said. "But we can wait for the others. In the meantime –" She looked guiltily at the bag, Charl still inside. "Fixit, if there's anything you can do . . ."

Emi and Cade were sitting at the edge of the courtyard, on the step, watching the rain. Smoking one of Emi's unusual pipes. That was one way to calm the sapper. Wish walked up behind them and stared out, too. The storm hadn't let up much, though the thunder had quietened.

"You kissed and made up with the midget?" Cade asked. More resigned than hostile.

"He's a lot smaller than a midget," Wish said.

"Probably not even worth eating."

"Now that we've been properly introduced, it'd be kind of weird."

"*Kind of* weird," Emi echoed. "But she'd still consider it."

"Hey, it's been a while since we were top of the food chain," Wish said, and Cade offered a dutiful snigger. Emi's efforts had worked to relax her a little, at least. Wish went on, "This has been really shit, no kidding. But we're not going to hurt them – this was a stupid mistake. I've got something you might like, though, Cade."

"What's that?" Cade rolled her head back.

"These guys want to blow the place to hell. Like, the entire abbey. I think you could get involved in that."

It took a moment for Cade to let it inspire her, but slowly the traces of a smile crossed her face. Bless her and the hell they'd all been through, at least you could still amuse the girl with explosions.

"Someone's coming," Emi said, though, no hopeful moment sacred. Wish followed her gaze to the front of the building, where two shapes moved quickly through the rain. The forward one held up a hand for peace.

Dakoda. She and Rue ran through the rain and into their shelter. They were soaked through, hair flat against their faces and boots squelching as they approached. Dakoda flicked water off her arms and said, "We're safe for a good distance, only activity we've seen is in the massive ugly building at the centre. Lights coming out the doors."

"You didn't test that barrier, did you?" Wish asked.

"Not on your life. One for her to investigate." Dakoda prodded Emi with a boot and the mage swatted her away.

"Hopefully not," Wish said. "We've got company, claiming they've got a way in."

Dakoda's brow knitted with concern, correctly assessing that out here company came with caveats. Rue said, "The fuck kind of company?"

"Waders. But . . ."

"They killed Pound," Cade said, bluntly. "Then Wild made friends with them."

"It was a mistake," Wish said. "The fighting, I mean. Pound killed one of them first. They're here for the same reason as us." Dakoda and Rue glared in a stony silence that had become far too familiar. At once disbelieving, could Pound really be dead, and accepting, of course she could.

"Waders?" Rue finally said. Wish nodded. "And you wanna work with them?"

A slight echo of her disdain at bringing a ringer on board. Wish hadn't heard Rue's take on the Gonish, but it was unlikely to be good. She said, "They have a plan, and we need all the help we can get."

"That's true enough," Dakoda snorted, wiping dripping water off her nose with an even wetter forearm. "Hope you know what you're doing, Wild. Because the nature of that energy shield tells me if we don't do things just right here, we're all toast."

44

The worst bloody bit is what you don't know for sure but can guess at close enough. Because you're smart to how the world and the war works now, but the details are lost to the dead. Algi's not coming back, for example. Renny's gone and Sable's dead. There's no proof, nor accounts of what happened, but there's no sense being naive. Only, no one can give you the peace of saying they died quick or clean; no one can stop you lying awake imagining it was slow and lonely.

**Extract from the Letters of
Major K. Tyne, Elmn, 720**

When Brade and Oksy returned to camp, everyone got into business mode, analysing the waders' information and settling on a plan. As well as all he'd told Wish, Hightower added that in watching the abbey they had seen a big, important-looking man, possibly a general, come and go, as well as a trio of what looked like mercenaries riding a wyrling. They would likely be camped with the nearby battalion, and there would only be a handful of soldiers in the abbey, at best. The only other authority figure of concern was the Dread doctor in charge. Vorhale, a madman with metal arms. He rarely left the main building, but they'd seen him outside once or twice giving impatient orders.

The added information heightened tensions as Brade barely hid his irritation at not having encountered the waders sooner. He grilled them on all they'd seen, confirming what Wish already had: that they'd have done a lot better working together from the start. Brade was aware of the site in Fever Forest but not Cleave City, and grumbled that his own inside man had proven less effective than he'd hoped.

"My operative in Null gave me dribs and drabs of information," Brade confided, "and said he was arranging something in Highscythe. But no mention of anything further east."

"We tried to get word out," Hightower insisted. "But the officers at the front –"

"The officers at the front are clueless," Brade scoffed. "All they care about is their particular little patch of trenches." He pushed down his frustration, though, and added, "It's incredible that you came this far. And whatever our fortunes were up to now, we're charmed by fate that we can finish this together."

There was a general murmur of agreement, and Brade was doing his best to stay positive, but Wish was undecided whether finding themselves in the same place at the same time had been lucky or not. Pound was dead. And the wader Robards. That truth hung over the scouts like a bad smell, and left them with little option but to morosely turn in, to rest before their dawn advance.

Wild Wish arranged patrols throughout the night, to give them the best chance to spot Sun and Sabre Squad coming to join them. Otherwise, the squad gathered together in one room, with Brade and the waders taking another. During Rue and Oksy's watch, Wish lay stiffly beside Newk, unable to sleep as she imagined some terrible fate taking Four Skills and the others. Newk shifted on the hard floor, shoulder brushing up against Wish's, an acknowledgement that she was awake and aware of her concerns. Newk whispered, "We're going to do good work tomorrow."

"Yeah?" Wish whispered back. Across the room, Cade gave an unpleasant snuffling snore, not far from Pound's old habits. Wish continued, "It's not so much what we'll do that's worrying me. It's who'll be left to celebrate it. You can stay at the tunnel entrance, keeping watch –"

"I didn't come this far to keep watch."

It was firm enough to silence Wish. The idiocy of her suggestion was tangible in the air above them. She finally said, "It's not fair, that's all. Back in Swelig, I had no one. I found *so many* friends out here. Special people." She rolled onto her side, to look into Newk's eyes. Amazing Newk. She smiled, sadly. "I couldn't have found you any other way."

"Mm," Newk said. Something like agreement. "And where else could a Fireti earn respect?"

"Racing horses?" Wish suggested.

"Ah, Fireti only ride scrap beetles," Newk said, mock-devastated.

Wish adored the response, and the tone, and crept closer, their bodies pressing together. She placed a tentative hand on Newk's shoulder. "It'll be just one more day, I guess. One more hurdle and we'll go home. All of us. You and me?"

"You and me," Newk agreed, quietly.

"You'll have all the respect you can imagine in Swelig," Wish promised. "We'll be heroes. Queens."

"I'd be happy with *equals*."

"Ha," Wish said. "Maybe that." And she wanted to promise more. Warm baths and foot rubs and open-air concerts. Cuddles by the fire and walks along the cliffs on bright summer nights.

But on the other side of the room, Emi whispered, as loud as talking, *"I am yet to meet my equal."*

Dammit Emi. Why was she awake? And if she was listening –

"Reckon if you did," Dakoda put in, against another wall, "would you be flirting with him and keeping everyone awake the night before a big operation?"

Shit. Were they all awake?

"I might," Emi pondered. "Either that or I'd ride him all night."

"Gross," Fixit groaned. "Don't give Wild ideas."

The girls sniggered and gradually quietened again. Wish exhaled, still smiling at Newk. She lowered herself down, resting her head against Newk's chest, and tried to enjoy being there. Soaking up her warmth and the calm of her breathing. Newk slid an arm around her and held her close.

Somehow, Wish slept, and she didn't dream.

She was stirred by Dakoda and Angles walking into the room, finishing up a patrol, with light creeping through the open doorway. Wish sat up, clearing her eyes, aware that if there was light, it was time to go. She tried not to get her hopes up, meeting Dakoda's eye with the question of if Sun or Sabre were out there, but when Dakoda shook her head, Wish's heart still sunk. Only Boot Squad had made it in time for Tate's dawn attack.

"Probably just been delayed," Dakoda said. "We can give them a nice welcome by finishing up before they get here."

Wish hummed agreement. Shame it depended on her leading them to victory without Tate or Larkin, or even Spyke, to take the reins. Still, dawn was always the plan, and she refused to consider complicating her life by waiting. The other scouts might be about to act, just really well hidden. No. Dawn it was, and the wader's plan was their best bet.

With minimal discussion, the scouts packed up the camp and headed out under the first light of the morning, leaving only Charl behind in the safety of the cloister. Hightower darted ahead of them, jogging to match their cautious walking pace. He took them through some trees to a narrow grate in a wall not far from the cloister. The rusty opening was some kind of effluence station, the bricks around it dark and ominously sticky-looking. They'd be lucky to shimmy through without getting stuck. Hightower told them he'd tested it, having gone under the magical barrier without problems. Though there were likely to be an unknown number of mages in the abbey, at least two, he remained confident there would be few soldiers, and the two roaming grekkels were usually resting at this time of day.

Not all of Boot Squad trusted his information, or this plan, Wish could see that plainly enough, but their patrols overnight seemed to confirm that activity around the abbey was sparse. They hadn't spotted the grekkels, even, which Wish really hoped meant he was wrong about them. She'd heard of such people, native to north-eastern Drail, but never seen one, and did not want to.

Whatever their misgivings, they had no better options, and everything about Hightower suggested a nervous person out of place, not a scheming mastermind. The waders' only weapons were small knives and sharpened metal poles. That and a little pack of explosives, barely four inches across, which Hightower claimed would cause a big enough blast to start a reaction. Cade scoffed and insisted *she* would take care of the explosion, showing off one of her packs, about the size of two Hightowers.

With the scouts gathered at the pipe, then, ready to blow something up, Wish had to take ownership of the plan. Cade would obviously be going in with her bombs. Oksy, Wish quickly decided, was the most obvious person to hold back, on watch, given that she could keep an eye out better than anyone. Angles could stay with her, because Wish had no idea how much of a liability she'd be. As for the rest of them, Dakoda didn't even want to be here, Fixit only wanted to help people, and Rue – Rue had bloody sent Newk into Wish's tent. And sure, Newk had already warned her she didn't want to miss this, but how could Wish put any of them in danger?

Looking into the grate, Wish said, "If just me and Cade go in, maybe, we can put down a few detonators unseen." She looked at Hightower, standing below her knee. "You said the other site you hit went up with a boom?"

"There are prisoners in there," Hightower said worriedly. Ah, right, the brother.

"And need I remind you of the actual mission here?" Brade said.

"Save the world?" Wish said.

"Recover whatever we can. Vorhale himself would make the ultimate prize. We've got a full squad, I'd suggest everyone does their part."

"We're not afraid," Newk said, to a ripple of agreement.

Wish nodded, of course, she wasn't really considering leaving anyone behind, silly suggestion. But dammit she wished Tate was there to send them in. "All right, but Oksy and Angles, you're keeping watch out here. We're not having grekkels sneak up on us. Everyone else, I guess tie your guns to your backs because it looks like we're going in on our bellies."

"And be careful not to do too much damage in there," Brade said. He looked pointedly at Emi. "The more we can preserve, the better we can understand our enemy and help the war effort back home."

Emi grinned like she wouldn't dream of bringing the whole abbey crumbling down around them, unless she got the opportunity.

"Yeah," Wish agreed with Brade warily. "Seriously, no one

touch or break anything unless it's necessary."

And with that, they levered the pipe open together, and looked deeper into the damp, dark space. Wish put her hands on the sides, taking a breath, ready to lead the way. Something tugged at her trouser leg. She looked down at Hightower, coyly smiling up at her.

"I can go first?" he suggested, quietly.

"*You* can definitely wait here," Wish said.

"This is my fight, more than yours."

Wish took a breath. Couldn't even keep the little people safe. She stepped aside and Hightower climbed into the pipe, and readied himself, a spear in one hand and a small but surprisingly bright torch in the other. It illuminated patches of old, innocuous waste.

Once he'd crept a short way in, Wish crawled after him. Her shoulders brushed the walls of the pipe, the tight space forcing her to shimmy like a worm. Hightower trotted ahead, his spear bobbing at his side, then came back, apologising for leaving Wish behind. Then he moved on again. The tunnel filled with Wish's loud breathing, and the huffs of the girls behind her as they writhed in. Squirming, uncomfortably getting there, little bit at a time. At least it wasn't wet. Only weirdly sticky. And impossibly cramped, and likely to collapse or suddenly get tighter and trap them in place with no way to turn or retreat or –

Wish gritted her teeth and called back in a whisper, "You all okay back there?"

"It's metal," Cade replied from somewhere around her boots, directly behind Wish. "Compared to the trenches, this is a luxury."

Maybe, Wish conceded. That was one way to look at it. But she had a feeling things were going to be just as bad when they got out.

45

Only the Dead Know Life

Azrian Idiom (Incomplete?)

It felt like they'd been shunting through the pipe for the better part of the day by the time Wish finally saw more light ahead than Hightower's beam. Getting bigger as she shuffled closer. A grated opening; an exit that they wouldn't be able to get out of? Alarm bells started to ring as Wish slid nearer. Even if she could break it, there'd be people waiting on the other side. Hell, this was an awful idea and there was no way back and –

"I can slip through," Hightower whispered, crouching by her face. "Gonna unscrew it from the other side. Be proper quiet."

Wish nodded, and hissed over her shoulder, "We're here, everyone quiet!"

Hightower crept ahead and up to the grate, and Wish shuffled right up to join him, pressing her face into the bars to look out. The pipe ran off a shallow gutter built into a tile floor, coming from the centre of what Wish already sensed was a vast room ahead. It was flanked on either side by tall metal walls and bits of machinery. Hightower stood next to her head, leaning out to watch for guards. He whispered, "Got a Dread soldier, on the higher walkway. Looking the other way. Ain't seeing anyone else from here."

Wish raised her eyebrows, suggesting he get on with it. He ducked outside and quickly undid a latch on the grate, then carefully pulled on it, the metal giving a small rusty shriek that made Wish wince. The wader checked over his shoulders, moving slowly, making sure they weren't heard, then returned to tugging. The grate swung out on a hinge, open wide enough for Wish to squeeze through. Hightower dashed across the floor to press himself against a metal wall and waved to Wish. She pushed out, blinking into the light, then she darted across to join him in the cover. She turned back and saw Cade squeezing out of the pipe, like the wall was giving birth. Cade's pack dragged out after her, and behind that a rifle was pushed across the floor, Rue following.

Wild Wish swung her rifle around from her shoulder and double-checked her surroundings. They were at the rear of a couple of free-standing metal chambers that had been constructed within the church room, a passage between them and behind them. There was a metal grilled walkway above, and beyond that the ceiling stretched to an incredible height, lined with morbid creature carvings that complemented the foreboding ugliness of its exterior. Leaning around the corner, Wish could see through the passage that the church hall had been gutted of its typical furniture to house these big metal cells, stacked in piles three tall, with small gaps between some of them. The gutter from the pipe ran to a cluster of machinery at the room's centre, crowded with cables and pipes that went towards the cells. As if all the metal rooms in this chamber were feeding whatever that central nonsense was.

Wish moved to the next cell, checking for the guard Hightower had spotted, on the walkway a storey up. The soldier was leaning on a railing, looking lazily towards the middle of the church.

"Another to the right," Rue whispered, appearing at Wish's side. The others were quickly coming out, taking positions along the back of the metal cells.

"Only two?" Wish said, suspiciously.

"Lot of places to hide, possibly some backrooms, but that's what it looks like."

"With that few," Wish said, "we could capture them. We could –" She turned a look to Rue and found the same concerned expression Dakoda had given her, skewing the aim of the Reaper at Green Rise. Rue's blue eyes said *no half measures*. This was not a time to take risks. This was war. Wish said, "No. You've got that one? I'll give the order."

Wish slipped back past Rue, crossed the gap in chambers and instructed the others. Dakoda to get the second guard, supported by

Newk. The rest of them to provide cover. They steadied their rifles as Dakoda and Newk sneaked around a big pillar, sticking to the shadows, and Rue climbed the rear of the metal chambers, pulling herself up onto the walkway. It creaked, just a tiny sound, making them all freeze, but the guard didn't react. Rue drew her knife and crept up behind him, then paused to give Wish a look. Wish nodded and the knife flashed. She winced at the sight, the man pulled back into Rue's embrace as she lowered him to the floor, neck gushing blood – did he look sideways into her face as she killed him? Did he have any idea it was Rue who was holding him?

Across the hall, the other guard made a noise – gagging as Dakoda struck. The man choked, short but sharp enough to echo far across the hall. Wish moved between the cells towards the centre of the hall, her footsteps sounding stupidly loud and bouncing off the walls of the otherwise silent chamber. She looked towards the front of the building, where two enormous iron doors stood, with regular sized doors leading to side-chambers either side of it. There were clattering footsteps coming from them, men responding to the sound of the solider gagging. Another soldier burst out of one of the side-doors, shouting with the incoherence of someone freshly woken, the meaning of his slurred Drail obvious: "Wassat sound?"

Disorientated and unsure, they just had to stay out of sight –

A gun went off, its shot explosively loud in the abbey's quiet dawn, and the soldier was thrown back across the floor. Another soldier yelled Drail threats, scrambling inside the doorway. Wish shot a glance sideways to see Fixit, the next cell across, gun shaking in her hands – she'd panicked and fired. No sense holding back now. Wish shouted, "There's at least one more in there! Boot, move!"

The soldier shouted, too, and Wish saw the barrel of his rifle poking out the doorway. Fixit fired again, to keep him hiding, and he fired blindly back. The walkway rattled above, Rue changing position. Rapid footsteps clapped against the flagstones opposite as the other scouts took up positions, everyone looking for an angle while staying in cover of the alleys between the cells.

A shot came from across the room and the soldier went quiet:

one of the scouts had got all the way around the room. They were still for a moment, waiting for more. Satisfied, Wish straightened up and hissed, "Everyone fan out, get this place secure!"

As one, they did – Dakoda and Newk raced out across the hall, jumped over the soldier's body and into the side chamber. Fixit, after an apologetic look for sparking the fight, turned and clambered up the stairs to another walkway, covering Rue as she thumped around the higher vantage point. Wish and Brade edged into the middle of the room, staring at the odd apparatus that the cells surrounded, while Cade started fishing through her explosives pack. Emi strolled nonchalantly in the other direction, hands in her pockets, while Dakoda and Newk re-emerged to dart across to the other side-chamber.

Moving through the room, Wish saw down one of the alleys between cells another soldier's body on the floor, hands at his neck. There was nothing above his neck but blood; Newk had evidently got ahead of Dakoda and done what she did best. No sign of where the severed head had fallen.

"Looks clear!" Dakoda called out, coming back into the main chamber. "Bunch of billets but no one here."

"Clear from here, too!" Rue shouted down agreement.

"I'm so sorry," Fixit said, a little distraught as she leaned on the rail of a walkway above. "I just saw him coming and –"

"It's fine," Wish said. "Dakoda, Newk, can you take a look out the back, make sure there are no other hiding places?"

"Check the cages, please!" Hightower said, appearing at Wish's leg.

Wish approached the nearest cell and looked in through the circular window in its bulkhead, to see a bare room inside. A body, human-sized, was huddled in the corner. Like a pile of sheets, empty of muscle. Refusing to acknowledge that, let alone try to explain it, Wish moved quickly to the next cell, empty. Better. She checked down the line of them. Emi had made it to the last cell, at the rear of the room, and was scratching her head in thought.

"This isn't right," Brade announced, climbing over the machinery in the middle of the room. It was a big, complicated-looking pile of metal, pipes and wires. "Look at this, parts are missing." He held up unconnected cables.

"No one in the rear," Dakoda called out, jogging back into the main hall.

"They're all dead," Fixit said, moving along the upper walkway.

"Good riddance to them."

"No, the prisoners," Fixit said, voice hollow. Wish looked up. Fixit was standing away from the cells. She'd been checking other windows, and had one cell door open.

"Not prisoners," a scratchy, high-pitched voice announced from the front of the church. The scouts tensed as one, rifles coming up, to see an opening in the main doors. At the base of the great height of looming iron ballast was a human-sized panel, with apparently well-oiled hinges. Framed in the entrance, a shadow stood against the low morning light. A man that didn't make sense, with an ordinary torso and legs but big square blocks where his arms should be, like a bathtub on legs. "They're test subjects. And of course they're dead. Or didn't you know the 64 has, at last, proved a flawless success?"

"Dread Doctor Vorhale?" Captain Brade took charge, hopping off the machinery. He had his sword drawn at his side, his pistol out in the other hand. "Come quietly, so we don't have to do things we'd regret."

"I wasn't the one making a noise," the doctor said, then gave a sinister, malevolent snigger. Wish shifted her rifle at her hip. He was a fair distance off, but she was sure she could at least clip him. There was something strange around him, though, the way the light glared behind him. "But if you'd like to save yourselves trouble, please, choose a chamber each. I can demonstrate our work. No? Pity. Dismember them, corporals."

Then the shimmering light erupted with a flare, as Vorhale charged into the hall, and chaos followed with him. A flurry of gunfire came from the doorway, sending the scouts diving for cover. Wish leapt between two cells while Brade ducked behind the machinery and Rue ran along the walkway above. The short salvo stopped and heavy footfalls followed Vorhale in – two, three people. Rue fired and shots cracked back at her. Wish leaned around the corner to see a big black shape flash behind a pillar as the mortar erupted behind it.

"Take them alive!" Vorhale's shrill voice ordered, and Wish picked him out, ducking behind another pillar, metallic armour sticking out at the edges where he was too big to hide. Brade fired a barrage of shots at him, clinking off the pillar or the metal, uselessly emptying his pistol – then Wish was distracted by a sudden pulse, metal bending loudly, and saw Emi struck. The edge of one of the cells had twisted out and hit the mage, knocking her into a roll across the floor. There was an enemy mage nearby – whoever had created the effect hiding Vorhale's reinforcements.

"Grekkels!" Rue shouted. "Coming on your flank, Dakoda!"

Wild Wish spotted flashes of a beast moving with bounding, leaping steps between the opposite cells. On the other side of the chambers, Dakoda fired, twice, before there was a crash of weight hitting home. A shriek of pain – Dakoda down – and Wish was sprinting, yelling as she charged between the cells and skidded out to face the monstrous creature. It stood nearly three metres tall, arms hinged like wolf's legs, maw stretched in a sharp-toothed sneer. Newk stood over Dakoda, down on the floor, fending it back with swings of her sword. It took a clawed swipe which Newk feinted, and she spun, stabbing through its gut. But even as its insides spilt over her blade, the grekkel twisted and backhanded Newk's head, sending her tumbling. The second she was out of the way, Wish fired a single, perfect shot that hit the monster in the eye. As it crumpled, Wish ran to Newk's side, to help her up, to cancel whatever had happened – but more gunfire made her skid to stop. She turned to the sound, had to run quickly back between the chambers.

Another grekkel was up on the higher walkway, metal bending under its weight as it bounced towards Fixit, the medic backing off and firing up, one shot missing, the next clipping its shoulder, then it was on her. Wish fired while still moving closer, bad shots, an awkward distance and a worse angle. The grekkel struck Fixit, knocking her down, but it bucked at the sound of a gunshot, arching its back as a bullet struck it. Rue stalked up the walkway behind it in a crouch, quickly firing and hitting it again, high in the shoulder. It slammed into the nearest cell, staggered enough for Rue to surge forward and smash her rifle into its face, throwing it back over the edge.

As the grekkel thumped dead into the floor, a shout snapped Wish's attention the other way. Vorhale was charging forward with his immense, unreal metal arms swinging. Brade hopped back, sprightly, turning around the blows, but when he struck back his sword scraped across metal. Wish steadied herself, aimed and fired, and her bullet likewise pinged off the man's wildly flailing arms. She tried again, but the gun clicked empty.

"Out the way, Captain, I can't get a shot!" Rue shouted, and as she did a flame burst from the main doorway, a great flash of light and heat that shot overhead, making Rue scream and drop back. Wish stared in horror as fire engulfed the upper walkway. A robed mage stood at its source: he'd been hiding near the entrance. He stepped out into the room, flicking his arms out as though shedding water, and he threw his head back to howl. A crazed dirt-minder, paying his magic's price. Wish sprinted towards him, rifle dropped, clawing to get her short-blade free. She sprinted past Brade and the man with mechanical arms as they duelled, the latter's brute force driving Brade back, punches cracking the walls and tiled floor as he missed.

The mage snapped his head around as Wish drew closer, and just as she jumped, blade cocked back ready to stab, he dropped and slammed both hands into the floor with a fierce snarl. She roared, airborne – and the ground cracked and lifted. She was slammed in the chest and thrown into the air. She flew so high up the action below suddenly looked tiny, Brade and his opponent doll-sized, the cell chambers like play blocks. Wish flapped her arms like she could swim through the air, gasping to regain her breath. Then her insides rushed up as she was suddenly falling, coming fast towards the rugged eruption of broken earth that had propelled her. As she hit it, bracing herself to splatter, the ground fell away, softening like a sponge. It bounced up slightly, and she rolled into jagged stone, cut and scraped.

Wish steadied her hands against the shattered floor, and looked up to see the Dread mage twisting away with a foul sneer, twitching hands bracing for another attack. Not directed at her, but towards the far side of the room – where Emi crouched, one hand on the ground after helping Wish. Emi wrenched her outstretched arms up in an arc, pulling a slab of broken masonry through the air, faster than the mage could defend. He got one arm up before the chunk of building pulped his torso. Then Emi was running to Wish's side, doubling over with giggles, and Wish clambered to her feet shouting, "Watch out Emi, there's more!"

Emi flapped a dismissive hand, almost in hysterics. Beyond her, Brade and the madman with metal arms were still duelling, as though this crazed mage's exchange had never happened. Vorhale's mechanical fist slammed into Brade's blade, tearing the weapon from his hand, and the captain was thrown into a sideways stumble. He kept his footing where any other man might've fallen, but was vulnerable, and the big metal arms were raised to strike him with skull-crushing power. Then Vorhale jerked aside with a high-pitched yelp, lifting a leg; Hightower hung off it with his spear jammed in the man's calf.

Vorhale kicked out savagely, throwing Hightower off and through the air, but as he brought the foot back down he yelled at the pain and stumbled, giving Brade a window to tackle him round the waist and bring him down. The doctor bucked, a mechanical arm slamming Brade off him with ease, and he turned to rise, but Wish was there, then, skidding across the floor, blade back in hand. She pressed it against his throat. She held off stabbing at the last second, looking into his eyes as she froze, and he froze too. They both breathed deeply, and his spittle sizzled angrily between his teeth.

"I'll do it, I'll fucking do it," Wish promised, but the look of frustrated fury in his eye confirmed he already knew that. She wanted to add something clever, a line of judgement to bring this psycho down, but nothing came. She merely stayed locked there, knife ready to kill. To move now, to do anything else, would be to accept the disaster all this had become. She would *have* to kill him.

Another blade slowly, gently slid before her eyes, pointed down towards Vorhale's face, breaking Wish from the trance. She looked up worriedly and found Brade had returned, standing over them with his sword poised. He said, voice gravelly from the action, "Stand down, Wild Wish. I believe the day is ours."

46

Purity is in the mind.
Purity is in the body.
Those that accept purity will be saved.
Those that reject purity will be burnt.
Those that do not know purity will be taught.
Ten Thousand Tenets of Purity, Official
Purification Handbook, Psalm 15

Maringdale remained restless even after they boarded the Iron Barge again. Everyone else was relaxing, and that put her more on edge. Even the 1st Wavecutters, spread out over a handful of carriages, softened their feelings. Between violent threat and flashes of hate, she read flashes of the ordinary from them: impatience, uncertainty, loneliness. Similar anxieties to those she felt amongst ordinary soldiers. The Dread soldiers had actively put up barriers in the village, she realised. Now she could more comfortably probe them for hints of betrayal. After all, there was no guarantee the insurgency ended with those scouts.

Netts and Donut were conversely eager to enjoy the now familiar comforts of the Iron Barge. Netts almost bounded for a leather-upholstered bench, but Maringdale swatted him off it, saying they'd not be sleeping on the job. He obediently slunk along with her, his feelings flashing that this was bullshit – they should be enjoying the spoils of success already.

Not that it wasn't tempting for Maringdale. After thwarting Stanclif's insurgents, Reeve had remained miserable and uncomfortable, with a constant sense of disquiet that blurred her senses. The previous days had been little better, travelling by air and settling in poky stop-offs. The Iron Barge, on the other hand, was luxurious, and steaming towards their final goal. Soon, Drail would have full control of the war and Stanclif would come to peace talks with a beggar's bowl outstretched. Then they'd ride the Iron Barge as victors, through a land ready to rebuild and advance. Soon, but not yet. She couldn't allow the slightest of mistakes before then, and determined to walk the entire train checking for trouble.

Once Maringdale had trekked three quarters of the bustling train, as packed and noisy as ever, it pulled into a station and the doors churned with soldiers coming and going. Hopping between pushing young men, as they raced to gather their things, Netts cried out, "Guess you gotta start over, now?"

The stop brought more than just fresh soldiers and supplies: it brought a giddy air of news from the front. The rumours started in excited whispers that quickly spread, nervous energy gripping everyone. The Battle of Wick had begun. Pressing through the crowds, still searching for any hint of ill intent, Maringdale became increasingly distracted by the varying accounts until she realised Netts had a point: it was folly to try and monitor the entire train's occupancy. She instead chose to resolve the rumours that had everyone so worked up. She sparked a conversation with an officer she sensed genuinely knew what was going on.

"Started with an air assault," he said, a twitchy man with a moustache that he kept touching. "Knew exactly what they were doing, sent a swarm of kite fliers, directly over the Basin Screw. A hundred airmen maybe, and I doubt any got out alive, but there was too many to stop all at once. They hit us bad. Bombs tore right through the artillery. Lost the best weapon Wick had." He spat in disgust, hitting the fine oak wall. "Then they reveal their answer to the weapon. Cowards didn't want it known till the Basin was done, otherwise the second that thing fired we'd have fired right back, wouldn't we?"

Not exactly cowardice, then, but rather sensible. Maringdale asked, "So what's the damage?"

"Put a hole in the western wall, half a mile wide. Must've wrecked a score or more homes, probably killed a hundred civilians, the bastards. But the weapon only got off a couple shots – figure it's burnt out, cheap Stanish engineering. That or they couldn't produce more than a couple rounds for it. Anyway, they're readying troops near this opening, and if the bastards don't flood in at first light tomorrow, it'll be the morning after. We're ready for them, though, ain't we?" He said it like a demand, scratching at his moustache with his forearm. Terrified.

"Definitely," Maringdale said. More than he could know.

She continued through the train, finding the soldiers' fear and eagerness for the coming conflict created a strong haze over any ill thoughts she could pick out. She found one or two considering deserting at the next stop, and one considering revolting against his sergeant, but didn't care to get involved in such menial matters. The latter wasn't likely to act on those feelings, anyway.

Finally, she made it back to the Dread Corps' carriages and found the Wavecutters' crowd had swelled, bolstered by increasingly menacing men and a renewal of that feeling she'd sensed in the village. Fuelled, now, by the confirmation that battle was coming soon, blood for them, *blood for all*. Maringdale paused, feeling her own anxieties growing, about to step into a sea of rabid thought. She told Netts and Donut, "You two should go back. Find the eagle's nest we used before, keep a lookout from there." Maybe it was a protectiveness she hadn't realised was blossoming, wanting to keep the pair out of trouble, or maybe it was just that she didn't want them to see her worried. Either way, it confused Netts.

"You serious? These are my people, I can –"

"You can pretend to do something useful there," Maringdale cut in harshly. "With a good vantage point that also lets you rest up for the battle."

Netts didn't shift, but Donut did, looking hopefully back the way he'd come, not wanting to enter the Dread carriages himself. It didn't take an intention mage to know the shocksmiths were the worst men on this train.

"They're not your people," Maringdale clarified for Netts. "They're the nastiest lot Ways could find."

He hesitated a moment longer, but as he looked into the carriage again himself, at those savage faces, he nodded, accepting her charity. "We'll see you up in the nest, then?"

"When I can get away."

Netts nodded, recognising the break at last for what it was. He thumped Donut's arm and directed him away. Maringdale waited until they were lost in the crowd before she pushed through the Dread soldiers, along a tight corridor passing booths packed with loudly talking men, their furious emotions even louder. She crossed to the next carriage and passed more booths until it opened to a broad dining area, with a round conference table at the centre and windows framed with gold.

Ways was sitting there, making the table look child-sized before his bulk, a mug of frothy ale in one hand. He had men either side of him: one bearded, in a green greatcoat with a flat cap and no sign of stripes, concealing his obviously high rank, the other bald and familiarly avian-featured.

"Maringdale," Ways boomed affably. "You've met Battle Chief Hark?"

"Sir." Maringdale nodded, edging closer. "We worked together in Highscythe." The buzz of shocksmith hate fogged her mind, but she caught Hark's self-satisfied malevolence clearly enough. He sat back, glowering with disgust that she was still breathing.

"And this is Lieutenant General Scathe. Both joining us to assist in the defence of Wick."

Without looking up, or acknowledging Maringdale in any way, Scathe snorted to suggest he didn't entirely appreciate Ways' wording. She had to push hard to pick out his feelings between the hostility of the surrounding men: this was not how he would do things. It was not an honourable war. It was unclear if he was concerned about the brutality of these Dread reinforcements or Vorhale's weapon. Maybe both.

"And where are your companions?" Hark asked.

"Patrolling the train," Maringdale said, then sensed the need to correct herself: "Actually, I've given them time off. Sometimes my work is best done alone." It satisfied him, evidently wanting Netts and Donut involved even less than her. Damn, why was he here?

He must've travelled a long way north from Highscythe only to be coming south again.

"Seem like a reasonable pair, those two," Ways said.

"Excellent support, sir, I'd be happy to recommend both of them."

"And I'll take that under consideration. But I'm glad they aren't here now."

The sense of trouble suddenly flashed on her – between the heavy thoughts, the impatient lust for violence – a clearer intention – to strike before she noticed – and as her hand gripped her pistol and she half twisted she knew it was already too late. A bulky shape had slid out from between the black-armoured men, a stubby, wide-barrelled gun held lazily at waist-height, aimed up at her chest. She knew the man who held it. *Thorn Red*. He was made fat by scarlet leathers, worn in layers to form armour as thick and impenetrable as any of the Dread plating, straps under and around various panels holding weapons. He had the face of a killer, rugged, stubbly and square, narrow eyes deep in his face above a thin, sharp nose, with a flat circular hat, moderately shorter than a top hat. Unlike the shocksmiths, his intentions came through strong, clear and sane. Smugly triumphant, but wanting her to make a move. Give him an excuse.

Maringdale relaxed her hand from the pistol and held it up in submission, glancing sideways to Ways. He was perfectly calm, another day at work. The rest of the carriage quietened, men turning their attentions to her, and the thump of their mixed-up intentions grew louder – *blood, death!*

"Constans Maringdale, you're under arrest for the murder of Sin Sight Panderlair, by order of the Purification," Thorn said.

"Murder?" Maringdale snarled. There couldn't have been evidence, no witnesses besides Donut. Ways himself had practically thanked her for it. "On what grounds?"

"On the grounds that you confessed to a Battle Chief," Hark said with mean satisfaction. That lying son of a – but as she spun to him, she saw it wasn't *he* who had betrayed her. Ways stared impassively as his intentions quietly rumbled for this to move on, *be done with her*, away.

"Battle Chief Ways?" she appealed for explanation, and hated the sound of her weak voice. He waved a dismissive hand, this matter beneath him, and turned to resume talking to Scathe. Maringdale surged forward, voice steeling, "Are you mad? Without me you'd have been –"

But Thorn Red was suddenly on her, twisting her arm around and up under the shoulder. She almost struck back with an elbow, but his gun barrel pressed into her neck and he growled in her ear, "You're done, Maringdale. Bloody traitorous scum."

He would do it. Any excuse and he would kill her. Him and the dozen Dread soldiers around them. Easier for everyone that way. She gave up, and let him guide her away, past the staring, judging soldiers of two carriages, stumbling until they reached a booth of only a few men. Thorn Red quickly cleared it out with a boomed command; even Dread soldiers scarpered at the mention of the Purification. He shoved Maringdale into a corner and shackled her wrists with old, warped cuffs that he chained to a radiator girdle between the booth's two benches. He locked the door and sat in the opposite corner, gun on his knee, aimed at her. He'd taken her pistol, now down on the bench beside him, but her sword was still awkwardly sheathed at her side, along with a handful of knives. It was deliberate: he wanted her armed so she might try something.

"You know there's nothing to bring to trial," Maringdale said.

"And you know there's never needed to be anything, as far as the Purification is concerned," Red replied. No – legal defence or not, to be arrested was to be damned. It would just be a smoother journey if she was dead.

"You're calling me a traitor." Maringdale shifted to get more comfortable. "Do you have any idea what I've been doing these past weeks?"

Red gave her an unimpressed look.

"Panderlair was the traitor," she spat, viciously. "He would've got in the way, focused on the Dread Corps themselves rather than the –"

"As he *should* have," Red cut in. "The Purification has concerns regarding their actions. A full investigation will be taking place there."

Maringdale went quiet, seeing the reality of her situation. Everyone answers to someone, even the Dread Corps, and Vorhale and Ways had most likely taken this project further than the Arrow Council had authorised. Perhaps the only public clue to their real progress – and defiance of the Council – had been in Cleave, as Panderlair had suspected. But she had preferred to help the war effort. Which is what they were doing, wasn't it? Riding rapidly towards striking a decisive blow at the heart of their enemies, thanks to her. She had done this, giving clear warning and transporting essential information, protecting the research. The weapon might not be what the Purification wanted, but Ways only intended to win the war – why had he sold her out now, so close to completion?

She asked, quietly, "When did Battle Chief Ways arrange this?"

Red considered if there was something to lose in answering honestly. He said, "I got word the moment you joined them on this train." So there'd been no reference to what she had achieved at Reeve. How she had worked *with* the Dread Corps.

"In exchange for what?"

"No exchange," Red said. "Just the Dread Corps doing their duty to the Purification."

So no one would be questioning them before Wick. Maringdale sank back into the seat. Once they reached Wick and set off the bomb, the Purification would no longer be able to do anything about Vorhale's project. The weapon would be proven. The war won.

She could, of course, expose the weapon now, and tell Red exactly what was going on. Vorhale's device sat not two or three carriages away, waiting to explode. A bastardisation of magics, something unholy and corrupt. But who would care, really, when they had a Battle Chief's word against hers – a rogue agent.

"What were you thinking," Red said, blandly. He was no intention mage – not magic at all, just a hunter like Panderlair. Men with her skills, after all, usually reached positions more prestigious than Purification drones. "That the Dread Corps would take you in? There's not a single woman amongst their ranks, you know that. And their mages are the most skilled in their respective circles. Trained to extremes."

Maringdale scowled. It wasn't so unlikely, was it? How much more skilled than her could those wretched mages be, after all? She said, "What happens next?"

"You know what happens next. We'll depart at Ark, one stop before Wick, then on to Hail."

Hail. Where they could perform an official trial. And her purge.

47

Necessity found The One War responsible for medical advances that changed the very fabric of society. The funicular plague, for example, may have killed as many people as the fighting, during the winter of 719 — but it was also finally eradicated with military-developed vaccines in 720. This, a disease that survived five centuries and killed millions. And that is to say nothing of the minor advances from field medics, gaining a lifetime's experience with every battle, improvising techniques that might have eluded doctors with ten years of scholarly education.
Sickness and Sin: Medicine and Religion
Through the Ages, Grunberg, p. 634

Winning the fight granted only a moment of calm before everyone was jolted back into panicked activity. Wish and Brade hurriedly bound Vorhale with cables from his own machine while Cade and Emi went running between the downed scouts. Rue was making the horrible noises of an injured animal up on the walkway, but at least that meant she was alive. Hightower scurried between Wish's boots to pull his spear free from Vorhale's ankle — which made him shriek loud enough to shake the rafters. Then the wader backed off, aiming it at him furiously like he might strike again.

"Oh fuck," Cade called from above. Wish flashed a look up and saw she was passing Fixit. Even from this distance, Wish could see the medic was bent lifeless against the rail, head at the wrong angle and eyes open. It must've been quick, so she hadn't suffered. But she had been the only one who knew anything about healing the rest of them. And they definitely needed help.

Reminded of Newk, Wish abandoned Brade and Hightower and

skidded as she ran around the metal cells, to where Newk and Dakoda and the grekkel lay. She sprinted towards them, faltering only momentarily as Rue shrieked and Emi shouted, "I'm trying to help!"

Dakoda was closest, rolled on her side, face pressed into the floor with her arms crossed tight over her gut. Her profusely bleeding gut. Wish started in horror as Dakoda coughed blood. Her eyes tracked up and she croaked, "Stomach's falling out."

"Shit," Wish gasped, and looked to Newk. Brave Newk, who'd stood up to a grekkel with a sword – she wasn't moving at all.

"Help her," Dakoda advised, then groaned. "Saved me. Kind of."

Wish ran on, heart pumping too loud for her to make out the other movements in the church hall, more voices calling out. She slid down next to Newk and turned her. Oh hell, her head was split open above the temple, gory and wet, eyes closed. Wish stared impotently. Not Newk, please not Newk. She raised a hand gingerly, not sure what to do – put pressure on it? Wrap it? How could she –

"Ah fuck," a voice said somewhere behind her, then footsteps rapidly approached.

Wish just kept staring. Another lost. They'd only just started . . . *No* –

"Here," Oksy said, pulling Wish back. Wish stumbled, clenching a fist to strike back, but Oksy held up a wad of bandages. "Let me see. I can help."

Wish caught her breath, watching as Oksy turned Newk one way and another, taking more supplies from her pockets. How did she get here? Wish said, "Why aren't you outside?"

"We saw the bastards come in," Oksy said, pouring alcohol over Newk's head. It drew no reaction, like Newk was in eternal sleep. "They were in the next building, the doctor, the grekkels, a couple more soldiers. I shot two outside, then we just braved the magic barrier. Ran down here to catch up."

"Oh," Wish replied, because what else could she say? That explained why the gunfire didn't continue after Vorhale charged in, and damn – Oksy had run through *magic* to join them? Wish looked the other way. Angles was crouched by Dakoda, whispering assurances, trying to tend her gut. Dakoda laughed bitterly. Wish said, "We should've hunted them all down before we came in here." Because it was her decision, wasn't it? Her bad leadership led to this. Never mind Tate's advance at dawn – she didn't have to do it.

"Hunted them how?" Oksy said, pulling the bandages tight. "They were all here and we couldn't have got to them another way. Not in time."

"In time? In time for what?" Wish snapped. "None of the other squads made it, Oksy! We could've waited! There was no need to move this morning!"

Oksy's expression said she didn't disagree, but it was what it was. Wish took a deep breath, trying desperately to keep calm. But it was a massacre. A disaster. Her eyes fell back on Newk. Please. Oksy said, quietly, "I think she'll be okay."

But there was no way to know that. Wish rumbled with anger and turned around. She snatched Dakoda's rifle from the floor and marched back between the chambers to the centre of the room.

Vorhale was propped upright, Brade to one side holding his sword, Hightower to the other with his tiny spear, less threatening in size but equally dangerous in intent. The doctor was talking to the wader, "If there were any Gonish here, there are none now. It's proved most effective against your people."

Hightower's face darkened, receiving all the confirmation he needed that his brother was surely dead. Another blemish on their shitty morning. Wish distracted him my stomping right up next to the small man, hands braced on the rifle. She breathed deeply, taking a moment to glare hatred at Vorhale. The doctor stared back without emotion. She snapped her attention to Brade and said, "You happy now, with our dawn-fucking-charge?"

"The weapon's gone," Brade said.

"Excuse me? What the hell difference does –"

"If anything, we should've attacked sooner," the captain told her. No apology at all.

Wish looked at the unholy mess of the workplace again. One cell was twisted out of shape and the floor near the entrance had been smashed by the mage; bodies were scattered about, blood on the walls. The unusual doctor, with his mechanical arms, bloody ankle and blotchy, malformed face, looked sickly amused. Wish said, "He's behind it all, isn't he? We've stopped him."

"We've stopped him," Brade said wearily, "but not the project."

"We satisfied our final tests days ago," Vorhale offered happily, accent the most untrustworthy kind of thick Slanik. "Bomb 64 is on its way to the front as we speak. You should be pleased, the war will soon be over."

"Bomb 64?" Wish replied, the name horribly cold and simple. She looked to Brade again. "Where on the front is it going? We can still stop it. How's it moving?" Wish recalled Hightower's comments about the mercenaries here. "If they've got wyrlings, we can find some too."

The suggestion made Vorhale laugh. "I apologise," he said, as though he'd misspoken before polite company. "But Bomb 64 would not travel by such pedestrian means. Only the finest, most defensible transport is worthy of my work of art."

"The Iron Barge," Brade guessed, and Vorhale's smug face confirmed it.

"That fortress on the rails?" Wish said.

"Exactly, exactly!" Vorhale said. "Even if you could catch up, there's no way you could *stop* it. When 64 reaches Wick, the world will bow to Slanik science."

Rue interrupted them with another pained, desperate sound. Wish didn't dare look her way, emotion clenching her face, but she called out, "How is she, Emi?"

"Lucky to be alive," Emi replied, loudly. "How's everyone else?"

"Same," Wish said, much quieter.

"Newk's stable," Oksy announced, coming out between cells, wiping her hands on her top. "And Dakoda's not as bad as she looks." Her approach stirred Cade to come down the stairs to join them. "Want us back outside, running another perimeter?"

"No, stay here," Wish said, adjusting her hold on the rifle. "This bastard's about to tell us everything and you can probably interpret his shit better than me."

Rue shrieked again and Emi laughed. Using her magic somehow, though dirt-minding could do little for flesh. Cade whispered to Wish, "Burnt up her arm and face. I think she'll survive all right but it's not pretty."

Wish nodded, expecting nothing better. The screams went quiet, then. She ordered Vorhale, "Talk."

"Oh, with pleasure. You're in charge, are you? That trollop of a Purification officer didn't do half the job she was supposed to, did she? No surprise."

"What job?" Wish frowned. Was someone supposed to have stopped them?

"Does it matter? Look at you all, you've saved the day. The mystery women of Stanclif. Well done, your mothers will be proud. Except the bomb *will* go off. A glorious combination of the forces of mind and earth, which they said could not be done. And not in the individual – oh no – but with the amplification of mechanics, the expansion of science, the –"

"What's it *do?*" Wish shouted.

Vorhale went quiet, only taking more pleasure in how his prattle had grated her. The walkway above squeaked with Emi's movements, the mage shushing Rue to listen in, and the doctor gave her a look before slyly explaining, "Why it kills, of course. It throws out a targeted pulse that no armour can defend against. Highly concentrated, to fry a brain."

Wish recalled Dollemore's arguments against such techniques, that using witlacing to kill was too short-distance and costly to have any strategic value. Unless it could be chained through dirt-minding, as Brade feared. She voiced his concerns, "You found a way to make it spread."

"Exactly," Vorhale said. "The same way the mindless channel energy through the earth. Once it hits one mind, it'll use the victim's own energy to jump to another. Latching onto whoever their thoughts go to. In their dying panic, they reach out to whoever's closest. Thinking *save me*. My friend, my officer, my close comrade-at-arms. Hoping for someone to protect them. That very hope creates the bridge that sends the pulse on."

"That's not possible," Emi called down. "Earth-minding is hard enough for a fully-focused mage to channel through solids, or liquids, let alone through the air, and witlacing is only done through pairing –"

"You don't *know* what's possible," Vorhale barked. "We've had all the freedom in the world to test the boundaries of the most devastating ideas, with the scale of this blessed war."

"Even if you *could* do something like that," Emi said, "the effects would be limited. It'd take all a mage's energy to hit two or three people that way."

"Yes, if you use a mage," Vorhale said. "So, so short-sighted. We have developed a way to store mortal energy, to send a blast *without* the mage. One that can build a huge reservoir of energy, giving it more power. So far we've contained our tests to these chambers; unleashed without boundaries, we can only guess how far the weapon's effects will spread. With everyone packed in their trenches, it could kill an entire army. But if a soldier dies on a nameless field in deepest Farne, thinking of his sweetheart back home on a Stanclif farm, will it reach her there?" He laughed again. "Quite possibly. Quite possibly!"

"By Bly," Brade uttered in quiet shock, the full potential of this weapon worse than he had predicted. "Surely even the Arrow Council couldn't condone this? It'll be even less predictable than gas."

"It takes courage to advance," Vorhale said. "The strongest prevail through such leaps. Those who lack the imagination must fall aside, to allow progress. You should be proud, all of you, that you get to see where it started. The dawn of a new world. Wait a few days and you'll see how it ends."

"Where?" Wish said.

"Where do you think?" Vorhale said. "Wick, of course, where your most valiant resistance is." But of course it was, where their forces were most effectively pushing forward – where the people Wish could actually put names to were fighting. Vorhale apparently spotted that in her face and bent closer, for all his binds allowed. "You have friends there? How delicious. Don't worry, it'll be over before you know it."

"Wish," Cade said, very carefully, "please can we blow this all to hell now?"

"And set civilisation back?" Vorhale said. "This is a necessary cull to end the war, you fools. Would you prefer to drag out the killing, the suffering, for however long it takes until everyone's dead? Bomb 64 will *save* lives."

"No," Wish said. A decisive, simple statement.

"No? What *no?*"

"No, no, shit-brain. It's not reached Wick yet and it's not ever getting reproduced here. Cade, yes, please, set the charges. Oksy, can you check the surrounding buildings? If there's a wyrling or anything else we can use to move fast, I want it found."

"Gather evidence," Brade came in, quickly. "Whatever reports you can find. And prepare to move the doctor. He'll testify before a war crimes tribunal in Stanclif."

"No," Wish heard herself say again. Brade's brow knitted. "We're not taking him. We've got enough baggage. And this isn't something that should be discussed in courts. Shouldn't be something of any public record."

"Then do you intend to execute him?" Brade replied, incredulous. "That's not your decision to make, Wild Wish. If they were capable of doing this once, we need to learn everything about it, to be able to counter it –"

"To use it for ourselves?" Wish suggested. His hesitation said yes, if it came to that. "No. We can wipe out every trace of this work here, and do our damnedest to track down the rest. I've crossed the line more than a few times, Captain. This time I see it, though, clear as day."

"The man's a monster," Hightower put in, by way of agreement. Vorhale merely grinned.

"Cade –"

"Stay where you are," Brade instructed, turning squarely onto Wish. "I'm the ranking officer here, and I have the final say, thank you very much. We go back with nothing, Stanclif might not even believe what we found. This man needs to be heard."

"There might be hope for you yet," Vorhale said. "Listen to your captain, dear; this is how the weak become strong."

"For once, Captain," Wish said, "I'm going to do something that will prevent nightmares rather than cause them. We came here to stop this. We lost people *to stop this*. Cade, would you –"

"Stand *down*, Wild Wish," Brade said through gritted teeth. "This is –"

The rifle went off in Wish's hands. Its violent crack echoed across the ceiling like the clang of a funeral bell as Vorhale snapped back against his equipment and went still. A single hole oozed blood from his forehead, brains spread behind him, expression stiffly surprised.

Everyone stared in silence. Then Wish finished Brade's sentence, "This is over."

Brade lifted his sword and Wish took a step back, rifle turned to him. Hightower darted to the side, out of the way, as Oksy and Cade closed ranks behind Wish, neither armed but both ready to scrap. Brade gritted his teeth, looking from them down to the dead doctor, and for a second the only thing in Wish's mind was that it was lucky Dakoda's gun still had bullets. Would've been embarrassing otherwise.

Angles came skidding around the chambers behind Brade, her own rifle up, eyes wide with fright. She looked unsure what to do, but removed any question that he had a chance of defying them.

The captain took a breath, swallowing outrage, threat, or another attempt to take control. It was clear none would do. He lowered the blade.

"I, for one," Emi called out from above, "am glad she shut him up."

"Agreed, a hundred per cent," Oksy said, quietly. "But I've got a practical question. How are we catching up to that bomb?"

"It's on the Iron Barge," Wish said, "so we can predict its route, at least." She looked down at Hightower. "You're sure there was a wyrling on site?"

"There *was*," Hightower said. "But I only saw one. Not gonna carry everyone."

Wish squeezed her eyes shut. Why couldn't everything just be easy and the war be over and none of this ever have happened in the first place? "Well we can get everyone clear of here, at least." She turned to Brade. "Is there a way we can get word to your people? Get someone ahead of the Iron Barge, put whatever resources we have into blowing up the tracks?"

Brade's icy stare said he was not over her rebellion, but she held his gaze until he answered, stubbornly, "No. There are no agents this far north who could send a message faster than that train."

"The Iron Barge could outrun anything," Oksy said helpfully, then added, "But it's a city on wheels, it has to make regular stops to refuel and supply. Between here and Wick, they'd have to stop for at least one night, I'd say."

"There's still a chance we could catch up?" Wish said, needing to hear it.

Oksy nodded. "If there's a wyrling here. We might do it."

"Could we get ahead of it? Blow the rails?"

"You'd have more chance bombing Arrow City itself," Cade put in with a shake of her head. "We targeted the Iron Canal from time to time back in 3rd Brigade – the rails are thicker and deeper than most of our charges can penetrate, even a dirt-minder would struggle with it. And anything you did try would alert every Drail outpost in a fifty-mile radius."

"Important question," Emi murmured, tapping her fingers against the rail, "is if anyone here actually knows how to fly a wyrling?"

That dropped the scouts into uncomfortable silence. Wish could've kicked something. Punched a wall. Simply screamed. But Brade cleared his throat, and admitted, "I can fly it." Wish waited to see if it would come with a caveat, but he added, with some hint at his formerly affable self, "We can argue about what this means for us, and Stanclif, once we're sure there's an us and a Stanclif left to argue over."

48

I went to war to fight for home, boo-rah, boo-rah!
I went to war to fight for home, boo-rah, boo-rah!
Saw a hundred dead and a thousand gone
Under the mud and lost to bombs
I wish I never went at all – won't please you take me home?
Traditional Stanclif Marching Song
[Updated Soldiers' Version]

Wild Wish longed for heartfelt goodbyes. The opportunity to tell each girl exactly what they meant to her. Dakoda, whose stoicism always brought her down to earth. Rue, tougher than a troll, inspired Wish to never give up. Fixit, most of all – Wish hated having said nothing to her before they went in. Fixit had done so much, not brave or tough or cynical, just trying to help people while they were all killing. She kept her faith not just for herself but for all of them. But she was dead and Dakoda's face was contorted in too much pain to listen and Rue had passed out, and Newk, though groaning, had never quite woken. Newk, dear Newk, Wish kissed her cheek and whispered everything would be okay.

It all moved too quickly, besides, from Vorhale's terrible threats to the realisation there wasn't a minute to waste. Oksy did indeed find a stabled wyrling, a disappointingly fat and ungainly looking one, while Brade plotted a course on his maps that showed the route the Iron Barge must've taken. Assuming its speed and one overnight stop, and their own predicted speed with the wyrling, flying directly over the Har Coul mountains with minimal rest, they might reach the train just before Wick. The chances of getting ahead of it with any meaningful time to spare were zero. So, they threw together packs of the barest provisions and quickly disguised themselves in scraps of Dread armour that only loosely fit Wish. She left her rifle in Oksy's care and took up a Drail weapon the equivalent of Pound's Rik Repeater, more suited to close quarters mayhem. This one had a circular chamber and wooden finishing that made it look slightly primitive, and the more dangerous for it.

They ran for the wyrling and took to the air, no time even to contemplate what they were leaving behind. It would be up to Oksy, Angles and Cade to carry Rue, Dakoda and Newk clear of the abbey, far enough away that Cade could lay her charges safely. Then they'd have a struggle all of their own, getting out of Low Slane.

Oksy was the only person Wish had offered proper parting words. She was leaving Boot Squad in her charge and they hugged before Wish boarded the wyrling and she had to, *had to* tell her: "I wouldn't trust anyone to lead them more than you, out of all our scouts – you're the best Oksy, I'm so glad you're with us, and I know you'll get them home." And she meant it, proved by the tears in her eyes not just as she said it but also when she remembered it, flying from Slane into Har Coul. If anyone could get the remnants of the Blood Scouts back to Stanish lines, it was Oksy.

But the wyrling was only capable of carrying three riders at any reasonable speed. It was down to Wild Wish, Brade and Emi, with Hightower stashed in a pack, to pursue the train. Exactly how the decision was made, Wish wasn't sure, except that she and Brade were in charge and Emi was bloody powerful, and Hightower didn't weigh anything so why not. His injured brother was left to Cade or whoever to carry home. Wish kept second-guessing the whole setup as they soared over Low Slane. Maybe Oksy should've been there instead of her. Cade with her bombs? Or should she have waited, in case the other Blood Scouts finally arrived? Tate or Larkin might have a better plan. Where the hell even where they? Should she have dropped everything to push north and find the other squads instead?

Wish found herself alone with those doubts, with Brade focused on flying and Emi conserving her energy. They were unreasonable doubts anyway, because the reality was there was a maniacal bomb on the way to blow up Wick and everyone around it and if they didn't stop it, no one would. They couldn't stay to see Cade's efforts in Reeve Abbey, which would surely create a spectacular explosion. They couldn't say long farewells or search for the other scouts or anything else.

After hours of private brooding, the mounted group passed out of Low Slane into Har Coul, which Brade announced with a shout despite there being no clear border markers to indicate it. Wish wasn't sure if she imagined it, but the grass beneath them seemed to be getting greener, the mills built with softer curves, the trees less prickly. Big boulders and cliff faces started rising up into the Kleb Range. From this vantage point, the world was simple and soft and beautiful. You could almost imagine it without people, without violence, a land where they weren't all murdering each other in the millions, and no one had cause to break Fixit's neck or melt Rue's skin or rip open Dakoda or crack Newk's skull. Wish had to pull up her goggles and smear a hand over her face, letting the tears whip away on the wind.

The war still found them in the sky, though, just as Wish was wondering if they might've all made this same journey to begin with, avoiding everything they'd been through. A pack of creatures flew towards them: four arrexes, smaller than their wyrling, wings flapping faster. They were Coulard creatures, with bat-like wings but coiled, insectile bodies like a bipedal wasp. Each had a single rider, men in heavy, fur-lined green coats, long rifles laid across their laps. Wish moved to ready her own rifle from the pack on her back, but Brade called out, "Act like we're friendly."

She held off, not liking it, and the arrexes swooped closer. Brade slowed the wyrling to accommodate them, the bigger creature evidently faster. One of the arrexes drew alongside them and the rider, features hidden behind big goggles and a scarf, shouted in Coulard, then Drail. Brade shouted back, answers Wish couldn't follow. They shared a little back and forth, and she stayed tense, waiting, ready for the shriek of action and the need to grab her gun and probably fumble it and fall off to a very dramatic death.

The man saluted, and the arrex banked and flew back to join the pack. They drifted to the side and kept following, only slowly falling back as Brade picked up speed again. Then, finally, the pack split off and dipped down through a cloud, out of sight again.

"What'd you tell them?" Wish shouted into Brade's ear. It made him wince.

"We're Dread Corps on our way to deliver an important message to Wick, what else?" Brade shouted back. "Like I said, no one wants anything to do with this armour."

Wish nodded, resting back into her saddle. He sounded more confident than her.

"They're going to radio ahead to the air gunners," Brade went on. "Instruct them not to shoot us down."

Great, Wish reflected, only now discovering there was such a thing as air gunners. A danger she hadn't known she should be afraid of.

Come nightfall, Brade insisted they were almost halfway to Wick, a phenomenal distance cleared, but they all needed rest, especially the wyrling. The Iron Barge would be settling into a station for the night, he expected, and while it would help them to gain on it if they pushed on, it was also essential that they have more than the brief comfort breaks they'd enjoyed so far. Wish ached like hell from being in the saddle for so long, and spent half their time on the ground doing stretches and groaning. With this promised longer break, she also took a minute to wash the most accessible parts of herself in a stream. Returning to the group, she found two new shapes in the dim light of their campfire. More men in padded Har Coul jackets, one leaning on a long rifle. Wish froze at the edge of the circle, not quite out of the shadow, as she assessed the short distance to her own gun, down by the sleeping wyrling.

She noted the lack of tension, though. Brade stood by the men at ease, smoking. One of them puffed on something, too, as they chatted. Emi leant against a rock, picking at her fingernails and ignoring them. She had her helmet on, so there was no way of telling that she wasn't just a regular Dread soldier. No sign of Hightower, but it wasn't exactly hard for him to hide.

Wish came over, because it'd be strange to stand and stare, but she kept her head down, hoping the shadows would hide her features and avoid questions like *what's with the woman?* Brade introduced them without fuss: Corporal Wild meet Sergeant Brisk and Private Dunn, patrol men who'd spotted them flying earlier in the day, caught up to check on them. It wouldn't have been easy flying over Drail after all, Wish conceded. Brade chattered away in Coulard like he was born there, laughing, telling stories, and it dragged on for far longer than Wish would've liked, until finally he sent the men on their way and she could breathe again.

The trio settled at their low fire and Hightower crept out from a saddle bag, whispering, "Thought they'd never bloody leave."

It didn't exactly put Wish at ease to sleep. She sat half awake for most of the short time they allotted to stay there, distracted by dark thoughts and jealousy over the others: the grumbling snore of the big wyrling, Brade sleeping upright against it like they were lifelong companions. Emi spread like a star fish on the ground, hands pressing into it like the world itself was hugging her. In contrast, Hightower was curled up so tight and tiny by the fire it took a big chunk of Wish's sleepy will not to pick him up and cuddle him. Wish wondered when the last time she'd properly slept was. If she'd ever sleep well again. Not if she died tomorrow, for sure.

Emi stirred first and stretched luxuriously, yawning loud enough it startled Wish from a half-dream. The mage caught her eye, grinned with a glint that said she was back in form, and said, "Today's the day we catch up to them. You ready to die?"

"That's bloody reassuring," Wish said. Dammit Emi. Of all people.

"You want *reassurance* taking on the Drail's most sophisticated war machine?" Emi gave a light laugh that woke Brade with a grumble, and uncurled Hightower like a flower. "We must be mad, Wild. That's all there is to it."

"Like you've always said."

"But it will be fun." Emi rolled her neck, popping cartilage.

"Sure. Maybe you can derail the whole train."

"With a bit of time, I might. If you can disable the half-dozen or so defensive mages on board. And provided I can get around their existing wards and whatever touched metal they've got in place. Which I believe, from the little I know of the Iron Barge, is a lot."

"It's not an option anyway," Brade murmured. He took a second to clear his throat and properly focus. "We have to be sure the weapon is disabled. Can't leave anything behind, nothing to chance." Which of course brought to mind that they had no idea what they were going to do once they got there, rushed as this pursuit had become.

"Onwards through the interior together, the old-fashioned way, I suppose?" Wish said. "Swords and clubs and a chestful of gung ho."

"That's the spirit."

"We going?" Hightower asked with a big yawn and a stretch of his own. "Don't even look close to light yet."

Brade checked the sky and the horizon and reached a conclusion the same time as Wish, but she spoke faster: "About two hours left till full daylight. Good a time as any to move."

"How you know that?" Hightower asked, impressed.

"Excuse me?" Wish leant a little closer to him, finding something of a smile. "You're shin high and crossed the whole continent to take on the Dread Corps. How *don't* you know how to tell time?"

Hightower took the question seriously, with a little shame. "Stuff like that ain't my area. I know how to blow holes in things and a little mechanics. Otherwise, I do what I have to. Got lucky more than a few times."

"Luck is *exactly* what we need now," Emi clicked her fingers, grinning. Because the small man had to be worth something, making up a quarter of their heavily reduced group.

Wish said, "I guess this is the last chance now. Anyone who doesn't want to come all the way can bail. We're as close to the front as we're likely to land again. Looking at you, Colm."

"I'm gonna walk home from here?" Hightower laughed. "Thanks."

"I've got every confidence in us," Brade came in more seriously. "I honestly believe if we can catch up in time, we can find a way to disable the weapon."

"If you're counting on *me,*" Emi said, "they'll know I'm there in an instant."

Brade nodded. "You're strictly backup. Which we hopefully won't need. Ideally, the Iron Barge rolls into Wick without them ever knowing we were on it. If they put all their faith into this weapon, not knowing until the last second that it's been compromised, then it'll leave them wide open for our forces to attack."

Wish tried to keep smiling at that. Tried to believe it as much as he did. Knew that he was more of a dreamer than her, right then.

49

Like all unstoppable giants of industrial success, the Iron Barge will ultimately be remembered for that which made it vulnerable. It was excess, in this case, rather than a particular design flaw, that led to the great train's downfall. After all, when a machine has the scale and complexity of a city but the infrastructure of a single, moving organism, then incidental crises are not merely likely, they are inevitable.

**Great War Machines of the Modern Era,
Little & Ganimese, p. 321**

By mid-afternoon on the second day of the train journey, with Wick approaching, Donut was well-ensconced in their viewing turret. It had been a comfortable ride, more so, he was almost afraid to admit it, since a messenger had found them and offered instructions from Maringdale that they stay put. For however long she needed to keep watch from the rear of the train. It didn't come easily to Donut, not chasing after her and providing her food and whatever else she needed, but he had gradually got used to it, and was aided by Netts' company and, without Maringdale to turf them out, the company of two green-coat sergeants. They played cards, which Donut was getting better at, though he didn't quite get the rules, and they drank, and they joked, often laughing at things Donut didn't follow. But he didn't mind. Mostly, he was smiling because he felt included, and he never sensed they were laughing at him. In fact, they offered him drink and food and didn't send him on errands, just let him be. Didn't ask him anything.

Donut didn't like to hear Netts' complaints about Maringdale, but he had to agree sometimes that maybe she was a bit too controlling, and didn't especially care for what was best for all of them. But then, she knew how to get a job done, and they'd always worked effectively following what she said – even when Panderlair had been in charge, it was usually her ideas that got things done quickest. She gave Donut extra hints and orders when Panderlair wasn't looking, to make sure he did his bit. And now she was keeping watch while they relaxed, and that didn't feel like something they should complain about. If anything, it tempted Donut to go and find her to make sure she had everything she needed, or just to lend an ear. She had a lot of emotion, Maringdale, which she rarely shared, and Donut sometimes felt she needed him nearby just to listen to her complaints. Same way Netts and these green-coats liked to complain, except with her it was a rarer and more meaningful experience.

But in her absence he had a lot of time to look out the window and appreciate the rising sun, then the falling sun, and the rolling beautiful green hills. He saw a field of windmills and a hill dotted with sheep like fallen clouds. Saw a regiment of five tanks rolling over the grass in a straight line, and one time a blade hawk, close enough to see the white feathers on its chest as it glided by. It reminded him of Gulvar, left behind, which was a real shame, because he'd seen someone else brought a griffox, which wasn't much smaller than his wyrling, and was tamely secured in one of the rear carriages.

Donut watched the sky as he wondered if she should look for Maringdale. Find some work to do. But it was nice here. The men were friendly. The sky was pretty.

With the train drawing Maringdale nearer to her fate, each option for escape fell away faster than the last. Thorn Red released her cuffs so she could eat, and so she could relieve herself, but he kept a close eye on her at all times. She never once felt a slip in his intention to finish her at a moment's suggestion. When he left her alone in the berth, she considered kicking out the radiator to get her wrists free, but they would still be bound, and where would she go? She considered kicking out the window, jumping from the train, but this was one of the taller carriages and it was a twenty-foot drop at least. She considered calling in other guards and persuading them, using intention tricks to woo them or pretend she could curse them, whatever – but if she got two, fifteen, a hundred soldiers on side, what then? There was no fighting her way off the Iron Barge. The other option, of course, was to sway Thorn Red himself, but he was single-minded, fortified against persuasion by some deep fervour that would only get stronger if brought into question. Panderlair had resented this man's success, a rival on the other side of the continent who did more for the Purification than anyone. He wasn't going to fall for intention tricks.

All that was left was to sullenly consider the life choices that had brought her here, and how exactly she wanted to play the trial. With a simple confession, she'd be hung, no fuss, no torture. If she denied it, they'd do whatever they could to make a proper example out of her, as a wolf in their own house.

So the day dragged to night and the night back to day until the train chugged to life to leave its latest port of call. Red told Maringdale they'd be arriving at Ark next. Mere hours away. Perhaps getting off the train would give her a new chance to escape, but she sensed Red thought the same thing: a new chance to thwart her.

Shortly after they set out, however, someone knocked at the booth and Red stepped out for a few minutes. His voice was raised and irritated in the hallway, and Maringdale sharpened her focus to pick out feelings: apology from the messenger. Fear. Frustration from Red, *their damn problem*, nothing to do with him. He returned with a face like he'd licked shit and she knew they weren't stopping at Ark anymore. It didn't bring her any extra hope. This situation had become worse if Red was concerned for his safety. It was supposed to be a routine arrest, not *this*.

"We're going all the way to Wick, then," Maringdale said. "The battle's heating up too fast?" No, it wasn't that – something more personal for Red. He had blamed others directly, not the war.

Something specific to the Dread Corps. "They're worried about the weapon making it in time. Do they still think it's possible the weapon's in danger from spies? Traitors?"

Red scoffed. "You tell me, they're your best friends."

"I think it is. They've done something, haven't they? Reminded everyone there are enemies among our own? Worse than the likes of *me*. I only wanted to forward the Drail cause."

"Save it for the court," Red said, thumping back down onto the bench.

She moved her sense past him. Spread her feelers through the carriage, through the train, trying to pick out intentions. But dammit, those shock troopers were still obtrusive with their hostile, nonsensical feelings. A barrier of such resistance two carriages down. She channelled back in, reading up and down her own carriage. Worries about what was coming. Two booths down, a man disgusted that they were fighting for *this* land. Maringdale scanned the rugged, rocky Har Coul terrain outside the window – nothing compared to the epic landscapes of Drail. Nothing at all worth dying for.

She closed her eyes, dipping deeper into meditation. Keeping watch, looking out for them in the limited way she could, to do the job she came here for, even if it was a farce, and they'd sealed her fate. That was one, faintly possible solution: be so valuable they can't ignore you. There was hope there, wasn't there?

Yes there was, she noticed, with widening eyes. Someone was approaching. Someone desperately concerned that they were going to be spotted.

Of the many things Wish had encountered since she first joined the war, the Iron Barge vied for a position as most incredible: a machine larger and more intricate than any she had seen in Stanclif or otherwise, sliding through the landscape like an unbelievably huge snake. A snake wrapped in layers of plated armour of varying shape and size, with gun turrets and towers and walkways and windows.

Stacked windows, carriages the size of houses. It curved on its trail towards them.

"Fuck," Brade grunted, ducking over the reins, trying to drive the wyrling to fly faster. That curse said they weren't in an ideal position, with the train ahead of them like that. They could cut the corner of its rails, but it might not be enough to slip on unnoticed. "Hold on."

Wish did so tightly as he angled the wyrling down and it slicked back its wings, streamlining, descending fast. Emi cried out a delighted whoop behind Wish. They sped towards the rails like a bullet, the train rocketing ahead, and Brade bent lower, lower, making Wish do the same. The Iron Barge looked even faster than them, still, but Brade was pushing the wyrling for everything it was worth, calling out to it with encouraging, desperate commands.

A gun turret turned their way – an orb on the side of a carriage, with a long barrel poking out. Brade banked the wyrling and the turret followed. Wish threw herself back, arms up, and slapped the chest plate of the Dread armour, screaming, "We're Dread Corps, Dread Corps!" As if anyone could hear her, with the wind and the train's trundling, monstrous roar of mechanical noises. The gun didn't fire, so maybe it worked?

"Hold on!" Brade shouted and dipped again, and they gave a last push, a desperate burst towards the roof of one of the carriages. For the panic in his voice, he brought them down calmly, and with a little bounce, a laugh, they'd made it, somehow, the crazy flight over.

Wish sat up, catching her breath, heart pounding, and saw a hatch open ahead. A green-coat climbed halfway out, big rifle aimed at them. He perched there as a second one climbed past him. Both of them wore goggles and fur hats. The forward one shouted and Brade shouted back, jumping off the wyrling. He quickly fastened something, a chain on the train's roof rings, designed for anchoring animals or balloons or what? Wish jumped down after him, wind beating as hard here as in the air, her legs shaking as she tried to stand steadily. Not sure if it was nerves from the flight or the rocking train beneath her feet. Brade did what she was learning he was very good at it, talking his way in, pointing back and forth, so Wish took that to mean they were a go. She quickly unfastened the Drail repeater rifle and her saddlebag, now empty of basically everything but their wader stowaway. Emi, behind her, jumped on the spot as though testing how strong the train roof was. Wish said, "Can you stop that?"

Brade shouted at them in Drail to follow, quickly, and they did so, passing the green-coats with nods, down a ladder inside. When the hatch closed above them, the tremendous noise of the vehicle was cut off, their world confined to this tight new space. The ladder dropped into a carpeted corridor with wood-panelled walls, more like a stately home than a train. Except there were other green-coats lingering around, a pair smoking by an open window, others pushed against the wall clutching their gear, in each other's way with no space to move. Brade gave more passing comments to the guards that had welcomed them, then slapped Wish's shoulder and directed her on. He whispered, barely audible with his helmet and hers muffling it two-fold, "We're three carriages down from the Dread Corps."

Wish nodded and let him lead the way.

The three carriages they passed through were incredible. Firstly, a maze of tight corridors and stairs, where occasional open doorways showed quaint little seating booths, but then, in the second carriage, something like a ballroom, complete with a crystal chandelier hanging in the centre, and concentric balconies housing crowds of soldiers for three tiers above. Emi elbowed Wish in the ribs as they walked through, an unsubtle hint that Wish was gawking. Good thing she had the helmet so it wasn't stupidly obvious. Except a lot of green-coats *were* watching them.

Onwards into the third carriage, more corridors like the first, passing doors and forcing them to squeeze between tighter and tighter groups of soldiers. If the whole train was like this, there had to be *thousands* of heavily armed men on their way to reinforce Wick. And a vast number between Vorhale's weapon and their single escape route.

The talk around them died down as they passed, men turning to whispers instead, not because there were two women parading through, for a change, but because of the armour. Maybe Wish's hefty gun, too, which was, frankly, heavy. How did Pound carry hers for so long? Maybe Wish *should* carry something like this more often, build up her muscles –

A man with a thick moustache blocked their path, slapping a hand into the wall and shouting, and Wish tensed, thinking for a moment they'd been rumbled. But he was making an announcement, which was received with excitement, as the men around them began cheering, shouting encouragement. Wish recognised the chant as a green-coat favourite: "Tat, brent, tat, brent!" Translating to *strength, power*. Brade didn't join in, as Wish thought he might, given his friendliness elsewhere, so she and Emi followed his example and stood waiting till the crowd calmed enough for them to press on. But as the noise settled, the men laughing and grinning where they weren't merely shit scared, Wish picked up another voice, through the walls, sounding considerably less happy. Someone who'd taken the announcement badly? It sounded like a *woman*.

Brade patted Wish to continue, and they did, leaving that behind, squeezing past Moustache as he shared bold comments with the closest men. An officer, assuring them this was going to be a great day. He went quieter watching them, though, apparently no friend of the Dread Corps.

The trio passed through a brass-framed doorway into a connecting corridor, a few metres before another bulkhead door, and Brade hissed over his shoulder, "If you didn't get that, we're approaching Wick."

"Ah," Wish replied. Because how else could you respond to the news that they were almost too late and all going to die?

"No," Brade said, "it's a good thing."

Either way, it was immediately irrelevant as he led them on into the waiting carriage, and they almost strolled right into a crowd of much grimmer men in armour that matched their own. These guys mostly had no helmets, and were otherwise dressed down, armour plating on the floor or against walls, showing off muscle-hugging black uniforms, with severe faces poking out top. Unlike with the green-coats, a hush didn't pass through, only a few curious faces turning their way, finally somewhere that they belonged. But as Brade continued through the crowd, Wish felt more and more of them watching.

"Got my first mage," Emi whispered by Wish's ear, almost making her jump. "On the floor above." Perfect, now that they were in the midst of the most terrifying soldiers Drail had to offer. Their equipment, Wish noticed, was designed to be horrible, with guns decorated with bones and sharp metal fetishes, blades with kinks that would rip as they withdrew. One man had a battle scythe propped against the wall, curved wooden handle as tall as him, with a three-foot blade that curled down with nasty ridges. How was that practical?

They made it through the carriage without event, though, these men not expecting trouble and not looking for it. Yet. But once Brade passed into the next carriage, with an open room, he stopped, and Wish bumped into him. Looking over his shoulder, she saw what he had seen: a man bigger than most on the train (in the world?), with a uniform marked for his rank. She didn't know Dread ranks, but the number of lines made him look important. With him was another man in uniform, bald, the pair with their backs turned, talking to some soldiers.

After the surprised stop, Brade quickly recovered, and went above and beyond keeping his cool: he bounced into the room, suddenly animated, and started shouting in Drail. Waving his hands. Wish followed hurriedly rather than get left behind like a weirdly uncomfortable spectator, but she cringed at the attention as everyone in the carriage turned their way. There was no hope, because who the hell were these three? And how clumsy was this armour, really, to hide the two women's curves completely? The big officer turned to them, with his hawkish-looking bald friend equally ominous at his side. Brade kept moving, barking commands as though he himself was in charge, and he barely skipped a beat even when the big man himself shouted over the growing hubbub. They stopped in the middle of the room, surrounded by tables, some kind of dining area, apparently more exclusive as there were fewer soldiers here. Wish noted the crockery on the middle table – actual plates, and a half-finished rack of ribs. She could almost hear Emi salivating behind her.

Brade exchanged a few more stern words, impossible to believe he was so confident in the face of actively encouraging *everyone* to pay attention to them. But he spoke persuasively, with just the right amount of subservience, and Wild Wish took his meaning, as the soldiers started moving. He was playing the role of an excited guard who was spreading the news that the battle was fast approaching – shouldn't they be getting ready? The Dread soldiers were reaching for their weapons and armour, as the officers decided whether or not to embrace or scold this intrusion. The hesitation lasted a moment that could've been a lifetime, before the big man erupted with rapid commands in Drail, spurring the room on the same way Brade had. And Brade continued walking. Wish let herself breathe again, and followed him through to the next carriage as quickly as she could. They went into another tight corridor, with less attractive, cheaper wooden walls, and sturdier metal doors. The hallmarks of a storage area, with only a couple of loitering Dread soldiers standing guard. Brade quickly issued them the same instructions, pointing back towards the officers' carriage, and the men hurriedly stood to attention and moved in the opposite direction.

"You're getting them all ready for a fight?" Wish hissed.

"Getting them to gather," Brade replied quickly, moving through to a stairwell. He checked back along the corridor – sure enough, soldiers were converging on the officers, packing into one place. Readying weapons and putting on their helmets. Wish saw then, it'd be better cover, for slipping out. She supposed. Brade said, "Almost there, I think."

He pushed into the stairs, metal rungs this time, less impressive than elsewhere, spiralling into where Wish immediately sensed they needed to be. Something about the equipment exuded importance, and deadliness, and ripeness for sabotage. More soldiers were down here, fussing over supplies with more purpose than elsewhere, between big cages stacked with crates and guns. And a machine on spiked metal wheels, the size of a small carriage, armour-plated on four sides with a confusing looking panel on the front and a big brass cone on top, like someone had fused a trumpet with a safe and stuck it on a trolley. Two numerals were painted in crude black above and to the right of the control panel. 64.

Well that was a rare gift of signalling.

Brade moved straight in, clapping his hands for attention, issuing the same orders as before. Two men towards the back of the room jumped up and quickly nodded, accepting his message and scrambling towards the stairs. Another man to the side, rummaging in a box, banged his head in surprise, and cursed but ambled after the others. That left two more men, a little less impressed, looking like they'd been in a heated discussion and didn't appreciate being interrupted. They were standing right in front of Vorhale's weapon.

One of them said something sharp to Brade, and immediately the two went back to chatting, one of them pointing at the 64.

"Yours is on the right," Brade whispered. He gave Wish zero time to process that before he stepped forward. Another second and he had his knife drawn, closing the distance to the men. They both looked up at the same time, and their argumentative bubble was popped. Wish leapt forward herself, no time to draw the blade now so she swung the repeater rifle up, leading with its butt. As the first man opened his mouth to shout and the second went for a weapon, Brade plunged his knife in and Wish cracked the gun into a jaw. Both men crumpled, Brade's fell more gracefully as he caught him, lowered him. Wish's went down clutching his face, trying to shout and curse but finding his mouth crushed awkwardly shut. She followed through quickly, slamming the gun into the back of his head. Again, as he still twitched. Once more and he was motionless, and Wish's heart was thumping. She looked from the man back to Brade, now casually turning his attention to the weapon, his victim lying on the floor. Emi was at the foot of the stairs looking up. No one had noticed this flash of brutality Wish had just lived through.

"Quickly," Brade said. Wish joined him and felt movement in her satchel bag. She opened it and Hightower jumped out, giving her a look. Maybe *he* had noticed her smashing the man's head in. He leapt onto the weapon, trotted over it, and assessed, "This thing looks impenetrable."

"There's got to be a few tons worth of explosives down here," Wish said.

"Yeah, but" – the wader stamped a little foot on the metal – "no guarantee they're gonna get through this. Looks like touched metal. And a blast might just set it off."

"It's a bomb, that's the idea," Brade said. He pried at the control panel with his knife, flipping it open. A simple box, riveted and secure as the rest of the lump of metal, containing an entirely rudimentary black dial with a white stripe indicating up, the Off position, and a series of numbers around the edges. Five, ten, up to fifty. Minutes? Seconds? That was the entirety of its controls.

"Captain Brade," Wish said slowly. "How do we sabotage *that?*"

"Simple," he said, though. As smoothly as he'd led them through the train and taken quick charge of that room of Dread soldiers, he did the unthinkable in one quick movement, and turned the weapon's dial. "We set it off early."

"What the hell are you doing?" Wish exclaimed, as Hightower cursed, but Brade stepped past her and strode to the stairs, casual as if he'd just posted a letter. "Captain, we can't –"

"We can't *stay*," Brade cut in, turning back. Emi stood aside, looking as stunned as Wish felt. He told them, "I've saved you the burden of responsibility this time, ladies. Now, I suggest we leave quickly."

Wish was already shaking her head, though, not knowing what she could do or how but knowing she absolutely couldn't just leave.

Brade's expression soured. "It's done, Wild Wish. Come on."

"You go ahead," Wish uttered, unthinking.

"Don't be ridiculous, you won't get back through this train without my cover."

"Just go," Wish snapped, looking into his eyes to tell him whatever she might or might not be able to do now, they were not together on this anymore.

Brade squinted at her, disappointed, then gave Emi and Hightower cursory glances. Thankfully, both were still too surprised to run with him, and the captain didn't wait for them to change their minds. He curtly nodded and said, "I'll be at the wyrling if you come to your senses in time." And with that, he bounded up the steps, leaving Wish to stare at the ticking bomb.

"Move your damn arse, you idiot, you've no idea the lives you'll cost!" Maringdale roared at Thorn Red, bucking in her seat, rattling her chains. "It's not a damn trick, shoot me if it's not true!"

He leant out the doorway, looking up and down the hall as men moved quickly, clumsily, a sense of energy sweeping through the train. Excitement and fear mixed together as they rattled closer and closer to Wick, almost overwhelming in its fervour, but beneath it Maringdale knew exactly what she'd felt. Passing them by, two or maybe more people with feelings of distinct trepidation.

"They were in this carriage!" she snapped. "Worried at being found out! Clear as daylight!"

"Convenient it should be right when this confusion starts," Red replied, though she sensed he had strong doubts. She was too adamant, too loud, to be faking.

"They were moving towards the weapon, you idiot! At least go through and warn them, check for yourself if you don't trust me!"

Red gave her a glance. Deciding yes, he could do that. He pointed at her to suggest she stay put, no words necessary, and he pushed into the throng of soldiers. Maringdale shouted again in frustration and twisted to the radiator, started kicking at it. This is what she was here for, this is where she could show value. However it had happened, there were traitors here, and no one else was going to stop them. She'd show them all, she told herself, with another kick at the rails. Save the damn war.

"Maringdale?" Donut's voice snapped her around. Her dumb aide was in the doorway, stunned to see her like this.

Netts squeezed past him, into the booth, and paused with equal surprise. "The hell happened to you?"

"Finally!" Maringdale spat. "They're here, on this train – get me free."

"Who's they?" Netts asked, rushing to her side and drawing his knife. He wedged it between the shackles, teasing at the lock. No hesitation; he'd done this before.

"I didn't see," Maringdale said. "I felt it though. They passed not five minutes ago."

"We just got boarded by some soldiers on a wyrling," Netts said. "Donut saw them coming in."

"Looked just like Gulvar," Donut added happily.

"Bunch of guys in Dread armour," Netts continued, chewing on his sticking out tongue as he focused harder. "Thought it worth checking out, considering Dread soldiers don't fly wyrlings. And here you are."

"What'd they look like?" Maringdale asked, but as she did the shackles popped open and Netts gave a little sound of success. Maringdale rubbed her wrists and shook them out, standing. "Okay. This way."

"They were armoured head to toe," Netts answered the question. "Couldn't see their faces."

"Think they might've been women, though," Donut put in.

Maringdale froze in the booth's exit. "Say that again?"

"We can't let it go off," Wish said, almost paralysed by the ticking bomb before her. Brade had twisted it to ten. That was how much time they had to fix this or escape. Emi was at her shoulder, equally unsettled, while Hightower paced in front of them. "It could kill *everyone*. Not just in Wick – everyone, everywhere."

"Didn't you already have that discussion with him?" Emi said.

Yes, but here there wasn't a squad of girls to back her up, and Brade likely supposed this was him compromising with her plan. That or taking it to an obstinate extreme. The last traces of the bomb would be gone, for sure, and he'd get his lethal, devastating blow delivered to the Drail. Except there was no way of knowing how lethal that blow would be. Enough to wipe out an army or enough to wipe out a country?

"I can stop this," Emi said, quietly, moving closer. She raised a hand to its metal, but didn't quite touch. "At least, I can create an opening."

"Get me in and I'll do something with it," Hightower said. "Disconnect the magic canisters or whatever's inside. Or, you know, blow it up before it blows itself up. Might help?"

"It would give us even less time to get away." Emi smirked, as if their increasing danger made it more fun. But she then gave Wish a serious look. "If I create an opening, they'll know I'm here. The chances of us getting out are nil." With a mage in the next carriage over, never mind the horde of Dread soldiers, it was suicide. But then, the 64 might kill them anyway.

"I've sacrificed so much to try and end this war," Wish said, almost under her breath. "Sacrificed so many other people. To get back, to find our . . ." Happiness. To see Rue and Pound sweating on the farm, Dakoda hunched over books, Newk smiling in the sun. Wheat blowing in the sea breeze, lush grass under bare feet, children's laughter pealing through the village. Clean clothes, fresh colours and smells. Wish closed her eyes. Were any of them getting back, ever, anyway?

"*I* don't mind dying," Emi said, prompting a decision. "How about you, little man?"

"I came to help. I ain't leaving knowing I dint do all I could."

"But I'm *not* taking responsibility for the choice," Emi went on, and she was grinning. Telling Wish it was all right either way, like it was a game. "You're the dreamer, Wild Wish. You tell me, can you imagine a world where we die glorious heroes?"

"Not really," Wish admitted. "Not sure death and glory can go together. But I guess it's another chance to find out. Do it, Emi. Let's fucking ruin this thing."

50

While many factors fed into the result of the First Battle of Wick, just as with the Battle of Green Rise, it is an event that could be said to have been ultimately decided by an unexpected complication which swept in from the least-expected direction. Just as General Amalric failed to predict Stanclif's ability to get around his position on the cliffs, so too Wick somehow found Stanclif forces ignorant of the impending arrival of the Drail's devastating war machine, the Iron Barge, and the ferocious new weaponry it carried with it . . .

Dueley's Comprehensive: The One War in 10 Volumes (Vol. 4), p. 289

Pushing against a sea of men, Maringdale reached the officers' carriage and broke into enough space to stand steady and refocus. Couldn't pick out those feelings again, yet, and it was only getting harder now, with the shock troopers' instinctive defences pressing in – *death, kill, render flesh!* Maringdale gritted her teeth against it and searched the carriage with her eyes – dozens of men now fully armoured, helmets covering their faces. There, towards the centre, Ways was turning about, issuing commands, a couple of messengers waiting to take orders away. A few paces back from him, turning impotently on the spot, was Thorn Red. He'd barely arrived quicker than Maringdale and looked disinterested in any serious attempt to find the threat. But his eyes ran over her and his face fixed in alarm.

"Battle Chief Ways!" Maringdale yelled over the general commotion. "There's a traitor aboard!" The soldiers quietened as Ways glared at her. Hark turned furiously from his side. For the relative silence, though, the murderous thoughts of the Dread soldiers hung like a dirty cloud. Maringdale shouted, "I need your men to stop being so bloody-minded so I can pick them out!"

"A thousand apologies, Battle Chief," Thorn Red called out, "I've no idea how she got free." He hoisted up his wide-barrelled gun and started to move through the crowd, hindered by motionless, uncertain men.

Ways raised a hand to stay him. "Let her speak. Go on, Maringdale."

"I felt them coming this way," she said. "And my men saw them, three newcomers dressed in Dread armour. They arrived by wyrling. Ten minutes ago?" She turned to Netts. He nervously mumbled agreement. "They were concealed, but I'm certain –"

"Concealed?" Hark snapped. "Conveniently hidden amongst our own, hmm? You'd have us perform a witch hunt. With battle rapidly approaching?"

"Better that than let them twist a knife in our backs," Maringdale snapped.

"My men *can't* stop being bloody-minded," Ways said, more calmly. "The entire point of their training is to resist wit manipulation. The 64 is well-guarded, Maringdale. I don't think you appreciated my point in giving you back over to the Purification. We do not need you." More than that, she felt his feelings come through. He let them flow, *wanted* her to feel it. Resentment. Whatever minimal use she had been, the Dread Corps was no place for a woman. It was insulting to suggest otherwise. His attitude was barely different to Hark's, he just afforded it the minimum emotion. She was a tool to be used and discarded, never their equal. Maringdale pushed down the flood of mean feeling, glaring at him. The fool didn't realise it was precisely this attitude that had compromised their weapon. It was women, after all, who had come all the way to thwart him. She would show him. She would find them, stop them, and prove once and for all how necessary she was to the Dread Corps.

"Dirt-minder!" a voice shrieked, a man barging into the carriage with a wave of shoving that pushed Maringdale aside. He skidded to a stop, a Dread mage with robes flapping, his heavily-tattooed face taut. "There's dirt-minding in the weapons cache!"

For a second, they could hear the clack of wheels against the tracks, the terrible men who had so quickly discarded Maringdale silently realising at last that she was right. Then panic hit them like a hammer, as half the men surged in the direction of the far exit and the weapons cache, jamming together to slow the whole effort down.

Ways yelled, "Show some order, you're Dread damn you, not common thugs!"

It scarcely calmed them, with many not even listening. Hark screeched his own commands to undermine the order: "Secure the weapon, secure the hold!"

Intentions flared towards killing the enemy, securing the train, and Maringdale found a gap in the shock troopers' fury. With their defences down, distracted, more raw, honest human emotions came through: general fear at betrayal, danger, but then a crucial one, distinctly different: satisfaction. Someone who knew it was too late, and was pleased.

Maringdale frowned at a pair of Dread soldiers seemingly stood still, the tide of bodies bustling about them, as though they hadn't quite grasped how best to use themselves. Except they were moving, slowly, against the tide. As she stared, one of them turned her way, and through the eye-slit of her helmet, Maringdale saw – those weren't a man's eyes. Exactly as she had feared. Stanclif's women had got on the train. Because the enemy weren't as close-minded as these fools. Biting down anger and frustration, Maringdale opened her mouth to shout, to expose the spies at last, as the woman caught her eye. Knew she had been spotted. Swung her rifle up.

It was one of the simplest bits of magic Wish had seen Emi do, but with the biggest consequences: with this gentle warping, opening a small hole in the metal of the bomb, she both put a target on their backs and created a chance to save countless lives. The world didn't implode the moment it happened, so Hightower swung into the hole and quickly went to work, as Wish crouched trying to shine a torch in. He called out what he found inside, a network of cables and strange objects. With none of them knowing what it all meant, he started setting charges.

Emi said, "No sign of trouble. Maybe their mages aren't good enough to sense me."

Hightower appeared at the hole again suddenly, making Wish start back with surprise. He said, "I got no idea how it all works, but I cut a cable that looked important, in case my charges don't atomise the lot anyway."

"It's ready to go?" Wish asked.

"Yeah. Given us slightly less time than's already on the counter."

"Great, then let's go." Wish grabbed the wader and he yelped in surprise, but didn't resist as she bundled him back into her pack.

Emi lifted her hand to the bomb to reseal the hole as Wish covered the stairs, then they ran up together. They slowed down in the corridor, seeing tension ahead. Through the door, the many men of the officers' carriage were focused on something at the centre of the room. Wish edged towards them, listening to raised voices, though she couldn't understand their Drail. No one bore them much heed as they slipped into the room, into the crowd. The big man was shouting, addressing a woman who looked like a pirate, flanked by a smaller Dread soldier and fat man.

Then a mage shoved into the room, screaming, and chaos followed. Someone *had* sensed Emi – but he'd been thankfully far enough away to give them a head start. Emi pulled Wish back, out of the way, as the room was animated towards the armoury, everyone suddenly upset, out for blood, readying weapons. The scouts weren't the only ones not jumping on this panic – some soldiers were looking to the big man for orders or simply twisting about in confusion – but most of them were flooding towards Bomb 64. Wish nudged Emi, trying to move the other way. The mage had caught Emi's magic too late, hadn't he? They were too late to fix it.

As the thought crossed her mind, Wish got an eerie sense of

being watched, and looked up to see the pirate woman staring her way. A look of recognition on her face. Fuck. It didn't matter how, but she *knew*. They were screwed. But for the briefest second, Wish still had the element of surprise, so why the hell not.

She pulled the trigger before she'd steadied the gun, the cracking gunfire producing a riotous arch of bullets. The first shot caught a man in the leg as he passed, the second shot tore through a table, the third was meant for the pirate. She was dropping to the side already, and the bullet hit someone behind her. The room's panic and confusion dipped into total chaos. Men started shooting madly at Wish, making men around her return fire, towards the scrambling pirate lady, assuming somehow that *she* had caused this. Everyone was shouting, and the pirate was screaming back, calling them names.

Wish dropped down, almost on all fours, trying to clutch the repeater to her hip as she pulled herself along with her spare hand, ducking bullets, trying to get desperately to the door. She was hit from the side and crashed through a table, rolled into someone's legs and tripped them over. Her attacker pulled the other man off her and clamped a big hand on her chest plate, hauling her up – the fat civilian who'd been with the pirate, now red-faced with a singular purpose: stop her.

He got another hand on her throat, and lifted her as she kicked feebly. He held her up on show, but too many men were shouting, shooting at each other, with the big officer roaring for order, for anyone to pay particular attention. Except, Wish saw from the corner of her eye, the pirate woman was straightening up, shoving soldiers out of her way, and she'd got a sword drawn. She grimaced nastily at Wish, gold teeth glinting. She barked in Drail and the man wrenched Wish's helmet off, but as he did she felt a rush of air and was suddenly released, falling onto her knees. She looked up in time to see the man crashing through a table of his own, chest caved in as though hit by a tremendously powerful hammer, shocked face already lifeless. A Dread soldier stood over Wish, one hand out to help her up, the other in a fist that had apparently delivered that death blow. Not a soldier – Emi – she'd thrown a deadly blast of magic through the man's chest plate. She heaved Wish to her feet as more men turned their way, noticing what was happening.

A man cried out in a high pitch, his meaning obvious: "That's them – stop her!"

The Dread mage was bumbling into the middle of the room, pointing, and with his intervention the mad infighting was redirected, soldiers regaining their senses to focus. Not quick enough: Emi pushed Wish ahead then slammed both palms against the floor, to send a pulse through the train that made the carriage shake. Wish ran, not stopping to figure out what was going on, only that she had to get away. The door was only a few strides ahead. The room listed like a boat caught in a wave, echoes of the disastrous barkmen's journey, and people fell over one another, furniture crashing into them. As Wish pulled men out of the way and leapt for the doorway, a soldier scrambled into her path, small in frame but teeth bared like an animal ready to scrap, hands up like claws. Wish ducked his reaching punch, coming inside his swing, and rammed her head into his jaw, not exactly on purpose. It knocked him back into the door-frame and he turned around it, but he rolled to grab her again as she tripped over him, out of the carriage. He got a hand on her ankle and yelled for his friends to join in. The carriage behind them shook again, creaking and pulsing with energy, and the Dread mage fired an answering blast of magic. It felt like the air itself would be torn apart any second. Wish kicked back, catching the soldier in the face, stunning him long enough for her to whip her short-blade from her thigh and stick it fast into his eye. He gave a sharp, short, final shriek.

Wish pulled herself out from his body and was immediately struck again, someone sweeping in with a gun butt to her face. It was a glancing blow that knocked her into the wall, followed by another, catching her in the gut. She caught hold of the wall and got an arm up just in time to block the third blow. Then Emi was at her side, reaching over her shoulder, laughing madly as she got a hand on the attacker's armour. A great whoosh of power threw the man back. Wish straightened up, clearing her eyes to see the soldier tossed brutally down the tight corridor of the next carriage, so hard that he ploughed through the men like a reaping blade. Blood and limbs sprayed up over the windows and walls, a moment of such sudden gore that Wish froze gaping. But Emi pushed her on, laughing harder as they skidded on the blood, barely able to stand straight for her hysterics.

They continued a few steps into the next carriage before Wish realised Emi had slowed down. She turned back, finding the mage pressed against the wall, doubled-over shaking with laughter or tears. Wish took her hand, dragging her on, crying, "Come on, move!" But behind them, the Dread soldiers were pressing in. One in the doorway tried to steady himself, rifle up, but the men behind jostled him – he fired and hit the wall. Wish dropped to a knee, then whipped up one of the fallen soldier's guns. She fired back into the mess, impossible to miss. Jammed back the bolt and fired again, an older gun, but powerful, ripping through armour and two, three bodies at once.

"Emi, go!" she roared, clogging the doorway with bodies as she kept firing. The mage lurched on like a drunkard, nodding, cackling and saying nonsense words.

She patted Wish's arm in passing, then stopped. "Uh oh."

Wish threw a look over her shoulder, just as the rifle clicked empty – more Dread soldiers, cramming into the corridor ahead, an endless swarm. They stalled where they were, mostly armed with blades, with one or two rifle barrels poking through. Likewise at the other end of the corridor, the few men who'd squeezed through the doorway held back, weapons ready. For their sheer numbers and weaponry, they were nervous about advancing.

"How much time you think we've got left?" Wish whispered, but Emi wasn't really there, swaying side to side, reciting some haunting children's rhyme under rasped breaths.

"Swing around the wither tree, won't you take my hand –"

A woman shouted, demanding in Drail to be let through, and the pirate lady pushed into the corridor, sword ahead of her, blood-splattered face furious behind strands of wet dark hair. This looked remarkably personal to her, and Wish had a strong sense that in the midst of this madness they'd just killed the lady's only friends.

Wild Wish braced herself, aching in places she didn't want to explore. Back-to-back with Emi who kept giggling and half singing to herself.

"– take my hand and swing with me, until we cannot stand –"

The pirate woman took a step closer, taking charge where before she'd seemed the target of the soldiers' concerns. A voice called out to her from behind, an order that had to be her name, *Maringdale!* She ignored it to address Wish in Stanish, "Is it just you?"

Wish frowned, as Emi's singing turned to a murmur, wondering for a moment if Captain Brade had got clear. Behind Maringdale, a man in elaborate thick leathers and the massive armoured officer found their way through, too, glaring fury towards the scouts.

Maringdale ignored them, eyes narrowing on Wish. "The Gentleman is here?"

"Only us," Wish said weakly, spreading her hands. Brade at least might get away, and tell the world what the Blood Scouts had done. This woman was too late, however much she might've pieced together of their efforts, aware as she was of a man's involvement here. Is that why they were arguing before? She'd figured it out and no one believed her? But they didn't predict the bomb was about to go off. If they knew, they'd all be trying to stop it.

"What have you done?" the woman demanded, moving closer. "What do we need to stop?"

Wish's eyes widened – she'd just read her mind?

"Yes, I know exactly what you're –" Maringdale paused, right before Wish, and her eyes widened. She turned with a cry in Drail. Suddenly aware about the bomb. She shouted proudly, triumphantly – this is exactly what she'd warned them of, and the men watched in shock, realising their mistake. Good for her. But it was a distraction, the chance for Wish to take a few more down with them, maybe give Emi a window to get clear – Wish grabbed Maringdale and pulled her back against the wall, grappling. The big officer was shouting, not at them, ignoring them, in fact, to send men back through the other carriage, and Emi screamed, a terrifying, horrible and feral sound followed by an immense cracking of wood and the screams of the men in the other direction.

Maringdale drove an elbow into Wish's ribs and threw her head about, trying to get another strike in, but Wish held on tight, merely trying to hold her as a shield, stop anyone else getting close. They tripped into Emi, and the mage spun and screamed again, as a large weapon fired, bullets tearing into the wall around them and making Maringdale shriek in pain. Wish kept backing off, the man in furs advancing, cocking his wide-barrelled gun for another go. She swung Maringdale around to put her body in the way, then tripped over debris and threw a look back – Emi was supporting herself with arms pushed into the walls at either side, and the corridor collapsed ahead. The ceiling above had fallen through in chunks of broken flooring that completely blocked the exit, but formed a ramp up to the hallway above. Wish backed towards it as Emi scrambled ahead, laughing.

The man in furs shouted, demanding Maringdale get out of the way, as other soldiers crowded in behind him, none able to get closer in the tight confines. She ignored him, bucking against Wish's grip, but weaker now, having taken a blow. Then the big officer pushed through, tearing a rifle from someone, and he fired without hesitation, less interested in saving Maringdale. The shot threw them both back, a hot punch driven into Wish's belly, but Wish held on tighter as she crashed down into the jagged chaos of Emi's makeshift ramp, just managing to swing her satchel out of the way at the last second, as Hightower shouted inside. The huge officer strode towards them, shouldering soldiers and then the leather-clad man out of the way. Wish kicked up the ramp, catching on shards of metal and wood as she dragged Maringdale with her, weaker but still struggling.

As the officer loomed towards them, Wish almost at his chest height in her scramble, he raised the rifle to finish her. Hightower erupted from the satchel like an animal, sprinting over her arm, over Maringdale, into a rapid sprint up the barrel of the officer's rifle. He leapt through the air with a small but ferocious battle cry. The officer stared in disbelief – Maringdale slackened in Wish's grip, marvelling too, no one quite ready for the spectacle of a leaping wader, driving a spear straight into the man's eye.

To his credit, the officer didn't go down straightaway, but swung the rifle up quickly to swat Hightower off. He missed, because Hightower was already bouncing back, falling through the air, and instead the officer hit his own face. Blood sprayed from the wound, and the man tripped into the wall, now doubly stunned. He dropped the rifle, caught the spike in his eye, and managed to pull it out with a sick squelch. The eye came with it, and someone retched further back, behind the big man blocking the corridor.

"Move!" Hightower cried, clambering over the debris next to Wish. She was buried under Maringdale, and realised now that the woman wasn't fighting anymore, the warmth of her blood spreading. Wish pushed out from under her, and Maringdale lashed out a hand, trying to stop her but getting nowhere near. Wish hit Emi, the mage huddled against the ramp further up, giggling to herself, and looked back. The big officer was heaving his last breaths, propped defiantly up against the wall by one shoulder. The man in leathers was trying to reach around him, to move his immense weight, but failing. Maringdale was down on the debris, a bullet wound low in her gut, another up in her shoulder, but some life still left in her eyes. Watching Wild, not quite comprehending, and strangely, impossibly, pleased.

Wish stopped, just for a second, to try and figure out why this savage woman, bent on killing her moments ago, on the cusp of dying, was smiling. But there was no time – men were still shouting, the train was shaking with the panic, and Hightower was roaring at Wish to keep going. She snapped herself out of it, grabbing the little man by his arm and carrying him with her. She grabbed Emi's elbow with the other hand and stumbled desperately up the wrecked floor, to the corridor above, where she found the area empty, soldiers having fled for safety or joined the fighting below. There was a ladder, not unlike the one they'd entered with, and she ran for it, pulling Emi along as the mage tripped and laughed. Moving on nothing but the sheer will to survive, Wish swung Hightower up and clamped his waist in her teeth to free her hand, then shoved Emi ahead, grunting at her to climb. The mage did so haltingly, barely able to focus, and Wish lifted her up, putting all her drained muscle into getting her to the top of the ladder. Wish got around her, one arm holding Emi steady and the other shoving at the hatch, desperate shouts muffled by Hightower squirming in her mouth.

The hatch opened and sunlight burst onto Wish's face, and suddenly she was up and dragging Emi onto the roof. The rush of the train's speed threw Wish back, the sudden movement making her gasp and release Hightower – he cried out, whipped away by the wind, but she got a hand up and caught him by the leg, then pulled him close to her. Wish ducked against the wind and kept pushing Emi with her other hand, the mage in a crawling crouch of her own. The wyrling was still there. Three carriages further on, with a figure next to it, engaged in a fight. Shit, Brade hadn't made it clear himself – someone must've been watching the animal, and he was now spinning on the spot, sword out, fending off green-coats. One fired a rifle from the nearby hatch, a loud but useless shot that flew overhead.

"Emi!" Wish screamed. "Get yourself together!"

The mage met her eyes, some sense returning, and nodded. The pair moved in a running, desperate crouch, over the roof of the first carriage and to the gap – almost two metres to the next. They jumped without thinking, without hesitating, and both landed clumsily on the other side. As she recovered her footing, Wish adjusted her grip on Hightower, tossing him up to catch his waist in her fist, then she kept running, Emi close behind. Ahead, Brade cut down his last opponent, knocking the man off the side of the train. Brade slammed the hatch shut and turned for the wyrling. He stopped when he saw them. They sprinted, screaming together as they leapt over the next gap, stumbling worse this time. Wish skidded and almost went over the edge, Hightower yelling panic from her hand. She steadied herself, crept quickly back, and saw Brade was undoing the wyrling's straps, readying to leave. Behind him, she finally noticed, the great walls of Wick rapidly approaching, making her pause.

"Today, Wish, today!" Emi cried, with a little laugh but definitely clearer senses. She sprinted for the next carriage and Wish followed. They were doing it, a short run away from the wyrling and freedom, with the massive black maw of Wick's gates opening to accept this death train. Emi jumped, cleared the gap and kept moving. Brade waved them urgently on. Pounding behind the mage, Wish saw the final obstacle to clear, that little gap between her and salvation, and as her feet left the roof of the train, the bomb exploded behind her.

Maringdale could just make out the sky through the rattling window, past trees of stamping legs rushing around her. Some soldiers were trying to give chase, racing after those violent women, but most were panicking, running one way or another to escape, without any real sense of direction.

Not her. She was down, done. Letting them walk over her, kick her ribs as they went. She couldn't feel much anyway, except coldness, a numb throb. When a boot hit her temple and smacked her head into the floor, she laughed. Give me another, why not. Of course it should end like this. So much she could've done, so much more they all could've done if they'd only listened to her. They were all going to die here though – she was as sure of it as she was that she could've prevented it.

Idiots. They deserved this, and maybe she deserved it too, for trying to help them. But at least she'd seen Ways fall. Taken down by the smallest of foes. And Thorn Red was thwarted; he'd have no medal for betraying her. The whole Dread Corps would suffer for turning on her. In Arrow City, Pace and the Purification, they wouldn't know all that Maringdale could've been, but they'd also never hear what these foul men thought of her.

They might yet remember her as a hero. Or at least as someone who tried to be.

If they remembered her at all.

As Maringdale focused on a white cloud, out in the blue, letting the chaos of the creaking, cracking train fall away from her senses, she wondered if those Stanclif women had it any easier. There were two of them here, young, desperate and wild. The handful abandoned to the slaughter in Low Slane were little better equipped.

Did they suffer the same weak support, the same traitorous, idiotic commanders? Probably.

Her vision was getting darker. Feeling fading away. For the first time in forever, the intentions of other complicated, messy people were getting quiet. Almost peaceful.

She hoped they'd escape.

She hoped they'd send this entire train to –

The world shook, and the train banked like it might fall over. Wish's landing was thrown, and she hit the side of the next carriage with her chest. She slid over its curved surface, caught her free hand on a rung and swung out, body in the air again. She came back with a thump, hitting the train, as sounds of twisting metal and blasts of air and secondary explosions rushed over her. Somehow she kept her grip on Hightower. The wader pushed at her fingers to release himself, and started climbing up her sleeve, offering rushed assurances, "You can do this, reach up, dammit!"

Momentarily dazed, Wish blinked hard to look back, seeing most of the rear of the train now obscured by an immense black cloud, armoured walls rent out, but the whole thing still moving – rushing on through the smoke even as it tilted to the side, coming down onto the tracks again. The thump jostled her again, and Wish cried and threw her other hand up as she lost her grip. Another hand caught hers, and she found Brade perched above, hanging over the edge with a grip on a rung further up. He yelled with effort as he lifted her, and Hightower shouted encouragement, now perched on her shoulder. She scrambled to get footholds, something to grip onto. They rolled back on to the roof and immediately ran for the wyrling; Emi was struggling to hold it in place by its reins. The carriage shook, wheels coming off the rails as the world's most powerful vehicle struggled to keep aground. Another explosion behind them, and both Wish and Brade jumped to avoid being tripped by the tumbling carriage. The wyrling screeched and launched up with a great beat of wings, just as they caught hold of the saddles. Taken up clear of the train, air beneath their feet, Brade and Wish scrambled for all their worth over the animal's straps, pulling themselves finally, breathlessly, aboard. Emi sat at the front, reins in hand, and yelled, "How the hell do I steer this?"

But the wyrling was taking care of itself, putting quick distance between them and the flaming train as it roared on towards the city. Wish watched with amazement as the scene unfolded before her. The higher they got, the more was revealed.

Wick was on fire, far away, a walled city cast in plumes of smoke, buildings crumbling and men swarming over the decay like ants, on the battlements, in the streets that were visible. Through a great hole in one wall, Stanclif soldiers were pouring in, tanks behind them, the biggest guns thundering shots overhead. And the Iron Barge, a fortress of gun turrets and packed with men, was racing towards it all with a gaping hole in one carriage, trailing black smoke. It was rattling all up and down its length, vibrating like it might fall off the rails at any moment. Then it erupted with a chain of extra explosions, one following another as pockets of fire tore out of the vehicle's shell. Men were climbing out of the roof hatches, jumping out of breaks in the shell, or from between the carriages, their only chance against spreading fire and a train that was, evidently, not slowing down. Maybe the blasts had shot the brakes, maybe the drivers had been injured, but whatever the reason, the Iron Barge was speeding into Wick without control.

Its front steamed through the massive gates waiting open to receive it, and the train disappeared into the madness of the war-torn city. Its flaming rear end caught up, and it caused a collision louder than anything the tremendous battle had to offer. As the Iron Barge tore an explosive, ferocious hole in the back of the Battle of Wick, Wish rose through the clouds, denied a view of the final disaster. But it was bad, tremendously bad, hundreds if not thousands dead bad. All those men falling off the train. All those people already dead on it. And the look in Maringdale's eye as she lay dying. Wickedly pleased, somehow, with the chaos Wish had caused. A small part of Wish questioned, pathetically, if anything at all that she'd done was good.

But she was out of breath, and energy, and slumped in her saddle behind Brade, who looked shaken and bloody, behind Emi who sat tensely holding the reins. And Hightower, still on Wish's shoulder, slumped against her, his little breaths coming ragged as he used her neck for support. They'd all made it through alive, at least. These four, if no one else.

Wish exhaled deep, terrible relief, and held in a trembling need to cry.

Epilogue

The city was not entirely decimated, if you knew the right places to look. Stanclif Command understood that, and fortified the most defensible neighbourhood, in the eastern quarter of Islang. There, tall frescoed town houses sat behind hedgerows and gilt-iron fencing, cobbled streets that almost resembled peacetime, if not for the occasional snowfall of ash and the traffic of military vehicles and running messengers in blue uniform. The streets were quiet and preserved enough, at least, that Wild Wish could pretend she was in one of the finer districts of Stanclif's capital, on her way to visit a moneyed uncle. Right until she was inside Hope Tower, a villa of archways and marble squeezed into a six-storey pillar at the north tip of Islang, where the area's incline formed one of Wick's tallest peaks. A rattling black metal cage carried Wish to the top of the tower, escorted by a female clerk with big round glasses and a kind smile, a girl who looked like she wanted to say something but didn't. Maybe to congratulate Wish for her many achievements. Or more likely to point out she had soot or blood on her somewhere, even after four days of scrubbing, seeing as she could not seem to get her skin nor her uniform, nor most assuredly her soul, completely clean again.

The clerk guided Wish through to a lavish suite containing delicate suede-padded furniture and a floor-to-ceiling window with a panoramic view of Wick. From the crumbling rubble of former buildings, piles of brick and broken timber, to the merely bruised homes being freshly barricaded with sandbags and razor wire. The enormous arrow of destruction caused by the Iron Barge's crash was also visible, the ripped train fragments at rest like the half-buried carcass of an unimaginably large serpent, picked over by scavenging soldiers.

"Lieutenant 'Wild Wish' Evans," General Easter announced his presence, making her snap to attention. He was in his wheelchair on the other side of the room, where maps and folders of documents were strewn about, amid canvas bags and parchment cases, radio equipment and the odd gun or two. The general looked considerably more tired than he had in Blythe, having seen a few things himself whilst she was away, though his voice remained uncompromisingly authoritative. She wondered if he remembered talking to her on the Blythe battlements. "I have your title correct?"

"Sir," Wish said, affirmative. Then reconsidered. "I'm not sure I was ever officially promoted. Or if that was the rank I was supposed to have."

"We'll clear that up, don't worry. You're in for the Valiant Star, you're aware? The first female soldier in the history of Stanclif to receive one."

Wish frowned, keeping her eyes a few feet above his head rather than make eye contact. She was quite sure plenty of women deserved it more than her.

"Decisive action taken at both Green Rise *and* Wick," Easter said, as though reading off a record someone had passed him. "And journeyed all the way into the heart of Low Slane. We're all very proud of you."

"Thank you, sir," Wish replied, not sure who *we* referred to. Did Command's stuffy generals sit about discussing the lowly soldiers' merits over tea? Maybe they placed bets, or collected trump cards with their traits.

"I shan't ask you to recount your adventures," Easter continued. "Captain Brade has been quite generous in all the detail of his debrief." Probably going to write a book on it, celebrating himself. "And he was quite clear about your particular role in it, though of course your comrades will be similarly honoured. I understand the decision to silence Doctor Vorhale and dispose of his research was yours alone."

Bloody Brade. Wish nodded gravely. Was this it, her retribution for insubordination?

"He explained your reasoning, and I commend your foresight. Some things are best buried. Likewise, I believe you are to thank for deactivating whatever weapon they had on route to Wick."

"You're not . . . angry?" Wish ventured.

"Definitely not. It was your unit to command; if anyone was out of line it was Brade himself. And I have no doubt you did the right thing. There's been no trace left of the weapon for us to say, for sure, what damage might otherwise have been done. Such is often the case with averting disaster – we shall never know the scale of what was avoided. And thus, we cannot thank you enough, the debt you're owed impossible to calculate."

Wish gave him a conciliatory smile. He said they'd averted disaster, but the state of the city looked pretty disastrous to her. The right thing she'd apparently done, like so many others, had cost an awful lot of lives.

"Your effectiveness can be recognised, though," Easter went on. "My fellow generals were wrong to underestimate Brade, and even more so to underestimate the Blood Scouts, I fear. I am guilty of that myself. It was folly to place you all together and push you aside, under the rug as it were. Even a handful of your number might make all the difference, scattered throughout the forces."

"Sir?" Wish replied with alarm. It sounded like –

"I'd like you to move east. We've done well here on the Western Front, and with Wick secure, and Farne in our hands, Stanclif has earned a respite that might tie us over until the spring. From there, we can push strongly into Drail territory, as far as Low Slane by summer. But there's a thorn in our side, as the Drail are dug in around western Garter, with troops dotted through the volcanic foothills of Lome. It's scrappy warfare with little room for pitched battle. The perfect place for spies and scouts to excel."

"The Blood Scouts are yours to command," Wish replied, imagining it might be how Tate would say it, though tinged with the regret that she wasn't sure what that even meant now. What were the Blood Scouts, after their devastating run into Slane? She was also wary that she wasn't sure she could follow *every* order she was given. Not now.

"You're to be reassigned," Easter went on. "Marksmanship and infiltration training. Camouflage, subterfuge, wherever your specialities lie."

"More training? Respectively, we're all rather experienced now."

"Not for you. Training *from* you."

Wish's eyes widened. He wanted her to be an instructor, like Major Hesketh?

"Now, as I hope I've made our very deep gratitude for your efforts clear, I need to warn you how this will play out publicly. You'll hear them talking in the street, praising Captain Brade, cultivating this Gentleman myth. It's good for morale here, and bad for morale over the line, this idea that he singlehandedly sabotaged the Iron Barge and thwarted a Dread Corps plot. But you and I both know where the real heroics lay. This is just policy from the top; it wouldn't do to have a group of women take credit for this operation, because most simply wouldn't acknowledge it. Doesn't give the young men so much to aspire to. Rather makes them feel ashamed."

"Bless their fragile egos," Wish whispered, and Easter eyed her in a way that said he'd heard. Nothing wrong with his ears.

He didn't comment, but continued, "Nevertheless, what you did for Brade, I'd have you do again. I have countless competent men spread across the continent who could use extra support. Reliable, exceptional support. Starting, as I say, by training those at Lome."

"Absolutely," Wish said. "But sir, do you want me to report this back to the other scouts? I'm not sure where I –"

"There are no other Blood Scouts," Easter said. "As of now."

Wish's heart dropped, suddenly faced with news she'd been trying to confirm since Brade had first reunited them with the Stanclif forces. No one had heard from any of the scouts pressing south from Slane, but she was counting on seeing Captain Tate triumphantly leading her friends in a column through the hills, past the bridge fortifications that now marked the new divide between the Drail and the Comity. She'd imagined hearing Rue's teasing voice in a mess hall, calling her out – or Newk, gently slipping into her room at night. Anything, any hint, to replace the things she saw and heard at night instead, the dark memories that crowded the empty space where her friends should be.

She'd been starting to think she'd been forgotten, left to eke out days picking up rations and loitering amongst guard posts, unable to find anyone to report to, with everyone too busy managing their own people. She'd not seen Brade since they arrived, and Emi had slunk off for R&R – classic Emi, she would resurface when she was needed – leaving Wish with only the diminutive Hightower for company. But even he parted ways with her, a day after their arrival, when he learnt where the Gonish refugees from Blythe were. He kissed her hand when he left and said it was an honour to have served with her, which was rather gallant even in his rough accent, but while he promised to reconnect once he'd regrouped with his people, she was left her wondering if that was another fleeting contact she'd never see again.

And so she had been totally alone when a messenger stirred her from half-sleep in an alleyway asking if she was Wild Wish. If so, she needed to report to Hope Tower to meet with Command. Hope Tower, perfect, the place she'd finally regroup with her friends! But was this all there was? Her standing here alone, to take orders that sent her far away. Were none of the others coming back?

"As and when others of your platoon resurface," Easter continued, though, "they'll be similarly reassigned, according to their skill sets. I'm not discounting having you work together again, but I won't be making the same mistake of wasting all that talent in one place."

"As and when?" Wish questioned, and Easter held her gaze. He did know something. He didn't want to tell her.

"I can't have you staying here any longer, Evans," the general said. "You're to leave tomorrow morning. Your mage will be sent with you, and –"

"Emi?" Wish exclaimed.

"*And* you'll reconnect with Captain Brade outside Lome. This is a great opportunity, for us and for you. Do us proud in Lome as you've done us here, and I'm certain this war will be entering its final legs."

Wish wondered how many times she'd heard that. How many times she'd done terrible things to ensure that. How little difference it made that she knew the truth of it, too. She said, "General. Can you tell me, honestly, if we're really any closer to the end?"

Easter stared back sadly for a moment. His lack of an answer gave her the truth.

"Then please," Wish said, "that's not what I need to hear. I fought alongside the best people I've ever known, travelling to Low Slane. They were my friends. If you know anything, please . . ."

Easter kept staring, torn between exercising the authority to not have her question him and a clear sympathy for what must be a wretched expression on her face. He said, "I can't have you staying here, waiting, and I definitely can't have you going out looking, understand?"

Wish frowned, not understanding for a second, before realising he was concerned she would go renegade to hunt for her friends. She hadn't considered that as an option before.

"You *will* be moving east," Easter confirmed, to dampen that impulse. "But, for what it's worth, we have heard from our spies in Oak Grove. Female soldiers have made it at least that far south. I can't say how many or exactly who, but they should arrive here within three weeks. To be absolutely clear: you won't be here to meet them."

Wish nodded. She didn't have to be here, that was enough, for now; they weren't dead. They were marching, sneaking south – Oksy, Cade and Angles upright and leading them, at least, Dakoda stitched up and learning to walk again, Rue now decorated by burn scars fitting to her toughness, probably enjoying getting closer to Newk, who of course woke up not long after Wish left, wondering where Wish had gone. Newk, strong and enthusiastic in navigating hostile land; she'd run into her arms when they met again. All of them would be enjoying the great green vistas of rivers and mountains Wish herself had flown over – they'd have more time to take in the enemy countryside than she had. And they were only the ones Wish *knew* were still alive. Probably by now Tate and Larkin and the others had caught up to guide them, Four Skills pushing out ahead keeping them all safe. They'd bring Hightower's brother Charl, too, of course, and she could reunite the waders and invite them to join her, demonstrating to Stanclif command that it wasn't just women they'd neglected, but the lesser races, too. She wondered, then, if that was why the pirate woman Maringdale had died smiling. Seeing in Wish some hope for what she couldn't find herself in Drail.

Wish was grinning then, imagining herself safely instructing young men to be the best soldiers they could be, changing the very nature of the fight in Lome, enjoying a hopeful winter, not having to kill anyone herself, waiting for her friends to return. They'd be together again eventually. When the war finally ended, they'd all be together. Exactly as planned.

Get More from the Rocc

Greetings, it's me, the author, Phil Williams. I hope you enjoyed reading *However Many Must Die*. If you did, please spread the word: leave a star rating or review, tell your friends, produce viral videos involving vicious animals, hang flags from your window, this sort of thing. In the rapidly changing world of global marketing, word-of-mouth still means everything for a fantasy author, so please rave about this book on any online store where you can, on Goodreads, and with all your friends.

All of them.

It takes a village/army to sell a book, but if we can boost this one enough, I've got plenty more I'd love to share from the world of the Rocc and the One War.

Speaking of which, I have a **special offer** just for you. You can return to this world with my prequel novelette, *Oksy, Come Home* available exclusively, and totally free, if you join my newsletter here: **https://phil-williams.co.uk/hmmd-offer**

You'll also be the first to learn about the next instalments in the series and any future offers.

Acknowledgements

This book was many years in the making, not least because it was a new departure – my first all-out secondary world fantasy in over a decade. As I stewed on it for a long time, before, during and after writing, I've benefited from input from a great many people all deserving of the highest thanks.

First and foremost, my friends, readers and fellow writers who've offered feedback on some or all of this tome: Richard Buxton, Wendy Swarbrick, Ian Black, Luke Scull, Adawia Asad, Travis M. Riddle and Phil Parker (yeah, you're still in even if you didn't like it, Phil!). Particular thanks to Patrick Samphire who did a full edit on the book, ensuring I did even more work but unquestionably improved the book. And special thanks to Dominic McDermott for a much-needed proofread; this book would've been much scrappier without him – and in turn thanks to Zack Argyle and Bookborn for setting up the Indie Fantasy Fund, responsible for connecting me with Dom.

Next, a huge thanks to my tremendous artist, Stefan Koidl, for the striking cover that so wonderfully captures Wild Wish's chaotic smirk. I feel blessed to have had him bring the book to life with his talented art. And a second thanks to Travis Riddle for putting up with all my back-and-forth over finalising the design work.

As always, thanks too to all my advance readers and reviewers, and all those who've supported me along the way, including Lynn Williams of Lynn's Books; Timy, Jen and all the team at Queen's Book Asylum; Mihir, Lukasz and all the team at Fantasy Book Critic; Julia Sarene; my ARC readers Ami Anger, Damo Larkin and everyone else; Mark Lawrence and everyone involved in making SPFBO great; and of course YOU for giving this book a go.

Beyond people I actually know, this book is also a product of quite a deal of research that likely isn't even apparent in the text. I naturally wanted to write an all-out fantasy so I could make things up, but, so it goes, I found myself relying heavily on historical texts to inform my chicanery. Specifically: *The World At War* by Mark Arnold Forster provides an understanding of the truly diverse nature of a global conflict. *The Unwomanly Face of War* by Svetlana Alexievich gives fascinating insights into female soldiering, with so much detail I wish I could've forced into this story (some of the things early readers considered most unrealistic were lifted from these real-life accounts). *Sniping in France* by H. Hesketh-Prichard provides a fascinating intro into sniping when it was an emerging discipline, which again scarcely features here but helped at least in my own head. I'm sure there are more I'm forgetting, too.

Mention should also go to the writers who've gone before and inspired me, not just in the world of fantasy (where my urge to write this book found roots in J.R.R. Tolkien and Glen Cook) but the historians I used to read. I'm quite sure some of the epigraphs here unconsciously borrow or abuse names of real historians I came across during my university studies. There are also some nods in here to real historical figures, most specifically Sir Richard F. Burton and his colleague John Speke who did, in fact, suffer bugs burrowing into his ear.

Finally, thanks as always to all my family and friends for their ongoing support, particularly my siblings Nick, Fran, Alex and Christen, and my father and Sandra, and most of all my amazing wife Marta.

Also By Phil Williams

ORDSHAW SERIES
The Sunken City Trilogy
UNDER ORDSHAW
BLUE ANGEL
THE VIOLENT FAE

THE CITY SCREAMS

The Ikiri Duology
KEPT FROM CAGES
GIVEN TO DARKNESS

DYER STREET PUNK WITCHES

THE ORDSHAW VIGNETTES VOL. 1

ESTALIA SERIES
WIXON'S DAY
BALFAIR'S CONFINEMENT
AFTAN WHISPERS

FAERGROWE SERIES
A MOST APOCALYPTIC CHRISTMAS